THE Fifteen-Minute RULE

DICKSON UNIVERSITY BOOK THREE

max monroe

New York Times & USA Today Bestselling Author

DEDICATION

To every reader who's ever yelled "JUST KISS ALREADY!,"
we're with you…
And to Ace and Julia, you'd better figure this out or we stg

AUTHOR NOTE

The Dickson book we've all been waiting for—*Ace Kelly*.

This book consumed us.

It made us laugh more times than we can count.

It is everything we thought it'd be—times a million.

You think you know what a best-friends-to-lovers book is like?

Ha. You have no idea what's coming.

Buckle up, Ace Kelly is about to take you on one hell of a ride.

Happy Reading.
XOXO,
Max & Monroe

THE Fifteen-Minute RULE

PROLOGUE

Julia

Sometimes, Ace Kelly is the most annoying best friend in the whole wide world.

I don't care if he gave me the last purple popsicle yesterday or told everyone at school that I'm the bravest girl in the second grade because I touched a worm on the playground. None of that matters right now because I am *so* mad at him. He just made his stupid Hulk action figure rip the hair out of my favorite Barbie's head.

"She didn't even do anything!" I yell, holding my partially hairless Barbie up in the air. "She was trying to do some yoga, Ace!"

"I'm sorry, Lia!" Ace exclaims. "But the Hulk gets mad sometimes! He can't help it!"

"Well, the Hulk has anger issues," I snap, scooting to the edge of the rug in his bedroom and turning my back to him. "And so do you. I'm mad at you, Ace Kelly. Really, *really* mad."

Instantly, he goes quiet because he knows the only thing he can do when I'm upset with him is to wait it out.

We have a rule called the fifteen-minute rule. It's not, like, a law or anything. We made it up. But between us, it's nonnegotiable.

Ace wanted to choose sixty-nine minutes because he says his dad tells his mom he likes that number all the time, but I told Ace that sixty-nine minutes is a really long time. Like, I'm pretty sure that's more than a whole hour, which is, like, forever long.

I guess we could've chosen the five-minute rule or ten-minute rule, but we both think fifteen is a cool number, so it won two to nothing when we took a vote. Now, we're not allowed to stay mad at each other for longer than fifteen minutes, and it all started over my sidewalk chalk drawing last summer.

Ace added a gross stream of boogers and snot to the pretty girl I drew on my parents' driveway, *ruining* all my hard work. One minute, she had beautiful long purple hair and big pink eyes and a yellow dress, and the next, she had a face covered in green slime because boys are gross.

The only problem with our rule is that Ace isn't very good at telling time yet, so I'm the one who always has to say when the fifteen minutes are up.

"Is it time yet?" Ace asks, scooting a little closer to me.

See?

I huff out a breath, but I don't answer him, concentrating on brushing my Barbie's blond hair in a way that will hide her new bald spot instead.

"Lia?" he tries again, quieter this time. "Has it been fifteen minutes?"

I sigh and glance down at my pink Hello Kitty watch. Only three minutes have passed, but when I look up, Ace is sitting there with big brown sorry eyes. He's not even playing with his action figures anymore, and his resemblance to Puss in Boots is growing by the second.

I cross my arms tighter and look away, determined to hold out until the time runs out or my Barbie grows her hair back—whichever is shorter—but when I glance back at Ace again, he looks even more pitiful. I crumble.

"Yeah," I lie. "It's been fifteen minutes."

"Really?" he perks up.

I nod. "I forgive you."

"Thank goodness, Lia. Fifteen minutes is so freaking long." His face breaks into a giant smile as he scoots right next to me again. "Wanna play action figures?"

"No," I say and quickly move my Barbie away from his angry Hulk and rise to my feet. "Thanks. You can play action figures. I'm going to play dress-up."

"You can borrow my Batman costume," he offers. "It's in my closet."

That might not seem like a big deal, but that Batman costume is Ace's favorite. He never lets his little brother Gunnar wear it. And one time, Ace had Kyle Collins over at his house to play with us and Kyle wanted to wear his Batman costume *so bad*, but Ace said no.

It's basically an honor. It's also one of the reasons why Ace Kelly is my best friend. He's always doing nice things for me that he would never do for anyone else.

I rummage through his closet, but instead of a superhero costume, I snag one of Ace's favorite T-shirts.

With the white fabric draped over the back of my head, I swing side to side in front of the mirror on his door and imagine myself in a big, fancy church with a handsome groom standing across from me. I'm more grown, of course, like a full-fledged woman with boobs like my mom's and lipstick and eye shadow and all the makeup my dad tells me I'm not allowed to wear.

I also have a big smile on my face because it's the happiest day of my life.

I don't know why wedding days are so happy for girls, but I've seen enough movies to know it's supposed to be the happiest.

I close my eyes and picture the whole thing.

My imaginary guy looks a little like a prince and mostly like Ace, and the flowers are so bushy that's all I can see other than my groom. He has Ace's warm eyes and Ace's big smile, and he's tall like Ace's dad. I lick my lips, trying to transport myself to the day enough to know why the guy looks so much like my best friend, but I can't quite get there.

Though, it feels good. Like, comfortable and stuff.

"Ace, we should get married," I say over my shoulder as my best friend sends his Spider-Man action dude flying into the wall.

"Married?" he complains, now in the middle of the Hulk attacking a block city instead of my poor Barbie's head. Spider-Man rolls and flips back into the action, and Ace makes punch, kick, and explosion sound effects with his mouth. "Why would you wanna do something stupid like that?"

"Stupid?" I ask, offended. My mom's magazine shows brides all the time, and girls at school were just talking about it because Mia Crawford got to go to her uncle's wedding and she said it was the most exciting thing she's ever been to. She even got to be the flower girl and wear a pretty white dress like the bride, and she said, after the wedding, there was food and cake and dancing.

"Getting married isn't stupid, Acer! There's a pretty dress and a big cake, and you get to dance with your friends and stuff."

"Uh, all that sounds pretty stupid, Lia." He scrunches up his nose at me. "Plus, don't you have to be, like, really old to get married?"

I frown, tossing my T-shirt veil behind me and spinning to face him. His knees are scuffed from playing outside earlier, and his hair sticks up in the front from sweat or slime or something disgusting. Still, his cheeks are full, and his brown eyes are warm in the same way they always are. He'll understand if I explain it to him. He always does.

"Our parents are married. They make it seem pretty cool."

"Yeahhh," he groans. "And they're old."

"Okay, fine. So maybe you have to be old. But I still think we should get married, and we should plan on it now for when we're old, so we don't have to think about marrying anyone else. I don't want to be with some stinky man. I heard my mom and your mom talking one day about guys who were their boyfriends and how they had a big ego or something. I think that's got somethin' to do with BO."

"Our moms don't have boyfriends. They can't. They're not allowed because they have husbands. And I've heard my dad tell my mom she can't have a boyfriend."

I roll my eyes at him. "They had boyfriends *before* they got married to our dads."

"Well, I don't want to marry some smelly girl. I don't even want to be a boyfriend or a husband. I just want to be your best friend."

"That's why we should get married when we're old people."

"Fine, Lia." He tosses his Spider-Man figure onto the floor and picks up the Hulk. "But not until we're realllyyyy old."

"Duh, you already said that, Ace. We'll be old, I promise. Like… twenty-five."

"*Twenty-five?*" Ace asks, wowed. "That is *so old*, Lia."

Ace is eight and I'm seven, and I think when we're twenty-five, we'll have our jobs and money and houses and stuff. Ace might even need to use a cane to walk around then; I don't know. But I'll still be his wife, even if he has bad legs.

"I *know* it's old." I put a hand to my hip. I always do this when I need Ace to focus on what I want him to do. "So do you promise or what?"

He stares at me for a minute, but the Hulk is still in his hand, and I can't tell if he's going to go back to playing or be serious. "Fine," he says through a huffy breath. "Yeah, I promise."

"That means you can date other girls and stuff for a while, but when we're twenty-five, you don't date any other girls but me."

Ace scoffs. "Yeah, no problem, dude. I'm not gonna date girls at all. Besides you, every girl at school is annoying as heck."

"Hey!" I protest. "Girls aren't annoying!"

"I said every girl *but* you, Lia." He rolls his eyes at me. "You're different."

"Why?"

He rolls his eyes again. "Because you're my best friend. *Duh.*"

"Okay, it's settled, then. We'll get married when we're twenty-five. What should we do to make it official?"

"Spit shake?"

I groan. "Absolutely not."

"Well then, what's your idea?" Ace shrugs. "I can't do the blood thing because I got in trouble the last time we did that."

"We'll make an official agreement. A decree."

"A de-what?"

"A decree, Ace," I mutter. "The royals do it."

"Oh. Yeah. Okay, whatever. Where's the degree?"

"*Decree,*" I emphasize. "Do you have a notebook or a diary or something?"

"A diary?" he questions. "That's fluffing girl stuff."

"Whatever." I sigh. "I have my diary in my backpack."

"You have a diary?" His brown eyes are huge as he looks at me. "Does it have a bunch of crap in it about girl stuff and sleepovers and, like, tampoons or something?"

"Tam-poons?" I question in confusion. "What in the heck is that?"

"I don't know. My dad always says they're a woman thing when we get them for my mom. I think you have to shove them in your butt when you're a woman."

"Shove them in my butt?" My mouth is wide open. "Ew. Gross. I'm not doing that."

"Good idea, Lia," he says, nodding with very serious eyes. "I wouldn't want to shove anything in my butt either."

I'm definitely going to have to ask my mom when I get home if she shoves tampoons in her butt too. But right now, I need to focus on the important stuff. Like marrying Ace when I'm twenty-five.

I pull the pink bound notebook out of my backpack, flip to the last page, and scribble down the rules.

Ace and Julia get married at 25 years old. No matter what.

It's a little sloppy, but my handwriting is getting better at least. I write my name at the bottom, **J U L I A**, and hand the notebook to Ace to do the same. "Sign your name at the bottom. That's your decree."

He has to concentrate to hold the pencil right, and I roll my eyes at how stupid he thinks school and writing are. His Hulk rests on the floor at his knee, and his tongue sticks out of his mouth as he spells aloud. "A-C-E, right?"

"Yes," I confirm.

"Julia!" my mom calls, just as Ace puts the pencil to the paper. "Come on, honey, let's go! Daddy's double-parked downstairs!"

"Coming!" I yell back, jumping to my feet and hovering over Ace.

It takes him a while to put his letters together still, and I know I need to get moving. "You write your name and then keep the notebook somewhere safe, okay? Then we'll have our official decree."

"Yeah, sure."

"Ace Tobias Kelly!" Ace's mom is now yelling for him too.

"I'll write my name, Lia. Promise."

"Okay, good." I lean down and push a kiss into his cheek quick, grab my backpack, and take off down the hall.

Ace Kelly is my best friend, and when we turn twenty-five, he'll be my husband.

As weird as it'll be to be old, I can't wait.

1

Over eleven years later…
Friday, June 6th
Julia

*h. My. God. He killed* Luna.

"Of all the irresponsible, unforgivable, unbelievable things my best friend could…" I whisper to myself as I walk across my bedroom at my parents' house in Short Hills, New Jersey, drop my overnight bag, and come to a screeching stop near my window. My hands shake and my exhale stutters.

Ace Kelly straight up murdered my plant, and the carnage of the crime scene is laid out like an episode of *CSI* right in front of me.

"Luna?" I whisper, staring in horror at the limp, drooping leaves of my once-thriving peace lily. She looks like she gave up on life a few days ago, which, incidentally, is exactly when I left her in Ace's care. I step closer and inspect the butchery. The soil is soggy and drenched, like Ace tried to water her with the tears of every woman in the city who's had to deal with the aftermath of dating an emotionally unavailable man, and you and I both know, that means Flood City.

I explicitly told him, *"Only a little water every day. She's very particular and only likes to be misted,"* and he straight up waterboarded her like he was trying to get state secrets.

Oh boy, did she ever break.

My poor Luna. She's been my go-to gal since I started my freshman year at Dickson University last fall. She was my study buddy for midterms and finals. She was my emotional support plant during Scottie's tragic cheerleading injury. And when I had to move out of the dorms in May, I brought her home to my parents' house, my intention to spend the rest of my college career with her.

And now, she's dead.

Damn you, Ace Kelly, you direction-avoidant moron.

I yank my phone out of the Chanel purse Ace's mom gave me for my sixteenth birthday and send a text to the offender himself, the heat of my anger shooting from my chest to my fingers. It'd probably be more dramatic if I called, but my generation doesn't do that.

> **Me: *Where are you?***

Because of my innocuous words, he misses the angry text memo.

> **Ace: *Damn Jules thank fuck you're finally home from the Catskills feels like you've been gone forever but good news already omw to your parents' place***

Having been gone with my parents for the last few days, I'd normally be worried about getting together to download all the tea I've missed and to hear stories of the antics Ace has gotten into without me, but this isn't any normal welcome home. This came with a housewarming gift from my nightmares.

> **Me: *You'd better turn around right now, then. You killed Luna!***

> **Ace: *What are you talking about? Gary can't turn around I'm on the bridge***

> **Me: *My PLANT, Ace. The PEACE LILY I trusted you with. She's DEAD***

> **Ace: *Oh yesterday She was looking kinda dry So I gave her a top off or 2. Did she not like that***

Ace makes a job out of not using proper grammar or punctuation when he texts me, and at first, I tried to fix it—which was both a thankless and fruitless endeavor. Now, I find it endearing because it's weirdly him—like he gets too excited to think it all the way through before hitting send. But today, it's annoying again. Maybe one day, when he has to get an actual job, he'll introduce himself to more than the occasional comma and period, but for now, they are rare acquaintances and almost never used correctly.

> **Me: TOP OFF OR TWO?? SHE'S A PLANT, NOT A TOYOTA CAMRY. I TOLD YOU NOT TO OVERWATER**

I don't hear back from him again, so I settle for cursing his name as I unpack all the stuff I brought on my trip to the Catskills with my parents and sister Evie.

Butt-munching, plant-abusing, psychopathic waterer…

It takes much longer than it should because, I swear, I am *the queen* of overpacking. Only two nights at our getaway cabin that already has everything I need, and I still managed to drag an extra fifteen pairs of underwear and four entire outfits that never saw the light of day.

By the time I have everything put away, there's a knock on my bedroom door, and despite my better judgment, I answer it.

Ace, slightly out of breath and holding a Whole Foods bag in his hand, stands on the other side of the threshold.

I cross my arms. "Well, look who it is. The *murderer.*"

"I'm sorry, Julia. And before you yell," Ace says, "I come bearing peace. And possibly Luna 2.0."

"You *killed* my baby," I seethe.

"I know. I didn't mean to. I swear. But…" He pauses, reaches into the bag, and pulls out a tiny pothos in a pink ceramic pot. A *starter plant.* "I Googled 'low-stakes forgiveness plant,' and this was the top result." He lifts it higher. "Pothos. Practically unkillable. Like your ability to hold grudges against me."

"I'm feeling very grudge-y right now." I glare at him. "You flooded my baby girl to an early grave."

"I thought she was thirsty!" he exclaims. "And Jersey isn't exactly a hop, skip, and a jump from Manhattan, you know. I had to consolidate my visits while you were gone."

I eye him knowingly. "Let me guess, you were busy schmoozing rando girls." Knowing Ace, he probably had two dates with two different women in the same stupid night, so of course, Luna got the low end of his priority totem.

"There was only one rando girl," he corrects. "Her name is Lindsey and she's a very nice gal, despite being a little too clingy for my liking."

"You think every girl you date is clingy," I retort and point toward where my dead plant sits on the windowsill behind me. "Clearly, even my beloved Luna falls into that category, and she doesn't even have a vagina!"

"I'm sorry, Julia. I really am." If I had a penny for every time my best friend has flashed those stupid, perfect brown eyes of his in my direction like a freaking irresistible puppy, I'd be richer than our parents' net worths combined—and they're billionaires!

I purse my lips. "Mm-hmm."

"So… Julia, my favorite girl in the whole world, my best friend, my best girl, my favorite gal pal, the wind beneath my wings, my angel, my—"

"Ace," I cut him off and cross my arms over my chest. "Get to the point."

"Are you going to let me come inside your room?"

"Nope." I shake my head. "Not yet."

He shifts his weight, his desperation building. "How long has it been?"

I blink rapidly as I'm transported back a decade to a time when I had to keep track of the minutes for him. "I…I don't know."

"You know our rule, Jules. Fifteen-minute limit. We can't stay mad at each other longer than that," he says, flashing me a hopeful grin. His brown eyes are still big and pleading, and I start to crack like he's Pavlov and I'm a dog.

Honestly, it's hard to believe that the Ace standing before me is the same boy from my childhood, because physically speaking, he's a full-fledged man.

He's wicked tall, muscular, handsome as hell, and has the kind of entrancing brown eyes that have made numerous girls at Dickson U fall to his feet. My beloved Luna alone was around for several of the random girls Ace has temporarily dated, and she only survived our freshman year of college. When we were in high school together in New Jersey at West Chester Prep, it felt like every week he had a new girlfriend.

"Time's up, right, Jules?" he pushes, and his pleading yet undeniably magnetic smile is still in place. "I'm positive you texted me over an hour ago. I mean, I ran to Whole Foods, for fuck's sake."

I purse my lips, considering the implications of him getting off that easily. "The timer started when you arrived."

"What?" he questions with a shocked laugh. "That is not how the rule works, Lia, and you know it."

I glare at him. "Don't you dare try to turn this around on me, you stone-cold plant killer. Our rule was invented to keep our fights in check, not to let you run roughshod over my feelings with a get-out-of-jail-free card anytime you like. The timer started with your arrival. Deal with it."

"Can you at least let me come inside your room?" He holds up the pothos again. "You know, so I can fully plead my case from somewhere a little more comfortable than the doorway?"

I sigh dramatically but step aside to let him inside my room. Immediately, he sits down in the cushy pink chair by my window. I don't miss the fact that he's making a strong effort not to look in Luna's wilted direction, his body turned almost awkwardly.

"I brought pizza," he says, pulling a box out of the Whole Foods bag. "And I made sure it has your nasty combination of pineapple and jalapeños. I also thought I could convince you to fully forgive me with a little evening o' rom-com."

I squint at him. "Define that."

"You yell at me about killing your plant—"

"*Luna*," I correct him. "She had a name. She wasn't some weed I plucked from an alley. She was my beautiful baby Luna."

"My bad," he says and holds up one hand in defeat. "You yell at me for killing our dear, sweet, beautiful Luna." He looks to the ceiling and makes the sign of the cross over his chest. "May she rest in peace. Amen." He meets my eyes again. "For however long you need. Then we eat pizza and watch *Grease*."

I snort. "Of course. *Grease*. Why am I not surprised?"

It's his *favorite* movie, though his love for love is born from both nurture *and* nature, so it's hard to point any blame or shame directly at him. His father, Thatcher Kelly, has a long-standing love affair with all things romance. At one point, my dad was forced to be in some kind of romance book club that Ace's dad was running. Not to mention, Ace's mom Cassie writes romance novels in her free time, whenever she's not busy doing her famous NYC photographer thing, and has force-fed beta reading sessions on both of us on more than one occasion.

Long story short, Ace has been inducted into a romance-loving cult from birth.

"Jules, shall I remind you that last rom-com movie night, we watched your favorite, *You've Got Mail*."

He's not wrong. When I die, I hope I get reincarnated as Kathleen Kelly, and we did watch it on our last movie night—two times in a row.

"It's my turn. And *Grease* is a classic," he adds, grinning. "It's my favorite rom-com. Hardly something to complain about watching."

"It's barely a rom-com."

"But it's *our* rom-com." He waggles his brows at me. "Remember Halloween? Fifth grade? You were Sandy. I was Danny Zuko. You had that curly blond wig and the candy cigarette."

I groan. "That wig gave me hives."

He winks. "But I looked incredible in that leather jacket. Don't lie."

"You looked like a kid trying to play dress-up in his dad's clothes."

"I looked cool, Jules," he retorts and reaches out to briefly hold my hand. "By the way, bestie, I missed you while you were gone. It was weird not having you around."

Oh, here we go… I should've known it would only be a matter of time before Ace started shelling out his charming voodoo to shove me more quickly toward compliance.

"Don't be dramatic." I roll my eyes. "I was only gone for two days."

"Technically, it was *three*." He grins up at me. "Trust me, I was counting down all 4,320 minutes until you were back."

Sigh. I swear, he really makes it hard to be mad at him, even knowing he's half full of shit.

"Well, I had to go with my parents to the cabin." I shrug. "It was family-only and full of Evie's bitching and bad Wi-Fi and not up for debate like *your* family trip to the Bahamas. I can't believe your parents let you stay home."

"Don't be jealous, Lia. You know what my family is like. Opting out is like a survival tool."

Once again, he's not wrong. The Kellys are both the *best* and certifiable on any given day.

"Anyway, I'm glad you're back." His eyes dance with mischief. "We're going to Groove tonight."

I raise an eyebrow. "You want me to go clubbing with you after you committed first-degree plant murder?"

"I have fake IDs for both of us." He winks. "I figured I should balance my crime with something fun."

"So, you want to balance the crime of killing Luna with the crime of underage drinking? A sin for a sin?" I question, and he just laughs.

"Fake IDs are barely a crime. Everyone on campus has one. Frankly, you should feel lucky that your best friend can always pull through with the right connections. If you ask me, while the day started out a little…bad…it's starting to feel like it's turning around." He grabs the pothos and holds it up. "And let's not forget about Luna 2.0."

"Fine. I'll eat your stupid pizza and watch *Grease* and go to Groove." I sigh again. "But I swear, if you manage to kill this Luna—"

"I'll buy you a whole fucking jungle, Jules."

I laugh. I can't help it. Ace Kelly is irresistible—just like he always has been.

2

 y phone vibrates in the back pocket of my jeans as my eyes catch sight of the sign for *Groove* in the distance. I pull it out to find missed text.

> **Lindsey: Hello? Ace? Don't leave me on read. When are we going out again?**

Like I told Julia earlier today, Lindsey is a nice girl—with great legs and a curvy ass—but she's not really my style. Frankly, this is the tenth text she's sent me in the past forty-eight hours.

> **Emily: Hey…**

And Emily is a girl I met at a frat party two months ago. We danced and flirted and kissed a few times, but we haven't managed to meet up again since that one night.

Now, I'm not a total asshole who ghosts girls, but when Julia nudges me in the ribs, saying, "Ace, now isn't the time to text your harem. Get your head in the game," I don't hesitate to slide my phone back into my pocket.

"Relax, Jules," I say, wrapping my arm around her shoulders. "It's all going to work out."

She flashes me a nervous look, and I pull her closer to my side. She's anxious about using a fake ID for the first time.

"The bouncer isn't going to know, okay?" I whisper into her ear. "I got you."

She rolls her eyes but follows my lead, officially allowing me back into her good graces after the fuckup with her beloved plant.

Luna's funeral was short but adorably dramatic in a way that only Julia Brooks can pull off.

She insisted on a eulogy, and I let her roast me the entire time while I buried the dead plant in the Brookses' backyard. We ate pizza, argued over whether *Grease* is a rom-com some more—it is—and then sat down and watched it for probably the hundredth time. I know every fucking word of that movie, and Julia still pretends to be annoyed by it even though I know she ships Danny and Sandy together as much as I do.

It was a great day, despite the rocky start, and now, with the night still young, we're with our closest pals and heading to one of the hottest clubs in the city.

The bouncer flexes and postures as we approach the front door of a brick building in SoHo. His mouth curls into a subtle snarl that accompanies the complaints from the people waiting in line behind us—otherwise known as the ones I'm acting like don't exist right now as I move our group toward the entrance where music pounds through the door and the flicker of strobe lights peeks through the bottom crack.

Groove is a college club that's well-known by the young and rich of NYC. No doubt, socialites, polo types, and American royalty have soured Mr. Muscles's point of view on groups that bypass the line, but I'm not fucking standing out here sweating my balls off in the June heat. And I'm sure as shit not letting our friend Scottie suffer through the wait in her wheelchair while people whisper.

Playing cutsies is the only way.

Luckily, I know I'll change the beefhead's mind—since he's already preparing to tell us to fuck off—because I, Ace Kelly, have a special gift for changing everyone's minds.

It's the reason broody Finn Hayes and star quarterback Blake Boden are my friends, the catalyst for my popularity, and truthfully, the only way I got into Dickson University last year.

In high school, I slacked a bit on my grades—*shocking, I know*—and landed myself on the wait list. But all it took was a quick trip to campus and a chat with the dean, and I was well on my way to my first semester of freshman year on time, with my parents none the wiser.

Which is good—because my mom would have fucking killed me. She's not the type of mom to whisper disappointment with clasped hands and pursed lips. Cassie Kelly is a stone-cold soul-snatcher. If she ever finds out, you'll be talking to my ghost. Seriously, R-I-P me.

"Hey, man," I schmooze, handing over my fake ID to Mr. Muscles, followed by Julia's as she passes it to me. "How you doing tonight?" Recognition hits me from another occasion like a bolt of lightning, and I use it. My mind is always networking and cataloging people I meet for the future, and the older I get, the more and more valuable the skill seems to be. "Your name's Bruno, right? I think I've seen you with my buddy Knox."

Bruno shrugs and holds his flashlight to my ID first before handing it back and moving on to Jules's. He glances at Julia and me, entranced by our good looks, I assume, and then to Scottie's wheelchair behind us.

I keep talking.

"I know it's busy. Friday nights are crazy base case, but I can't imagine what it'll be like in August when all the college kids move back in to town, you know?"

His ice cracks slightly. "Yeah, this is nothing. Line will triple by September."

"Triple?" I scoff, really leaning into his plight to earn some brownie points. "You're fucking kidding."

"Nope." He shakes his head. "Even come December, they'll all be out here, freezing nipples off for a chance to get inside."

"Standard turnover, though, right? People out before people in, and if it gets late enough and a good DJ is on, no one is leaving."

He nods his big head. "Exactly."

"Shit," I say with a laugh, patting him on the shoulder as the corner of his mouth turns up. "I'll remember you. Maybe even bring you some HotHands or something if I'm in the neighborhood."

He chuckles, and I shake his hand, leaving behind the hundred-dollar bill folded there. Without acknowledging it, I turn back to Scottie and Finn and Blake and wave them forward and through the door, and Mr. Muscles claps me on the shoulder, not even bothering to check their IDs. "Enjoy yourselves," he says as we all head inside.

"Thanks, Bruno."

I follow the group in, but Julia hangs back, excitedly bouncing high enough to put an arm around my shoulder. This is our first official time sneaking in anywhere with fake IDs, which is actually remarkable, given we're so close to of age now. I mean, I'm nineteen and she's eighteen, but Julia is clearly jazzed over our fake-ID rebellion.

"I can't believe it worked!" she squeals and squeezes my shoulder. "I'm so excited!"

I smile. "Come on, Jules, you know I'm unstoppable when I'm on a mission."

She laughs, and the vibration makes her shimmery gold dress shine even more under the lights of Groove. "I'll give it to you tonight, Acer. You pulled it off, and I love you for it." She smacks a kiss on my cheek, and I lift her into my arms to spin her around before setting her back down on her heels.

Finn gives our name to the VIP host, who walks us to our table in the back center of the club, and lights strobe across Julia's face as she shimmies her way across the dance floor in front of me, the tan of her thighs' exposure inching higher and higher as she raises her hands above her head.

Several idiots glance in her direction, and I don't hesitate to move a little closer to her as a douche deterrent. I don't know everything, but I know with certainty that there's not a single fuck in this club who is worthy of my best friend.

Jules is magnetic—she always has been—and seeing her having

a good time is half the reason I'm as unhinged as I am. As her best friend for her entire life, I see it as my duty to make her days better. She's always returned the favor effortlessly and is the only person who truly makes space for me to be myself. That doesn't stop me with other people—I create space on my own—but it's nice to be understood.

Scottie looks back over her shoulder at Finn as he wheels her through the crowd on the dance floor, barking at anyone who dares to take half a second too long getting out of the way or flat-out running over their feet if necessary. She's pink with embarrassment, a perfect match to her magenta shirt, but somehow accepting and grateful at the same time, both of which show in the twinkle of her eye.

Blake walks behind them, high-fiving a couple of randoms who recognize Dickson University's Golden Quarterback and tilting his eyes to the floor to avoid calling any more attention to himself than necessary. I don't know why he doesn't soak that shit in more—I sure as fuck would—but I guess his humble nature is part of why we all love him so much.

"I'll go get drinks," I offer, settling Julia into the VIP booth in front of me with a hand at her upper arm to help her get her purse off her shoulder.

"I'll help," Finn offers, tucking Scottie into her spot on the other side of the table and leaning down to place a kiss to her lips. Her presence is like the sun on hard butter, softening him considerably.

We scoot down to the crowded bar and shove our way into the only hole we can find on the opposite end of the bartender. I put my tongue to my teeth and whistle, effectively grabbing her attention. She's short, absolutely stacked in the chest department, and sporting black bangs that have to be annoying as fuck as they tangle in her eyelashes. Her smile is big when she spots me, though, and I know I can have her eating out of the palm of my hand if I want to.

I bump Finn in the chest when she abandons her other customers to head in our direction, and he scoffs.

"I don't know what fucking voodoo you have, dude, or who the hell you bribed to get it, but I'm a little scared of its power."

"You should be," I advise seriously. "It's backed by the most powerful witches of the highest world order."

He rolls his eyes. "Fuck you."

I laugh. "It's raw sexual charisma, Finn, not magic. Don't be jealous that you don't have as much of it as I do."

"That's cute, Ace," he retorts. "But I'm pretty sure I'm the one with the beautiful, perfect girlfriend, and you're the single bastard. So, who's really winning?"

I roll my eyes. "I don't have a girlfriend because I have the entire playing field, dude. Don't get it twisted."

"Right, sure." He makes a show of looking around me. "But… that still doesn't explain why you're standing here. *Alone.*"

"You and I both know I could take this bartender home if I wanted to."

"So do it," he challenges.

I snort. "And leave you to enjoy the VIP table I got for us all on your own? Get real. Maybe at the end of the night."

"Hey, guys," the bartender in question greets cheerfully, making Finn waggle his eyebrows and me sigh. "What can I get for you?"

"I'll take a rum and Coke and something called a cosmopolitan." I gesture toward Finn, and he shakes his head at my "off switch," as he calls it. Once I get what I want out of certain women, I dip. She came to wait on us. I placed my order. That's all I needed, really, since I don't have the time or energy to hang on her periphery until closing just to take her home. "You order your shit, dude. I gotta take a quick piss, but I'll be back to help you carry."

The bartender's smile deflates considerably at both my cold shoulder and my secondary, very obviously girlie drink, but I bump Finn on the shoulder and beat feet anyway. It's not my job to cushion the blow of reality for everyone I come into contact with. *Fuck me, that'd be tiring.*

I make quick work of the bathroom and flirt harmlessly with a few dancing ladies on the way back to Finn, and then we carry our drinks to our booth. Finn's eyes are both shrewd and disgusted, and honestly, I take that as the highest compliment.

Dudes like Finn are simple. They're biological. They're the type that imprint like fucking werewolves and then roar at anything that comes within five feet of their woman. I'm more complex—universally attuned. I use what I'm given and move with the tide, you know?

I pass Julia's drink to her and set mine on the table, before making her scoot to give me room. She laughs as I continue to shove at her until she's crowded into the back, and then she punches me in the shoulder to make me quit.

"God, you're such an ogre, Acer," she huffs, but she also laughs.

I wink at her and look out at the club before us.

"Gah, this feels so good!" I exclaim, rubbing my hands together.

Red velvet ropes are stretched out in front of us to block off the steps to the dance floor, effectively keeping us out of the hustle and bustle. This is our first real group outing since the tumultuous end to last semester, and I figured paying for VIP would hedge our bets for a fantastic fucking time. Plus, my dad left behind a credit card for "emergencies" while they're away in the Bahamas with my brother, and showing Scottie a good time after all she's been through is of the highest urgency.

Our good friend Scottie wasn't always in a wheelchair. When we all started Dickson at the beginning of freshman year, she was a star athlete on the prestigious Dragons' cheerleading squad. To say life handed her a bag of shit a few months ago would be putting it mildly.

"The gang is back together!"

"Four friends walk into a bar…" Scottie adds, sipping the drink Finn and I just delivered through a tiny black cocktail straw. I pick up my own rum and Coke to do the same. "And then one more rolls in."

Blake stutters, Julia squeaks, and I dump the liquid from my drink right back into my glass to keep from spewing it everywhere as my eyes shoot to Finn. Jokes about paralysis are touchy—even if you're the one without use of your legs.

Finn guffaws, devolving into hysterics rarely seen from the straight-faced friend of mine, and I do my best to lean in to the awkwardness. If I'm anything, it's wildly inappropriate and bold when everyone else is timid.

"Oh, come on," Scottie says, reaching over to shove Blake in the shoulder. "Lighten up and take the joke. Please. For the love of God. I need everyone to be normal."

She's not completely off base in assuming we've been uptight, but I don't know why she'd think it's because of her. Her boyfriend's main hobby is carrying a stick in his ass.

Don't get me wrong, he's had reason, but I've been surgically removing the damn thing all year long. Scottie in a wheelchair is nothing in the buzzkill department compared to Finn's proclivity for wanting to kill everyone.

"You're right," Blake agrees. "Sorry, Scottie. I'll lighten up."

"Thank God." She sighs dramatically. "I was starting to worry that pod people had invaded your bodies and turned your likable, playful personality into a typical jock."

"Ouch." Blake laughs. "Low blow on the sports, babe."

She wags a finger. "You remember who I used to date. Other than you, I don't hold out a lot of hope for muscle-bound lovers of pigskin."

"That's because Dane was a douche burger," Blake remarks before Finn can stand up and flip the table for old times' sake. I swear, my buddy Finn Hayes has been hard at work beating the shit out of that kid Scottie was dating when we first arrived at Dickson last August for going on eleven months now. I'm glad Dane the Douche finally got kicked off campus for good since I missed the opportunity to invest in stock for that New-Skin shit you put on torn-up hands—and for Finn's and Scottie's sakes, of course, since he was a tormenting asshole. "It had nothing to do with football."

Finn nods and winks at Blake. "I shoulda killed that kid."

Yep. So close to the table-flipping.

I reach around Julia and pat Finn on the chest. "No, no. You got in enough trouble with that tool as it is. No need to spend life in prison, buddy."

"You would've gotten me out, Acer. Just last week, you told me your dad has a separate lawyer on retainer for whatever trouble Gunnar gets into," Finn says confidently, drinking from his glass of ice and brown liquid, his handsome, edgy fucking eyes running roughshod all over my sensibilities. He's right. I'd do anything for him, even when he's grumbly. We have a bond, a kismet, a wholly symbiotic, fated-but-platonic love story.

"Just when you think a guy likes you for *you*…" I joke. "You find out he's only with you for what you put out."

Blake rolls his eyes and laughs.

"What are you drinking, Scottie?" Julia asks cheerfully from beside me.

"It's…oh… Well, it's a virgin Dirty Shirley," Scottie admits. "I'm still not big on alcohol."

"What?" I ask, shocked. "Finn told me virgin was just part of the name. You're not drinking?"

"Neither am I," Finn admits softly, putting his glass to his lips. "This is just soda."

"What!" I exclaim, my arm flying out to the side as I inspect the traitor's glass a little more carefully.

"I'm not drinking either," Julia says then, nodding toward her untouched cosmopolitan and grabbing my forearm. She looks up at me through her long-as-fuck lashes as she rubs a hand over her stomach. "I can't."

I don't know what the fuck she's doing or if she's gassy or something, but when she keeps rubbing at her stomach, my own pitches to the side. *She's not saying she's baking a fucking kid, is she?* Surely I'm fucking mishearing things because of some earwax-buildup bullshit.

My dad had earwax buildup five years ago, and it drove my

mom fucking nuts. He couldn't hear for shit. Well, it's either that or he lied about the whole thing and spent two months acting like he couldn't hear anything my mom was telling him. Truthfully, knowing my prank-loving father, it could go either way.

"You're…you're pregnant?" Scottie asks, her voice jilted. Immediately, my hopes of clogged ears are dashed, and a red mist vaporizes my lungs.

What…the…*fuck.* Last I checked, housing a kid in your uterus requires a cock and balls or a turkey baster, and the idea of either one in Julia's *tunnel* is making me feel like cosplaying my good buddy Finnley for a little while.

Murder. Mayhem. Lots and lots of bleeding bodies.

"Jules…"

She purses her lips and then licks them dramatically. "Yes. I'm…"

"Who the hell's baby is it?" I scream, the question bursting from my lungs like a Jack jumping from his box. This is…unbelievable. Inconceivable. Just…not possible. Julia Brooks has been my best friend my entire life. We've grown up together, leaned on each other, been the one thing we could count on for as long as I can remember.

She's beautiful and smart and…way too fucking single to be pregnant. I'd know if some fucker slipped her the greasy knob. I'd *know.*

Right?

Right??

"Ace—" Julia starts, but I can't fucking breathe. This VIP booth is suddenly the size of an anthill, and I am King Kong. I need space. I need air. I need answers.

"Whose is it, Julia? Because I'll fucking kill him myself."

Scottie leans toward Blake, but I barely hear her as she asks. "Is it just me, or has this night had a lot of talk of killing?"

My eyes are too clogged, my vision too red.

"Who, Jules? Tell me who. I swear to fucking everything, I will strangle whatever motherfucker—"

"Oh my God, Acer, relax!" Julia snaps, finally breaking character and sucking in her stomach. "I'm just kidding! I'm not pregnant!"

"You're not?" My whole body shakes, sweat beading on my forehead and forcing me to wipe at it. "You're not pregnant?"

Julia rolls her eyes like she didn't just scramble my insides like motherfucking eggs. Hell, with the way I'm feeling, I'm certain she added an entire bottle of hot sauce on those fuckers.

"Of course I'm not freaking pregnant, Ace," she responds through an oblivious snort. "I'm on birth control."

Fucking birth control. *Birth control.*

Of course, Ace. I'm still sleeping with all these no-good fucks, but I'm protected.

I know Julia isn't a virgin—I was there for the aftermath of senior prom and Tommy Gerkin's little dick—but fuck me, she's not a sleep-around type of girl. She's not even a date-around or hookup kind of girl, and the mere idea of her having sex with rando college dudes makes me want to puke. Or break shit. Maybe both. I tug at the collar of my shirt. It's hot, and I can't swallow. For some reason, my tongue won't allow it.

"Goodness, Jules," Scottie says through a giggle. "You're crazy, girl."

Julia laughs and shrugs, taking a drink from her fancy cocktail and turning to face the dance floor, where the DJ is doing a remix of a familiar song.

My limbs won't move, and my jaw has a permanent tic. The good vibes of the night are gone, and all I can see are visuals of my best friend—the most beautiful woman in the world—on her back with wide blue eyes and splayed blond hair while some schmuck pile-drives her on his patchwork dorm room couch.

My *God.* How didn't I… How couldn't I…

Julia. Jules…

Blake grabs Finn's shoulder. "Hey, uh, why don't you hold down the fort here with the girls while I take Ace outside for a minute?"

Finn nods, I think, but all I feel is Blake's gentle guidance as he grabs on to me and moves me out of the booth, down the steps, and through the crowded club.

A few women brush up against us on our way out, but I can't see anything but Julia's face. Her smile, her laugh, her big blue eyes.

Our lives together, intertwined like vines, dance inside my head like a montage over the vibing crowd on the way to the exit.

We walk down the long hallway to the front door and step outside, moving down the sidewalk toward a group of people who've come out to smoke their cigarettes.

I welcome the cloying smell of smoke, hoping it'll suffocate me. This…this feeling is not good. It's not good at all.

Blake ushers me down the wall past them and into our own area and pushes me into the brick with a gentle hand.

"Take a breath, Ace," he instructs, squeezing my shoulders tightly. "Come on, buddy."

I shake my head and finally manage a breath that racks my entire body. As oxygen returns, panic invades with it. I pace from side to side, yanking at my hair with my hands as a million thoughts torture me.

Fuck. Fucking Julia fucking Brooks. Am I…am I in love with her?

She's been my best friend since before I even knew what a best friend was. We've been attached at the hip since we were kids. Wherever I went, Julia followed. Whatever I did, she was doing it with me. And no matter how hard I try, I can't come up with one singular childhood memory that doesn't include Julia Brooks.

But the idea of her pregnant. The idea of another motherfucker enjoying her body and leaving her. The idea of some fucker falling in love with her and stealing her right from under my nose…

I suck in air.

Shit. Shit. Shit.

I spin in place, my whole world falling away with every turn.

"Dude, are you okay?" Blake asks as calmly as he can, but I am anything but composed. I am coming apart at the seams.

I shake my head. Back and forth, back and forth, back and forth. It's like I can't stop.

"Blake," I say in this strange, completely pleading—though unintentional—way. I just...I need him to fix this. To fix *me*. I need my blinders back on, my happy attitude, my plausible deniability that the world—*my* world—is a narrowed channel of me and one other person while the rest of it means fuck all. I need...I need to be able to breathe.

"Yeah, buddy."

"Blake."

"Yep."

"I...Jules...me...her."

He nods. I keep trying to string shit together. We're practically Moe and fucking Curly right now.

"She's... I... My heart...might explode."

"Okay, buddy," he says, moving immediately to shove me past yet another group of huff and puffers. "Just relax and breathe. I think you're having a panic attack."

Yeah. A scream escapes. *Yes. This does very much feel like an attack of panic.*

"I...Julia."

"Yes," Blake agrees. "Julia."

"Me and...Julia."

I rub at my eyes. "When she said she was pregnant, I...saw red. And then black. And then blue and green and every color of the rainbow. Fuck, I might have seen my own fucking stomach at one point. I always thought... I thought we were just friends. I thought..."

Blake smiles, the fucker. "Oh, I know. We all know what you thought, but we also know you thought wrong."

"You've known?"

"Oh, Acer, we all know, buddy. You and Julia are the *only* people who don't know, and I mean that with every literal fiber of my being." He points back at Mr. Muscles. "You see the security bouncer guy?"

I nod.

"Even he knows."

"Well, fuck! What am I supposed to do now? Just go back in there and act like everything is the same as it's always been?"

Blake's shrug is so fucking unbothered, I want to punch him in his perfect Dickson Dragon dick. "That part is up to you. How do you handle being in love?"

I scoff. "If I fucking knew that, I wouldn't be asking you. I mean, what would you do?"

"I'm still trying to figure it out, Ace. Just like you."

Well, *fuck*. He doesn't have the answer either, and it's because we're a couple of dumb fuck guys who know fuck all. It's the women with the knowledge, the wisdom, the value. Our dicks might as well be wind socks for as much control as we have over our hearts.

Usually, when I need help, I ask Julia. But it feels a little fucking different asking her this. And for the first time, maybe ever, Ace Kelly is at a complete and total loss for what to do—and talking my way out of it isn't an option.

Holy shit, I think I'm in love with my best friend.

Gary backs the Escalade into the spot in the garage under my parents' building and shifts into park. I stare out the window at concrete pillars and shifting earth and try to find the will to move, but the magma of tonight's momentous epiphany has a pull so great that even a hundred-thousand-dollar vehicle can't protect me.

Julia. *Jules.* My best damn friend and my girl Friday.

Am I really in love with her?

What do you think, dickwad?

Fuck me. How in the hell haven't I seen it before now?

"You okay, Ace?" Gary asks, insight into my mood going well past that of some rando Uber dude. Gary's been driving me since I was fourteen years old, and despite having been through *a lot* of weird, questionable, freakish shit in that time, I can guarantee he's never seen me like *this.*

He knows it. I know it. The universe knows it.

I'm…lost. I'm found.

I'm confused as to who I even am and truly questioning the fucked-up nature of being able to lie so well you even fool yourself. I've heard of fast-talking—I'm a master—but I never thought I'd been consuming my own bullshit.

But it seems so obvious now that the girl I've turned to for every major milestone…is *the* girl. The one I can't see myself living without, the one who changes all the rules—the one who turns boys into men.

The thought of losing her to someone else, the thought of her settling down and making a family with someone who's *not* me? Unbearable.

"Y-yeah." It's a stutter and so pathetically false I'm disgusted. But it's all I've got, and Gary doesn't press. "Just a weird night. Thanks for picking me up."

I made it another two hours at Groove before texting Gary to come get me early, my whole being a shell of its usual persona. My laughs were forced, my body might as well have been controlled by an alien life force—but I managed to hold on long enough to keep suspicion to a minimum—at least, I think.

"Of course."

Ugh. My stomach feels like I ate spicy Chinese takeout with an ulcer.

Gary's been driving me around the city for an hour and a half at my request since we left SoHo, which I know is obnoxious, but now that I'm back at my parents' place in Manhattan, all I can think about is Julia being out there without me.

Fuck me, should I go back?

What if some asshole is grinding on her? What if she falls in love with a sweaty dumb fuck with a goatee and bad cologne? What if…?

I shake my head at myself. The last thing I need to do is go back to Groove and act even weirder than I already was. No doubt, Julia will sniff me out. She'll know something's up.

And fuck, what would I tell her? "*Oh hey, by the way, when you pretended to be pregnant and then I started thinking about you with other dudes, I realized that I might be in love with you.*"

Yeah. No. That's not going to work. I need time. I need space. I need to figure my shit out before I toss myself over the fucking cliff.

"Can you…can you also… I'm sorry, I know it's late, but can you go back to Groove and make sure Julia makes it home okay too?"

"Of course."

"Thanks, Gar."

With a pat on his suit-clad shoulder and a heavy sigh, I climb from the Escalade and drag myself through the underground garage to the penthouse elevator twenty feet away. I scan my access card and ride the lift to the top, stepping out into my parents' place with quickly tiring limbs and an anxiously rapid heart.

My phone vibrates in my back pocket, and I scramble to pull it out, damn near dropping the fucker on the marble floors.

> **Bridget: *ACE KELLY! Where are you?? I thought you were going to be at Groove tonight!!***

But when I see it's not Julia telling me she's on her way here to profess her love for me, I don't even bother sending a response back. The pull of some pretty college girl is nothing compared to the pit of unrequited love that now sits in my stomach for the girl who's been my best friend for my whole fucking life.

This is uncharted territory—a new land with different rules and laws and norms. I feel overwhelmed at the idea of finding my way, so it's probably best if I can con myself into getting some sleep before diving in.

I drag myself to the kitchen to heat some milk to hopefully ease my mind into slumber. I have no idea if milk helps you fall asleep, but with as many times as Julia has made me watch *White Christmas* during the holidays and I've seen Bing Crosby say it helps with nightmares or some shit, I figure it's worth a shot.

Once the milk is heated, I take a sip and try to revel in the quiet, begging my mind to find some of the same. I have the place to myself, since my parents and Gunnar are on vacation in the Bahamas, and the peace of an empty home in the world of the Kellys is an unexplainable boon. We are loud. We are boisterous. We are fucking unbearable at times.

With my parents and brother out of town, the difference is even more noticeable. They, of course, asked me to go, but I reneged to stay here and hang out with my buds. And Julia.

Which makes sense now that I know I'm in love with her—who wants to go on vacation with their family while the woman they love stays behind to be potentially wooed by a bunch of swing-ing dick wielders?

"Am I really in love with Julia?" I ask, my head now in the fridge and my heart in my ass. I already know the answer to that ques-tion. Which brings up another question. "Fuck me, how long have I been in love with Julia?"

"Forever, bro."

Startled, I jump back from the fridge to find Gunnar just standing there in the doorway that leads to the bedroom hallway. A smug, casual smile is plastered on his stupid fucking face. He's shirtless—he's always shirtless—and a Cheerio clings to his chin, still wet with milk.

"What the fuck?" I exclaim, my heart pounding in my throat. "What are you doing here?"

"I caught a late-night flight home from the Bahamas. Thatch and Cassie were getting on my nerves."

This fucking kid. He's fourteen years old, but he seems to think he's thirty. Honestly, my baby brother makes me look normal, and let's be real, we all know I'm not.

"Do Thatch and Cassie know you left?"

He shrugs. "I should probably text them."

What the fuck?

"Anyway, good night." He just shrugs, drops his bowl in the sink, and leaves.

I fall back into the cabinet front of our giant fridge. The sound of the elevator dinging thirty seconds later is both a shock and a con-cern. It's two o'clock in the morning, and again, he's only fourteen.

I grab my phone from my pocket quickly and shoot him a text.

> *Me: Where the fuck are you going at 2am?*

> *Gunnar: Taco Bell. You want some?*

> *Me: You were just eating fucking cereal!*

Gunnar: Yeah, but I haven't shit since yesterday morning. It'll clean me out.

Gunnar: Actually, it'll clean you out too. Maybe even wash down some of your lovey dovey panic.

Me: Fuck off

Gunnar: I'm trying to, dude. YOU texted ME

Me: Because you're fourteen! It's my job to look after you

Gunnar: I'll be fifteen in August, bro.

Me: Oh my bad Mr. Adult. You can't even legally vote you dumb fuck.

Gunnar: And it's Mom and Dad's job to look after me. Which, clearly, they failed since I'm here and they're in the Bahamas. Just let it go.

Let it go.

I know it's not the responsible thing, considering he's not even old enough to get a fucking driver's license and this is New York and it's the dead of night, but I'm kind of in the middle of a crisis and he's been in situations like this more times than I can count…so I do.

I let it go.

My phone pings with a text.

Gary: Julia is home safe.

I breathe a sigh of relief. And I go back to my milk and existential crisis and dreams of a simpler time.

You know, before I realized I'm head-over-heels, eat-shit-and-smile, I-am-so-totally-fucked in love with my best friend.

Summertime, wealth, and the freedom of a weekend when you're a college student is a dangerous combo.

It's pushing noon by the time I finally drag myself out of bed, last night's makeup smudged and blond curls a mess. I'm still a little groggy from staying out way too late dancing at Groove, but I'm ready to see what today's entertainment will hold.

I know not everyone lives like this—I'm truly not that self-absorbed—but I'd be a fool not to enjoy it while I can. Dickson University won't last forever, and according to my parents, the "real world" comes at you fast. Like, horrifyingly fast. With taxes and meetings and a Roth IRA.

I'll have plenty of time to be steady, reliable, and respectable—*boring*—later. For now, I'm young, alive, fairly responsible, and excelling in my only obligations of good grades, good vibes, being kind, and hanging out with my friends.

My dad owns Brooks Media, one of the biggest tech strongholds and in-house marketing firms in the world. His dating app, *TapNext*, basically invented online romance, and now he's worth literal *billions*.

Sometimes I forget we're rich. Like...obscenely, whateven-is-money rich. But that's probably because my dad's idea of luxury is a well-seasoned grill and his favorite hoodie from college. I'm incredibly privileged, but I'm privileged in a Ford, you know?

We don't own a yacht. We don't summer in Monaco, and our

yearly holidays revolve around my parents forcing my younger sister Evie and me on trips to our cabin in the Catskills. It's the opposite of what you'd think a billionaire would do with his money. But that's my dad, Mr. Humility.

However, the fact that my dad's wealth could have us sitting on our own superyacht in the South of France is freaking insane when I let myself really think about it.

Once I'm awake enough to focus, I do what I always do first thing in the morning—grab my phone and text Ace.

Our families are practically fused at this point. Our parents fell in love around the same time, built their empires of wealth at the same time, and popped out kids who were apparently soul-bound from birth. Ace and I grew up together. We've been best friends since before we knew what friendship was. Since before we had teeth.

Me: Gooood morning! Where did you go last night? Gary said you sent him back for me but didn't say why you ghosted.

When he doesn't answer almost a minute later, I send another.

I'm not afraid to be myself with Ace. I can be demanding and demon-text, and I don't have to choose my words carefully. We've known each other since before we could toddle—before we could think—and I know he'd never judge me for something so stupid. He might *fake* judge me, for the sake of a joke or running commentary, but he'd never do it for real. He's the most open-minded, kind-hearted guy in the world. It's not just forced proximity that makes him my best friend—he earns the title too.

Me: Hellooooooo. Earth to Ace! Time to wake up, sweetie pie! Rise and shineeeeee. You know I'm going to keep texting until you answer, so you might as well just roll over now.

Me: No, don't be rude and smack me off the nightstand. Just answer me and I'll stop pinging you!

Me: Ow, buddy! That hurt. Am I damaged? Do you need to take me to the phone store?

An answering message finally vibrates in my hands, and I celebrate, throwing my arms up over my head and doing a little dance before pulling them back down to read it.

Ace: You think you know me huh? I'll have you know I'm well-rested Up conquering the day

Me: Where did you go last night?

Ace: To crazy town dude. I got home to Gunnar here back from the bahamas without Cassie or Thatcher's knowledge

Me: WHAT? How did he get back?

Ace: Spirit Airlines or some shit I dunno I don't know how we have the same dna

Me: Haha. Okay, then. Let's move on to what's really important. What are we doing today?

Ace: No clue. Something together tho

Me: Well, duh! How about I get ready and meet you at your parents' place in an hour?

Ace: No, I'll come pick you up

My eyebrows draw together, but I shrug. I'm all the way at my parents' house in Jersey, but whatever. If he wants to come pick me up, it's probably because we're going to end up in Ocean City, Maryland, eating crab or something. Ace is always dragging me along into spontaneous shit, and as much as I pretend to protest, I secretly love it. He's controlled chaos, and my life would be far too boring without his brand of fun.

Me: Okay. See you soon!

Stretching widely, I get up from my bed with a toss of my white comforter and run on my toes across the air-conditioned hardwood floor to my bathroom. I flip on the light, and the heated floor, and turn on the shower to scalding levels.

While it warms, I admire my youthful glow in the mirror, despite still being covered in last night's makeup. I know rolling out of bed and looking this bright-eyed and bushy-tailed won't last forever either, and Ace's mom is always reminding me to *"kiss my tits while I can still reach them."* Seriously, her words, not mine.

"Maybe I should be a little sluttier," I whisper to myself cheekily before shaking my head with a laugh. I've never been the loose-as-a-goose type, and sleeping with random guys at the drop of a dusty, crusty dinner date seems like the very thing that would make my father's humble-billionaire head explode.

But I've never had an actual long-term boyfriend. Not even in high school. I've hooked up. I've even had sex…once after senior prom with underwhelming results. I've gone on dates but never actually *dated* anyone for longer than a month or two.

And I can't decide if that's a good thing or a bad thing.

Like, should I be putting myself out there more? Should I be dating? Lord knows, Ace has been balls deep in the dating pool since we hit puberty.

"Julia!" my sister Evie yells, the shrill panic in her voice making me hold my ears. She's fifteen—almost sixteen—and perpetually in crisis these days.

"Jeez, Evie," I complain as she comes bursting into my bathroom without invitation. "I'm about to take a shower."

"Thanks for the update, sis, I never would have guessed by the running water," she replies smartly, her attitude temporarily pissing me off. "Though, I'm thankful your tits and bits are still covered."

"Hey, genius, you're in my room, on my time, without invitation, and clearly freaking out about something. If you want me to listen without kicking your ass out, you'd better take a chill pill."

"Ugh, fine, sorry." She huffs out a breath. "Queen Julia, master of your lair, may I please bestow my problems upon you?"

Poising my face with regal conviction, I bow. "That's better. You may proceed."

"I know you've been out of high school for a year, but this gossip has the kind of big boobs and an even bigger ego that's unforgettable." My eyebrows draw together as she continues. "Heather Donovan is running for class president against me this year, and she just put up a website claiming to have dirt on our *father*."

The big boobs are making sense now, as Heather was always well-known at West Chester Prep for her G cup. I can't even imagine the back problems she's going to have in twenty years, but for now, she relishes the attention too much to get them reduced.

"It's summer, Evie. School isn't back in session for, like, two months. Why are you busy with your reelection?"

"Did you just hear anything I said?" Evie glares at me. "Heather Donovan says she has dirt on Dad."

"Dirt on Daddy?" I shake my head. "That doesn't exist. Don't stress."

Evie rolls her eyes. "Wow, I never thought of that, thank you. Come on, get real! I looked at the site, and she's got screenshots of Dad sending ugly dick photos to women on TapNext! It's his profile, his picture, his username! All of it!"

"Get real. That's got to be AI."

She purses her lips. "Well, I ran it through that AI-detection app that Lexi made, and it says it's legit."

Lexi Winslow is the daughter of my parents' other best friends, Wes and Winnie Lancaster. She's twenty-six, finishing up her second doctorate degree at Dickson, and quite literally the most brilliant human being you'll ever meet.

She's not just smart. She's the smartest person in the room, always. So I can understand why Evie is freaking out, but I still have a hard time believing that our father has sent dick pics. Ever.

"Evie, come on." I shake my head. "This is Kline Brooks we're talking about, for Pete's sake. He doesn't do dick pics. He doesn't do scandal. He does socks with sandals."

"You're wrong, Julia," she refutes and starts typing something on her phone. "Just look at the website. Look at the photos before you make any assumptions."

"Look at the dick pic photos?" I say on a disgusted laugh. "No way. You can leave now."

"Just look at the photos!" she exclaims and starts moving toward me with her phone held out.

"I said no, Evie!" Immediately, I cover my eyes. "I am not looking at dick pics some high schooler is claiming our father sent!"

"Just look at them!" She's all up in my personal space right now, trying to tug my hand away from my eyes. "Don't be such a prude!"

"Don't be a prude?" I retort on a screech. "Evie, this isn't me being a prude. This is me protecting my freaking sanity!"

"Just look at them and tell me if it's Dad's dick!"

"Oh my God, Evie!" I shout and push her hands away from my face as I back up so far that my ass bumps into the glass shower wall. "Have you lost your ever-loving mind? Like I'm going to be able to pick our father's dick out of a lineup? Fucking gross, Evie! And I highly doubt whatever photos Big Boob McGee put on that website are real!"

She finally drops her phone to her side, and I breathe out a sigh of relief.

"Are you done, you psychopath?"

"Not even close. Even though *you*—" she glares at me "—won't help me figure this out, I still have investigating to do."

"Well, good luck with that." I let out a deep exhale and point my index finger toward the door. "I have to get in the shower, pronto. Ace is on his way to pick me up now."

"Of course," she whines. "Summer plans with the dude you literally spend all your dang time with are so much more important than the internet downfall of our father."

"Evie, you're being dramatic. I assure you. Nothing, and I mean nothing, on the internet will be the downfall of our father. He's Mr. Do-Right. He's not a PR nightmare. He's the PR manager."

"Something tells me you won't be saying that when his face is plastered all over everything—"

"Girls, are you in here?" our mom calls, her footsteps just outside the bathroom door.

"Don't you dare tell her about this," I whisper and put a finger to my lips to shut my sister up and open the door. "Why, yes, we are. Apparently, we're due for a family meeting, and everyone decided my shower time was the most convenient. Where's Dad? Is he on his way?"

"Did someone say Dad?" my dad asks then, just a few footsteps behind my mom and turning my bathroom into a full-blown clown car.

I swear, if my grandparents show up, I'm calling the police.

I shove through Evie and over to the shower, shutting off the water and crossing my arms over my chest. "I guess the shower can wait."

My dad laughs, slinging his arm around my mom's shoulders. "It's so tough living in these conditions."

I roll my eyes as my mom purses her lips, expecting some big, dramatic reaction from me. But she's not going to get it. There's no point anyway.

I sigh. "So, what can I do for everyone?"

"Mom, Dad, how did you guys meet again?" Evie asks instead of giving them a chance to speak. "Were you friends first?" Her eyebrows draw together as she hops up on my bathroom counter and continues. "I know you worked together, but who made the first move? What was the power dynamic? Did HR get involved? Sexual harassment, perhaps?"

"*What?*" My mom's shocked laugh is high-pitched and awkward. "What are you getting at, Evie? Where are all these questions coming from? And sexual harassment?!"

"It's fine," my dad says, his unshakable calm practically palpable in the bathroom full of fluctuating female hormones. "Yes, I was your mother's boss, so I suppose there was a bit of a power dynamic, but there was no HR involvement and everything that happened between us was consensual."

"TMI," I mutter under my breath, making my mom blush and smack my dad in the chest while he laughs.

"I actually asked her out the first time so my mother wouldn't set me up with someone else."

"A last resort," my mom says teasingly.

"And what else happened?" my sister pries. "You just started dating, and that was that? Or was there online sexting involved?"

Our parents share a look.

"What kinds of details are you after, Evie?" my dad asks. "Because I'm pretty sure you don't want to know all of it, but I'll be happy to share the play-by-play if you want. But I should warn you, there's a lot of NSFW material in it."

My dad saying NSFW makes me groan. "Please, no. Let's not go there," I say and turn to my clearly insane sister with gritted teeth. "Evie. We *don't* need to know the details."

"I'm just trying to piece it together," she retorts, and when I widen my eyes at her, she softens her voice and her interrogation direction. "To, you know, get an idea of what you were like when you were young, I mean."

"As opposed to old and decaying like we are now?" my mom asks, a mock act of affront bringing her hand to her chest.

"Jules?" Ace calls from my bedroom, his eyes widening as he pushes open the bathroom door to a crowd. "Oh wow. Hey, everybody. We having a bathroom party or what?"

"Everyone was just leaving," I say, taking command. "I still have to jump in the shower, Ace. Sorry. But I'll be quick."

"Hey, no rush," he says breezily. He's hard to ruffle, honestly, and I don't know that he's ever complained about having to wait for me before, but I could have been ready thirty minutes ago at this point.

"How's it going, Ace?" my dad asks, immediately kicking into his reliable adult mode. "Everything okay at home with your parents out of town?"

Ace scoffs. "Great, except my brother came home unexpectedly on his own."

"What?" my dad questions in surprise. "I just talked to Thatch this morning. He didn't mention anything about Gunnar leaving."

Ace just shrugs. "Yeah, well, he probably hasn't realized it yet. Knowing Gunnar, he set up some elaborate ruse. But he's very home, unless I was hallucinating last night."

"Which is also very possible," my salty sister mutters. "You are a Kelly. Crazy is in your DNA."

Ace scoffs through a chuckle. "Thanks, Evie."

She sticks out her tongue, and I'm officially tired of sharing my bathroom. "Okay, seriously. Can everyone get out of here so I can shower?"

"Fine. But Mom, Dad, you come to the kitchen with me," Evie orders. "I have more questions."

"Oh jeez," our mom remarks teasingly. "I sure hope I pass the test."

"You always pass my test," my dad flirts, pushing his chest against her back as he guides her out of the bathroom with his hands at her hips. Their affection is bold and unabashed, and for as disgusting as it is for me, their eldest daughter, to watch, I have to say I appreciate and respect it. After all the Scottie and Finn family drama I had to witness last year, I can't imagine how it must feel to come from a broken home. The shit her mom did to her and the horrible things his father has done… Well, it's the exact opposite of what I've had growing up.

I've never experienced anything but love and support in my home. And I know, more than all the money we have, that's what makes us truly wealthy.

Ace lingers a little as I turn the water back on, leaning a hip into the counter and smiling at me. "What?" I ask, rolling my eyes at the scrutiny of his stare.

"I'm just marveling at how good you look when you wake up. I had a mohawk and a six-inch trail of drool crusted on my chin."

I shake my head. "Oh, come on."

"Seriously, Lia, I don't even know why you're worried about showering. You're gorgeous."

"Uh…thanks, weirdo, but I smell."

"You smell *good*."

"Excuse me?"

"I said you smell good, Jules."

"I heard you," I say on a confused laugh. "But I'm still wondering why you're acting so…"

"So…?"

"I don't know…different."

"Different?" he questions and shifts on his feet. "I'm not different. I'm…chill. I'm cool. I'm Ace motherfucking Kelly. I'm your best friend who hasn't changed or had realizations or anything. I'm—"

"Leaving the bathroom so I can take a shower?" I cut him off with a smile.

"Yeah." He runs his hand through his dark hair, grinning as he does. "That."

"Perfect." I squeeze his shoulder and spin him around, patting his butt lightly to send him toward my bedroom. "Don't worry, buddy. I won't be long. Just a quick rinse-off and I'll be done. I won't even wash my hair."

"Ace!" my dad's voice booms from downstairs. "Why don't you come to the kitchen and eat some lunch with us while Julia gets ready?"

It's my father's obvious attempt at keeping things PG between Ace and me. Even though I'm in college and Ace and I have been best friends our whole lives, Kline Brooks doesn't take any chances when it comes to his daughters.

Ace just grins. "Looks like I'm being summoned."

"Yep. And while you enjoy chatting it up with the Brookses,

I'm going to attempt to take the shower I've been trying to take for the last thirty minutes."

He hovers near my bathroom door for a long moment. He searches my eyes, and he opens his mouth like he wants to say something.

"What now?" I ask, raising an eyebrow. "Did you forget how to use stairs?"

"Nah." He grins, but it doesn't quite reach his eyes. "Just making sure you didn't forget this is supposed to be a quick shower and not one of those long-ass hour-long showers you take when you have to shave your legs and shit."

"Rude," I say, already laughing. "This is a precision operation. And it's not my fault I've been interrupted like three times. Or that you're *still* standing here."

"Fine, fine." He backs away, hands raised. "But if you're not downstairs in twenty, I'm sending Evie in here with a bullhorn."

"Trust me, Evie has already done enough damage today."

He winks. "You say that, but no matter what Evie tries to throw at you, I'm certain you've survived worse."

The trauma of the dick pics flashes behind my eyes, and I shake my head. "Ace, you don't even want to know what Evie just tried to throw my way."

"It can't compare to that time you gave yourself bangs with kindergarten scissors and blamed it on me."

"Hey now!" I point an index finger in his direction. "I was five, and you dared me to."

"And I thought you looked cute when it was all said and done."

"All said and done?" I question on a laugh. "My mom lost her mind when she saw that my hair looked like a mushroom."

"But you were a cute mushroom."

"Out," I say, giving him a playful shove toward my bedroom, and he starts to head on his merry way.

"I'm going to check on Luna 2.0 real quick. And…" He turns

back one last time. "Don't forget to sing loud enough for me to hear you downstairs. You sound like dying sea life, and it calms me."

"Leave, Ace."

"Going, going." He shoots finger guns at me. "But if brunch turns into a Kline Brooks' interrogation, I'm throwing you under the bus."

"Wouldn't expect anything less."

As I shut the bathroom door, I hear him mutter through the wood, "You're lucky I like you so much, Lia."

I smirk, turning the shower handle all the way hot. "You're lucky I haven't murdered you with my loofah!"

His laugh fades as he walks away, and for the first time all morning, the house feels quiet.

But not in a bad way.

In an Ace-is-here kind of way. And somehow, that's always been enough.

Ace

The pool shimmers in front of me, water lapping at the edge and flickering in the overhead sun. It's three o'clock, and Julia and I have been at Manhattan Elite Swim Club for an hour. I'm in the pool, and she sits on a lounger under a cabana canopy twenty feet away. Her skin is still dewy with undried pool water, and I do everything in my power to keep my tongue in my mouth and my dick—constantly threatening to salute her—within the confines of my trunks.

I haven't gotten a hard-on in public in five years, let alone for my best friend, and the feelings of pubescence, I have to say, are not a comfort.

Her skin is tanned, and her legs are long, just like always. And yet, today, I can't seem to make myself look at anything else. There are other girls here. Hell, there's one five feet away who's been doing her best to grab my attention, but all I can see is Julia.

Jules.

Lia.

My best fucking friend and, evidently, the love of my life.

Fuck.

When I woke up this morning, I tried to tell myself I had just lost it a little last night and what I thought I was feeling for Julia was, like, temporary confusion or misplaced feelings or a non-life-threatening stroke.

But then I went to her parents' house in Jersey to pick her up, and I caught sight of those big blue eyes of hers and heard her gorgeous fucking laugh and I couldn't bullshit myself into thinking my feelings for her weren't real.

They are real. Too real, if I'm honest.

Of course she wanted to do something in a bikini today. *Of course.* Only thing worse would have been a nude retreat, and with the minuscule size of her orange-and-white cheeky bottoms, I'm not entirely sure we're not on one.

But seriously, why does her ass have to be so…perfect?

I bite my lip and swim over to the edge to get a little closer, but she's just out of range, behind another couple of rows of busy chairs and a mesh curtain she's just rolled down from our poolside cabana to keep more of the sun at bay. Our parents have been members of this club for as long as I can remember, and the perks are awesome. A running tab to get food, all access to a private pool, and some of the finest sporting equipment in all the city are always at our fingertips.

I know we're a couple of spoiled rich kids, but I try to use it to my advantage for other people too when I can. Just today, I invited Finn and Scottie to come with us on our guest passes, but they both declined, citing plans to hold hands and kiss or some shit.

Lucky, reciprocated-love bastards.

I sigh, putting my cheek down on the hot, wet concrete and willing myself to calm down and come back to center. This is Julia.

My Lia.

Yes, she's hot. Yes, she's beautiful. Yes, she's smart and funny and interesting and amazing in all the ways that count. But she's also my pal. She's the person I can trust and *have trusted* my entire life. She knows all my secrets and faults and failures. She knows the best of me and the worst of me, and she knows that they often come in tandem.

She knows me. She's always known me.

And I *know* her.

She's not different, we're not different—even if it feels like *I* am—and if I'm going to be a good friend, I need to keep the space between us unbetrayed by my sudden crush. She needs me to be steadfast. She needs me to be reliable in all the ways I always have been.

I can do that. I can handle that. I am peace. I am calm. I am rationality.

And if I can just get my dick under control, I can go back to being her pal.

I pick up my head again, dunking it under the water and coming up renewed. My chub is only at half-staff, and I can think thoughts again, and pretty soon, I'm going to be good as new.

I'm strong. I'm adaptable. I'm—*who the fuck is that?*

Two guys fill the space on the lounger next to Julia now—*my* fucking lounger—leaning in close and chuckling at something she's just said. Her big, obnoxious sunnies she got on our last trip to Fifth Avenue block her eyes, but her body language is open and inviting and turned toward them. My brain buzzes with dangerously loud white noise, and I lift myself up and out of the pool in one smooth motion.

The girl behind me still tries to get my attention with some kind of laugh and throat-clear-led boob hoist, but I pad on hot, smoldering stone toward Julia without looking back, ignoring the sound of singeing skin coming from my screaming feet.

My territory is being invaded, and with war comes pain.

Prick One and Prick Two have smiles the size of Texas as they get up and exit the cabana, and Julia lies back, her stomach stretching out to toned and flat again.

I should go gently. I should lead in like a Roman or a Victorian or whatever the fuck the dudes were on that show *Bridgerton* that Julia loves so much. Because the cold hard facts are that as far as Julia's concerned, I don't have fuck-all reason to be in a piss-poor mood.

Sadly, I don't listen to my own advice. I steamroll in like the New Yorker I am.

"Who the fuck were those dudes?" I ask, sitting down on the lounger next to Julia.

She sighs before opening her eyes and pulling her sunglasses off. She leans forward, closer to me, and it takes every ounce of will-power I have not to glance down at the way her perfect breasts are being pushed out toward me like they're on my own silver platter.

Fuck, is it just me, or is this "I'm in love with my best friend" shit getting complicated?

"They go to Dickson," Julia eventually answers. "Drew Bettencourt and Gregory Allister. They're in Sigma Tau, and Drew was in calculus with me."

I forget the names as soon as she says them. As far as I'm concerned, they're Tweedle D and Tweedle-I-fucking-hate-him.

"And what are they doing *here?*"

Julia laughs, unaffected by my *fuck-them* attitude. She's used to my mood swings, my bluntness, my damn near inquisition. We've done so much together in our lifetimes, frankly, I doubt anything from me would come as a surprise.

Except, I suspect, my newfound undying, obsessive, completely soul-crushing love for her. *That* might be a bit of a shock.

"What do you mean, what are they doing here?" she retorts, and one of those adorable snorts she always makes leaves her cute fucking nose. "Swimming. Hanging out. Like us. Greg's dad owns that really popular kids clothing company now, and Drew's family—"

"Yeah, yeah, whatever," I interrupt. I don't want to hear shit about those assholes. I don't care about them or their hopes or their dreams. I care about Julia. *My* Julia. "I meant, what are they doing talking to *you?*"

She shrugs. "They just wanted to say hi. Recognized me. And Drew wanted to…" She sits up slightly, looping one arm around her knees and adjusting her sunnies on the top of her head. "He wanted to ask me out for tomorrow night. And, yeah…we're going on a date." She claps her hands like the news is something other than abominable. Like it's *good* news.

It absolutely, most decidedly, is motherfucking not. In fact, it feels like someone just told me I have terminal cancer and have ten more seconds to live.

It feels like fucking dog shit.

"You're going on a date? With *that* guy?" I scoff. "He looks like a douche, Lia. In fact, I can still smell the linger of Axe body spray and protein powder in his wake."

"He's a nice guy," she contests with a roll of her eyes. "So what if he's a little stereotypical? I could say the same for Scarlett, you know. Big, fake tits and a smarmy smile."

"I haven't talked to Scarlett in months," I hedge.

"And what about Lacey?" She quirks a brow. "Or Kristen? Or Bailey?"

"Who the fuck are they?"

Julia rolls her eyes. "Oh, you know, just girls you were literally flirting with and talking to at the beginning of freshman year."

"Jules, honey, if I can't even remember them, I don't think they count." It's a stupid argument, even I know it, but it's all I have. As far as I'm concerned, there's pre-epiphany Ace and post-epiphany Ace, and the two shall not mix.

"Yeah, well. Maybe in a few months, I won't talk to or remember Drew either. But tomorrow night, I'm going on a date with him."

"Whatever," I agree with a pout and shove back into my seat. The only thing stopping me from throwing myself at her feet and begging her to reconsider is the deep, deep desire not to come off as an absolute lunatic. I mean, I'm trying to make her love me, not feel like she needs witness protection.

"Don't be such a downer, Acer. We can still hang out during the day," she tries to console, nudging me with her perfect foot. "The date isn't until tomorrow night."

I grit my teeth against seven different curses and take a deep breath. It's not going to do me any good to make her angry. I need to be understanding, present…perfect. I need to be so good to her, all the other fuckers don't stand a chance. Basically, I need to become the human version of a golden retriever with abs.

Which, thankfully, good genetics, good nutrition, and the occasional workout already have the abs issue under control. I just need to figure out how to make her love me.

"That works," I eventually say, taking the calm, cool, and collected approach. "We'll do something fun, then. Maybe make a quick trip down to Ocean City for some crab or something."

"Oh my God!" she shouts, jumping up and spinning toward me. "I was just thinking earlier that you were going to end up taking us down there for crab today!"

"Really?" I laugh.

"Yes," she agrees, shaking her head. "We're starting to get too in tune, Acer." She taps her temple. "I don't know if the world can handle that level of friendship."

"It can," I assure. "If it can handle what happened at the paint-and-sip my mom signed us up for when we were sophomores in high school, it can handle anything."

"Oh my God! I almost forgot about that. You got so drunk on wine before your mom even realized we were drinking something other than grape juice."

"She claims she had no idea she was condoning underage boozing, but I'm not sure what to believe."

Julia snorts. "You got so wine-drunk that you tried to turn your butterfly into Batman halfway through."

"Listen, I maintain that was a creative pivot."

"Your butterfly had one normal wing and one that looked like it belonged to a melting spaghetti noodle."

"Hey, limp wing is still better than limp…" I trail off, waggling my eyebrows.

"Oh God, please." Julia slaps her hand on my thigh with a playful roll of her pretty blue eyes. "Come on, let's go in the pool again. I'm getting hot."

I agree easily, straddling my chair to climb to my feet and offering a hand to steady her while she gets up. I walk behind her to the pool, keeping an eye on the fucks who stare a little too long at her ass, and hold her hand while she climbs down the steps at the side, before following her in. She dunks under the water and comes up with her hair slicked back, and I immediately post up behind her to smooth it out of her eyes.

"Thanks," she says quietly, turning to look at me over her shoulder as my hand grazes her shoulder.

I smile. "Of course."

I want to lean down and kiss the water-dotted skin, but I don't. Not that I wouldn't normally—our friendship has always crossed societal boundaries—but with the way I'm feeling inside, I'm not sure I would survive it.

Julia spins in the water, her fingertips dancing on the surface, and then leans onto her back to float. Her feet kick up in front of me and land on my shoulders, which she uses to glide herself back and forth.

Her feet are so dainty, her toes long and pink-tipped with magenta polish. I grab on to both, my thumb working subconsciously over the freckle on the top of her left big toe. In a vast expanse of perfect tanned skin, this one freckle stands out like a landmark of our lives together.

She ab-curls up, her thighs pressing against my chest until she can replace her legs with her arms, hanging off me in a hug. I hold my waist back, careful of my newly renewed fucking rager.

We're the same. This is how we've always been. Close. Easy. Effortless.

Except, at the same time, I can tell this is the beginning of something different.

Now I'm on the edge of a cliff, staring down at what I can't have. This, for better or worse, is the beginning of my ruin. Because, unlike before, my mind races at every touch, analyzes at every moment, and obsesses over her wildly.

Because I love her. I love Julia Brooks.

And tomorrow, she's going on a date with another dude.

Fuck.

Sunday, June 8th
Julia

I didn't plan to spend my whole day with Ace again. It just…happened.

One minute, we were eating bagels from our favorite bakery in SoHo and arguing over whether the everything bagel is the best bagel you can get, and the next, we were watching people play chess in Washington Square Park before picking up tacos. And then somehow, we ended up at a pet store holding a chameleon Ace named Mr. Slippy.

It was a lot. It was also…fun. So much so that I almost forgot I had an actual date tonight.

Almost.

Ace, of course, made sure I didn't forget—by accidentally spilling salsa all over my shirt and making me change, which started a whole debate about outfits, and then he said I should let him do my makeup, which turned into another argument because, frankly, Ace's over-the-top hand on my eyelids would've been a war crime.

Long story short, I was a little late for my date with Drew. Not egregiously, but enough to make my palms sweat when I realized he was stuck in my parents' living room talking to my father for ten whole minutes.

Now, I'm sitting across from him at a cozy table in a fancy restaurant called Olivette, trying to focus on conversation and not the vibrating phone in my lap that's been lighting up like Times Square on New Year's Eve.

Drew offers the bread basket, and I take a piece and a pat of butter on my plate gratefully. My phone buzzes in my lap again—the same thing it's been doing for the last half an hour—and I do my best to glance at it discreetly as messages dance across the screen.

Ace: Did you know the Romanovs were like actual killers?

Ace: I thought with so many names that ended in The Great they'd be like legit and stuff, but according to this thing on Netflix they were pretty ruthless

I grit my teeth, trying not to fidget in my chair too much while Drew looks on.

Ace: Do you need to heat hot dogs long enough to actually cook em or just get em hot? I can never remember

Ace: Do you think that chinese food place on fifth avenue will deliver all the way over here? I want egg rolls

Either my phone is lagging in delivery or Ace's fingers are literally moments away from falling off because the speed with which his messages are landing is something to be marveled at.

My smile twitches at the corner. Drew's in the middle of explaining something about his macroeconomics professor last semester, and I really try to stay tuned in, but Ace is chaos in text form. I click the side button on my phone to darken the screen again, but it goes off immediately, lighting back up.

"So, what classes are you looking forward to most this year?" Drew asks, chewing his bread completely and dabbing at his mouth with his napkin before even starting to speak. He's been working hard to keep our conversation going despite my level of distraction, and I swear, even though he should be annoyed with me, he hasn't broken his smile once.

I don't know if he's going for sainthood or if he's actually this chill, but I appreciate it either way. I never dreamed Ace would be texting this much—or that anyone would. In fact, I don't think anyone in the entire world has ever texted this much in a one-hour time frame. It's probably in contention for a Guinness record.

> *Ace: I'm worried the Armani suit for Lexi's grad thing might be a little too casual. I mean I wear Armani to class sometimes. You think I should go with the Gucci or keep my options open*

> *Ace: Do you think testicular torsion is something you can talk through? I just pulled my nuts BAD but like I can still talk through my teeth you know*

God help me.

"I'm really looking forward to psychology. I never thought I'd be interested in it, but when my peer counselor told me about the curriculum, I knew I had to take it," I manage to say, still distracted by my phone but vying for something, anything, to erase Ace asking about testicular torsion from my memory.

I type feverishly across my keyboard, knowing I can't keep this up much longer without ruining the date completely.

> *Me: Ace, can this wait? I'm on my date with Drew, remember?*

> *Ace: OH SHIT SORRY totally forgot. Mums the word and shit. I'll wait for you to text me unless it's something really urgent*

I tuck the phone away and smile softly, apologizing. "Sorry about that, Drew. Won't happen again. I think he's done."

"He?" Drew asks, but it's not unkindly. "Please don't break my heart and tell me you have a boyfriend."

"Oh, no." I laugh. "No boyfriend, just a best friend named Ace. We've known each other since we were born, practically."

"Ace Kelly?"

"That's the one." Obviously, everyone on campus knows Ace

Kelly, just as he intended. He told me at the last party we attended together that his aura arrives ten minutes before his physical body.

"Got it." Drew smiles. "I was just making sure I wasn't being unknowingly cockblocked by a six-foot-tall problem."

"While my best friend is *technically* six-three, and a very loud, very chaotic problem, I'm single."

He chuckles. "Good to know."

We settle back into conversation, and it feels like we're finally getting into a groove.

I've done little more than glance at Drew this whole time, which is truly an injustice to his good looks. He's got that blond, preppy, rich-guy style with pressed pants and loafers and the perfect collared shirt. He has a dimple in his left cheek and Caribbean blue eyes and the kinds of muscles born from a strict gym regimen.

He picked me up from my parents' Manhattan apartment in a Bentley with a driver and brought both flowers and candy for the occasion. We left them in the car—in the built-in refrigerator so they wouldn't melt—but I'm still amazed he was thoughtful enough for the gesture.

It's not that I don't know good guys—I know the best of them, really—but college-aged jocks aren't usually in the most romantic of subsets.

"Ugh. I'm so sorry," I say when my phone buzzes obnoxiously again from my purse.

And once again, Drew is gracious, waving a hand and scooting back just enough to cross one ankle over the other knee. "Oh, no problem. Is it an emergency?"

"I… No. I should put it on Do Not Disturb." I wince. "I'm sorry I didn't before. Let me just do that really quickly, and then we can focus on us and dinner. Anyway…you were asking about classes. I haven't picked my major yet, so I'm still kind of exploring, you know? What about you? Do you know what you want to do?"

"My dad's in private equity. I'm kind of thinking I might go

that direction too. The pay is good and stuff. But I don't know…
I'm not really passionate about anything yet, I guess."

"Would your parents be okay if you decided to do something
else? Or is there, like, pressure there?" I ask, but I'm also fumbling
with my stupid phone, trying to discreetly find the setting to put
Ace on Do Not Disturb.

"They're pretty cool. My dad might be a little disappointed, but
overall, I think he'd support whatever I wanted, however begrudg-
ingly. Are your parents cool with you taking your time deciding?"

My phone buzzes with another message from Ace, and re-
gardless of whether it's a good idea or not, I find myself glancing at
it. His last message said he wouldn't text unless it was urgent, and
believe it or not, he's usually pretty trustworthy. People mistake his
goofiness for something else, but he's solid. I've never had anyone
I could count on more.

> *Ace: Oh jeez I think I need help you might need to come
> over here… Gunnar is fucking nuts and I'm in over my
> head, Jules!*

My heart kicks into overdrive as possibilities of trouble Gunnar
has found run through my head. They are endless and varied in danger, but seeing as he's shown up at home with a few members of the
Pagans—a very real 1% biker gang—gone into anaphylaxis because
he took some random food from a random stranger outside of a
Dollar General, and painted their entire house with baby powder
just to make a YouTube video before, I can't just assume it's nothing.

Right now, there's a very real chance that Ace could be texting
with his hands behind his back while being held at gunpoint.

"Shit. Drew, I'm sorry, but I need to cut our date short. There's
kind of a family emergency I have to tend to. I'm so, so sorry. I feel
terrible."

"No, no, of course. I understand. Don't feel bad. Can I help?
Do you want me to come with you?" he asks, shoving to his feet and

jumping to my side of the table as I sling my purse on my shoulder and stand.

"No, thank you. Really." I shake my head. As much as some extra hands could be useful, I hardly think it's smart to enlighten Drew on just how much ridiculous fucking drama comes with the Kelly family at this stage of the game. I'll need to ease him in—soften the blow. One of Gunnar's emergent situations with undisclosed details is not at all a gentle introduction, seeing as it has a very real possibility of ending in a cavity search. "I appreciate it so much and how understanding you're being. I really hope we can reschedule?"

"Of course. I'd love that."

I smile, leaning in to place a kiss to his cheek. "Thanks again. I promise not to be on my phone next time. Hell, maybe I'll just leave it at home."

"Julia, don't worry about it. I've… Well, I've had a crush on you since we first met last year, and I've been around you enough to know you wouldn't be leaving right now without a good reason. I'm good. I promise. We'll do this again."

I kiss his cheek again. He's just so…*understanding*. That's nice.

"Thank you, Drew. Really. I'll call you."

I take off on fast feet, shoving through people in the front of the restaurant waiting for tables and out onto the sidewalk. I scroll through my phone to Scottie's number and hit the green phone button to call her. Drew may not be an option for backup, but I'm definitely going to need it. Finn is the best set of muscle I can think of with Ace's dad out of town. If things get really dicey, Finn'll be able to get his newly discovered brothers—the Winslows—involved too.

"Hello?" she answers on the third ring, slightly out of breath.

"Scottie, is Finn with you?"

"Yeah, why?"

"I need him. In fact, I could probably use both of you. And Blake, if you can get ahold of him, as impossible as that's been this summer. But I need everyone you can get to meet me at Ace's parents' house pronto."

"Why? What's going on?"

"Something with Gunnar, and Ace's parents aren't home."

"Ohh boy."

"Girl, please." I blow out a breath. "You have no idea. Tell Finn… well, tell him to bring at least his fists, but if he's got a weapon, that probably wouldn't be bad either."

"Jesus, Julia!"

"I've gotta go! I'll meet you there!"

"Fine. I'll tell Finn to call Blake too."

"Perfect. Bye."

I hang up before she can say anything else, and I don't know if she was intending to or not. But I've got to call Ace, and I've got to call him quick. I need some kind of clue as to what we're walking into. I need to know if I need to call the cops.

I need to know if I need to call my dad.

I need to know if I need to alert the mayor or call in a favor to the National Guard.

I dial the number and put the phone to my ear, and he answers in two rings, his voice hurried.

"Hello? Jules?"

"I'm on my way. Finn and Scottie are on their way, and they're trying to call Blake too. What's going on, Ace? How bad is it?"

"It's bad, Jules. I think I'm going to have to call the cops."

"Oh God." As bad as that sounds, it could sound worse. Police are local. When we up the ante to federal agencies, like the FBI, I'll let myself panic. "Just do your best to contain the situation until I get there with backup. And whatever you do, do *not* take off your clothes."

"What? Why would I take off my clothes?"

"I don't know! You're the one with the information, but I keep picturing some very rough strip searching!"

"Noted. And…honestly, probably pragmatic, knowing Gunnar. I'll keep my clothes on. At least until you get here."

"Getting in a cab now!" I yell. "Bye!"

I hang up and put my hand in the air for a cab, but Drew steps out in the street in front of me, putting his fingers to his lips and whistling so loud his car pulls away from the curb down the block and floors it toward us immediately.

"Drew. What are you doing?"

"Coming with you."

"I said you didn't have to. I don't—"

"Jules, there's no way I was sending you out of here to rush to some emergency on your own. I just stayed back to pay the bill."

"Drew—"

"Don't worry about it, babe." He opens the door for me and holds out a hand. "Come on, get in."

I climb in the car and slide across the seat, and Drew gets in behind me. "Where are we headed?" the driver asks, and Drew turns to look at me.

Ready or not, I guess Drew's getting thrown into the deep end of the Kelly pool.

I sure hope he can swim.

"520 Park Avenue. And hurry."

"520 Park Ave?" Drew asks. "Isn't that on Billionaires' Row?"

"Yep." I nod.

Big money. Big hearts. Big trouble. That's the Kelly family in a nutshell. But hey, at least it means we always have bail money.

7

Ace

I swear, I tried to keep it cool. I really did. But when Julia asked me to stop texting her and reminded me she was on a date, I panicked. I couldn't just sit there and do nothing while she's across town eating garlic breadsticks with Drewchebag.

Now, my palms are sweating, and my shorts are clinging to my thighs, and when I hang up the phone, the guilt of what I've just created almost chokes me alive.

Good Lord, what have I done?

I've just made her abandon her date because I'm a jealous little fuckboy.

My chest grows tight, and the rubber band of injustice snaps me in the dick.

I pace the room like a caged animal, dragging my hands aggressively through my hair. If I made her leave that date for anything short of Armageddon, I can kiss my chances of making her love me goodbye. I've got to mobilize. I've got to improvise.

And I'd better do it fucking quick.

I transition from an aimless march to an all-out sprint out of my bedroom. I've just insisted she come home to help me with the party that Gunnar is throwing, and there's no party. There's no anything but me with my dick in my hand.

Shit! Shit! Shit!

Upon arrival to Gunnar's room, I'm disappointed to find him doing nothing other than lounging on his beanbag chair, some sort of fucking documentary playing on the TV at a neutral volume.

There's no fire. No belly dancers. There's not even a vape pen. I'm in big, *big* trouble here.

"What are you doing?" I shout, and Gunnar looks up at me in confusion.

"Uh…" Gunnar shrugs. "Watching the making of the International Space Station."

"You're fucking kidding me!"

Gunnar's brows draw together. He's obviously not kidding me, but of all the times for him to act like he's not the biggest menace to society on Planet Earth, he picks tonight. This is the kid who egged the governor's mansion on his school trip to Albany, for Pete's sake.

"Okay, fine. You're not kidding. You've gone through a metamorphosis from you to a…vegetable. But I need you to do something. Anything but this."

"I'm not following, bro." He's detached. Uninterested. Making my fucking heart burn.

"Can you, like, I don't know…light something on fire…steal a car…throw a party? Be you, for fuck's sake!"

"You want me to throw a party? Like, right now?" He mutes the TV and turns himself in his chair to face me fully. I don't like the look in his eye, but I got off the phone with Julia at least two minutes ago, so I don't really have the room to start thinking through how bad of an idea this could be *now*.

The train is in motion, and baby, it ain't stopping.

"Yeah."

Gunnar shrugs and gets out his phone, scrolling so calmly my balls shrivel into my body. He's either going full sociopath or fucking me over by being the most normal he's ever been, and right now—I can't believe I'm saying this—I need it to be the latter. I need him to be less contained. Pronto.

"What are you doing? Now isn't the time to play fucking Pokémon Go, bro."

He sighs. "In order to have a party, I need to invite people."

"Oh. Hitting up the group chat?"

Gunnar snorts. "I invited the whole contact list, excluding Mom and Dad."

"You *what?*"

He sighs again, this time rising from his beanbag chair and pulling off his pants until he's standing in nothing but his underwear. "You're really starting to annoy me. You wanted a party, and I'm throwing a party. What's the problem?"

"Your contact list? The entire thing? Our fucking grandparents are in your phone. Julia's parents. Dad's assistant."

He shrugs and pulls a different pair of shorts from his drawer, slinging them on. He doesn't get a shirt, though. He never gets a shirt, and he never responds when I try to explain that we're all tired of seeing his nipples. It's like his vocal cords stop working. "It'll sort itself out."

"Into chaos! You think Kline Brooks is getting a text about you throwing a fucking monster party at our house and not contacting our father? Dad's assistant Madeline? She's worked for him since before we were born!"

Gunnar shrugs. "Maybe they'll finally realize I'm gone, then."

Fuck me. He's not entirely wrong. It's been almost twenty-four hours at this point since he up and mysteriously flew back to New York from the Bahamas on some random airline while my parents slept or partied or who the hell knows. My parents are a unique set of individuals—I know that—but I can't *believe* they haven't noticed him missing yet. It just doesn't track.

For all I know, Gunnar blocked both of us as contacts in their phones and the Bahamian authorities are dragging the whole damn ocean right now.

"They probably *did* realize but have the Bahamian authorities doing an island-by-island grid search. Have you called them? Texted?"

"No. Have you?"

"Well, no. I've been…busy." Obsessing over Julia, trying not to self-destruct. It's been a *very* crowded agenda.

"Then it is what it is. If they find out, they find out."

"How are you the most casual human on the planet at fourteen? Like, are you missing the gene that synthesizes consequences? Are you a fucking sociopath? I really don't get it."

"You don't get it because you take life too seriously."

"Me? Take life seriously? Do you know who the fuck you're talking to?"

Gunnar scoffs. "Think what you want, but you're living in a tiny little box created by the nuances of societal expectation. I live without boundaries."

"I am not conventional," I protest. Ace Kelly is a fucking wonder. A visionary. A man with his own drum. Just ask anyone other than this fucker. I don't know what the hell he thinks he's talking about.

"Please. What have you done since the moment you realized you're in love with Julia? What are you doing right now? You're not throwing the party. I am."

I shake my head, aggravated. "Never mind. Just…invite whoever you want and get fucking chaotic, for the love of God. Julia's on her way over here now expecting you to be flashing the neighbors with a porn star's twig and berries or some shit."

Gunnar laughs, shrugging. "Suit yourself."

Shoving past me, he heads for the living room and starts pushing furniture out of the way piece by piece. I stand and watch, my hands on my hips and my heart in my throat. He opens the glass expanse back doors to the patio and turns on the string lights my mom hung as soon as they moved back into the city last summer.

For years, we lived in Jersey while my parents worked in New York, just so we could be in the same neighborhood as the Brookses. But with me going off to college at Dickson and Gunnar fucking disappearing to the city all the time anyway, they decided to stop phoning it in as commuters and take the plunge back into city life.

They changed our Short Hills estate into some kind of investment property that does luxury vacation rentals and Hollywood film sets and relocated to our penthouse in Manhattan. I won't deny it's a pretty bougie version of "city life" in this mega-penthouse, but it's still the city. And with all the New York debauchery at his fingertips, who the hell knows what Gunnar is going to have showing up here in the next few minutes.

Gunnar passes by me on his way to the front door, and I pivot like a flag in the wind. "You ever seen a peg-legged stripper before?" he asks.

"What?"

"A peg-legged stripper. She's got a leg that's a peg."

"Jesus, Gunnar. You're fourteen. How have *you* seen a peg-legged stripper?"

He rolls his eyes. "Little tiny box, bro. Little tiny box."

"I'm starting to think I'm okay with my box," I say, my voice escalating as he disappears into the hallway. "If the outside looks like whatever fresh hell you're living in," I finish on a mumble.

Moments later, he's back, with a cooler and two strong guys wheeling a hand truck full of liquor. My eyes bulge. "What the hell?"

"Don't worry," my underage brother says. "The kegs will be here in five minutes max."

"The kegs?"

He rolls his eyes. "Yeah, Ace. The kegs. How else do you think we're going to have enough supply for a thousand people?"

I gulp. "A thousand people?"

"What's with the shock-and-awe act?" he asks, getting frustrated with me. "You told me to throw a party. A rager. To create chaos, did you not? What did you expect? A group of old ladies knitting?"

"No. Fuck. I just didn't think you'd invite our fucking dentist."

He laughs. "Dr. Bunnfield can get down."

"God help the profession of dentistry. God help us all."

Our elevator dings open, and an onslaught of girls in tiny dresses disembarks, right into the apartment like it's their own. They give Gunnar air kisses on the cheek, promptly steal cans of wine spritzers from the coolers the two hulky guys are loading and retreat to the patio. Within three minutes, two more cartfuls arrive, and the noise level in our previously quiet penthouse ticks up ten decibels.

When a fifth cart of people shows up and makes themselves at home, I finally find Gunnar again and ask another question. "How are all these people just getting up here without you escorting them?"

"I gave out the elevator code in the text."

"You… Did you set a new one?"

He laughs. "No. I just gave the code."

"Fuck me, Gunnar." A deep sigh escapes my lungs. "Mom and Dad are going to kill us."

"You. They're going to kill *you*. Because one, I don't care enough to be killed. And two, you're the catalyst for this little soiree. I was happy watching my doc about the space station." He shrugs. "Just think, if you'd just had the balls to tell Julia you didn't want her on some date with some other dude, you could have avoided all this trouble."

"Screw you."

Gunnar laughs and wiggles his fingers. "Toodle-oo! Have a good night!"

"Toodle-oo? *Toodle-oo?* Where the hell are you going? Gunnar? Gunnar!" I yell as he officially disappears.

I am so, so fucked.

Within ten minutes, the entire 12,000 square feet of living space of my parents' Central-Park-adjacent penthouse is teeming with people. People I know, people I don't, and people I'm fairly certain found their way in off the street.

Gunnar's violin teacher from six years ago dances in the corner with a group of women I've never seen before, and the man—*boy*—who set it all in motion is still missing.

I have three missed calls from Kline Brooks, ten from Georgia

Brooks, and I just got a text from Julia that she *and* whatshisface will be here any minute. Apparently, *his car* got stuck in traffic on their way uptown.

My ears buzz, and my throat is thick with danger. I don't know how I'm going to get myself out of this one, and she's not even coming by herself.

Gunnar is right in one way—this was not a good plan.

I need a new plan. One that has fewer outside factors and more Ace factor. One I'm in complete control of. It'll be a grand plan. The best plan.

I just don't know what that is yet or how I'm going to put it into action with all these fucking people inside my parents' penthouse.

But surely I'll figure something out. I hope. I pray.

Succumbing slightly to the error of my ways, I head for the kitchen and fill a cup from the kegs that arrived right when Gunnar said they would. I haven't seen him since he disappeared, but I have seen a blind woman, a stripper with a peg leg, and a man with a fortune-telling goat. I've been too busy, you know, *freaking the fuck out* to let him read me yet, but he seems to be a big hit with all the ladies in attendance.

When the elevator opens and reveals Julia, I set my cup down on the counter, smooth my hands down my shirt, and rush over to her. Crusty McJockface follows her like a poodle on a fucking leash, his big, beefy hand at the small of her back. I see red and blue and green and every other color of the damn rainbow as I try to keep my tongue in my mouth and my brain from exploding.

"Oh my God, Ace. This is…insane. We were downstairs waiting for a turn in the elevator for, like, ten minutes before Drew forced our way into this one."

My teeth clench. "It's fucking Ripley's Believe It or Not in here tonight, Lia. There's a man with a goat somewhere, and if I'm not mistaken, I saw our middle school principal coming out of the bathroom before. Gunnar invited his entire contact list—including your parents."

She laughs. "Well, that explains the three screeching voice mails I've gotten from my mother and the cryptic text from my father about 'these damn Kellys.'"

"Did you talk to your dad? Has he talked to my dad?"

"Yes. He just texted me that your parents were in a helicopter after landing in Westchester."

"Oh God. So, they'll be here soon."

"According to my dad, yes. They left the Bahamas earlier today. They thought Gunnar fucking drowned. My dad is the one who told them he was home."

"My stomach hurts," I mutter as the meat sweats bubble my guts. I haven't had any meat—or any other food for that matter since Julia's date had me all fucking torn up—but it doesn't matter. I'm one sighting of my dad away from explosive diarrhea. I'm a big dude, but Thatcher Kelly is bigger in all the ways that count. Muscle, sheer determination, number of fucks he's lost the will to give.

I might as well make peace with God now because I'm pretty sure I'll be meeting him soon.

"Are you okay?" Julia asks, pushing me toward the couch that's officially relocated to the wall by the linen closet and sitting me down. "You look clammy."

As she finishes asking, the elevator doors open again, and a pig with a service vest comes running out. My parents' pig Philmore, a pet born of a ridiculous prank war between my parents, is in his twenties and aging considerably, but he's still got some pep in his step. Especially, I suppose, when he's arriving to a party in his home with all manner of YouTube starlets and TikTok influencers in attendance.

People start cooing and freaking out at his cuteness, but I feel a different sense of doom. His arrival heralds the arrival of my parents.

Julia stands at my side, a hand squeezing steadily at my shoulder as my parents step inside, surveying the scene around them. They're both wearing sunglasses—even though it's ten p.m.—so I can't get a good read on them, but they don't start screaming right away.

I pat Julia's hand twice before standing and turning to whisper in her ear. "If I don't make it back, just know that I loved you."

She giggles, not taking me seriously at all, which is just fucking perfect, really. Truly, it's right on par for how this whole damn night has gone anyway.

"Go on, buddy," she reassures. "It's going to be fine. This is Thatch and Cassie we're talking about, not the Kennedys. They've seen this before." Her head whips around as the pirate stripper walks by. "Except maybe that."

"Yeah," I say.

"Are those your parents?" Whatshisface asks in his big, lumbery, dumb voice.

I don't nod or answer, but Julia does, her little laugh making my skin crawl because it's directed at the wrong fucking guy—*aka not me.* "Yes. They are two of the wildest people you'll ever meet, which honestly explains their youngest son. It's the full power of their DNA combined. I think—"

As she keeps talking, turning to look into his eyes while he plays with the ends of her hair like he has any fucking right, I walk away. Toward the flogging. Toward the yelling. Toward hell.

Honestly, at this point, even a bloody beating from my parents seems like a better option than staying here and watching them re-enact an episode of *Love Island.*

My dad spots me pretty easily as I head for them—we're the two tallest people in the crowd—and waves me over with a crook of his fingers. I gulp and comply, heading toward him and my mom in the back hallway that leads to the movie theater.

Did I mention that my billionaire investment and accounting firm father also moonlights as a tattoo artist in his free time? Or that his and my mother's favorite pastime is playing pranks on each other?

And I'm not talking sitting on a whoopee cushion pranks. I'm talking hiring a mariachi band to follow their best friends around on their Valentine's getaway trip. I'm talking, when they were first dating, my mom bought my dad a mini pig that ended up being a real-sized pig and got him certified as an emotional support animal for my father's nonexistent depression and anxiety just to screw with him.

Not to mention, the first day of my freshman year at Dickson, my dad showed up to my first class with a fucking backpack and school supplies, saying he'd enrolled himself in all my classes and was going to experience college again with me.

I don't know for sure what my punishment will be, but I know it won't be good, and it won't be swift. I'll probably be paying for this for the rest of my natural-born life.

"What the ever-loving fluff is going on here?" my dad asks, moving me into a scary place against the wall. His hand doesn't press on my throat, but it lives on my shoulder, perfectly in pouncing position. "Kline texted. Said there was some big fucking blowout going on at our place."

"Without us!" my mom adds, as though the primary complaint is that there is a big party happening *without* her.

My dad tsks. "Like always, Kline and his big dick are right."

"Yeah, well, you know Gunnar," I lie. "He's unhinged. He… I tried to stop him, but he…he's not right. One minute, it was just the two of us, and the next, half the city was here."

"Is that Dr. Bunnfield?" my mom asks, watching with interest as our dentist keg stands in the kitchen.

Something smacks me in the back of the head, and when I notice Gunnar standing in the vicinity of the origin of the projectile, a wave of panic washes over me. His eyes say I owe him, and owing Gunnar is absolutely terrifying in every imaginable way. Plus, I owe him for the actual party and the lie about him being the reason for the party too. So, I owe him twice. And if you include my parents in the payback-punishment scenario, it's safe to say *I am fucked.*

I'll probably have a tattoo of a unicorn on my ass by Tuesday.

Or a septum piercing. Or be running drugs for the Colombians through Newark airport.

"Where is Gunnar?" my dad asks, his voice stern.

I look back to where he just was, but he's a phantom. If I know my brother, he's halfway out of the city by now on one of those rickshaw carts, headed for a Devils game or something. He doesn't give a fuck. And when he doesn't give a fuck, it's as if he has magic powers. "I don't know," I answer candidly. "I really don't know."

Thatcher sighs, and I take a deep breath. Sighs are better than rage. Sighs are a sign of defeat.

"Well, shit. I guess we might as well get a beer, hun."

My mom nods. "I've been reaming out the Bahamian police's asses for a day straight. I need a drink. Did your brother get Heineken?"

I swear, my life is an early 2000s comedy starring Stifler's mom.

"Uh. Yeah." I run a hand through my hair. "Pretty sure the keg in the kitchen is."

"Perfect. Come on, T-bag. You can hold my legs when I keg stand."

I watch as my parents head for the party in the kitchen and take turns handstanding on the big silver drum while chaos reigns supreme around us. Philmore oinks and scurries around them, and whatshisface holds my dad's legs when he takes a second turn.

It is hell on earth, and Finn and Scottie haven't even managed to make it up the elevator yet. The night is so, so young.

And the only thing that could make it worse, does.

Julia hangs there with my parents and whatshisface, laughing and smiling and possibly falling a little bit in love...

With the wrong fucking guy.

My plan...foiled. Couldn't have gone worse, actually.

Guess I'd better get busy coming up with a new one—one that'll work.

My mom sits spread-eagled in sweatpants and a baggy T-shirt, a bag of peas at the apex of her thighs and a sleep mask with cartoon bug eyes strapped on her head. She lies back, groaning lightly, and I sneak on light feet through the hall at the back of the couch to try to avoid conversation.

She pops up quickly, resting herself on one elbow and pulling the mask up off her eyes, and I freeze, a cramp in my toes forming immediately.

"Where are you going?" she asks, accusation making the words lash.

"I…uh…out?"

"Nope. Nuh-uh. We need all hands on deck cleaning this place up, and I'm, as you can see, vaginally indisposed."

"Ugh, Mom." I groan. I'm still tired, drained, and fucking bleeding from the eyes and ears over the things I saw last night—over the things that were still happening up until three short hours ago when my dad and Finn finally managed to kick the last group of lingering people out of here. I don't need my mom saying the word "vaginally" any time of day, but of all the times of day I don't need it, this is the pinnacle.

"Don't *ugh, Mom* me. You're on Solo cup duty until I can get my feet back under me. Your father is vacuuming." She adjusts her position on the couch and nods down the hall, where the faint hum of the vacuum moves slowly closer.

"Vacuuming? Does Thatch even know how to vacuum?" I can hardly picture my big, meaty-handed father operating such a short domestic device with any skill, let alone to the tune of 12,000 square feet of living space.

"Please, Ace." My mother sighs. "Ask something that makes sense. Of course he knows how to vacuum. As a matter of fact, suction is one of his specialties."

"Oh-kay. Jeez. Really?" I cry. "Must you?" I know I left myself open by interacting at all, but you'd think the universe, having seen Julia hand in hand with Colonel Frat Mustard for so many hours last night while Finn and Scottie did an excellent job of reminding me exactly the kind of loving relationship I'm missing at the same time, would cut me a break. I'm a walking wound. My pus is festering among the mess and infecting my whole life.

She laughs, unbothered. That's one thing about my mom—she's *never* bothered. It doesn't matter if I'm on the brink of the most formidable moment of my manhood. That's a me problem.

An overwhelming hum enters the room briskly, my tall-ass father behind it with big black headphones on. He shoves and wields the vacuum wildly, ramming it into furniture and concentrating more on dancing with high knees than what he's sucking up.

The machine grinds and bogs down as it picks up something bigger than its hose can handle, but he's undeterred, pushing onward toward us while he swings his hips back and forth.

One thing I know for sure: our housekeeper is going to be so pissed when she comes in to a broken vacuum and scuffed-up baseboards.

His gaze flickers up and locks on my mom and her ice-pack-covered hoochie, and he switches off the vacuum immediately, removing his headphones and tossing them among the other debris on the coffee table.

"What are we doing here?" He grins. "Cooking up my favorite meal?"

"Oh God," I groan, and my mom laughs riotously.

"You wish. I'm sore from last night."

"Sore? Did we fuck and I forgot about it? Pulled a you and fell asleep while my dick was still in ya?"

She shakes her head, and I don't bother asking. In fact, I avoid asking so hard the job is practically a paid position.

"No, you big oaf. I pulled my groin trying to outdo your keg stand."

"Ahh." He nods proudly. "Yeah, your first mistake was trying to outdo me, sweetheart. You know that's impossible."

"Shut up. I don't have the patience to argue with you *and* ice my vageen, okay?"

My dad shrugs, latching on to my shoulder instead just as I'm about to escape. "What about you, son? Pretty big to-do last night. Did you have a good time?"

"Hardly," I grumble under my breath before I can think better of it. The whole thing was a fucking debacle and a half, and *I'm* the reason it even happened in the first place. Not only did I *not* make any progress with Julia, I earned myself fucking cleanup duty this morning while Gunnar is God knows where doing God knows what. And yet, even not knowing where he is, I know my fate from his revenge lingers in the distance like a sniper in the mist.

I'm scared. And shaken. And this is only the beginning.

"What? You didn't have a good time?" My dad shakes his head. "Julia looked like she had a good time with that Chad guy."

"Chad?" my mom asks, popping up from her forlorn spot and entering the conversation again. "Who's Chad? I thought his name was Brad."

"Chad, Brad, whatever." Thatch just shrugs a shoulder. "He seemed like a cool dude."

"Who?" I ask, only half cognizant of the conversation. I'm too busy picturing Finn and Scottie chumming it up on double date-ish terms while they chatted with Julia and whatshisface. And to think I've spent the last year considering Finnley Hayes my bestie. My brother from another mother.

He'll be hearing of my feelings on his betrayal. That's for sure.

"The guy Julia was with," my mom clarifies helpfully, snapping me both into awareness and an All-American rage.

"Fuck that guy," I say simply.

"Whoa, bud. I don't know if we can condone this language," my dad jokes, and I roll my eyes.

"His name isn't Chad or Brad. And he's not fucking cool. Not even a little bit."

"Oh jeez, sorry, Mr. Name Police. Did I strike a nerve or what?" my dad asks, glancing over his shoulder at my mom conspiratorially.

I shake my head and move away to start collecting Solo cups while they continue to bicker back and forth.

"Go easy on him, you fuck," my mom chastises. "Remember how pathetic you were when you were in love with me?"

"Pathetic?" my dad scoffs. "I was not pathetic. And what does love have to do with Chad?"

"Please!" my mom volleys back. "You were the most pathetic! You practically begged me to live with you. Sent me flowers all the time. Kept sleeping with me even though I continually fell asleep on you. You were desperate. Hard up."

"Uh-uh, honey." He waggles his finger at my mom. "I think your memory is taking creative liberties, because the way I remember it, you were the one doing the begging. You moved in with me without invitation, sent *yourself* flowers from my dick, and got me a pig so you could baby-trap me."

Philmore oinks with perfect timing, cruising through the room on the way to his playroom down the hall.

I sigh and pick up more cups, my mind whirling on a new plan for setting Julia's love train back on the right tracks—the ones that lead to me.

Most people would say I need to tell her how I feel, but I know with every ounce of my being she is *not* ready for this kind of intimate knowledge. And I *can't* ruin our friendship. Before I realized I was in love with her, I could barely stand to spend a day without her. Now that I'm privy to my heart's one and only true desire, I'd put Julia in my pocket and carry her around all day if I could.

Which, frankly, would be incredibly helpful when it comes to keeping her away from Dicky Drewlface.

You're an idiot. Julia is petite, but she's not Tinker Bell.

Against my better judgment, I turn back to my parents, reengaging them in conversation. "When you guys were dating, what changed your mind from just fucking around to it being the real deal? I mean, why do you love each other?"

My mom flashes a look to my dad, moving the peas on her vagina enough to sit up straight. "Well, son, your father, despite his many, many idiosyncrasies, is a capable man. He's a good lover, a good heart, and a really good sportsman."

"Sports—" I shake my head at myself and cut the question short. "You know what, never mind. I don't wanna know." I sigh. "I just thought…you guys seem happy and…" I huff as my mom's eyes get wide. "Forget it."

"What's on your mind, Acer?" Thatcher insists, waving a hand at my mom to keep her quiet. "Having trouble with the ladies?"

I roll my eyes. "Don't worry about it, Dad."

"I'm sorry, buddy, but I can't do that," he says earnestly.

And I thaw a little, wondering if my initial idea to bring my parents into the problem/solution brainstorm wasn't such a bad idea. Maybe they can help—

"I have to worry about it because your erectile dysfunction could sully the Kelly name."

"Dad!" I shout, all my good feelings officially gone and beaten by a dead horse I should've known they'd kill. "I'm not suffering from ED!"

"Well!" he shouts back, shrugging at my mom with a playful wince.

"Forget it." I hold up a desperate hand. "Just go back to your icing vaginas and shitty vacuuming and forget I said anything."

"Come on, now, Acer." My dad sits down on the couch beside

my mom and pats the cushion next to him, and stupidly, I take him up on the offer. "Let's have a real talk about what's going on."

I shake my head. I'm not ready to have a real talk. To confess my love for Julia or beg for help or ask them how I could have ignored it for so long. So I just sit there instead, soaking in the silence. For the first time maybe ever, they soak it in too.

"Maybe you should talk to Julia," my mom suggests lightly, but her eyes are far too knowing. "If you're not ready to talk to us."

I snort. "Yeah, Julia is the last person I'm ready to talk to about this."

"I knew it!" my dad yells, snapping his fingers and playfully shoving my mom before pretending to motorboat her boobs.

My head falls back on a grimace.

"You love her, don't you?" My dad claps with glee. "You love a little Brooks girl, and I'm going to get to rub this in Kline's big dick and face for the rest of our lives, aren't I? Tell me, son. Tell me you're going to marry her, and Kline is going to have to officially call us family. Make your daddy's day."

I hate that he knows. But according to Blake, everyone but me knew for a long fucking time.

"Everything feels so fucked." I let out a deep sigh. "Honestly, I don't know how I didn't realize it sooner."

Thatch jumps up from his seat and thrusts his arms in the air, spinning in a circle. "Yes! Fuck yes! All my dreams are coming true! My manifestation journal is working!"

My mom laughs. "Great. You've done it now. Now we'll never get rid of that fucking journal."

"I am wealthy. I am worthy. I am horny." He flashes my mom with a wink. "Can you help me with any of those, honey?"

"I'm currently indisposed, Thatcher," she retorts. "And frankly, the fact that it took you this long to figure out your son is in love with Julia makes me wonder if I married below my IQ level," my mom adds on a sigh. "Ace has been in love with Julia since before he could even write his name."

Apparently, Blake was right.

"I knew," my dad refutes. "Of course I knew." He moves his eyes back to me. "On a side note, Acer, it was wild how long it took you to figure out how to write your name. I mean, it's three fucking letters, you know? Your mother and I were worried there for a bit."

"Jeez. Thanks for that. You're really helping boost the confidence." I groan, but I also laugh. For as wild as my parents both are, I'm still thankful they're my parents. "Just forget I said anything, guys."

"No, no. Now, Ace of Base. There's no need to be insecure. You can spell your name and even tell time now and shit. We didn't think you'd make it past second grade, and you're in college, buddy! You're doing the damn thing!" He pumps a celebratory fist in the air.

"Wow," I deadpan. "Thanks."

"Though," he adds with a shrug, "you clearly have some work to do if you don't want Chad edging in on your tail."

"I'm going to tell Kline you called his daughter tail," my mom mutters, which makes my dad pinch her nipple and rip the bag of peas from her vageen.

Never mind, I take it back. I regret that these two are supposed to be my guides in life.

"Acer, what you need to do is prove to Julia that you're more than the man she knows," my dad continues trying to give me advice. "You're more than the funny, plucky friend. You are a strong force of safety and love, do you hear me?"

I roll my eyes and climb from the couch to start collecting cups again. Suddenly, that sounds like the better option.

"You are a wildflower, just waiting to sow your seed!" my dad shouts, well after I'm out of sight. "Be the wind, son! The wind beneath her wings!"

"Dad! Just let it go!" I call back. "Seriously. And do not try to intervene! I will handle this myself!"

You'd think I wouldn't need to say that, but this is Thatch and Cassie we're talking about. If I left them to their own devices, they'd end up outside Julia's window serenading her with fucking Air Supply songs on behalf of me.

"You can do it, Acer! You're a Kelly, son! And Kelly men have a long-standing track record of proving they're worthy of only the best women!"

I roll my eyes. Though, for all the bullshit he's spouting, some of it is producing a by-product of sense.

Maybe…maybe he's onto something.

Maybe I just need to prove that I'm love-worthy to Julia.

And how in the hell do I do that? By showing her how great I can be. By proving to her that I'm the man she needs. Then when I finally tell her I love her, there'll be no chance she'll reject me.

If I'm the perfect guy, she'll have no option but to love me back.

I start by texting her dad some very important information. In with him, in with her. The Brooks family is a package deal, and I'm shipping myself overnight, next day air if I have to so I can be part of it too.

And then, I take to Google, searching up, **What do women love in a man?**

Instantly, I'm given a lengthy list, with things like **responsible, protective, trustworthy, makes her feel safe, handsome, kindness, good sense of humor, self-aware, authenticity, good hygiene and grooming, emotional intelligence, stability, supportive, good communication skills, shows vulnerability, and verbalizes his thoughts and feelings.**

I pull up my notes app and start adding key things to the list that I know I need to prove to her.

Clearly, shit like good sense of humor and handsome are already done, but I can be a better communicator. I can be more responsible. I can be more protective. I can be more self-aware.

I can be a lot more things. I'm *going to be* a lot more things.

For Julia.

Ace's Plan to Woo Julia is officially in session.

Julia

"What the hell happened at the Kellys' last night?" my dad asks, pulling the newspaper down from its spot in front of his face and downing a swig of orange juice. We're in our Manhattan flat this morning, which is much smaller than our house in New Jersey, but fun to get away to every now and then. Plus, it makes it easy when I don't leave Ace's parents' place until four a.m. Not that Ace wouldn't have let me sleep over—he would have. But with Drew there, I felt like it was less awkward to leave together.

"Cassie texted me forty times while I was asleep," my mom chimes in. "Each one getting more and more manic about icing her vagina. I swear I don't even know how they've been our best friends for this long, Kline."

I roll my eyes and laugh as Evie repeats ice and vagina like it's a tic. She doesn't have one, but she's been watching old episodes of *Malcolm in the Middle* lately and has a habit of assimilating her real life to go with her TV fixation.

"Gunnar came home from the Bahamas early and threw a party for like five hundred people at their house last night," I update with the straight facts. "Ace panicked, of course, so I went over to try to help calm it down, but Thatch and Cassie ended up coming home and kind of joining in, so it was just a party." I shrug. This isn't that outside the realm of normal for the Kellys.

"Cassie said some guy was there with you too," my mom

remarks what she thinks is carefully. It's hilarious how obvious it is she's dying to know about him.

"I swear it's like a CIA network around here. It's no big deal yet. He's just a guy from school."

"Ace texted me about him too," my dad admits. "Asked me if I own a shotgun. Something about not trusting anyone and doing my dadly diligence."

What the hell?

I roll my eyes. "He's being a weirdo. Drew is fine. You don't have to bust out shotguns or be dadly, I swear. We've had one interrupted date and then partied with Ace's parents. I'd hardly say you need to be knitting grandbaby clothes."

"Julia!" my mom whispers, but my dad just laughs.

"Well, okay then. Let me know if it gets more serious, and I'll get involved."

I giggle. "Thanks, Daddy."

He winks at me over the paper and goes back to reading it, and I jump up to grab an omelet from the pan and a couple of pieces of bacon. My grandfather, Dick, got up and made them earlier while he was waiting for my grandmother to come back with their travel trailer during street cleaning. He finished breakfast and then went down to save the spot for her to park in right after the sweeper went by.

It's funny, really, but they're a great example of real love. Of give-and-take. Of fun and acceptance. It probably doesn't hurt that my grandmother has been a sex therapist for her entire adult life, and because my grandparents have zero filter, I have too much knowledge that their sex life reflects that.

And yes, that is very much both disturbing and endearing.

I take my plate and move over to the window seat overlooking the street.

My grandpa moves out of the spot he's been saving and waves my grandma in with their truck and trailer, a bright-pink sign with a vagina-shaped flower on the side declaring "Heals on Wheels."

My grandmother, Savannah Cummings, my mother's mother, is one of the most popular sex therapists on the East Coast. Since hitting the road to see the country in their camper, Savannah has taken her therapy to the streets as well. She's helped people in forty out of fifty states, according to her records, and I can practically hear the satisfied moans from here.

My phone buzzes from my lap, and I pick it up to look at it while I watch my grandma park their massive trailer in the middle of Manhattan. Honestly, she's pretty much a badass the way she can handle it.

Ace: What a fucking shitshow. You would not believe the amount of stuff there is to clean this morning and Gunnar is nowhere to be found

I giggle and type a message back.

Me: He's probably back in the Bahamas.

Ace: Holy shit don't even joke because that is so possible

Me: If it makes you feel any better, you're not the only one with family tales. My grandparents are backing in their Heals on Wheels travel trailer in front of our building as we speak, and a guy in a blue Buick LeSabre just got out and kissed my grandpa on the mouth before going into the trailer with my grandma. I'm pretty sure it's therapy happening in there, but it could be a swingers moment.

Ace: Savannah and Dick are in town? Are you in Manhattan still because if you are you should meet me for breakfast. My mom is passed out on the couch with a bag of peas between her legs and my dad is singing Britney Spears at the top of his lungs while he destroys our baseboards with a vacuum I'm pretty sure I can escape unnoticed

Me: Yeah, we stayed in the city. My mom and dad came in when they started getting the texts about the party, so I could come back here and my dad could come over and intervene if needed. I'm already having an omelet my grandpa made, but you can come over. We'll go do something.

Ace: Sounds good I'll be there in 30

Me: Cool. Just one thing, tho… Why are you texting my dad about Drew and shotguns? You don't trust your own best friend's judgment?

Ace: New number who dis

Me: Ace. Be serious. You don't like Drew?

Ace: He's fine I was just hyped up from the party. No worries okay

Me: I don't like it. In fact, it kind of made me mad. You should trust me more.

Ace: I'm sorry. You know I trust you. I trust you more than anyone. Even more than Finn and that kid is pretty fucking stand-up you know. This had nothing to do with me trusting you and more me having a hard time trusting other people to treat my best friend right.

Not going to lie, I was pretty pissed off he'd texted my dad about Drew, but I get what he's saying. And it's kind of sweet he was being protective of me.

Ace: Fifteen-minute rule?

Me: Yeah. No worries. I'm already over it.

Ace: Fanfuckingtastic. And seriously I'm sorry Lia. I crossed a line I know I did

Me: Water under the bridge.

Ace: Perfect. I'll see you in 30…unless my mom kills me on the way out and in that case it's been nice knowing you

I smile and laugh. Cassie's been threatening to kill her whole family since before I was born, and it hasn't happened yet. I have a feeling my buddy will make it out alive and well.

Me: See you soon.

I put my phone away and jump up, rinsing my plate in the sink and heading for my room to get dressed. Evie calls out after me. "Where are you going?"

"Out with Ace!" I call back.

It's no surprise. It's steady. Ace and I, we've always been a set. And I don't see that changing anytime soon.

After Ace picked me up, we took the subway over toward campus to have breakfast at our favorite hangout spot. Zip's Diner is basically a rite of passage for any Dickson student. It's greasy, it's kitschy, and it never fails to feel like home whenever we walk inside.

Ace doesn't hesitate to head over to our favorite booth, and I slide in across from him.

"When did Finn say they'd be here?"

"Any minute now," he answers and sets his phone on the table. "They tried to back out, but I used my sappiest complaints about all the time they've spent without us this summer and needing to download after last night's party. Plus, I guilted them that Zip would be sad if they didn't come."

I laugh. "You are the man with the powers of manipulation."

"Hey now. I prefer to recognize it as the power of persuasion. It's what they already want, I just make it more obvious for them, that's all."

"That's how you got Blake Boden to be your friend too, isn't it?"

Ace laughs. "It might be."

"Yo," Finn's voice greets, pushing Scottie in front of him in her chair and tucking her in her spot at the table before shoving in next to Ace. They do a little bro-hug battle thing before settling down, and Zip comes over to take their drink orders.

We all order our food too, since we've been here so many times before and don't even need to look at the menu, and Scottie starts talking about the party last night with stars in her eyes.

"Listen, I just want to know where Gunnar found some of these people. Lilian Latrain was there. Lilian Latrainnn. Do you know who that is?"

"Obviously not," Ace says, chewing on a piece of buttered bread and licking his lips when the butter smears on his chin. I hand him a napkin around the table and then take a baby wipe out of my purse for him to use. He *hates* the smell of butter on his face.

"God, you're a fucking animal," Finn teases. "Can't even keep the food in your mouth, for fuck's sake."

Ace gives him the finger and focuses his attention back on Scottie, taking the wipe from me gratefully. "So, who the fuck is Lilian Latrainnn? We're all waiting. I could stand to hear something fucking good from that shitshow of a party after all."

Scottie laughs. "Finn knows who she is."

"Yeah." He grins at her. "Because you stalk her videos constantly."

Scottie squeals. "You say that like it's weird. She has eight million followers, Finn. The equivalent of New York City's population."

"Eight million?" Ace shrieks. "Say what now? Who the hell is this chick?"

"She's a beauty influencer," Scottie explains. "And a travel influencer. And kind of an entrepreneur. She comes from a rich family, but she's built so much wealth of her own."

"Oh yeah!" I say as realization sets in. "I've seen her! She does videos with all the emojis, right?"

"Yes! Her editing skills are top-notch, but she really took off because she was doing a whole skit where she'd make herself look like an entirely different person with makeup and play two parts. Like, we're talking Hollywood-level makeup. At first, it was just two-person skits, but then she started doing full-cast things. I can't even imagine the time she put into all the makeup and editing."

"Oh my God. Yes! I remember now. She did that scene from *She's All That*. Somehow, she looked like Freddie Prinze Jr., Rachael Leigh Cook, and Matthew Lillard all in one video."

"Yep. That's one of her most viral. I think like a hundred million views or something crazy. And then she did one like all the ladies from *Sex and the City*. And full-on looked like all of them! I couldn't believe it."

"So, Finn," Ace interjects, cutting off Scottie's and my Lilian Latrain talk before it devolves into discussions of the luteal phase. "How about those Mavericks?"

Finn laughs. "It's okay, Ace. You don't have to act manly for me. It's not even football season."

"Yeah, well, tell that to Boden. The fucker barely answers my calls. Didn't even text me back about the party last night. My life could have been in danger. He didn't care."

"He's got, like, two-a-day practices," Finn argues. "I wouldn't want to drag my ass out in the middle of the night to deal with your shit either."

"Don't say that, Finnley. You love me."

"Yeah," he grumbles. "Against my better judgment."

"Oh, stop. If you hadn't have seen Scottie on the first day of school, you'd be in love with me right now."

"And what?" Scottie scoffs through a laugh. "I'd still be with Dane?"

"Don't even fucking joke about that shit," Finn mutters, his mood sullied so much that Ace and I make wide eyes at each other.

"I should'a killed that kid."

Ace jerks his chin at me to create a distraction, so I say the first thing that comes to mind.

"Drew asked me out again last night." A different kind of silence falls over the table, but I keep talking. "Our actual date got cut short by Gunnar's party, and he says he's had a crush on me since he met me last year—"

"He's had a crush on you for a—" Ace starts to ask, but Scottie cuts in before he can continue.

"Well, of course he's had a crush on you, Jules. You're the best. Right, Ace? Right, Finn?"

"Right," Finn says immediately.

Ace watches me closely. I don't know what he's thinking right now, but his silence makes me chew on my bottom lip and twist my straw in my water. I don't want to care so much about what he thinks about every little thing, but I do. He knows me better than anyone.

"Of course he's had a crush on you, Jules," he eventually says, and his face softens. "There's no one better than Julia Brooks. I'm a close second, of course." He winks at me. "But you've always been number one on my list. And I was number one on Finn's list until Scottie came along."

Scottie snorts. Finn elbows Ace in the chest.

"Ow," Ace mumbles, rubbing his chest with his eyes on me. They dance with affection, and I count my blessings that I've had a best friend as awesome as him for my entire life.

"I'm sorry I ruined your bromance with Finn, Ace," Scottie comments with a mischievous smile. "I know the two of you were quite the couple at the beginning of freshman year."

"Oh God," Finn mutters. "Please do not encourage him."

Ace just laughs. "Oh, c'mon, Finnley. You know you miss being my roommate."

"I miss being your roommate as much as that peg-legged stripper from last night misses her left foot."

"She was oddly talented, wasn't she?" Scottie questions.

"From your lips to God's ears, babe," Finn comments through a chuckle. "I almost forgot her left leg was wooden when she was playing backup dancer and singer with Thatch and that old dude with the glasses."

"Dr. Bunnfield," Ace chimes in.

"Excuse me?"

"The old dude with glasses is my dentist. Dr. Bunnfield."

"Your fucking dentist was at that party last night?" Finn questions in a shocked laugh.

Ace nods. Scottie starts asking him a bunch of questions about how his dentist ended up at that party last night, and while Ace tries to explain how truly unpredictable his baby brother is, I discreetly pick up my phone to open my text thread with Drew.

> **Drew: So…have you come to a final conclusion on my second date chances? Not trying to pressure you, but also, if it isn't obvious already, I really want to see you again, Julia.**

I didn't give him a real answer last night about rescheduling, but that's probably because I was distracted by how everything was going to turn out for Ace and Gunnar in the light of day.

Now that I know Ace is alive and well and thriving as usual, I feel okay to say yes.

> **Me: Tell me the time and place, and I'll put it on my calendar.**

10

Gary drops me off at the curb of Brower Center, the student union building for Dickson University, and then pulls away to find a place to park and hang out while I do my thing. I say *thank you* and *see you soon* because I'm not an impolite fuck, but I have to admit, with the text that just came in from my best friend—and recent LOML—Julia Brooks after asking her what her plans are for today, I don't have much space to handle anything else.

> **Julia: At the swim club with Drew, actually. You should come meet us when you get done on campus! Did your peer counselor say why she wanted to meet and go over your schedule again? I only had to meet with mine once.**

Since the failed party initiative at my parents' place, Julia's gone on another date with the fuckbag and hung out with him and his fuckbag friends twice, including today.

I'm annoyed, but I'm also optimistic since starting the next phase of my plan.

Now that I'm balls deep in trying to make my best friend fall in love with me, I'm putting everything I can into action that will paint me in the best light possible and keep me close to Julia.

I wouldn't say I have my plan all plotted out into a bullet-point list, but I know it's multifaceted and I know it's in motion. Creative inspiration takes time to prove that you're a responsible, trustworthy, perfect, love-worthy man. And whenever that inspiration strikes, I'm grabbing it with both hands and running with it.

Trust me, it hasn't been easy being *very* supportive of Julia's new dating status, but I'm doing it as a keystone of security. Close is the place to be, even if I'm secretly the enemy. I've smiled, I've congratulated, I've checked in and done it often. And I've held back the urge to ask Gunnar to help me kidnap Drew mafia-style, put cinder blocks on his ankles, and toss him in the Hudson.

I hate knowing she's spending five percent of her time with someone else—but ninety-five percent has still been with me. She texts and calls when she's with him, and we haven't fought or needed the fifteen-minute rule at all.

I am Zen. I am steady. I am everything she needs and then some.

> **Me: Sounds good babe. I dunno she wasn't specific but I'll meet you there when I'm done**

I stroll through the food court and grab a quick bite of oatmeal—this level of sleuthing requires fueling—and when I realize I've only got two minutes until meeting start time, I head back out of the cafeteria in the direction of my peer counselor's office.

I'm excited.

In opposition to what I told Julia, I am the one who asked for this meeting, and I did so with purpose. It's all a part of the plan, of course—*oof.*

Like two concrete walls being slammed into each other, I run into a body with the force of my distraction. I push back gently, ready to apologize for having my head too far in Julia's ass to pay attention, but the voice that greets me is a sound for sore ears.

"Hey, Ace."

"Holy shit, everybody, it's Blake Boden!" I yell dramatically, cupping my hands around my mouth to fashion a makeshift megaphone. Blake blushes, and I get my jollies. I fucking love how bashful he is about being a football star. Not to mention, it feels like this bastard has been avoiding me since final exams were over in May. "How's it going, man? You're up and about pretty early."

"Me?" he questions, glancing at me and then at the bustling people behind me and back again. "What about you? What are you doing on campus this morning?" He's right to be suspicious, though I don't appreciate the distrust to my vision. If Blake should know anything at all about me by now, it's that I always have a plan and a reason. Always.

"I have a meeting with my peer counselor in a little bit to go over my schedule for the fall. I'm planning to make some changes to my original plan, so I wanted to get ahead of the game."

"Changes? You switching majors or something?"

I laugh. *Majors.* This fucking kid with his "societal norms" and shit. "Oh. No. I'm putting myself in a position to be in every single one of Julia's classes, that's all."

His face is a mask of both judgment and appreciation, and I revel in both. I don't hide from my ways—I embrace them. The only thing I haven't quite mastered yet is how to confront Julia, but that has more to do with positioning myself away from failure than embarrassment.

"Ah. I see we're still coming to terms with the Julia thing."

"Oh no. I've come to terms. The thing is, she doesn't even know the terms exist, and all these fuckers all over this campus sure as shit don't either. No way in hell I'm letting some preppy kid with bad breath scoop her out from under me before I have the chance to convince her to love me back."

Blake nods and chuckles. "Well, as long as you're handling it reasonably."

"Reasonable is my middle name, bro."

"Of course."

"What are you doing? Grabbing breakfast?" I ask. He's been keeping to himself this summer, despite our constant pestering. I know he's been busy with football, but I also have to make sure he's not just bullshitting me. Nobody avoids Ace Kelly and gets away with it.

"Yeah," he agrees easily, nodding toward the buffet line behind me. "Grabbing something quick so I can chill a little before practice."

I jerk up my chin and hold out a hand for him to shake. It's nice catching up, but I've got an appointment to get to upstairs posthaste. "All right. Well, hit me up later. I think we're all going to get together and do something. Feels like we've barely gotten to see you this summer, you've been so busy acting like you're a fucking football savant or some shit."

Blake laughs. "I'll see what I get into later and let you know."

"Fine. But you have to at least come to Fourth of July with us," I insist, pointing a finger in his chest. "We're all going to Finn's uncle's lake house. It's a big Winslow family tradition that now includes the Hayeses, my crazy-ass parents, and Julia's mom and dad. Despite the parental units being there, I swear it'll be a good time."

"I'll see if I can make it, but it sounds as if it has potential," Blake replies with a sexy hotshot wink. He plays the humble part well, but underneath it all, he's a cocky little shit like the rest of us, I know it.

"*Potential?*" I scoff. "It's going to be a good fucking time, Golden Boy. My dad and Gunnar went out and bought a shit-ton of fireworks. Your ass needs to be there, bro… Anyway, I gotta run. I'll catch you later." I slap him on the back and run toward the stairwell by the door. A quick glance at my watch reveals I'm two minutes late, which isn't exactly the best start when you're trying to talk people into shit they aren't technically allowed to do.

My phone buzzes in my hand, and worried it might be Julia, I open the screen to read the message and climb the stairs all at once.

It's not Jules, though; it's Finn. And while I do read what he has to say, I put off responding until I'm out of this fucking meeting. He should know by now that friendship with me is meant to be a roller coaster of highs and lows of fun.

> *Finn: I really will kill you if you don't stop signing me up for subscriptions I don't want. Fucking jam? What about me makes it look like I'm a jam guy, Ace?*

Tucking my phone into my pocket, I scoot up to the receptionist inside the poor counseling office and engage my smile. "Hi, there. Ace Kelly here to meet with Mrs. Patreetus. So sorry I'm a couple minutes late. I ran into my good friend Blake Boden downstairs and didn't want to be rude by not saying hello."

I name-drop Blake like a celebrity in Hollywood, and I do it without an ounce of shame. Around Dickson's campus, he is an enigma.

The receptionist meets my eyes, her smile growing when I throw her a wink, and then scoots her chair back to guide me down the hall. "Right this way. I'll show you to her office."

Mrs. Patreetus is mid-chew on a hot dog the size of Gary's Escalade when receptionist girl opens the door and leads me inside. A dollop of mustard falls on her sleeveless sweater, and she wipes it away with a dry napkin and a bun-filled, awkward smile. It's a little weird that she's eating a footlong this early in the morning, but *a little weird* is my love language. The tension in my shoulders leaves, my objective more in reach than ever.

Me and Mrs. Patreetus are about to get down. I can feel it.

"Welp, what brings you in today, Ace? Feeling nervous about your schedule? Thinking about picking a major? I know it's a big decision, but—" She launches in, setting aside the jumbo dog and pulling her laptop to the center of her desk to get it fired up.

I don't bury the lede—I know now I don't need to. Clearly, Mrs. Patreetus can swallow it. Plus, I've got a fluffing pool where Julia's currently unsupervised in a bikini with a bunch of fuckbags to get to.

"I'm here to change all my classes."

Her eyebrows draw together. "Change…all your classes? Did you pick something that has some different requirements?"

"Oh yeah. I picked something different, all right." I pull the crumpled piece of notebook paper from my pocket and smooth it down on the table between us. "These are the ones I need to be in."

"Calculus 2? Physics? Psych 201?" She shakes her head. "Ace, these are some pretty tough classes. I thought at our last meeting we decided to steer clear of advanced math and stick with something more fitting of a communications major?"

"Yeah, well, I changed my mind. I want to challenge myself. Really lean into my education and stuff. I mean, why else am I here, you know?"

"I don't know that you're qualified to move on to Calc 2—"

"Mrs. Patreetus, please. I'm begging you. I can't…" I bite my knuckles. "I can't quite explain the shift in my mind-set in detail, but I can tell you with certainty I'm dedicated to this."

She doesn't quite take the bait, so I keep going.

"I'm going to give it my all. I'm going to seek help when I need it." *From Julia as often as possible.* "I'm going to dedicate my life to these classes…" *And making the girl in all of them fall in love with me.*

"This is quite the big challenge, Ace," Mrs. Patreetus says. "But I don't know if this is a good plan. I'm not so sure it's setting you up for success."

Shit. It's time to really lay it on—thicker than the mustard that's currently sitting on her footlong.

"Mrs. Patreetus, you know, I really appreciate that your goals revolve around setting me up for success. I can't tell you how much that means to me," I say and avert my eyes for a long moment, my gaze a little hesitant, a little shy, a little Hollywood Oscar-worthy. "I don't have a lot of people in my life who do that for me. It makes me feel really comfortable around you, Cynthia. Do you mind if I call you Cynthia?"

"Uh. I—"

"My dad owns Kelly Financial," I cut her off on purpose. "One of the biggest investment and accounting firms on Wall Street these days. It's quite big shoes to fill, you know?" I sigh. "Of course you know. You've clearly worked your way up to success. Yours is the kind of job that you have to be incredibly qualified for. And I guess, in a way, when I first started here at Dickson, I was afraid to challenge myself. Afraid of failure because of how high my father has set the bar. But making decisions out of fear is never a good idea, you know?"

She lifts one shoulder in acknowledgment. "You're right, Ace. Fear can be a big deterrent in reaching your full potential."

"And that's all I want to do, Cynthia." I smile at her, really smile at her in a way that begs and pleads but also slowly pulls her into my web. "I want to reach my full potential. I want to create my own path. I want to step out of the shadows of my father's big fat feet and be the best version of Ace Kelly I can be."

She's nodding along with me now.

"And when I set my mind to something, Cynthia? Well, there's not much stopping me. It's a familial trait. DNA coded. And I don't think we should fight it. Do you?"

Cynthia stares at me for a long moment, before letting out a deep exhale of air and moving her focus back to her laptop screen. "Well, Ace, I can't make any promises, but I can certainly try my best to get you in all the classes you want."

Hell fucking yes.

"You're the best, Cynthia." I flash her my most charismatic smile. "See? This is why everyone on campus says that you're the best counselor."

"No one says that," she responds, and a faint hint of a blush touches her cheeks.

"Trust me, Cynthia. Everyone says that."

She smiles as she starts to work on updating my schedule, and I have a sneaking suspicion that my sweet Cynthia is buttered up enough to secure all the classes I need to solidify another phase of my plan to win Julia's heart.

11

Julia

My mom walks around the apartment I'm nearly certain is *the one*, while I hang back to give her space. Her mouth is set in a firm line as she moves from the living room to the kitchen, opening each cabinet like she's inspecting them for hidden sins.

My phone buzzes in my purse.

Ace: *how's apartment hunting going*

I glance toward my mom, who is now inspecting the freaking range hood over the stove. She squints up at it like it's personally offended her.

"I wonder if this is up to code," she mutters to herself. She knows jack shit about range hoods or stoves or anything that requires technical knowledge, but she's certainly putting on a good show of testing the fan.

Me: *I mean, I found a place I love, but Georgia is still a skeptic.*

Ace: *you think you found THE place???*

I move my eyes around the apartment, taking in the way the sunlight casts gorgeous shadows across the hardwood floor. Goodness, I can picture myself living here. I can picture myself making this space my own.

Me: Yes. I really want this one.

"Are you sure you don't want to live at home, honey?" my mom asks, wringing her hands with nerves as she continues to move around the kitchen, running her fingers across the small butcher-block island in the center of it. "I'm sure your dad would pay for a driver or even bring you in himself when he's coming into the office."

I smile toward the living room windows and adjacent fire escape without turning around so she can't see, gentling my response appropriately. My mom means well in every sense of the phrase—she is kind, generous, patient, and honestly the best mom I ever could have asked for. She's not trying to control me or cramp my style or keep me a kid like I know some other moms might be if they suggested I stay home instead of spreading my wings—she's just a worrier. She wants the most for me—safety, happiness, success—and is downright terrified of making a decision in opposition to that goal.

For my freshman year at Dickson, I lived in the dorms. Which is still technically moving out, but it's not as big of a deal as moving out into your own apartment. Which is what I'm trying to achieve right now. I can imagine it's creating a little bit of an internal crisis for my mom.

Her job for nearly the last nineteen years has been to mold her life around mine, and now I'm just moving on? I get it. It's got to be hard.

"I'm sure. We researched, remember? This place has a doorman twenty-four hours, good lighting, and is really close to campus. I can walk or, if the weather's bad, take the subway because it's right downstairs."

I also happen to love the arched doors and windows, the hardwood floors, the wainscoting, and the open concept kitchen. It's not enormous—this is New York after all—but it *feels* big. The landlord doesn't mind if you paint or personalize, so long as you put it back as it was before you move out, and I like the idea of choosing everything for my own space. I've been looking at places since May, and *this* is the one. I'm sure of it.

"You're right. I know." I look back at her, and she winces. "I'm sorry. I don't want to be a buzzkill, really. You're an adult, and I respect that. It's just my lifelong job to worry about you."

"I know, Mom. But this will be good."

"Okay. Maybe I'd feel better if one of your friends were living here with you, but I understand you not wanting a roommate. It's a lot. Even the best of friends can be too much sometimes, and you know I know—"

"Just what do you know, Wheorgie?" a too-familiar voice calls, making me jump.

Cassie Kelly strides in like she owns the place, her giant sunglasses perched on her head and an iced coffee in hand.

I'm used to the Kellys being in close proximity at pretty much all times—hell, I was just texting with Ace—but having them materialize out of thin air seems a little much.

And a little poltergeist, to be honest.

"Cassie? What are you doing here?" my mom asks, evidently feeling the same confusion as me.

"Ace told me you guys were looking at apartments today and says he wants to live off campus too, so I tracked your location."

"You…tracked… How do you have my location?" my sweet mother asks, her hand to her chest. I, for one, am not even a little surprised, and for as ridiculous as it is, it makes me smile. I never have any doubts about why my best friend is the way he is—the proof is in his DNA pudding.

"Are you kidding?" Cassie laughs. "I've had that setting turned on for years. I always know where you are. Always."

Georgia Brooks is not amused. "Do you even hear yourself right now?"

"Of course I do, Wheorgie," Cassie says, a proud smile on her lips. "I sound like an intelligent goddess."

My mother's best friend has been calling her variations of

Wheorgie and Whorge and basically any combination of the word whore and Georgia combined. It's their thing. Well, it's Cassie's thing. Though, I've certainly heard my mom drop the nickname Casshead a time or two.

But to prevent any emotional damage, I refuse to ask them where the nicknames came from. I mean, there're certain things you don't want to know about your mom. Or your mom's best friend—even though Cassie Kelly doesn't hold much back.

"No, Cass." My mom shakes her head. "You sound like you belong in a true crime documentary."

"Oh, please," Cassie says, waving a hand. "It's for safety. And also because I'm nosy."

My mom shoots her a look, but I've long stopped being surprised by Cassie Kelly's antics. She's chaos cloaked in Chanel perfume, and Ace is basically her spiritual clone.

Which becomes even more obvious when he strolls through the door right on cue.

I aim a finger at him. "Of course you were in on this."

He grins. "You called it *the one*, Jules. And who am I to deny my mother her God-given right to stalk your mom?"

I roll my eyes at him, but Cassie is quick to take over the conversation again. "You two have been friends since you came out of us. I honestly quite like the idea of you being in the same building."

Ace nods like this has been the plan all along. "If you're taking this one, I'll take the one across the hall."

"Have you even looked at it?" I ask with a scoff.

"I'm looking at this one. It's got floors and a kitchen and, most importantly, you. Feels like a win."

I gawk at him. "That's your entire decision-making process?"

Ace shrugs like he hasn't just completely hijacked my solo-living fantasy.

Leave it to my best friend to take my months of research and narrow it down to a split-second decision for himself. I guess he figures I've done the legwork, but I can't imagine being that loose with my future *home*.

Don't get me wrong, it's not that I don't like the idea of having him close. I mean, we spend every freaking day together as it is. But I kind of thought moving in here on my own might give me a little independence going into the school year. My introspection has been hard at work since I started hanging out with Drew, and after inviting Ace to join us at practically every opportunity, I'm starting to wonder if I've become dependent on using him as a crutch.

And things are going well with Drew. I really don't want to ruin it by being so insecure in my own independence that I'm constantly obsessing over where my best friend is and what he's doing and wishing he could be there too to carry the conversation more.

Drew's a great guy—with unfettered interest in me. And he's the first guy I've dated in college. I don't want to ruin it.

"Lia?" Ace says, eyes searching mine. "You cool with me living across the hall?"

This is it. My shot to say something. To stand up for the very independent woman I'm pretending to be.

"Yeah. Of course." I smile. "You're my bestie. It'll be great."

Ace beams like I just handed him the deed to the building. "Get your Amex, Cassie. We're going housewares shopping."

His mom groans. "Maybe I should assign that to your father."

Ace snorts. "If you want the centerpiece of the apartment to be a stripper pole, then sure. Grand idea."

"Say your goodbyes, Acer," she says, already halfway out the door. "We're hitting Target before I change my mind."

Ace pulls me into a hug, warm and familiar. And I let myself melt into it for just a second.

"You good?" he asks quietly, and like magic, I actually am.

Living near Ace will be amazing. Any problems I have with exerting my independence are my own, not his.

"Yeah," I say. "We're going to have the best year."

He kisses my temple and backs away, only half listening as

Cassie calls for him again. "There's a party on campus later," he says. "You coming?"

"I have a date with Drew."

He lifts an eyebrow. "Another one, huh? That makes three, right?"

"If you count the first one, which I'm not sure we should."

"It counts. All things interrupted by Gunnar still have to count or none of us would ever have anything, you know?"

I laugh. "True."

"Well…" He shifts toward the door. "Text me or call if you get done with him…or done with the date…or whatever…and want to meet up. I'm hitting up Scottie, Finn, and Blake too."

"Okay. I'll let you know."

As the door shuts behind him, I lean against the kitchen island and stare at the hardwood floors I love so much and sigh.

It was silly to think there'd ever be a phase of independence anyway. Ace Kelly has a way of making it feel like he's there even when he's not, and now, he'll just be doing it from across the hall.

12

The bass from the speakers rattles the old pipes in the ceiling, and half the crowd is already dancing like they forgot this is a historic brownstone and not a New York City club. Dickson athletes and random city kids are packed shoulder to shoulder, shouting over the music, spilling drinks, and pretending this isn't the third party this week hosted by Greg Landers and Holden Olsen.

Greg and Holden moved in early for soccer preseason, and apparently that means they're determined to make this place the social nucleus of the summer. I met them in Rocks for Jocks last semester—formally called Intro to Geology—and got added to the VIP list.

Which, yeah, not a big surprise there. It's me.

I haven't had a chance to attend one of their parties before this, though, because of my busy social schedule, and for as much fun as it seems like everyone else is having, I'm fucking miserable.

I sip my soda and scan the crowd again. Still no Julia. Obviously. She's on a date with…whatshisname.

"I just…don't know what she sees in him is all I'm saying," I complain, sipping from my soda again while Finn and Scottie briefly share a look. "He looks like the kind of guy who plays acoustic guitar on purpose. At parties. And he's kind of weird-looking too, don't you think?"

"He's not that bad, Ace." Scottie chews her lip. It's almost like she's fighting a smile, which, clearly, I'm seeing things. There is absolutely nothing to be smiling about right now. "And he's a pretty nice guy. I met him a couple times last year, and he's not like most of the other rich jocks I've met."

My blood runs cold, and Finn clears his throat, evidently choking on what a fucking idiot I am to convince myself Julia fucking Brooks, a goddess if I've ever known one, is giving time and interest to a loser.

"And," Scottie adds, leaning into Finn's side, "he does seem like he really likes her."

I narrow my eyes. "Yeah? Well, so does every other guy who's ever seen her walk into a room. Doesn't mean he's qualified."

"Qualified for what?" Finn smirks. "To be her boyfriend—or survive a conversation with you about it?"

"All I'm saying is he's not right for her. Even if he's a saint or some shit like you're saying, he's still a bad match," I counter, trying to knock some sense into their heads. I don't know why they're even attempting to defend that douche. "I mean, he wants to be with Julia. Immediate red flag."

"Why is that a red flag?" Finn asks, searching my face closely.

Why, Finn? Because I want to be with Julia. And only one of us gets to win that game.

I clear my throat. "Because Julia is too sweet and kind to be with a frat guy like him. His formal wear collection probably revolves around a toga and golf polos. There's no style. No pizzazz. No fucking personality. He might as well be a cardboard box."

"Technically," Finn cuts in, "that attire thing is kind of accurate."

"Finally, man." Eyes wide, I nod. "*Finally*, you're seeing what I'm seeing."

"I don't know if I'm seeing what you're seeing," Finn retorts. "But sure."

"You are, Finn," I tell him. "Trust me, you are."

Finn doesn't say anything to that, and Scottie just nods. Clearly, the two of them are just coming to terms with the fact that my beautiful Julia is on a date with a frat douche.

I take another swig of soda to finish the can and crush it in my hand. Music pounds so loudly in my ears, I can hardly think, and my anxiety feels like it's running at an eleven.

What would normally be a fun environment feels like a torture chamber.

"Hey, Ace," a girl in a hot-pink dress and brown hair says, stopping just inside my personal space. She has a flirtatious smile on her lips, and I'm pretty sure her name is Penelope. "I didn't know you'd be here."

"Surprise." I smile to be friendly. "I'm here."

"Well, it's good to see you." She giggles and twirls a strand of her hair around her finger. "Want to come dance with me?"

"Penelope, I appreciate the offer," I answer, doing my best to still be friendly and let her down easy. "But that pretty dress of yours deserves a guy in a better mood than I am tonight."

"Oh no," she says, her lips turning into a pout. "What's wrong?"

"What's wrong?" I laugh despite myself. "What isn't wrong, Penny?"

"Maybe I can help lift your mood…?" she offers, and her eyelashes flutter over her green eyes. "You know, I can be a lot of fun."

"I'm sure you can be, but I'm going to sit this one out." I flash another smile at her. "Though, it would make my night if you make sure you have a good time for me."

She smiles back. "I think I can do that."

Eventually, she walks away, and both Finn and Scottie stare at me.

"What?" I question, and Scottie cracks up.

"Pretty sure most guys would kill for that kind of attention, Ace," she says, and all I can think is, *most guys aren't trying to win the girl who already knows everything about them.*

"Okay, Ace. What the hell is going on?" Finn claps a hand on my shoulder. "I'm starting to get the feeling we need to stage some kind of intervention, but I don't know what the fuck the intervention is for. Are you on drugs? Drinking? Porn addiction?"

I sigh. "Finnley, I wish I had a porn addiction."

"Ace Kelly, you do not mean that." Scottie cracks up, but I'm not laughing. "Okay, yeah, what is going on with you?"

I look at Finn and Scottie, at their happy fucking faces, at the way their hands are clutched together, and they probably don't even realize it because everything is perfect in their happy little love bubble.

"I want what you two have."

Finn furrows his brow. "Common sense?"

"Love," I say, completely ignoring the teasing jab.

"You want to be in love?" Scottie questions.

"I want Julia's love." The words come out as a whisper, but somehow, they both manage to hear it over the party. "Because I've had the earth-shattering realization that I'm in love with her."

I wait for their shocked reactions. I wait for Finn's eyes to bulge out of his head and Scottie's jaw to hit the tops of her knees. I wait and I wait and I wait, but it never comes.

And then I remember what Blake said to me that night outside of Groove.

"You guys knew too, huh?"

They both nod.

"Well, fuck," I mutter and run a hand through my hair. "Would've been nice if someone would've let me in on this very important information."

"Pretty sure you had to have that realization yourself, man," Finn says and squeezes my shoulder.

"Oh, don't worry. I have." I sigh, and for once in my life, the sounds of the booming music and people laughing and chatting aren't music to my ears. "This party sucks and I'm itchy." I pull at the collar of my shirt. "We texted Blake, and he bailed. Half these people are freshmen trying to impress seniors, and I just don't have the energy for it. Are you guys having fun? Or can we beat feet and shit?"

Finn and Scottie share another look—always with the fucking telepathic conversation bullshit—before Finn speaks as a representative of their couple council.

"Sure, man, we can leave. You wanna go to Zip's and get some food?"

"Yeah," I agree, my wheels spinning. "Whatever. Let's just get out of here." An idea hatches. "Actually, you know what? I know exactly where we can go."

"All right, dude. Lead the way."

———

"Ace, why the fuck are we in Central Park?"

"Don't worry about it, Finn," I say, scooting a little deeper into the bushes to get a good look at Julia and the fuckface on the other side of the grassy lawn. He's got a stupid picnic set up, while other people chat and lounge and throw Frisbees around them in the moonlight.

"Ace, isn't this where Julia said Drew was taking her?" Scottie asks.

After we left the party, I was able to keep my idea to come spy on Julia's date under wraps because of the proximity to my parents' penthouse. Finn and Scottie assumed we were either going there or to an establishment close by that I frequent because of living in the neighborhood. Neither of them said anything or asked any questions to confirm, though, so really, it's on them for trusting me so much when they should know how impulsive I can be.

"What?" I feign confusion. "No. Is it?"

"Oh my God, Ace. You didn't." Scottie's voice is soft and defeated and more than a little disappointed.

The funny thing is, it doesn't bother me, even though I know deep down in the land of rational thought that it should. Right now, all that matters is Julia and my obsession over the fact that some other fucker could be putting his tongue down her *very* perfect throat at this *very* moment.

"I didn't what?" I ask, playing the part of the innocent fool just like my father taught me.

"Ace, I'm telling you right now, it is not a good idea for us to interrupt Julia and Drew's date," Finn insists. "It will not go over how you'd like, I promise."

"That's not… Oh my goodness, Finnley. You don't think I planned this, do you?"

Scottie grimaces and shakes her head. "Oh man, we're in trouble. We're all in *a lot* of trouble."

"No, no," Finn corrects. "Ace is in trouble. You and I are smart enough to stay right fucking here in the bushes Ace put us in. Julia's never going to know we were a part of this, and if she ever does find out, I will tell the tale of our hostagehood."

"I'm not going to go over there." I hold up both hands in the air. "I'm not."

Finn lets out a heavy sigh. "Sure."

"What? You don't believe me?"

"Not even for one fucking second."

"Smart," I finally admit. "Because I definitely have to go over there."

I lean into the bush as Drew brushes some hair out of Julia's face, and my stomach clenches. *Fuck that guy! Fucking fuck that guy for thinking he is deserving enough to even lay a finger on her!*

Scottie reaches up and touches my arm gently, and I do my best not to flip out on a friend who doesn't deserve it.

"Ace," she says gently. "I know it's tough, watching her like this now that you've realized. But please, take it from me, you'll get a lot further being supportive than being annoying. Drew's just a phase. Just some guy to occupy her time. But if you're there, steady and compassionate and a good ear when she needs one, she'll realize that you have all the qualities he doesn't."

Shit. Her words hit me square in the chest.

"Thanks, Scottie. Really. I… Just hearing you say that helps. And for what it's worth, I'm sorry I've involved you two," I apologize. "You're sweet friends, who just thought you were joining me for a party tonight, and here you are, playing super-secret spy from the bushes. So, I'll just watch here a little longer and then head home.

I'm close, you know? But if you two want to go do something else—something more worthwhile, I understand."

Finn's eyes narrow as he sighs. It's the *double-double bullshit, you're in trouble* meter in his head going off with bells and whistles and alarms. "You're going over there as soon as we leave, aren't you?"

"What? Finn? Please. I'm giving you my word." I know it's childish, but you can bet your ass my fingers are motherfucking crossed behind my back. "You don't trust my word?" The real problem is that I've trained him to understand me too well—forced him into the recesses of my psyche as a method of trauma bonding the two of us.

"No. Not even as far as I can throw you, and you're a big motherfucker so I don't imagine I'd get you that far."

"Maybe we should stay, Finn," Scottie hedges, watching me with skepticism.

"No, babe," my best buddy says gently. "Once Ace's crazy horse is out of the barn, there's no containing it. We're going to go have a late dinner and head home. Ace is going to do what Ace is going to do, even if going over there is the biggest dumb fucking move he could make."

He's probably right. Maybe I shouldn't go over there.

My eyes jump back to Julia and Drew. She laughs, and my chest squeezes.

Or maybe I should. Maybe I need to find a way to stop this before she gets in too deep with this fucker.

I swallow hard against the burning pain in my chest and look back at Scottie and Finn, handing her my phone. "Before you head out, could you check to see if my DoorDash guy is coming?"

Scottie's jaw drops. "You *ordered food here?*"

"I was hungry," I answer with a shrug. I'm not going to crouch in a bush for hours on an empty stomach, you know? I'm not a savage.

Finn blinks. "What did you even order?"

"Just some lobster rolls and a Coke."

He shakes his head like I've personally offended his ancestors. "You're fucking *gone,* man."

But I can barely hear him over the ringing in my ears as I go back to watching Julia through the bushes. "Are you fucking kidding me?" I hiss, pointing toward the stupid picnic blanket scene. "He's brushing her hair behind her ear. I swear to God, if he kisses her, I'll throw this entire bush at him."

Scottie puts a hand on my shoulder, gently but firmly, before holding my phone out to me over it. "Ace. You're spiraling. I know you love her. I know this hurts. But you've gotta play the long game. Be the guy who's always there, not the one hiding in shrubbery with shellfish."

Finn nods. "Yeah. You jump out of these bushes, you're not the knight in shining armor. You're the weirdo with leaves in your hair and lobster breath."

I sigh, my eyes locked on Julia like she's the sun and I'm a moth with no concept of fire. "I just… I don't get it. What does she even see in him? I mean, he's *beige*, like if khakis became a person. His biggest personality trait is *being present*."

Finn raises an eyebrow. "That's a little rich coming from a guy who will be living across the hall from her now because of a secret plot to always be present."

I didn't even give Finn that information, but it's obvious he's put all the pieces of my win-Julia's-heart puzzle together. The sage bastard.

"I'm not saying I'm *not* unwell, Finn. I'm just saying Julia deserves someone with depth. With passion. With—"

"An arrest record for stalking?" Finn cuts in.

"Listen. I know I'm a little off the deep end right now, but I can't help it. I've been in love with that girl since she used to share her Fruit by the Foot with me in kindergarten. It just took me a while to figure it out."

Scottie's expression softens. "You're not wrong for loving her. Just…don't let it make you the villain."

I sigh, the weight of my own madness settling in. "You guys can go. I'll hang here for a bit, let the agony marinate, and then go home."

Finn narrows his eyes. "Don't go over there after we leave."

"I won't."

"Don't lie to me. I know that look. That's the 'I'm about to crash a date and call it fate' look."

I raise my hands. "Swear on the lobster rolls."

Finn looks at Scottie, then back to me. "We're actually leaving this time. But I swear to God, Ace, do *not* go over there."

"I won't." *Probably.*

Scottie sighs. "*Ace.*"

"You're right. You're right. I'll leave soon. I promise. Talk to you guys later." I say with a wave of my hand, not even looking at them as they start to move away. A Frisbee match has started up on the lawn on the other side of Julia and Drew, and I bet if I sweet-talk the guys playing, I can join in to get a better vantage point.

For now, my obsession reigns supreme.

They start to move away, and I watch them go, my eyes drifting back to Julia as she laughs at something Drew says. My chest squeezes like I'm the one under a microscope and not the one hiding in shrubbery.

But before Finn and Scottie disappear completely down the trail, I whisper after them, "Hey, on the Fourth…you guys are gonna hype me up, right?"

"Oh yeah, man." Finn doesn't even turn around. "I've got red, white, and blue body glitter with your name on it."

Scottie lifts a hand. "We believe in you. But, like, go home, Ace. Seriously, go home."

I don't answer. I just turn back toward the girl I can't seem to stop chasing.

"DoorDash for…Acer?" a voice whispers behind me.

I grin. It's a confession written in buttered seafood and soda.

Clearly, I have no current plans of leaving anytime soon.

13

Today is my dad's birthday.

Which means, in the Brooks house, things are chaos.

Not because my dad cares—Kline Brooks is the most low-key, under-the-radar, "please don't make a fuss" kind of guy in the universe. But because my mom insists on making a fuss for him anyway. Every year. Without fail. This year's fuss is a dinner party for thirty-five of his "closest friends," a signature cocktail called The Brooksberry Mule, and a custom ice sculpture in the shape of a K.

She's been spiraling since sunrise. Which is exactly why I snuck out of the house the second I saw the opportunity. I slid into my sandals, grabbed my purse, and whispered a quick "love you" toward the general chaos of the kitchen before disappearing into the sweet, quiet freedom of my car.

I left my sister Evie to fend for herself, but she's probably already faked her own death or at least a severe gastrointestinal emergency to get out of helping.

Last Thanksgiving, she claimed she had explosive diarrhea and stayed locked in the downstairs bathroom for four straight hours. Meanwhile, I was elbow-deep in potato peels and hand-whipping mashed sweet potatoes like I was training for the Great British Bake Off. When I finally went into the bathroom afterward, expecting it to smell like a garbage truck lit on fire, it smelled like vanilla. She'd lit a candle, put on spa music, and read an entire Sarah J. Maas novel in the bathtub while I got barked at about undersalting the gravy.

I had to get out of there, and thankfully, my nonnegotiable plans with two of my best friends made it temporarily possible. It's remarkably quiet here at the mall with Scottie and Kayla, flipping through racks of clothes.

So, so quiet. I sigh.

The three of us have been trying to plan this little Fourth of July preparation shopping trip for a couple of weeks, and with my dad's birthday party tonight and no outfit to wear to that either, today was an opportune time. Kayla's doing a summer internship here with some sunglass company, which means she's busy during the week, and Scottie's physical therapy is usually reserved for Monday through Friday too.

I flip past a navy halter with little stars on the hem, my phone buzzing in my back pocket for what has to be the fiftieth time today. I pull it out, glance at the screen, and smile despite myself.

Scottie looks at me curiously and asks, "Drew?"

"Just Ace. He's been texting me nonstop since Wednesday night. Funny memes, jokes, and yesterday and today, all different stuff for my apartment. I showed him my Pinterest vision board on Thursday when he came over to formally apologize, and he's been busy looking for stuff from it ever since."

"That's…really sweet," Scottie says, glancing to Kayla out of the corner of her eye before looking back at me. "Um…wait… What happened Wednesday that Ace had to formally apologize for?"

I laugh. "Oh, you know, just Ace shit. I made the mistake of telling him where I was having my date with Drew, and he interrupted in spectacular fashion by trying to catch a Frisbee and landing in the middle of our picnic. Smashed the cake Drew got and busted open the chips and dip. Drew had French onion all over his shirt and had to take it off for the ride home, it smelled so bad."

"My God," Kayla mutters with a shake of her head as she thumbs through red, white, and blue bathing suits. "Ace Kelly is something."

"Don't I know it," I agree with a laugh.

"So, was it just Ace who crashed your date?" Scottie asks, and when I look over at her, her gaze is fixated on a cute red crop top. "Or were there other…people involved?"

"Well, if anyone else was involved, Ace's body was the only one that dive-bombed into the center of the blanket Drew had set up," I answer with a roll of my eyes.

"So…were you mad?" Scottie asks. "Like, really mad?"

Kayla laughs and nudges Scottie playfully. "At least she got a shirtless Drew Bettencourt out of it."

"I was definitely a little pissed," I answer bluntly. "I mean, I have no idea why Ace felt the need to crash my date. But we have the fifteen-minute rule, so I got over it pretty quickly. All the stuff he's been doing since is sweet, but it's overkill. I've moved on."

"A *fifteen-minute rule?* What the hell does that mean?" Scottie asks, wheeling around the rack of bathing suits to look me in the eye. I avoid hers, knowing the explanation I'm about to give is a little farfetched for anyone outside of the Ace and Julia duo and feeling a little embarrassed by it.

"It started in second grade after our first real fight over a sidewalk-chalk masterpiece. I tried to break up with him as a friend, and he cried and said that wasn't allowed unless we both agreed. So, we came up with the fifteen-minute rule to keep the grudges from getting out of control. Fifteen minutes, and then you get over it."

"Let me get this straight." Kayla cracks up. "You guys have a time limit on being mad?"

"Yeah…technically, we do." I shrug and smile, but internally, I'm realizing how crazy it all must sound to them. "We knew we were going to fight. It's inevitable when you've known someone your whole life. So, we made a rule. Fifteen minutes to be pissed. Yell. Ice out. Dramatically slam doors. But at the end of the fifteen minutes, the wrongdoer has to apologize and mean it, and the other person *has* to forgive them."

Scottie and Kayla share a look I can't quite discern, probably because they've never experienced a best-friendship with someone like Ace Kelly.

"We didn't need it for a few years at the end of primary school, but it had to be reinstated in sixth grade," I add, concentrating hard on a red halter with white stars all over it instead of polka dots. "I tie-dyed his signed Mavericks jersey. I thought it would be a cool surprise. It was…not."

"Wow," Kayla says. "And you two really stick to this fifteen-minute-rule thing? Like, you've never been mad longer than that?"

I snort. "Sure, sometimes the anger simmers a little, but we've always kept up our end of the bargain. Most of the time, I'm over it before the fifteen minutes are even up because Ace starts apologizing with his big brown puppy-dog eyes."

"Not gonna lie, girlfriend," Kayla teases with a smile in my direction. "The two of you are quite the pair. Your friendship is…"

"A little weird?" I offer.

"I was thinking more 'hard to define,' but sure, I guess weird works too."

"And just think," I add with a self-deprecating smile, knowing full well that this story will truly blow their minds. "I haven't even told you guys about our official decree notebook we made when he was eight and I was seven and we agreed to get married at twenty-five."

Scottie chokes. "You agreed to what?"

I laugh. "Yeah, back then, we thought twenty-five was *really old*—like decrepit. So, we decided that's when it would be a good idea to pack it in, give up on singledom, and just marry each other. Signed our names in the notebook and called it a day." I shrug.

"And you still have this notebook?" Scottie questions, and I shake my head.

"Actually, no. I'm pretty sure it's somewhere at Ace's parents' house." I shrug. "We added the fifteen-minute rule to the official declaration at ten and a couple other promises over the years after that. But once we hit high school, we never really needed it anymore. I guess all our rules had become so ingrained they were unspoken by that point."

"And you just trust that he's going to follow it?" Kayla asks, skeptical. "I find it hard to believe that boy has any interest in settling down at twenty-five, some official agreement or not. At the beginning of June, Lindsey Boggs and Bridget Sanders told me he was texting with both of them. They knew, and they weren't even upset." She shakes her head. "He has some way about him."

My stomach pitches slightly but finds its feet again as I look through the rack of denim shorts. "Oh, come on, Kayla," I say, laughing it off. "I don't know if any of it means anything other than that we were a couple of silly kids with codependency issues. I'm just explaining the history of the fifteen-minute rule and everything attached to it because you asked."

"And you're dating hot Drew Bettencourt now," Kayla adds with a waggle of her eyebrows.

I wink. "Exactly."

"Is it serious with Drew?" Scottie asks from behind me, following my lead to the corner with the white outfits.

"I wouldn't say we're exclusive or anything, but he's a really nice guy and he makes me laugh." I smile. "Not a bad kisser either."

Both Kayla and Scottie giggle.

My phone buzzes again, and I pull it from my back pocket to check it.

> *Ace: This is the comforter you wanted right? I just happened to notice it through the window at Macy's. Do you want me to get it? It's the only one left the lady says*

I scan the attached photo and text him back with quick fingers.

> *Me: Oh my gosh, yes! I haven't been able to find it anywhere else online either!*

Ace: Ok I got it I'll put it with my stuff and bring it when we move in after the fourth unless you need it before that?

Me: I was just going to wash it, but I can do that when we move in since I was smart enough to find us apartments with laundry in unit!

Ace: HA Yeah yeah I guess it's good one of us does research

Me: And that one of us is always me.

Ace: That's because you're better at it than I am

Me: Sure. A likely story. Anyway, I'm out shopping with Kayla and Scottie. I'll see you at my dad's party tonight, right?

Ace: Are you kidding? There's no way I'd even be allowed to miss it. My dad's working on some special friendship bracelets or some shit

Me: Oh yeah, Kline Brooks is going to loveeee that.

Ace: It's his fault for not kicking the Kellys to the curb sooner. If you ever want to get rid of me and can't you can blame your dad too

I laugh.

Me: See you tonight.

I tuck my phone back into my pocket and look up again to find both Scottie and Kayla watching me with smiles. "What?"

"Drew?" Kayla asks.

"Ace still. Just confirming plans for my dad's party tonight. You're both coming, right?" I turn and start flipping through racks of clothes again, my need to find an outfit worthy of tonight's party renewed.

"Yeah," they both say in unison behind me. "Is Drew coming?"

I frown, holding up a white skort with a rippled front next to a matching cowl neck halter. "Nope. He has a thing upstate he has to go to for his grandparents. I'll probably see him sometime next week, though, before we head to Winslow Fourth of July." I shrug, spinning around and holding up the outfit against myself. "What do you guys think?"

"I think it'll look *killer* on you," Kayla encourages. "It works for the party or for a date night."

"I'm too excited about it not to wear it tonight," I argue. "But you're right. Maybe I can wear it again next week."

A good outfit gets more than one use, right?

Music plays at a reasonable volume, and catered snacks litter the kitchen as I cruise by for another carrot dipped in ranch, waiting for my friends to arrive.

My mom and dad laugh with their friends Wes and Winnie Lancaster, and their daughter Lexi and son Wes Jr. post up on the couches in the living room. A chef works on the main courses on the backyard grill, and my new white skort and halter highlight my summer tan perfectly.

Evie is still in her room getting ready, claiming some kind of online emergency yet again, and I text Ace for the seventh time to get an update.

> *Me: Where the hell are you guys?*

> *Ace: The traffic on the GW was fucking bananas. Thatcher hung his head out the window on more than one occasion saying he needed air like he's a fucking husky or some shit. Gunnar is wearing five tons of Axe body spray though so I can't even really blame him*

> *Me: Okay, I'm just bored!*

Ace: TRUST ME when I say you wont be bored when we get there. My parents are fucking psychopaths

Me: Is my dad gonna flip out?

Ace: Most DEFINITELY

Me: Oh Jesus! Can you give me a hint?

Ace: Steve Irwin?

Me: The Australian guy who died? Did they exhume his body?????

Ace: Trust me Lia. Let yourself be surprised

Me: Fine. But you better be here soon.

Ace: We're pulling into the front gate of the neighborhood now

I jump excitedly, grab another carrot dunked in ranch, and run for the front door to be waiting when they arrive. If Ace is saying something crazy is going down, I can trust that it really is unhinged, and I want to be the first person to know the details.

As I pull the heavy wooden front door shut behind me, the Kellys' Escalade pulls up at the curb. Ace is the first to get out, and Gunnar is right behind him, strolling casually in an open button-down shirt. His whole chest is still out, but his shoulders are covered, so I guess he's at least taking the occasion semi-seriously.

Thatch and Cassie get out the other side, and Nathan, Thatch's driver, gets out and heads for the back hatch. I watch with pointed interest as he opens the door and then hesitates, Thatch stopping behind him and rubbing his hands together with excitement.

"What the hell is about to happen, Ace?" I ask, terrified.

"Well, Thatch says, at our parents' age, if you're not crockin', you're not rockin.'"

"Yeah. I've heard that before. About those shoes, right? What'd he get him, a bunch of shoes?"

"Oh, Lia. I beg of you…just wait."

I turn back to the car just as a huge Rubbermaid bin is lifted out by Nathan and Thatch, holes drilled in the side and, if I'm not mistaken, a crocodile inside. A little baby crocodile, of course, but one, I imagine, will grow into an adult at some point in the not-so-distant future.

"Is that a—"

"Yep. It sure is."

The Steve Irwin clue suddenly makes a whole lot of sense.

"My dad is going to lose his shit."

"Yes. Yes, he is. There are also three pairs of Crocs, in varying colors, because as Thatch says, 'Every good birthday deserves a theme.'"

Ace and I split apart, jumping to the sides of the front porch as Thatch and Nathan carry the crocodile box through the front door, Cassie holding it open for them with a smile on her face.

I rush through after them, not wanting to miss a moment of my parents' reaction, and Ace crowds me at my back, positioning us just to the side of the kitchen with his hands at my hips as Nathan and Thatch set the container on the kitchen counter among the appetizers. It jumps as the little croc lashes out at the plastic sides of its container, knocking the carrots I was just eating to the floor, and I put a hand to my mouth. "Oh, dear God."

Gunnar leans against the living room wall, talking to Lexi, and my mom comes down the stairs, her attention turned back toward Evie, who's yapping behind her. "Evie, please. I need a break from the interrogation about your father and me. If you're that concerned about something, why don't you just come out and say it?"

"Evie!" I caution quickly, pulling her up short before she can add to the already tense moment with questions about dick-pic screenshots. "Not now."

"Julia, if your sister has something she wants to ask me, she should just—"

"Mom," I interrupt. "Look at the counter."

She spins to face the island, spying the mess first and then trailing slow eyes up to the culprit. Thatch and Cassie stand proudly on the other side, a pair of Crocs on their hands so they can dance them around.

"Is that a…"

"Hey, Georgie," my dad calls, his voice rising as he makes his way down the stairs. "Have you seen my green tie? I can't find the one with the—"

My mom smacks his stomach, and he stops talking, his keen eyes falling directly on the box on the counter.

"What in the *fuck* is that?"

I choke on my saliva, and Ace squeezes my hips behind me as we all brace for impact.

"Happy birthday, T-bag! If you're not crockin', you're not rockin.'"

Oh my God. "Things are about to go nuclear," I whisper.

Ace provides the countdown. "In three, two, one…"

14

"What the hell is wrong with you?" Julia's dad yells, the volume well outdoing the music and bringing everyone else up silent. I cover Julia's ears with my hands as a makeshift pair of those protective mitts, but she moves them away, fear that she'll miss something being said. "Seriously, Thatch. You need a diagnosis! That's a fucking crocodile!"

"Fluff yeah, son. I picked it out special, just for you," my dad booms. "But why are you screaming, Special K? Maybe you should lower your voice."

"Why am I screaming?" Kline Brooks keeps shouting. A prominent vein is now bulging from the center of his forehead. "Because you brought a fucking crocodile to my house!"

"His name is Crocky," my dad corrects him. "And he's a little sweetie pie. A little snappy at times, but sweet."

"Sweet?" Kline questions in outrage. "He's sweet? He's a reptile with fucking teeth, Thatch! Pretty sure he almost bit Nathan!"

"At least he's not a sex offender," Evie whispers into the small void.

Julia gasps in front of me before whispering, "Oh, Evie. Nooo."

"What?" Kline asks, his head whipping around lightning-fast. "What did you just say?"

"Don't, don't, don't," Julia whispers.

But Evie is undeterred. One hand to her hip, she keeps going despite her father's pulsating forehead vein and wide eyes. "I said at least he's not a sex offender," Evie repeats, this time at full volume.

Oh boy. Is it just me or is this going somewhere ugly fast?

I suck my lips into my mouth before releasing them on a whistle and wrapping my arms around Julia to protect her from whatever shrapnel is about to fly our way.

"What in the hell are you talking about, Evie?" Kline is clearly confused but still very, very mad. "A sex offender?"

"Yes!" she yells back at her dad, her path officially set. "Heather Donovan found all your old messages on TapNext and has been posting on the internet about you sending unsolicited dick pictures, Dad!"

My jaw drops.

Julia gasps again.

"Oh shit," my dad mutters under his breath, and I know with sudden clarity that whatever dick-pic bullshit Evie is currently talking about is something my father hatched in his terrible idea factory years ago. It's probably why he's now pretending to be incredibly interested in the crocodile, even choosing right now to try to feed Crocky a fucking carrot that he picked up off the floor. Crocky hisses and chomps loud enough to startle everyone in the room, and my dad just shrugs. "I feel ya, Crocky. I'm more of a meat guy myself too."

And Kline, well, he's still standing there with a face that looks combustible enough to power the whole fucking city.

"She started a website with it all to discredit my run for student body president!" Evie exclaims, now in her own version of outrage. "Dad, your dick pics are ruining my reelection chances!"

"Evie," Georgia says softly, cautiously. "Let's everyone calm down and take a breath."

But Kline is done.

"I'm all out of fucking breaths, Georgia," he shouts so loudly, even Crocky appears to cower in his box. "You wanna know what that is, Evie? That's good old Thatcher Kelly. When there's a problem in my life, it's *always* fucking Thatcher Kelly." Clearly, the man is fed up to the point of overflow from years and years and years of torment at the hands of my father, well-meaning as he might be.

"Hey now, Special K," my dad chimes in. "I only sent that one batch of gargoyle dick pics, and if you'll recall, I thought they were going to my future wife. And let's not forget they're technically the reason you're even with Georgie. Clearly, they made you a stand-out. You should be thanking me."

"Thanking you?" Kline repeats, and I swear, if his eyes bulge any farther out of his head, they're just going to pop right out and land by the discarded carrots Crocky knocked off the table. "I know you're completely delusional ninety-nine percent of the time, but let me straighten this up for you, Thatch. Your gargoyle dicks did not help me land my wife," Kline says through gritted teeth. "I landed her all on my own."

My dad laughs. He just fucking laughs. "Oh my, how the memory fades, K. But that's okay, you are really fucking old."

All our heads swing from one end of the kitchen to the other as the two of them volley back and forth, hurling insult after insult. The tension is so thick, we nearly all get sucked out the front door when it opens for Finn, Scottie, and Kayla's arrival.

"Sorry, we're late," Scottie announces good-naturedly. "Traffic was murder."

I turn to face them and shake my head, and Julia reaches back to squeeze my hand.

"Whatever, Thatch. I'm old. And boring. And I'm not fucking crockin'," Kline says as he rolls up a sleeve aggressively. "This party is over. And you're taking this fucking reptile home with you, and you're doing it right now because I want you to get out of my house."

Shit. This isn't good. This isn't just tension. This is war. And a war between our families is the last fucking thing I need. I give Julia one last squeeze and then step around her to intervene, hoping I can salvage something from this shit before it goes too far.

"Mr. Brooks, sir. I'll handle the crocodile. I won't let it stay here, I promise."

My dad's chest puffs up to say something, and I cut him off. "Dad, not now."

"Not now," Kline repeats then. "Not ever. I know you have some sort of fantasy about our kids ending up together, but I'm telling you right now, I'll put myself in the grave before I let us become actual fucking family."

"Kline," Georgia whispers, grabbing his forearm and glancing to me and Julia with worried eyes. My heart jumps to my fucking throat, but I do my best to keep my composure.

"I'm serious! I won't be fucking related to this man, and if any of my daughters want to be, they will have to do it over my dead body!"

Kline's words hit me square in the chest, leaving debris of forbidden love and despair and downright desperation behind. The Brookses and the Kellys have been friends for the entirety of my life, and now what? We're switching fucking storylines and becoming the Capulets and Montagues?

Romeo is a cool fucking name and Julia is eerily close to Juliet, but I don't want us to have to die at the end of this semester because our parents have forbidden us from being together.

I want to be with her. For a long and happy life. Once I convince her to love me back, that is. Though, it's becoming difficult to get Julia to love me back when our parents are in an outright war.

"Like I'd ever date a Kelly," Evie mutters, her verbal choices today feeling very confrontational if you ask me.

"Like a Kelly would ever want to date you," Gunnar chimes in.

"Gunnar, you and I both know I'd be the best you ever had," Evie says, blowing a kiss in Gunnar's direction, and her mom Georgia screeches in shock.

"Evie!"

My mother, on the other hand, provides a fucking slow clap of admiration. "Damn, girl. Aunt Cass loves the confidence."

Kline watches the whole exchange go down before storming out the back door on a huff. The door slams behind him and leaves the rest of us standing there speechless. Or what should be speech-less. My father, unfortunately, is missing the gene.

"After all I've done for that fluffing asshole," Thatch mutters. "This is the thanks I get? Come on, Cass, we're leaving."

Cassie and Georgia make apologetic eyes at each other, and Gunnar shoves away from the wall to follow my dad, flipping Evie the bird. To which she just blows him another kiss. And I linger there, unsure what to do or where to go from here that won't make things even worse than they already are.

"Lia," I turn to whisper, hoping she'll have some kind of answer.

"It's okay," she whispers back. "I'll cool him down. Just…make sure you get rid of that fucking crocodile and pronto."

I jerk my chin at Finn, and he moves around Scottie to come help me lift the offending Rubbermaid off the counter and carry it outside.

But Nathan is already pulling away from the curb when we get outside, and my dad is hanging out the back window, shooting me the finger.

I sigh as Finn and I set Crocky on the ground, and I pull my phone out of my pocket to call Gary.

"So…fun party," Finn says as Crocky hisses and thrashes his tail around in the container so hard that both Finn and I have to place our hands on the top to keep it from falling on its side.

Oh yeah. A fucking thrill and a half.

Especially considering my goal to win Julia over just got ten times harder. I'm not in the fold—I'm officially removed entirely.

15

The Fourth of July at Aunt Paula and Uncle Brad's—*aka the Winslow family's*—lake house isn't so much a holiday as it is a generational event. A full-cast production of chaos and food, laughter and fireworks explosions, and overrun with more relatives and friends than should be able to fit in the cabin.

Everyone's here.

Julia's family—Kline, Georgia, and her sister Evie—claimed the guest rooms with lake views. My parents and my lunatic brother Gunnar, who set up a floating beer pong table in the shallow end of the lake the instant he got here.

Finn's whole family—his mom Helen and his siblings Reece, Jack, Travis, and Willow—rolled in with enough snacks to feed a teenage militia.

Of course, the Winslow clan descended in full force. Wes and Winnie are here with their kids, Lexi and Wes Jr., plus the Winslow brothers—Remy, Ty, Jude, Flynn—and their spouses and kids.

And Scottie and my good buddy Blake Boden are here too.

It's loud. It's crowded. It smells like sunscreen, burgers, and the practice fireworks my dad and Gunnar have already shot off.

In the water beside me, Julia floats on a pink flamingo inner tube, looking like summer incarnate. The corner of her mouth curls up as she laughs at something Blake says, and I watch in awe. The sun reflects the lake water in her blue eyes, and her blond hair looks lighter by the day from all the time we're spending outdoors this summer. She has it loosely tied on the top of her head, and her bright white and red-striped bathing suit sticks partially out of the water as she continues to float on the bright-pink inner tube.

Finn, Scottie, and Lexi have posted up on the deck, watching us through keen eyes and shaded sunglasses, and all the other Hayes siblings are on a mission to the grocery store two counties over for more beef since we've already bought out everything within a twenty-five mile radius.

I feel badly for Scottie—wondering if it makes her sad to think about how she would have been in the water with us, swimming, if things were like before. She's handling it well, and Finn would more than willingly hold her in a doggy paddle of his own for sixteen straight hours if she wanted him to, but I can't help but feel like this is one of those reminders of her rapidly changing world because of her tragic spinal injury.

Nothing is promised. Nothing is guaranteed.

And if you're me, you might just realize you're in love with a girl you've known since you were born in one flash of an instant. She's been texting whatshisface on and off today, and I'll be fucked if I can't come up with a way to distract her completely. I need to be funnier. I need to be more interesting. I need to make big moves.

I need to move on to the next phase of *Ace's Plan to Woo Julia*.

Especially given that our families are practically the fucking Hatfields and the McCoys since my dad tried to give Kline Brooks a crocodile for his birthday last week. After the big blowout at the Brookses' house, I ended up taking Crocky to a reptile habitat in the city, where he is now safely living his best life. My dad was annoyed—the big bastard thought we could just keep the fucking crocodile—but when I explained that our pig might end up bacon, he gave up on the wild plan.

Truth be told, the fact that both of our families are even here together is a minor miracle all on its own, one I spent many days and nights facilitating in every way possible, but I am officially behind the curve in the race to be the guy Julia Brooks ends up with one day.

And I don't like it. I don't like it one bit.

I swim over to the edge of Julia's flamingo, my arms draped over a pool noodle, and look up at her as she tips her sunglasses down the length of her nose. "Your shoulders are getting a little pink," I tell her. "In a few minutes, we should get out so I can put more sunscreen on for you."

"Okay," she agrees easily. "I'll put some on your shoulders too."

"Thanks."

"Who's going to put sunscreen on my shoulders?" Blake complains, glancing up at the deck to, I assume, Finn and Scottie. I imagine he's feeling kind of third-wheelish, seeing as all the friends around him are falling in love and stuff.

I laugh a little and jerk my chin up at Lexi, who's so smart she makes chatting people up while leaning on the deck rail look like a way to tell IQ. Scottie and Finn, God love 'em, look hopelessly dumb compared to her. "How about Lex?"

From the deck, Lexi glances my way at the sound of her name but doesn't engage. Blake looks like a pig in shit at the suggestion, though, since he's been crushing on Lexi from the first day he met her at the beginning of fall semester last year. Think brilliant, older woman running the Double C show and in her last year of grad school and the sophomore star quarterback smitten from the moment she didn't give a shit about who he was, and you pretty much get the gist of Lexi and Blake.

"Now, that's an idea, buddy," Blake says with a grin. "One I approve of wholeheartedly."

Obviously, he's still very much smitten with Lexi Winslow.

Julia laughs and rolls her eyes, and it makes me wonder if she would do the same if someone told her I was in love with her. For the first time since watching Blake pursue Lexi to great ruin at a Double C event, I find myself rooting for him.

So what if he's the underdog? So what if Lexi is too smart for him? So what if it's the longest shot since the first person brought up going to the moon?

A man in love deserves a chance. A man in love—

"What time are the fireworks set to go off tonight?" Julia asks, interrupting my runaway delusion. "The real ones, I mean. I heard plenty of verbal ones between your dad and mine in the kitchen this morning before the rest of us got up."

"My dad says at dark."

Julia nods toward the dock, so I swim and hold on to her flamingo at the same time, bringing us both close enough that she can climb out while I hold her float steady. She grabs the mesh bag of sunscreen while I heft myself onto the hot Trex surface of the dock and set my pool noodle to the side. She hands me the bottle of SPF 30, and I squeeze a blob into my hand to rub on her shoulders.

Down the dock, Jude unties the canoe while chucking in a pair of oars, and from the house, my dad and Gunnar burst through the back door like a cartoon duo. My dad's in swim trunks that say *FUCK YEAH* across the crotch, and Gunnar's sporting a full Joe Dirt mullet. Naturally, they're carrying a box of fireworks so big it requires co-parenting. There's a verbal exchange between my dad and my mom that only God knows the meaning of, I'm sure, and then they head toward us and Jude and the canoe.

Jude screams something. Thatch barks. Gunnar howls.

It's like watching the evolution of man in reverse. Frankly, it's the most insane exchange I've seen from men of their age and wealth, and as I gaze into the future, it shrivels my balls a little bit. I'm going to be responsible for all of them for the rest of my life.

"We'd better watch that Julia's dad doesn't rig the canoe to explode when Thatch rows out to set the fireworks off," Blake says as Thatch and Gunnar make their way down the dock stairs toward us.

Julia and I both laugh, but internally, I groan. I'm more than ready for the feud between the two of them to be over, so I can restore some glory to the Kelly name. Right now, I don't think Kline Brooks would let me propose marriage to his fucking driveway, let alone make a bid to spend the rest of my life with his daughter.

"Things are easing up," I say, my tone blatantly hopeful.

Julia pats my shoulder. "They've been friends since before we were born, and your dad hasn't changed. My dad is temporarily tired, but he'll get his energy up again. It's going to be okay. I mean, we're all here together, aren't we?"

I nod, even if it's just to make Julia feel better. She doesn't know the fast-talking I've been doing behind the scenes or the promise I made to my dad to handle anything that comes up with Gunnar for the next month if he could just behave himself while we're here to keep the peace.

"I'm glad you decided to come, Blake," I say, spinning around to face him. The change of subject and direction are both warranted—to cure my depression and my growing hard-on. I swear it's like my dick's never seen Julia in a bikini before. "Seeing as you've been too good for us the rest of the summer."

He chuckles, unoffended. "Listen, Ace, some of us have shit to do other than bounce from party to party and hang out with our friends."

"Oh, please. I bet you've been sleeping your way through Manhattan."

He pauses briefly, glancing to Lexi before his shade-covered eyes come back to me and move back and forth. "Nah. I'm laying low. Focusing on football and academic pursuits."

"Academic pursuits?"

"Oh yeah. I've been broadening my knowledge base on a lot of topics…primarily the viability of takeout spots around campus."

Julia groans. "Now, that's research I can get behind. I'm starving, but I'm scared to go up to the house while our moms are still talking on the deck. They're being…suspiciously civil."

I think it's a good sign that our moms are still sitting with each other and talking despite our dad's rift, but the opportunity to show off some of my boyfriend-worthy qualities is too good to ruin by sharing that with Julia.

"I'll go up and get you some food. Anything you want in particular, or should I just surprise you?" I ask, making sure to touch on all the positives of our lifelong relationship—I'm both considerate of her wants and needs but knowledgeable enough to get something good if she doesn't want to have to think.

"Really?" She squeals. "That would be so great. Maybe some berries? Or something refreshing? But honestly, I'm not picky."

She leans over and kisses me on the cheek before flopping back on her towel, arms outstretched like a sun-soaked goddess.

It's *almost* the fantasy.

Except in the fantasy, she confesses she's been secretly in love with me for years and wants to elope immediately.

Still, I'll take it. For now.

"Do some recon while you're up there," she adds. "See if forgiveness is in the air."

"Copy that." I nod and slide my sunglasses on my nose to hide my eyes as they wander over the droplets of water dotting her skin. *She is perfection in every humanly way possible.*

Blake clears his throat.

I turn and find him smiling knowingly behind his shades.

Shit. Right. I'm probably giving myself away in more ways than one. I adjust my shorts and my gaze and my soul accordingly.

"You want anything while I'm up there, man?"

He shrugs with a laugh. "I wouldn't mind if you could talk Lexi into coming down here for a little while."

I laugh from a deep, dark place of understanding. "You got it."

We're just two saps on a dock, in love with girls way out of our league, yearning, pining, and trying to look casual while drowning inside.

16

The fireworks went off without a single call to the fire department, which, by lake house standards, is basically a national achievement.

No wayward bottle rockets. No flaming s'mores flying through the air. No Gunnar launching Roman candles from the grill.

Even more shocking? My dad and Thatch *laughed together*.

Well, it was more my dad laughing at Thatch right after he slipped on the dock, tripped over a string of unlit fireworks, and cannonballed into the lake fully clothed *while* holding a heaping plate of ribs that he was in the process of eating, but it's better than no laughter at all.

When Thatch popped back up like a deranged seal, with barbecue sauce still smeared across his mouth, my dad lost it. I'm talking full-on, clutching-his-stomach, laughing his ass off. Kline Brooks, the man who has barely spoken a full sentence to Thatch since the Crocodile Birthday Incident, doubled over laughing so hard I thought he was choking.

Ace and I made eye contact across the dock, both of us hopeful that it was a sign the feud was coming to an end.

"They're either making up," Ace had whispered, "or your dad is plotting my dad's murder."

Now, it's really late, and the lake house is quiet. Everyone's asleep. The moonlight spills through the window of Scottie, Evie, Willow's, and my room like silver mist. Scottie's snoring softly across the room, Evie's tangled in her blankets, dead to the world, Willow's passed out with socks all over her head in an attempt to master heatless curls, but despite shutting off my phone and rolling over to fall asleep an hour ago, I'm still wide awake.

Maybe it's the leftover energy from the day. Maybe it's the fact that I keep overanalyzing every text from Drew and wondering why I feel a weird combination of excitement and indifference. Maybe I'm traumatized from watching a shirtless, mullet-sporting Gunnar eat fifteen hot dogs in two minutes on a dare from Thatch.

No matter the reason, no counting of sheep or lack of blue light has been enough to lull me into submission.

The stillness is interrupted by the door creaking open, soft and slow.

Ace walks on quiet feet through streaming moonlight after shutting the door behind himself, lifts the thin white comforter off my bed, and climbs in beside me, staring up at the ceiling. I roll onto my side to face him, and he does the same, his big mouth curving up into his signature grin.

"I have something big. Huge. A secret. And I think I need to share it with you," he whispers into the quiet of Aunt Paula and Uncle Brad's big, old house. A gentle hum of the air conditioning working against the heat and humidity of July at night is the only sound I hear other than Ace's excited breathing.

For the first time tonight, I'm kind of glad I didn't fall into a sound slumber. If he'd come in and found me passed out, he might not have stayed to share his news.

"What? What is it?" I search his eyes intently. "I thought everyone was asleep."

Ace shakes his head, joining our hands up by my head and making me smile. His lips are curled so high it's bringing light to his eyes, and even in the dark of this quiet room, he manages to glow. I don't know anyone else with this much natural charisma. Even his parents, whom everyone thinks he matches apple for apple, come from a crazier, more unhinged, unpredictable place than he does.

His energy is chaotic at times, but it's also centered in warmth and kindness and love in ways I don't really know if I can explain.

He always makes me feel safe to be myself and makes me lean into the enjoyment of life in the best way. I don't know what I'd do if we weren't friends, which is probably why I had a private talk with my dad tonight before coming to bed. I didn't beg him to find forgiveness for Thatch—and I definitely didn't belittle his feelings over how often he's gotten the short end of the stick over the years. But I did remind him of all the good, irreplaceable things the Kellys have brought to our lives—of all the things I'd miss if they weren't a part of our world like they are now.

"Jules, you're never going to believe this," Ace whispers, his focus understandably on telling me the secret he has. "But I saw Blake getting up out of his bed in our room and pulling on a T-shirt before he snuck out the door."

"Where did he go?"

Ace smiles, his hand squeezing mine with renewed excitement. "I got up and looked out the window just in time to see him and someone else climbing into a canoe and taking off out across the lake."

"Who?" I ask, the gossip getting juicier by the second.

"Lexi."

"What?" I breathe, trying to keep my voice quiet and failing spectacularly. Ace puts an excited finger against my lips, and I grab his wrist tightly and squeal. "Do you think… Are they fooling around?"

Ace shrugs. "I don't know, but they looked pretty freaking friendly. Like, not Lexi-friendly. *Really* friendly. I think they might be dating behind all our backs or something."

"Oh, come on," I breathe. "Lexi? She basically hates Blake. She's always giving him shit and turning him down."

"Yeah, well. I think that might just be part of the plot. Part of them throwing us off their scent."

"Should we follow them?" I ask excitedly, sitting up and throwing the comforter off in one smooth motion.

"Definitely not," Ace disagrees, catching me by the forearm before my toes can touch the floor.

"What?" I turn to face him, my waist twisting. "Definitely not? Are you kidding? I thought you'd be all for this."

Ace shakes his head. "Both Blake and Lexi have abilities that scare me. He benches 250. She can almost undoubtedly kill me without a forensic trace. We sit this one out. But we know what we know, and that's better than nothing." I frown, but he pulls me back down into the bed and tosses the comforter over both of us. "Think about it, Lia. We know a secret that no one else knows about *Lexi*. I didn't think that was possible."

"It's amazing, actually," I agree, my adrenaline calming enough to see the wisdom of his approach. Light sways through his eyes in a slow dance as he watches me talk. It cradles me gently, holding space for me to ramble on and on for as long as I'd like. "I feel like a spy. Or a—"

Ace's lips crash into mine with surprising accuracy. My head goes back as I let out a gasp, and his tongue moves inside, touching just the tip of mine.

I pull back, shocked, an electric current running wildly through the entire top half of my body. Hands to his chest, I hold him at bay as though he's going to launch toward me again. "What in the *fuck* was that?"

"What?"

"Ace, you just *kissed* me."

"We always kiss."

"Not on the lips and *not* with tongue."

"What's the difference?" Ace argues, purposely dodging the point completely as though he can't tell how thready my pulse is under his fingers.

"Ace," I whisper. "Why did you kiss me?"

"Because this moment felt too perfect to pass up. Because I wanted to. Because..." He pauses, and I hold my breath against a deluge of coulds and shoulds and maybes. He searches my eyes, and I know they harbor a touch of wildness. "We're best friends, Lia. Inseparable and unstoppable and…it was a best-friend kiss."

"A best-friend kiss?" I repeat as my mind races with the reality that it didn't feel like a kiss of friendship at all. It felt like…*a kiss*. "Ace, our dads are best friends, and they don't kiss with tongue."

"Well, they're currently still in a fight, so that's like comparing apples to oranges, babe."

I sigh. "Fine. Our moms are best friends, and they don't kiss with tongue."

"That you know of."

"Ew." I groan, and he shrugs.

"Hey, my mom is too unpredictable, and you know it."

"Please, for the love of my sanity, change the subject."

He smiles at me. And then he whispers, "We know a secret about Lexi that no one else knows."

"We do." *And you kissed me.* Though, I don't dare say that out loud.

"Now, we should go to sleep," Ace says, snuggling me closer to him. His eyes meet mine again, searching, but then they stop searching altogether and go from open to shut.

An unexpected disappointment racks me, and I swallow hard against it to trap the urge to say something—to tread into dangerous territory with the boy I've known my entire life—deep down by my stomach. A burn sizzles as the acid there works to destroy the uninvited hope.

"Night, Lia." He moves his hand from mine to the side of my head, where he strokes my hair mindlessly.

"Night, Ace." I force my lids closed too, letting my body settle into his warmth as he caresses the strands.

As confusing as the kiss was, I still find comfort. Ease. Companionship. Peace.

And it doesn't take long before I fall asleep in his arms, everything else forgotten.

17

The hallway of the fifth floor of the Holloway Apartments just off Dickson University's main campus is busy today, the two doors farthest from the elevator on the campus end of the building propped open with doorstops as Julia and I carry up load after load from the cars as we move in.

I've been waiting for this day with little to no patience since leaving the lake on Sunday and dreaming of Julia's and my brief but perfect kiss since it happened late Saturday night. I know my tongue didn't work any miracles on its own, but I do feel like it started a mental tangent in Julia's brain not previously there—a possibility. A suggestion. A tease of what something more than friendship between us could be.

"Ow, T-bag, watch where you're putting your clown feet!" my mom shrieks, sidestepping my dad and dropping her end of the nightstand she was carrying with him.

"You don't complain about the size of my feet when we're in bed, sweet cheeks, so I don't know why you're acting like they're the next act in the freak show now."

"Because you clobbered my toe. It's smashed. I just got a pedicure yesterday!"

"Well, honey, maybe focus on carrying a little more than you're focused on your pedicure, and I won't—"

"Guys, please," I cut them off before they really get on a fucking roll. "Can we not?"

"Don't you dare complain about your mother complaining," my dad launches in, setting down the nightstand and gearing up to be even more ridiculous. "She's lifting shit for your ungrateful ass, and she just got a pedicure yesterday!"

I roll my eyes. "I'm not complaining. I'm very grateful for both of you," I say by rote, knowing it's the quickest way to nip their spiral in the bud. "I was just wondering if we could focus the energy a little more internally until we're fully inside my apartment to keep from upsetting my new neighbors?"

"Your new neighbor is Julia," my dad points out brusquely. "And she's known us her whole damn life. I don't think she's motherfluffing surprised by any of it." Raising his voice and canting his head, he asks her directly. "Are you, Jules?"

"No!" she yells back from across the hall, where her mom and dad have the enviable ability to be quiet.

I sigh. "She's just saying that because she's scared of you."

"Scared? Of me?" He turns fully toward the door this time. "You're not scared of me, are you, Julia?"

"No, sir!" she yells back.

"But I am," Kline, her dad and my dad's involuntary best friend/current enemy, adds. "And Ace is right. You're louder than hell right now."

"Oh, whoops," my dad says, seemingly taking Mr. Brooks's word over my own. "I'll take it down a notch." This level of compliance is in no way normal, but since the rift, and my five hours of *begging* him to make it right, he's been making an effort to be a less pointy version of the thorn in Kline Brooks's side.

Even amid the display of my worthlessness in the behavior-influencing department, I'm thankful he's at least taking that seriously.

"Hey, Kline!" my dad calls out.

"Yeah?" The response is more of a grumble than anything else from within Julia's apartment, but still, Kline Brooks is speaking words—okay, one word—to my father, and that's progress.

"Do you love me again yet?"

"No."

"Okay, buddy!" my dad calls back and swipes a bead of sweat from his forehead with his hand. "But I want you to know that I love you very fluffing much!"

"Thatch?" Kline tosses out, still not even bothering to peek his head out of Julia's open door.

"Yeah?"

"Shut up."

"Okay, buddy." My dad is smiling for some strange reason, and when he meets my eyes and sees the way my eyebrows are furrowed together, he just claps a hand to my back. "Relax, son. That, right there, was a bridge being built over a gap."

I have no idea what or why or how he thinks being told to shut up is in any way a good thing, but I don't fight it. I don't have the energy.

"I'm going to head back down and get one of the kitchen boxes," I announce. "Those and the bed frame are all that's left, I think."

"Good," my mom says, flopping down on the couch. "I think you two can handle that while I relax, then."

I don't complain. Not only is it not worth it, but in less than an hour, if I keep working diligently, my parents will go home, as will Julia's, and we'll officially be alone and living across the hall from each other for our sophomore year of college.

I'll be perfectly poised to move on to the next phase of my plan, in which I am at a whim's notice for anything she may need. I will be a safety net. I will be a tool. I will be a confidant. I will be anything she fucking wants me to be and, maybe, some things she doesn't know she needs yet.

I'm still hatching the specifics, but I've spent the last two days since we got home from Aunt Paula and Uncle Brad's lake house hypothesizing scenarios in which I could be useful. A broken air conditioner? A fire? An emotional emergency?

I will be more than just the man of the hour—I will be the man of every hour.

My dad hip checks me as he heads for the door, and just after he steps out into the hall, Julia peeks her head inside. "Hey, Ace, do you have the stuff you got for my apartment up here yet? Or should my dad and I run down and get it?"

"I'll bring it up," I offer quickly, only to be cut off by my mother.

She groans as she climbs from the couch, stealing my thunder right out from underneath me. "I'll get your stuff, Jules. Ace, go down and help your father with your own shit so I can get the hell out of here and home to a bath."

"Yes, ma'am," I agree through clenched teeth as I head for the door. Julia waits there, patting me on the shoulder as I pass her by. I turn to meet her eyes just one more time, but she has her phone out instead and is smiling down at it while her fingers fly over the screen keyboard.

"Scottie?" I ask hopefully—foolishly.

"Drew," she corrects, not even looking up from the screen. "He's thinking about coming over tonight after we get all settled."

"Great," I say through unshed tears.

I don't know if my tone is different or if she's just done with her message, but she looks up right before I turn to walk away and tucks her phone into her pocket, shrugging. "I told him I'll see how I'm feeling. I don't know. Might just wanna have the first night to myself."

While a fist pump would make the victory sweeter, I withhold the urge. "For sure," I agree simply, acting way cooler than I feel.

"Ace!" my dad yells from the elevator as soon as the doors open. "What the fluff are you doing? Stop fluffing around and come help me carry *your* shit!"

I laugh and smile at Julia before jogging away. I jump into the elevator my dad just departed before it closes and watch with a renewed sense of drive as Julia lingers in the hall, watching me go.

Maybe, just maybe, that stolen kiss a few nights ago got me somewhere after all.

18

Oven towel set, I move to the sink, where I have my new pink-rimmed dishes drying, and load them into the cabinets. I rearrange the flowers my dad gave me in their ivory vase on the counter and sigh. I'm happy—elated, really—but I have that feeling of not knowing what to do with my hands.

There's always been someone around. A roommate, a neighbor, my mom or my dad or my sister. I've pretty much never been left alone in any space to think, and tonight is my first official night to do just that.

My parents left three hours ago with a kiss from my dad and tears from my mom, and my sister Evie texted two hours ago to tell me my mom had been in a dimly lit bath ever since.

It's a new era, a new stage, and all of us, I suppose, are figuring out how to live in it.

I pluck my phone from the butcher-block-topped kitchen island and type out a quick message to Drew.

> **Me: Thanks for understanding about me wanting to be alone tonight. It just feels like a rite of passage or something idk.**

His response is immediate.

> **Drew: No prob. I understand completely. I'll come over tomorrow night maybe.**

I smile.

Me: That sounds great. I'll text you tomorrow to come up with a plan. Have fun at dinner with the guys.

Drew: Thanks, babe

I exhale loudly, contentment and confusion melding into one hot pot. I may not know what to do with myself with this new-found freedom, but I still have it, and in a weird way, that makes it feel even more worth celebrating.

I'm growing. Learning. Evolving into an independent woman with—

A soft knock on the door arrives with irony, and I know without looking who's most likely to be on the other side. My parents have gone home to New Jersey, Ace's parents left an hour ago, and Drew's at dinner with his friends at the Manhattan Club.

That leaves only my best friend and new neighbor, Ace.

I round the kitchen island and move toward the door, checking the peephole for safety purposes despite my certainty. My dad's safety speech about living in the city as a young woman, given only three and a half hours ago, is still fresh.

Ace's face is rounded and distorted, and he surveys the length of the hall on both sides as he waits for me to answer. Seemingly hearing me on my side, he leans in, his nose stretching and exaggerating, thanks to the lens between us. "Juliaaaa. It's me. Can I come in?"

I chuckle as I move back and undo the dead bolt and chain, pulling it open for Ace to step inside.

He lets out a low whistle, spinning in a circle as he takes in all the decorating I've already done. "Holy cow, Lia, this thing is already better than Pottery Barn. You should see my place. It's still ninety percent boxes."

I snort. "And yet, you're over here instead of unpacking them."

"Yeah, I just felt like we should chill for a bit. It's a lot of work moving in to a new place, especially with my parents at the helm."

I giggle.

"Anyway, I thought we could get a game plan for being across the hall and everything."

"A game plan?"

He nods like this is all very serious. "Yeah. Alternating dinner spots. Shared laundry days. Maybe we just leave both doors open at all times and treat it like one big loft. Like a commune. A hot-people commune."

I hum. "This is my first time living alone, Ace. I don't know about being so rigid with a schedule or anything. I kind of want to be on my own time for once, you know?"

"I get that. The independence hits hard and all that. But I don't intend to cramp your style, and I know you know it's not exactly *Leave It to Beaver* here in the city. The more I know about your shit, the easier it'll be to make sure you're safe."

"And leaving my front door open all the time is safe?"

"Good point." He puts both hands to his hips. "You need a dead bolt. Ten dead bolts and I need all ten keys to the dead bolts."

"I have a dead bolt," I explain carefully. "And a chain. Now, I don't imagine they'll withstand a battering ram or anything, but I'm pretty sure they'll do in a run-of-the-mill situation."

"Okay, well, that's good. I should still have the spare key. Just in case. I'll give you mine too."

I think it through for a few seconds before ultimately deciding he's right. Just because I'm looking to do things my way doesn't mean I shouldn't be practical. I have a great emergency contact right across the hall, and should anything go wrong—or something as simple as me losing my keys while I'm out—I'll have a backup plan.

I nod. "You're right." Grabbing the spare off the hook next to the door, I take my pink keychain that says *Love* off the set and hand it to him. "Here. That's my spare to the knob and the dead bolt."

"Great. But can you leave the keychain on it? That'll make it a lot easier to know what it is than if they're just keys floating around in my drawer."

"Your drawer?"

Ace smiles. "Yeah. My kitchen filing system, as it were."

I roll my eyes. "Oh my God."

"Don't worry, Jules. Your key is very top priority. I won't lose it."

"I guess you'll give me your spare too?"

"You bet, babe. I'll go get it in just a minute," he says, stepping deeper into my apartment and looking around. "Just wanna check some shit first…"

"What are you doing?"

"Making sure your smoke alarms are up to code. You're supposed to have one in every entry to a new room."

"What? How the hell do you know that? Did you do a stint in firefighter school that I didn't know about?"

He laughs. "We all have our niche obsessions, Jules. Mine happens to be fire safety."

"You seem weird today," I say, no longer able to ignore the manic energy that appears to be vibrating off his body.

"What? Weird in what way?"

"I don't know. I can't put my finger on it, but something is different. Are you stressing over going back to school?"

"What? No. I'm excited for the year to start, actually. I have a feeling it's going to be a great year."

"Really?" I'm shocked. Ace has never loved school. In fact, he's barely tolerated it up until now.

"Yeah. I know. It's a new thing I'm trying," he says with a chuckle. "Be more like Julia. Smart, funny, reliable. You know?"

I blush lightly at the unexpected compliment. "Will you be working on your tan? Because I'm also working on my tan."

"Until the good weather heaves its last breath. We could go to the swim club tomorrow if you want."

For the first time in our friendship, I hesitate to confirm the plan right away, and I don't know why. It's not like I don't want to spend the day with Ace at the pool—it sounds amazing—but I'm a little afraid since we kissed at the lake that maybe I want it too much.

Maybe, somehow, under the radar, I've let myself get too

attached to Ace, and one day he's going to meet some other girl who pulls the rug right out from under me.

"We'll see, I guess. I told Drew I'd check in with him tomorrow too. Maybe he can come."

"Oh. Yeah," he says. "Sure, thing. Maybe I'll invite someone too."

Yep. There's the rug, tight weave and fringy edges in all its glory.

"Well, thanks for looking out for my fire safety, but if it's okay with you, I think I'm gonna lie low and go solo tonight. It feels like a big deal, you know? The first night in my big-girl apartment."

His eyes soften, and the corners of his mouth lift. "It is a big deal. And you should spend it however you imagine it should be." He exhales loudly and shrugs. "Well. I'll be going, then. Maybe unpack some of my boxes." He laughs. "But if you need me…"

I smile. "You're right across the hall."

Ace Kelly has always been the boy I could count on. I have to wonder how I'll handle it one day—when he's the man at the end of someone else's calls.

When he's the man *another woman* can count on.

19

I sit on my couch in my apartment, staring at the paused show on Netflix, one ear to the door and my heart in my throat. Julia just got home from lunch with Scottie and Kayla, and while she was gone, I did a little *work* on her window air conditioning unit using the spare key she gave me the night we moved in.

Now, I know entering her place without her knowledge was a huge violation of her privacy and, well, the law, but I am in a desperate place, which has pushed me past the brink of the cliff above an ocean of poor choices. And in my defense, I didn't rummage through her panty drawer; I legit just did a little "work" on the AC.

And since this is technically included in the next phase of my big plan to make Julia fall in love with me, one might say it's a necessity.

Three days have passed since we moved in to our new apartments across the hall from each other, and if anything, Julia has been spending *less* time with me. I haven't been able to show off any of my manly, partner-esque qualities like reliability or integrity or my protective instincts or even my good sense of humor, and because she doesn't have to text or call to check in and see what I'm doing in the mornings, she doesn't.

I've popped over and knocked a few times, but the urge to sit in her lap and wait for her to love me is becoming unbearable, and believe it or not, I don't think it would help.

So, I've stooped. I've connived. I've crossed four different lines.

My knee bounces violently up and down as I listen intently, hoping to hear her door opening and her coming across the hall any minute. And she will. I know she will because I've made sure of it, but still, I'm nervous.

Visions of her smiling face as I solve her problems dance in my head along with the accompanying tongue-filled kiss that follows. I imagine us falling into each other, our sweat-slicked bodies fighting for more contact as we declare love and monogamy and an intent to have lots and lots of sex for the rest of our lives. She laughs at all my jokes and tells me she can't live without me, and I tell her she doesn't have to because I'm kidnapping her forever.

It's an elementary story at best, but I'm no fucking romance novelist, okay? I've read a few of my mom's—when forced—but I don't know how character arcs or climaxes work. I just know I'd like to be with Julia. Forever.

I adjust my backward hat again, smoothing it at the tops of my ears and making sure it's giving the appropriate amount of *sex symbol*. This look has been a weakness for Julia since high school, and given the tropical climate I've set across the hall, it should be perfectly on trend for reminding her what's normally hiding under my style.

A sudden bang on my door sits me upright like a slingshot, and I unpause the video on Netflix to sell the vision that I've just been chilling and watching TV as Julia's voice rings through the door. "Ace!"

I move with both speed and casualness to answer her call.

All right, boys and girls. It's showtime.

"What's up?" I ask, dialing concern into my tone and flexing the muscles of my abs as tight as I can manage at the same time. She pauses briefly, taking in my low-slung basketball shorts, shirtless chest, and backward hat before shaking her head and focusing.

I flex a little harder, hoping to regain some quick attention as she runs it down for me. "I just got home, and my AC isn't working."

"What? Really? Mine is working just fine…"

"God, that's so strange," she says and blows out a breath of air from pursed lips. "I don't think mine's been working since I left to meet Scottie and Kayla because it legit feels like a sauna in my apartment. Do you think you can come help me try to figure out what's going on?"

"Why, of course I can," I say, clearing my throat to force some of the nagging guilt down with my saliva. I'm going to fix it for her—obviously—so it's not like I'm really messing with her. I just want to show her how useful I can be. This is a little reminder that she can count on me in times of need.

I follow her across the hall, shutting my door behind me, but leaving hers open. Crossing the threshold is like stepping inside an oven as the July heat does its worst against her unprotected space.

It's just as intended but also makes my butthole clench a little bit with the pressure to get things circulating again *after* we have a little sweat chemistry.

"Wow. It'll fucking roast your ass in here, huh?"

"I think it might be hotter in here than it is outside!" Julia complains. "I'm pretty sure you could fry an egg on my boobs right now."

I grit my teeth to stop myself from saying we should try.

"Go change into a bathing suit or something if you want, and I'll get to work on this thing."

"Good idea!" she agrees readily, running to her bedroom while I take the cover off the front of her unit and pretend to start looking at it. When I'm sure she's gone, I find the reset switch on the back edge of the left side I disengaged earlier and push hard against it with my thumb.

I shoot forward as it breaks under the pressure, slamming my fucking forehead into the hard plastic grate on the front as the switch officially lodges itself in the off position. Panic seizes my already struggling lungs as I fight to get a grip on the now-broken shard, but that only pushes the switch deeper inside.

Fuck, fuck, fuck.

Genuine sweat pours from my forehead now as I wrestle with

the unit, my plan crumbling along with the frail, dry-rotted old switch. Not only is my easy little fix dwindling quickly, so is any chance of me looking like a fucking capable helper—which was the entire point of this whole endeavor. I didn't go to HVAC school. I don't really know how to fix this shit.

"How's it going?" Julia asks, returning from her room in a tiny green bikini with a wet washcloth around her neck. She looks amazing, as expected—it'd be nice if my huge fuckup weren't getting in the way of my enjoying it.

"Oh, I'm just troubleshooting right now," I bullshit, turning back to the unit and pretending to twist and turn knobs. "If you have a screwdriver, I bet I can get it taken care of."

"Oh my God, I do have a screwdriver!" she says excitedly. "My dad was insistent on me having a toolbox full of stuff, and I guess this is why! Let me grab it."

I watch as she runs for the laundry closet on fast toes, but I'm surprised when she stops to pull out her phone just short of the white latticed doors. She reads quickly and then spins around, heading for the speaker panel beside the open front door.

"Oh, hold on. Drew is here."

"*What?*"

"Drew. He's here. I have to buzz him in. We were texting earlier and planned for him to come over, and then I got distracted with the AC being out when I got home. Hey, maybe he knows something about how to fix it!" she suggests happily, practically skipping to the door in her bikini top.

Oh, no, no, no! This isn't good.

Drewgie Schnauzer was not part of the plan. I wasn't looking for a three-way, and if I were, it sure as fuck wouldn't be with a guy who looks like a dog with big, bushy eyebrows. Hell, I might as well have hand-tied Julia's tiny fucking bikini myself. *Go change, Jules! Get comfortable because Drew is coming over!*

I'm a fucking idiot.

"Maybe he, uh, should wait for us downstairs…" I scramble

to find any reason I can grab from my asshole to keep Dumbnuts away. "It's pretty hot up here, and I don't know if renters insurance covers heatstroke of guests."

Julia snorts, rolling her eyes. "I don't think I have to worry about Drew suing."

When she turns back to the open door and leans out into the hall, I let out a giant, openmouthed, silent scream into the void.

As Mr. Best in Show arrives and she ushers him inside with her hand in his, I consider slamming my head back into the front of the unit again. It'll either knock me out or magically fix this fucker, and at this point, I'd settle for either one.

I glance back and catch the tail end of his lips on her cheek, and his stupid fucking grin only grows at the sight of all of Julia's skin. Whatever part of my balls hasn't yet succumbed to heat withers and dies right then.

"What's going on?" he asks, but I don't miss the way his eyebrows furrow when he finds me shirtless inside Julia's apartment.

I don't hesitate to smile at him. Smug, confident, and silently saying, *Hi, fuckface. That's right. I'm here. And Julia is mine.*

Or, well, she *will* be mine. Soon. Once I can fix this damn AC and make her fall in love with me.

"The AC is out," Julia explains. "Ace is working on trying to fix it now, but it's hot as hell in here. We had to take a couple layers off."

"Oh, shoot. Yeah." He steps inside, feeling the muggy, stale air and capitalizing immediately. "It is hot in here."

He grabs the material of his T-shirt between his shoulder blades and pulls his shirt over his head, flexing his stupid muscles with every subtle move. Julia watches with a smile on her face, and a frog lodges itself in my throat as I try to find the words to say, *it's not that hot, so everyone should put their fucking clothes on!*

"Do you want a glass of water or something? Some lemonade?" Julia offers graciously. I can't help but notice she didn't offer me any chilled beverages.

"Lemonade sounds great," Shirtless Caveman grunts like a buffoon. "Did you make it?"

Did you make it? I silently mock the Dummy Drew in my head. *Did you make the lemonade, Julia? Do you want to see me flex my biceps, Julia? Oh, by the way, I have a teeny-tiny dick, Julia.*

"Nope, sorry. That's all Whole Foods," Julia says through her giggles, not at all clueing in to how stupid Drew sounds every time he speaks words.

Honestly, I wonder if I should suggest she get her ears checked. Maybe *she* has wax buildup or something.

"That's still awesome. You should see my fridge. It's practically barren. Probably a guy thing, though. Right, Ace?"

I grunt. *Fucker.*

So much for making progress today. I'm trapped in an avalanche of my own making—coasting toward death in a wild ride.

Julia, of course, will probably bring fuckface to my funeral, and the bastard will hover over my casket shirtless and flexing his fucking biceps.

20

Ace and Drew chat at the thermostat, picking through the settings to see if they can figure something out. Drew is calm and cheerful, his muscles flexing in every direction with even, subtle movements, but Ace seems agitated as he moves him out of the way.

He's shirtless too, and the sweat that beads on the back of his neck makes his hair curl at the ends under his hat. Ace looks hot, as always, but his lack of smile is stirring me in a way I don't expect. I love when he's joking and smiling and in a good mood—but something about him looking serious is making him seem grown up in all the ways I've been avoiding.

He's not the boy I played with anymore; he's all man. I knew the transition happened, but right now, it feels like I'm really seeing it for the first time.

"Any luck, guys?" I ask, fanning myself with my *Cosmo* magazine. "Maybe we should just call a repairman."

"I know a guy," Drew starts to offer, but Ace cuts him off.

"I already called someone, Lia. Why don't you go hang out in my apartment until I either get it figured out or they come? Feel free to snag one of my sweatshirts if you get cold. I mean, you usually steal them from me and wear them anyway. My sweatshirts. On your body."

I scrunch up my nose in confusion. *What the hell is Ace even talking about right now?*

"That's okay," Drew volleys back before I can answer. "Julia and

I already had plans to go to the pool, so we can just do that while you wait for your guy to come."

"Of course, Drew," Ace comments. "Since you don't want to hang around here being busy with adult man stuff, you go ahead to the pool so you can play in the water. I'll wait here because I'd wait all day to make sure Julia's AC is fixed. Hell, I'd wait all fucking week if I had to."

"I'd wait all day too," Drew comments. "Of course I'd wait all day. I'd—"

"Uh, guys…" I interrupt. "Why don't we all go to the pool? I'm sure the landlord can let the repairman in when he comes."

Ace stares at Drew for a beat before turning back to me and softening his face into a smile. It's different from the ones I've seen him use over the years—maybe even a little sad around the eyes—but beautiful all the same. "That's okay, Jules. You go have fun. I'll see this through and make sure it's working when you get back, okay?"

"No, Ace," I refute. "There's no way I'm leaving you here while I go to the pool."

"Lia, go have fun at the pool," he repeats. "I got this. I promise."

"Are you sure? I feel so bad I charged over there demanding your help, and now I'm just going to leave you here to deal with it?"

"No big deal, babe." He shrugs and winks at me. "That's what best friends are for, you know?"

Drew frowns a little before grabbing his shirt from the kitchen island and holding out a hand. "Should we go?"

"Yeah. I guess," I agree. "If Ace is sure?"

He nods. It still feels a little wrong to leave him here, but if I confirm that's what he wants any more times, we'll be dancing dangerously close to making the world's most annoying sound from *Dumb and Dumber*.

"Let me just grab my purse from my room." I pause. "Ace, you'll call or text if you need anything, right?"

"Of course," he says easily. "And I'll see you tonight. When you get home. I'll be here."

"You can call me if you need to too," Drew adds helpfully.

"She won't need to because I'm right here, but thanks for the offer," Ace replies.

"Okay," I declare, feeling like we could be stuck in this loop of them offering to help me for hours if I don't do something about it. I rush to my room, grab my purse and tank top and shorts off the bed, and then rush back out to the front door, scooping Drew out of the kitchen as we go. I wave enthusiastically at Ace and point to the front door behind me as we scoot through it.

Ace gives me the thumbs-up, effectively communicating that he will make sure the door gets closed if he leaves or the air gets turned back on or whatever.

I hand Drew my purse as we approach the elevator, stepping into my shorts and pulling my tank top over my head as we walk. "Thanks," I say, taking the bag back as he holds open the elevator door for me to step inside.

"You're welcome."

He stares at the doors as I apply lip gloss, and we start our descent to the ground floor. This building is great but old, so it moves like molasses, and when we're halfway down, he starts to talk.

"Ace likes you, you know."

I scoff and laugh at the same time, and he turns to face me, grabbing me gently by the bicep to get my attention. "Julia, I'm serious."

I laugh again, shaking my head. "Oh, I know you are and I'm sorry for laughing, but you just don't know Ace. This always happens, people thinking we're something that we're not. We've been friends since utero. He knows everything about me, and I know everything about him. Whatever that was back there was just him protecting me." I shrug. "He'll probably have two girls over while we're gone today, I'm telling you. He's charisma in a bottle, but it doesn't mean anything. You'll get used to him."

"Okay," he agrees easily because that's what Drew does, but I can tell he doesn't believe me. But that's not new. No one ever believes me.

I pat his hand and reach up to touch my lips to his cheek just before the elevator doors open to the lobby, my goal to put him at ease. "I know you don't believe me right now, but it's so sweet of you to pretend. I'm telling you, though, if you hang around long enough, you'll see."

"Okay," he says, holding me back when I go to step off the elevator and pulling my gaze to his so he can look me in the eye. "But just so there's no confusion…Julia, I *like* you. And if things keep going the way they are, I want to be more than just a friend."

My chest buoys and my stomach drops all at once, and I smile through the feeling like it isn't one of the strangest in the world.

Drew Bettencourt likes me.

And yet, in my mind, all I see is a vision of the kiss Ace gave me at the lake house. The *best-friend* kiss that didn't feel like friends at all.

What the hell is that all about?

21

As I spritz on my favorite Dior cologne, a text vibrates my phone on my bathroom counter.

Boden: Some of us don't have the summer off, dude. I've been breaking my back at doubles every day. What the fuck have YOU been doing?

His text is in response to the text I sent him three fucking hours ago, asking him where in the hell he's been and berating him for completely ignoring Finn and me when we tried to reach him last night and this morning.

Me: Mostly fucking off. Getting my shit twisted over Julia. You know the deal. Anyway are you free right now? I've got a whole fucking thing happening in Central Park in tminus 25 minutes and I need as many hands on deck as possible.

Boden: Sorry, I'm busy. As appealing as "a whole fucking thing" is. Truly reassuring, actually. Have you gotten any takers with that sales pitch?

Me: Finn's helping me

Boden: That tracks. You made him a hostage last year. Probably got Stockholm syndrome by now.

Me: Hey jockstrap he gives his friendship freely and willingly. I can't help it if he's unconscious when he agrees to things sometimes. He should sleep harder so he doesn't answer me

Boden: LMAO. Good luck, dude. With whatever it is.

Me: Yeah wahtever. Fuck you too

I slide my phone in the back pocket of my jeans, take one final look at my appearance in the mirror—*I look fucking good*—and head out my door and across the hall.

I knock three times, fast and hard, on Julia's door, calling through the wood to emphasize our need to hurry. We're already running ten minutes late, and I know for a fact that old Finnley Hayes isn't going to be happy about wrestling a goldendoodle puppy in the middle of Central Park for any longer than contractually agreed upon. "Come on, Jules! You ready?"

"Coming!" she calls back from somewhere inside. "Just a second."

I bounce on my toes and glance down at my watch again, willing my heartbeat to stop counting the seconds. I can feel it in my lungs, my wrists, my jugular. I am a walking pulse.

She's been talking about getting a puppy since the day we moved in to our apartments, and the idea of getting to see her face as she realizes it's happening is…overwhelming.

I never knew it could be like this—that it could *feel* like this. I've always loved Julia, but I've undoubtedly spent the majority of my life focused on myself. My reactions, my happiness, my wants and needs. Spending the time focusing myself on her has been enlightening in a million ways I didn't expect.

I'm learning new smiles, seeing new depths of her dimple—realizing she finds joy in the simplest of things, even when I get frustrated or upset.

She's sunshine in a bottle, and I've taken that for granted for a hell of a lot of years.

Today, though, I get to see a dream of hers come true.

And if I were a betting man—which I totally fucking am—I'd put a couple hundred grand on the fact that being the one to be there when this puppy dream comes true is going to bring us even closer together than we are.

Which is good, because I need to be reallyyy close to her—our bodies practically smashed together, really—to fit between her and Fuckface McGee most days.

"What took you so long?" I ask as soon as the door opens, making her roll her eyes and laugh at me as she pulls it closed and uses her key to lock it.

"Would you keep your panties on?" She huffs. "I don't know why you're in such a hurry in the first place."

"Because, Juliaaa," I sing. "The sunset is in twenty minutes, and if we miss it, a baby loses its wings."

"Babies aren't supposed to have wings."

"They are, actually, but since so many people miss the sunset, they never get to keep them."

She snorts. "You're bizarre."

"What else is new?"

"I'll be honest, you've been surprisingly calm lately. It's like Ace, but not, you know? Zen Ace. Zace, if you will."

"I'm just maturing, Lia. I mean, we're about to be sophomores in college. We live on our own in apartments in the city. I can't be out here just acting like a kid anymore. You'd kick me to the curb."

It's a little test, of course, to see how I've been doing for the last ten days in my plan to persuade her to love me. It's a check in on the flowers I've gotten for her vase when the ones her dad gave her died, and a query about the takeout I brought her the two nights we were at home for dinner, and a thermometer to read if I need to turn up the heat and get even more serious, but she doesn't give me much to work with other than simple reassurance.

"It'd take a lot to kick you to the curb, Acer. Especially since I have to get over anything you do that makes me angry in fifteen minutes or less."

"Believe it or not," I hedge with a laugh, "I'm really working on trying not to make you angry with me at all."

She smiles and pinches my cheek. "You have been very sweet lately."

I push the button to call the elevator and, when it dings, hold the door for her to step inside. She digs in her purse to pull out her lip gloss—something she always does on the ride down to the lobby—and I swallow hard.

Her lips, her hair, her eyes, her smile. I can't help but stare at every bit of it and wonder if I should just man the fuck up and tell her how I feel. I mean, maybe all this bullshit is dumb. Maybe Gunnar—as wild as this is to say—was right. Maybe I'm over-complicating the hell out of a situation that doesn't need complication at all.

I love her. I should just tell her.

"Julia?"

"Yeah?" she asks, her head still down as she replaces her lip gloss and digs through her purse until she comes out with her phone.

"Can you look at me for a sec?"

Her eyes jerk to mine at the seriousness of my tone, and I take her free hand—the one not holding her phone—in mine.

You can do this, Ace. You can do this.

"I... Well, see...I..."

"Yeah?"

"I just... I wanted to—"

Lady Gaga's "Bad Romance" plays obnoxiously in the space with a sudden jolt of violence, and the screen of Julia's phone lights up so hard it pierces the tenderness right out of my eyes.

She glances down at the screen, winces, and then apologizes

while ripping her hand from mine to hold up a finger. "Sorry. It's Drew. Just one second."

Every vestige of the urge to confess my undying love takes a knife to the chest. The love may still be there, but the courage to confess it is currently receiving last rites on life support.

She babbles and chats to Dr. Weasel, and my brain fogs like it's being fumigated. When she hangs up and looks back up at me, I startle.

"Sorry about that. What were you saying? It seemed like it might be important."

I shake my head. "Don't worry about it."

"Are you sure? I'm sorry I even answered, but he's about to get on a flight to Aruba. Family vacation."

Suddenly perkier, I ask, "He's going on vacation?"

"Yeah. For a week, I think. They do it every year before school starts, and he says his parents say it's nonnegotiable that he keeps going until he's married."

I don't give a shit about any of that—other than the fact that I'm about to have Julia to myself for the next week.

Operation Lost Puppy is just the beginning.

If this doesn't work, my next move is to fake a coma, request her as my emergency contact, and hire a George-Clooney-looking actor to play my doctor and tell Julia the only way to bring me back to consciousness is to kiss me and tell me she loves me.

But it *will* work.

I don't know what phase of the plan this is, but it's a big one. Maybe a *slightly* emotionally manipulative pièce de résistance, but I have no doubt it will prove I'm responsible and kind and trust-worthy and reliable and will one day make a killer anecdote in our wedding vows.

I casually guide Julia toward the exact place I mapped out yesterday in Central Park. It's the perfect little spot, near the west-facing path, that has the best view of the skyline because the trees part like the gates of heaven.

Golden hour is about to hit, and Finn is in the bushes with a goldendoodle puppy I bought off a woman named Felicia on Long Island. Thankfully, Julia and I are only a few minutes away.

My phone buzzes violently in my pocket, and then it pretty much keeps buzzing so much that I pull it out and discreetly look at the screen while I continue to guide Julia where I need her to be.

> *Finn: Where the fuck are you?*

> *Finn: It's hot. I'm sweating. And this dog is staring at me like he knows I have no plan.*

> *Finn: This is insane, Ace. Like really fucking insane. You know that, right? I already have enough to deal with, preparing to have all three of my brothers at Dickson this year, and yet, here I am, with a fucking dog, waiting for you in the middle of Central fucking Park*

> *Finn: I don't know how the fuck I let you get me into these situations.*

> *Finn: I swear, if you don't show up in 2 minutes, I'm naming him Todd and giving him to Scottie.*

I text back one-handed while pretending to point something out on the skyline for Julia.

> *Me: YOU CAN'T KEEP HIM. OR NAME HIM TODD.*

> *Me: Just chill for like a few more minutes and release the dog when I text "sunset"*

> *Finn: A few more minutes? I've already been standing here trying to keep this puppy hidden behind a fucking bush for like thirty minutes. This plan is UNHINGED.*

Me: *This plan is perfect. You'll see. Just wait.*

Next to me, Julia stretches her arms overhead and takes a deep breath. "This was a good idea," she says, sighing like peace incarnate. "I always forget how much I love Central Park."

"Same," I say. "It's even better when you're not dodging tourists or rogue saxophone players or those nice ladies who are always trying to sell mangoes."

She smiles, and the light hits her just right, and I swear to God I almost abort the mission just to blurt out, "*I love you! Here's a puppy and my soul!*"

Instead, I keep my shit together and text Finn one word.

Me: *sunset*

Nothing happens.
I text again.

Me: *SUNSET*

Me: *GO*

Me: *UNLEASH THE BEAST*

Finn: *Hang on, he's tangled in the leash.*

Oh my fucking God. Get it together, man!

Finn: *Okay. Okay. RELEASED.*

And then, like a miracle, he appears. The cute, adorable goldendoodle puppy bounds across the grass like a teddy bear on a sugar rush, ears flopping, tail wagging like he's never known sadness.

"Oh my God!" Julia gasps when she spots him running toward us. "Look at that puppy, Ace!"

And since he's the best dog in the whole damn world, he

literally runs straight to Julia's feet. We don't share DNA, but he's clearly my son.

She crouches down and picks him up, snuggling him into the crook of her neck.

"He doesn't have a collar," I say, eyes wide like I didn't orchestrate this entire thing. "I wonder if he's lost, Jules…"

"Aw." She cuddles him closer. "Are you lost? Did you lose your mommy or daddy?"

Technically, he just found his mommy and daddy, and I've been training him for this moment by having my mom put articles of clothing I've been stealing from Julia's closet with him every night since I got him from Felicia and stashed him at my parents' place.

The puppy immediately launches himself at her and starts licking her face with joyful abandon. She laughs so hard she falls onto the grass, and he climbs on top of her like he's found his soul mate.

I kneel beside them and point out his tag-less neck again. "He doesn't have a collar or tag." I make a show of standing to my feet and looking around the park. "And I don't see anyone looking for him."

"Aw, poor baby," Julia says, rubbing his fluffy head. "We can't just leave him, Ace."

"No," I agree solemnly. "We *definitely* can't leave him."

"Someone must be missing him."

"Or…" I say, voice low, heart racing, "maybe he was meant to find us."

She looks up at me slowly. "Are you saying this is fate?"

Yes. Yes, Julia Brooks. I am.

"I mean, if we *had* to take him, we'd have to co-parent. Like… full joint custody."

"I think I could handle that," she says, smiling. "He's literally perfect, but surely this is someone's dog, Ace. I mean, what are the odds that a puppy just finds its way into Central Park without an owner?"

"I'll check shelters tomorrow, just in case he's lost or someone's looking for him."

"Good idea." Julia nods, still cuddling our furbaby son to her chest. "And what if we don't find anyone?"

Internally, I'm screaming in excitement. Externally, I say, "Well…then I guess we need to give him a name."

Her answering smile is blinding. I casually pretend I'm chill, while internally, I'm thinking, *this is it.*

This is one of the moments Julia will remember when she tells our future children how she fell in love with me.

22

I light the last candle and turn off the lights, running to the coffee table where my two favorite gal pals are waiting. Scottie is reclined on her wheelchair, legs propped up on a carefully stacked set of pillows, and Kayla leans on the couch behind her.

I plop onto the pink pile rug on the kitchen side of the table.

The Ouija board Kayla brought sits menacingly in the center like it knows we're not ready, but I swallow down the nerves and rub my hands together dramatically. "Let's do this."

Yoko Ono—the dog—is bouncing beside Kayla, desperate for attention. She scratches the back of his neck lovingly, but it's not good enough for him. He starts licking her ear like it's steak, and she giggles and pushes him down lightly.

"Yoko, come here!" I call, fully aware that he's about as obedient as a windstorm. But maybe one day he'll listen. Manifestation is key. I circle the table and grab him, holding his thrashing little body in my lap as I take a seat next to Scottie again on the pink pile rug.

"I still can't believe you have a dog!" Kayla squeals. "And that you just *found* the breed you've always wanted in the park? What are the chances of that? Like one in a million?"

"I know." I smile hugely. "It's so wild, but Ace and I were just walking along in Central Park, and he came running over, straight into my arms. I swear it's like it was meant to be. I was really nervous that he belonged to someone, but Ace called all the shelters around the city to see if anyone was looking, and he wasn't wearing a collar or anything. I guess someone could turn up, but until then, I'm claiming him." I pet his head and shrug. "Technically, Ace says he's both of ours since we both found him, but he ran straight to me and barks every time Ace tries to hold him, so I don't know if that'll stick."

Scottie licks her lips and nods, her expression a little suspicious, so I babble on quickly to keep her distracted. Finn explicitly tasked me with occupying her tonight so he could do the last-minute work for her surprise birthday party on Friday, and if she somehow finds out on my watch, Finn is liable to flip out.

"Anyway, we settled on Yoko Ono, even though we know that was a lady and our Yoko is a boy, because she didn't really break up the Beatles like everyone said she did, and since Ace and I are un-breakable, her being part of our union without breaking it up feels like it brings some justice back to her name."

"Okay," Scottie laughs. "That's an Ace Kelly explanation if I've ever heard one."

I giggle and shrug. "I liked the sound of it because it felt like some kind of win for women, so I went with it. My only other op-tion was Bernie Barks-A-Lot, but that might have just been a gate-way to failure. Like, hello? Am I *asking* the universe for a dog that barks all the time?"

"So, what now? You just have a dog?" Kayla questions with a laugh. "What are you going to do if you're out?"

"I already talked to my mom and Ace's mom, and they both said they'd dog-sit whenever I needed. Cassie already has Philmore and Thatch, per her own explanation, so *what's one more animal.*"

Both girls laugh, and I cuddle Yoko a little closer. "So…who's going first?" I jerk my chin at the Ouija board. I've never used one be-fore, and for some reason, it's making me super nervous. But maybe that's just because my period is imminent and I'm a hormonal, emo-tional swamp monster whenever I'm in the middle of my flow.

"Not me," Scottie says, grinning. "I've got enough problems

without hearing from the other side. Someone else can vibe check the ghost energy first."

"Fine, I'll do it," Kayla volunteers. "I don't have that much to lose. What's the worst that can happen? It tells me my ex-boyfriend is going to break up with me again?"

"Oh, Kayl—"

A rapid knock on the door cuts off Scottie's sympathy, and Yoko goes absolutely berserk. He's yapping and jumping and flipping and flopping, and it's all I can do to keep him out of the appetizers and Ouija board.

"Jiminy Cricket, Yoko, it's okay! Relax, relax. It's probably just Ace anyway."

"Ace?" Scottie asks, glancing at Kayla and back at me again. "I thought he was with Finn."

"Yeah," I call back over my shoulder. "He texted earlier and asked if he would mess up girls' night too badly if he dropped by. He promised to be quick because he's supposed to meet Finn." I giggle nervously. "Sorry in advance if Finn's upset later because his buddy was late."

"Oh, no issue with me," Scottie says. "Right, Kayla?"

"No issues."

My eyebrows draw together. "Okay, I can't put my finger on it, but you guys sound weird." Ace knocks again, soft but loud. "Remind me to interrogate you later."

The two of them devolve into giggles, and I chalk it all up to pitcher margaritas and charcuterie. We've been gabbing for two hours now, and the two tiny shots of tequila I poured in the mixer—which Scottie approved of—must finally be hitting us.

When the door swings open, Ace is smiling so big I can see his molars. I laugh. "Hey, buddy. What's up?"

"Sounds like you're having a big time in there," he says, still grinning. "Want me to take Yoko for a little while so you don't have to worry about him?"

The offer is both considerate and unexpected, and I find myself swooning a little over Ace's ability to know what I need without my having to ask.

Still, I have a part to keep up, and that includes the white lie that Ace is supposed to meet Finn to do guy things—not work on Scottie's secret party that she's not supposed to know about. "What about Finn?" I ask loudly, just in case Scottie heard him, and he raises his voice back, thankfully catching on.

"I'll just drop Yoko off at my mom's on the way to meet him. No biggie."

I lower my voice to a whisper. "Okay, actually, yes. Please take him. He's fine, but he's been a little rowdy and won't stop licking Kayla's ear."

Ace chuckles. "I hear Harry Wethers from Chem One had the same problem our first semester."

I shove his shoulder. "Stop. Let me get the dog."

"Wait. Here," he calls, stopping me in my tracks and spinning me back toward him. "I brought some chocolate too. And a warm compress. And I know you guys had your own food planned, but I brought a couple steaks from that place you love. On the corner."

"Brasilia?"

He winks. "That's the one."

"Oh my God, that's amazing."

"I had a feeling all of it would be beneficial today. You know, because it's about that time of the month."

Whenever I'm on my period, red meat is my go-to. It's a trick I learned from my grandma Savannah. But how in the hell Ace knows all that is beyond me.

"Wait…*time of the month?*" My jaw drops. "Are you… Are you tracking my cycle?"

He holds up both hands defensively, a freedom he has because I'm now holding the heating pad, bag of steak, and box of expensive chocolates. "Not tracking. I just…kind of know now. I've been around a long time, remember?"

"Yeah, I guess you have." I shake my head, incredulous. "Pretty wild, though, that you remember that shit."

"Of course I remember that shit, Lia." He wraps his arms around my shoulders and presses a kiss to my forehead. "Anyway, I thought this stuff would be comforting, but if you're not into it, feel free to give it to the girls or get rid of it. Whatever."

"No. It's...great. Honestly. I can't believe I didn't think to get steak myself. The charcuterie was good but a little fluffy."

"That's what I'm here for, Jules. So you don't have to think about it." He winks, and I melt a little inside. Even on me, his winks have always held a certain level of power. "If you need anything else, just text or call, okay?"

I nod.

"Have fun with the girls." He leans down and kisses me on the forehead again, and then in no more than a moment, he and Yoko are gone.

But thoughts of him linger. Dangerous, scary thoughts of what it'd be like if we were more than just friends.

I go back to the girls and the Ouija board, and of course, we start asking it questions. They're throwaways at first—channeling our ancestors for basic hellos like it says to do in the instructions.

Is anyone there?

Are you friendly?

Can you tell us your name?

But as the night goes on, and the second margarita pitcher gets lighter, we get bolder and bolder.

Am I on the right path in life?

Do you use your spirit to guide me?

Is fate fair?

And finally, I work up the courage to test the scariest question of all.

"If you are able, and it's not too much to ask, could you tell us the first letter of the name of our soul mate? Kayla first. Then Scottie. Then me."

We watch as the planchette moves around the board in a circle. It stops first at the letter C, then an F, and then an A.

I gasp, and then we all erupt into hysterics. Kayla accidentally knocks over the hummus, and the planchette flies off the board like it's had enough of us.

I know it's silly. Probably not real.

But that A?

It scrambles something inside me. Not in a big, meaningful way or anything. Just in a tiny, oh-no-my-heart-did-a-weird-flip kind of way.

It could've been D. Probably should've been D. Logically, D made more sense.

But nope. There it was. *A.*

And now I'm sitting in the flickering candlelight trying *really hard* not to read into anything.

It's fine. Everything's fine.

Nothing to see here, ghosts. Move along.

23

"**S**urprise!" we all yell as Finn pushes Scottie inside Zip's Diner and the door closes behind them. He's been planning this party for a minute—wanting something special and unexpected for Scottie in the middle of her finding her new normal—and freaking out to me every five seconds in the process.

"*Do you think she'll really be surprised?*"

"*Is Zip's special enough?*"

"*Should I have told her instead of surprising her?*"

My best bud is normally composed as fuck, but my God, he's been a whiny weenie about this shit, and really, with everything I'm juggling on my own, it's been a lot. It's like putting on your oxygen mask before helping others on a crashing plane—I can hardly save someone else from hysteria when I'm on the brink of breakdown myself.

Last year, when he was in the throes of drama with Scottie, it was easy. I was composed. I was promiscuous. I was naïve. I was, however, in love—I just didn't realize it yet.

But when I'm honest with myself, I know I've been in love with Julia since the beginning. Since we first made our decree. Since we first laid eyes on each other.

"What?" Scottie exclaims, over the moon at our turnout and the volume of our yell. "I thought you were all out of town!" She looks over her shoulder and meets Finn's eyes, and he's looking like a proud Pete. "This is your doing?"

Finn grins, the cool customer extraordinaire, and I nearly roll my eyes.

Oh yeah, like he hasn't been losing his fucking figs over this shit for weeks. I haven't dogged him about it too much, though. Number one, he'd beat the shit out of me. And number two, I'm a fucking weenie too.

I've been officially in the game of pursuing Julia for almost two months, and this shit isn't getting easier. If anything, it's getting harder and harder to keep myself under wraps.

Drew isn't here tonight since he's still in Aruba—thank fuck—but he's always there in the background, lingering on her phone with texts and calls and surprise flower deliveries to her apartment. She deserves all of it, but I fucking hate that it's coming from him.

I should be *the guy*. I should be *the one*. This should be us and our families still all together in twenty years with Julia as my wife and our own kids in the mix. Sure, I'd probably have our fathers talking to each other instead of still kind of fighting over a crocodile, and Julia's mom here instead of dog-sitting Yoko for us, but the bones of the evening really are perfect.

Finn winks and leans down to kiss Scottie, and Julia nudges me with her elbow, the excitement over seeing our friends finding some normalcy again overwhelming her. It's been a rocky road for Scottie, especially, but Finn too. I'm happy they're both finding some footing in each other, even if my smile isn't as chummy as my girl's.

"Happy?" I ask, slinging an arm over her shoulder and rocking her into my side as Kayla claps in front of her face before teasingly punching Blake in the shoulder.

Julia is nearly bursting. "Are you kidding? I'm freaking ecstatic. I haven't seen Scottie this happy in months."

Tell me about it. Julia is the first to take off for the birthday girl when Finn finally stops monopolizing her space, trapping her in a hug and nearly squashing her limbs with the force of her love. Scottie laughs and, if I'm not mistaken, even squeaks out a few tears.

I wait my turn along with everyone else—there are so many

people in here, I can barely fucking move—but when we're all done with our initial hugs, Julia steals Scottie from the front and wheels her toward the cheerleading squad over by the big speaker in the corner.

Zip's Diner is literally packed to the brim with friends and family, but my focus, for now, is on Finn and making sure he takes a well-deserved fucking breath. Blake Boden follows me over, evidently having the same instincts as me.

"You pulled it off," I congratulate, clapping Finn on the back and rocking his big body gently back and forth. "She didn't have a fucking clue." I watch as a little stress leaves his shoulders, but then quickly returns when Blake's face turns angry.

"Nope."

Finn and I, both trying to suss out the problem, follow Blake's sight line to Lexi, who stands beside some dude at the other end of the room. Honestly, Blake looks positively fit to be tied, and I should know because I've had the same constipated look every time Julia and whatshisname are cuddle-y and shit in front of me. It's the *I wanna fucking kill* someone face.

It would be a little more confusing if I hadn't seen him sneaking out of the lake house with Lex on the Fourth of July. I know some shit is going down between them, but I haven't asked him about it and currently see it as my job to cast enough doubt to maintain his secret.

Lexi, for as sweet as she can be, would absolutely murder me if I were the one to out her secret dalliance with the star quarterback of our school.

And it wouldn't be quick—it'd be gruesome. She's too fucking smart not to know all of the very worst ways to torture someone without getting her hands messy.

"Who's that guy?" Blake asks Finn, his voice all growly.

"What guy?"

"Seriously?" he questions, frustrated. I laugh. I can't help it.

It's like looking in a mirror, he's so damn pathetic. "The one talking to Lexi."

I shake my head. The three of us. It's incredible. We're all fucking pitiful these days, and we all used to be so strong. It's amazing what the power of a once-in-a-lifetime girl can do. Truly.

"You're fucking intense right now, Boden," I suggest gently, trying to encourage him to rein it in before the whole party explodes.

"I don't care." He meets Finn's eyes again, desperate. "I need to know who he is."

"He works at the Hodge Clinic, dude," Finn explains. "He just came because he's been working a lot with Scottie."

Blake nods.

Finn laughs. "You know you sound a lot like a jealous boyfriend right now, right? For a girl who won't give you the time of day."

Blake smiles, and I know the edges of the secrets it carries. For all intents and purposes, I'm guessing he *is* the jealous but secret boyfriend. Or at the very least, secret hookup. Fucking hard to imagine with Lexi, but I'd say by the caliber of his glare, the lake house wasn't a one-time thing. "We must not allow other people's limited perceptions to define us, Finnley," Blake says. "There are things known and there are things unknown, and in between are the doors of perception."

"The fuck did you just say?" I ask, trying to follow his philosophical bullshit and getting lost somewhere in the middle.

Blake shakes his head. "Never mind. I'm going in."

"You're going in? What does that mean?" I ask, scared for him. Lexi is going to eat his fucking shit for breakfast if he fucks up whatever little secret agreement they have by outing their relationship in the middle of Scottie's party. "What is he doing?"

"I think he's asking her out."

"Oh fuck," I manage with a laugh, trying to play up Blake's innocence with Finn. "Why do I feel like he's going to crash and burn?"

"Because he is," Finn says with a laugh.

We both stand there, watching from a distance as Blake

interrupts Lexi and Hodge Clinic Dude's conversation. It feels a little like watching a car wreck as his hands gesticulate and his face gives 99 of his 100 secrets away.

Lexi's face doesn't give anything back, which isn't a shock, but in the grand scheme, I'm guessing neutrality is the best of all scenarios. It lacks blood. And gore. And Blake's carcass sprayed all over the place. We're too far away to hear what either of them says, but when Blake turns back around and heads in our direction, he has a big-ass smile on his face.

Mentally, I pat him on the back. I guess, this time, his bravado actually got him somewhere. I'm impressed.

I glance at Julia, wondering again if I'd do better to take the same approach—if I should just finally tell her that I've realized I'm in love with her. Whatshisface is still away, and I'd have time to prove my seriousness without interruption if I hid her phone...

It's a path a lot of people would've already taken, I know. And yeah, it has merit, but it's also such a shake-up from the status quo, *and* my worst fears are tangled up in that route. What if she cuts me off completely? I mean, fuck, we've been steady best friends for nineteen fucking years, and then I'm just *in love with her?* If she doesn't feel the same, she might not even want to hang out with me anymore.

"Holy shit, did she...?" I question, looking at Finn and wondering if we're about to hear the news of a lifetime from the man himself. Blake Boden and Lexi Winslow, an official couple?

Finn just shakes his head. "I don't know, man, but he looks thrilled."

Blake comes to a stop in front of us, his whole body a picture of relief.

"So...?" I urge, watching and waiting as Boden casually slides his hands into his jeans pockets and rocks back on his heels.

"I obviously asked her to share our love with the world, and she very graciously said no."

"What?" Finn blurts out on a snort while I suck in a huge breath of air at the unexpected honesty. "Get real. You got rejected."

I wheeze, trying to find the strength to go along with Finn to protect Blake's little secret a while longer. Funny thing is, I'm a man of secrets—my own and everyone else's. It's not an easy load to carry, but it's been one of my roles for my entire life. I'm just a vault like that. "Why do you look so happy about that and, please, even more than that, why are you talking like a fucking poet tonight?"

Blake smiles. "Because it's only a matter of time."

I look down, just barely meeting Finn's eyes as he gives me the *get a load of this guy* look. I know it, I respect it, I am it. But it's not my shit to tell. Not this time.

"Mark my words," Blake says confidently. "That girl will be mine."

I imagine this is his way of telling us without telling us. Of plausible deniability when we find out eventually and freak out that he's been keeping such a big secret from us all.

It's a great plan—one I'd utilize myself, to be honest.

"Finn. Help me out here. Bring this man back down to earth." I play my part, just as a dutiful friend is supposed to—just as Blake has been doing for me since the moment I flipped out in the club nearly two months ago and had an epiphany about Julia.

"Dude, I can't judge," Finn chimes in, bending in his way to make Blake feel better. "I spent four weeks in hospital waiting rooms for Scottie."

"That's what I'm saying." Blake wraps his arm around Finn's shoulder, happy with the solidarity. "When you know, you fucking know. Right, Finn?"

Finn looks across the room at Scottie, I look at Julia, and Blake looks at Lexi. Three poor saps, just begging the universe to put them out of their misery.

"When you know, you know," Finn agrees.

Yep. When you know, you motherfluffing know.

Now, I just have to convince Julia to get rid of the guy she's dating, fall in love with me, and somehow maintain the years of trust, comfort, and assurance our friendship has brought to our lives. *Easy, right?*

Mercifully, thanks to Cynthia Patreetus, come the start of the semester, Julia will be seeing me all day, every day, and I'll really be able to kick this dog and pony show into gear.

Speaking of dog, we also have our furbaby son, Yoko. Another important reason that keeps us bonded together like glue.

But when it comes to my best friend and love of my life, I'm not a slacker and I'm not just going to leave anything up to chance. I'm going to keep finding ways and reasons and situations—even if I have to create them—to put me in her vicinity and showcase all the important traits that make me the perfect man for her.

Day and night, my plan to win Julia's heart no longer holds regular office hours. This is twenty-four seven, baby, and the stakes are higher than ever.

24

ello, sophomore year.

I can't believe summer is done and today marks the first official day of my sophomore year at Dickson, but here I am, bright-eyed and bushy-tailed for my first class of the day.

Students filter into the classroom ahead of me, taking seats in the last three rows mostly, and chatting animatedly with their friends. Since this is a nine a.m. class, everyone is a little more awake than the poor souls who didn't know better than to skip first-hour sessions and excited to be back for another year of parties, sports, and maybe, if they have time, a little bit of learning.

Always a bit of an anomaly, I take one of the free seats in the first row and put my backpack in the chair next to me to save it for Drew. He texted before and asked me to save him a seat since he got held up at the coffee cart grabbing us both drinks, and I've never shied away from a showdown for a seat when necessary. Movie theaters, planes, trains—I have no problem saying something is taken.

Maybe it's my best friend Ace's influence, but for some reason, it's one of the only forms of confrontation that doesn't make me the least bit uncomfortable.

I survey the group around me surreptitiously, looking for familiar faces from last year, and a few stand out immediately. The only problem? They don't stand out in a good way. Higgins and Holston Hobbs are notorious class clowns and interruption seekers. I have no idea who they paid off to pass last semester, but I don't remember them passing even a single test in Calc 1. Today, they're wearing matching penguin pajama onesies.

I take out my phone and text Drew quick.

> *Me: Got our seats in the front row secured.*

> *Drew: Awesome, babe. Be there shortly.*

Smiling to myself, I toggle over to my message thread with Scottie to answer the one that came in right before I got into the building.

> *Scottie: If Dr. Nick can't heal me like he says he can, I hope he can at least write a prescription for a lightning-fast motorized chair. Getting around campus in the rush is a PITA.*

> *Me: Now, now, none of that talk. We're staying optimistic, remember? These are Lexi's genes we're talking about. And you said he sounded super confident.*

A little under a week ago, Scottie had her first consult with Lexi Winslow's dad and renowned neurosurgeon, Dr. Nick Raines, about her paralysis from a traumatic cheerleading injury in the spring. All the doctors involved in treating her before said the chance of getting any use of her legs back was extremely limited, but Lexi's dad isn't convinced. He's been working on new research in Germany, and he thinks there's a chance for surgery and rehabilitation. After everything Scottie's been through—her family trauma is so unimaginably heavy—I want it for her more than I've ever wanted anything for myself.

She's an amazing person. She deserves every opportunity in life and to actually catch a break for once.

> *Scottie: He did. But I guess I just…don't wanna get my hopes up too high, you know?*

Me: I get that. But I'll hope for the both of us, okay?

Scottie: Thanks, Jules. ☺

Me: Are you kidding? You're my girl.

Just as I'm finishing typing, there's some movement next to me, a hand moving my backpack out of the way out of the corner of my eye.

I smile and tuck my phone away, my head jerking as my gaze makes a bumpy landing on a face I'm not expecting *at all*. It's not Drew. It's Ace.

Which does not compute.

"Ace? What the hell are you doing here?"

He waggles his eyebrows and lifts his backpack into his lap, undoing the zipper slowly. "Getting ready to get my learn on. What do you mean?"

I swear, my eyebrows might as well be singular, they're so close together. "You're in this class?"

Ace shrugs, taking out a pen, notebook, a pair of tweezers, a turkey baster, an…*is that an unopened slip 'n slide?*…and his laptop in answer. I have questions, lots of them, about the contents of his bag, but compared to the giant pink elephant of his presence, they're inconsequential right now.

"But…how? I don't understand." This is Calc 2, which means you need to have taken Calc 1 to be in it. Unless he managed to fit in summer classes I didn't know about, Ace has *not* taken Calc 1.

"You've rubbed off on me, I guess, Jules." He grins at me and flips his baseball cap around so he's wearing it backward. I swear, I hear three girls behind us sigh dreamily when he does it. "I know I've been pretty lax about it in the past, but I'm going to start taking my schoolwork more seriously. Shooting for good grades, taking the hard stuff. You know a student's effort in college is a good sign of how much they succeed in life?"

"It is?" I question, but I don't even really know what I'm saying.

His ramble and unexpected presence are making my brain feel like scrambled eggs.

"No." He chuckles softly. "Well, I mean, at least I haven't heard anyone other than me say that. But it makes sense, doesn't it? Life is ninety percent effort, ten percent ability."

"I don't know that that's—"

"Good morning," the professor announces from the front of the room, effectively cutting off our discussion with a finger to the lips and a pat on my knee from Ace. He turns to the front, his pen at the ready, the random smattering of items tucked back into his backpack and notebook opened.

I turn to look for Drew as someone else takes the seat on my other side, effectively leaving him without a spot. I don't say anything, my shock over the whole last two minutes robbing me of my normal vocal abilities.

Drew comes in just as I'm about to turn back to the front, confusion spreading across his handsome face. I wince, mouthing an apology across the space as he's forced to find a seat in the second row on the far side of the room.

I sit quietly for a little while as Professor Emmsy introduces himself and the class basics, but as the intricacies of Ace's presence hit me, I have to delve deeper. I quiet my voice to a whisper and start to talk, but Ace shakes his head, his eyebrows forming a sharp wrinkle with their severe pull.

He points to the professor again and cups a hand around his ear, mouthing, "I'm trying to listen."

Frustrated, I reach over and rip a piece of paper from his notebook and steal his pen, scribbling my thoughts down quickly and handing it back to him.

> **How are you in this class??? This is Calc 2, Ace. You haven't taken Calc 1.**

He scribbles back and shoves it toward me, shaking his head seriously this time and pointing toward the board where the professor has started to outline the course's expectations and syllabus.

I worked it out with my peer counselor. I'm getting dual credit for Calc 1 at the same time

My chin jerks back. "You're in both classes?"

He points to the paper with a stern pen, and I sigh heavily before complying.

You're in both classes?

No. Private tutor for Calc 1.

Ohhhh. Who's the tutor?

Suddenly fine with direct communication, he turns to me and waggles his eyebrows.

"What?" I ask, confused. He goes back to the paper, jotting quickly.

You. You're the tutor.

"I'm sorry, what?" My voice is much louder than intended, and several sets of eyes jerk in my direction, including Drew's. Seemingly for the first time, he recognizes the guy beside me as Ace, and his consternation grows.

But Ace just goes back to writing on the paper before sliding it back my way.

Relax. You don't have to actually tutor me. At least not really. You just have to help me through this and teach me what I need to know and then sign off that you tutored me. If I pass this my peer counselor said they'll go ahead and credit calc 1

I blink hard as my vision blurs for a moment. *I'm supposed to be his tutor?* Like, what the hell is going on? I scribble down a response.

I don't know how the hell you pull these things off. That's insane. No college would EVER go for that.

He just grins at me again before jotting something down.

Until now. It would seem they're actively going for it

I blow out a breath.

I truly can't believe you and how you manage these things. You don't even know how to use commas.

It's a genetic gift Jules. I can't explain it any other way. As for the commas you can teach me that too.

I grab his paper and add them where they're needed in that very statement, circling for dramatic effect.

Which only makes Ace's nearly permanent grin grow more.

See? You're already teaching me things. This is going to work out great.

He turns to face the front again, and I do my best to shift my focus to my new teacher and the board as well. Evidently, I'm in charge of two people's college fates now, whether I like it or not.

The teacher continues his first day spiel, assigning us a practice sheet and several pages in the textbook to read before next class so we're not going into the lesson blind, and I jot the information down in my planner on autopilot.

For Ace's part, he takes active notes—not that I can make any sense of them—and focuses hard on Professor Emmsy's every word, but by the time he dismisses class fifty minutes later—declaring his congratulations that the seats we've picked today will be our official seats for the rest of the semester—I feel like my skin is crawling.

I'm confused. I'm a little angry. And I don't understand what the hell is happening at all.

Ace hands me my pen when I accidentally knock it on the floor and packs up his own belongings, and then he stands in expectation, waiting to walk me out of class. Drew packs up his own stuff, too, and heads toward us, and truth be told, I feel a little like I might explode.

I take a deep breath, willing myself to maintain some semblance of decorum since our professor still lingers at the front of the room, but I can't deny that my voice is cutting as I ask, "Why didn't you check with me before signing me up to be your tutor, Ace?"

He jerks back at the tone, and I suck my lips into my mouth before adding, "I just…I already have a full schedule on my plate, and now I'm going to be helping you with this class too."

"I know," he apologizes softly. "And I should have asked. But I'm going to pull my weight, I swear. I'm going to pull my weight in all our classes."

"What do you mean, *all our classes?*"

"Ace," Drew greets, finally making it over to us against the stream of students leaving the room. "Surprised to see you here."

"Oh hey, man." Ace smiles at him, clapping a hand on his back. "Yeah, I'm changing it up this year. Focusing harder, you know?"

"Mm-hmm," Drew hums, handing me my coffee and wincing as he checks his watch. "I'm sorry I have to run, but I've got physics to get to. It starts in five minutes, and I have to make it all the way over to Vincent Hall. Everyone says Grudeau is a hard-ass about being on time."

Both Drew and I are taking physics this semester, but we didn't end up in the same class.

"Of course. I'll text you later."

"Yeah," Drew agrees. "Maybe I can come by tonight." My cheeks feel hot. I'm annoyed at Ace; I'm feeling a strange jealousy vibe coming from Drew. It's all too much.

I nod. It's all I can manage.

We're not officially a couple, but I do like spending time with him. But I've explained the situation with Ace before, and he needs to trust me too.

I don't know. I'm just…caught off guard. And overwhelmed.

Drew leans down and kisses my cheek before taking off for the back of the classroom on fast feet, glancing over his shoulder at Ace and me when he gets to the door. I sigh, slinging my bag up on my shoulder and willing myself to get over this in less than fifteen minutes. I mean, I'm going to get over it anyway; I may as well get over it now before it stresses me out. *Right?*

"Do you not have class this hour?" I ask Ace as he puts on his own backpack, letting me go up the aisle first and following behind me. He's quiet for much longer than he's ever quiet, so I stop dead in my tracks and turn to face him, his earlier words of *all our classes* hitting me again like a Mack truck.

"Ace, what's your next class?"

He smiles sheepishly. "Psychology 201."

"Ace! Are you in…are you in *all* my classes?" I ask, outrage making the pitch of my voice much, much higher than normal.

He winces. "I'm guessing from the way you said that, that's a bad thing?"

"Ace!"

"Yes. I…yes. I'm in all your classes. But you're my best friend, Lia. And I want to get better at being a student, and you're the best student I know. It felt like the best place to start—the best of both worlds, you know? Are you mad?"

"Yes!" I snap.

"I'm sorry!" he apologizes, reaching out for my hand that I jerk back.

"Really. I didn't think it'd be a big deal, but I can see now I should have considered the extra strain on you. But I promise I won't make you babysit me. Swear. I'm gonna handle this shit on my own for the most part."

I sigh. His face is so earnest, so Ace. It's *hard* to stay mad at him. I don't know if my brain chemicals are just used to getting over it quickly after this many years of our rule or what, but it is what it is.

I love him, for better or worse. He's my bestie.

With one more deep heave of air, I reach out for his shoulders and pull him into a hug. He returns the gesture, wrapping his arms around my back and tucking his face into my neck. I soak in the comfort of him for a long second before pulling back.

"I just have one question."

"Yeah?"

"The tweezers, I can get. The slip 'n slide, even. But why in the fresh hell do you have a turkey baster in your backpack?"

"It's all for later. Me and some other sophomores decided on an innocent little slip 'n slide event by the new fountain on the pedestrian court to welcome some of the more interesting freshman. I was obviously going to tell you about it. I just didn't get a chance. The turkey baster was the best way I could think to surreptitiously steal some water from the fountain to wet the slide."

"The group of *more interesting freshman* you're referring to wouldn't happen to include Finn's twin brothers, would it?"

He smirks. "I don't know. Trav and Jack *are* pretty interesting."

"What am I gonna do with you, Ace?" I ask, mystified. "Finn's liable to cut your throat if you get them in trouble."

He smiles and slings an arm around my shoulders. "Aw, that's so sweet of you to worry about me, but Finn loves me too much to really hurt me. At least, not without ample warning time so I can run to Central America first. Now, come on. Walk with me to our next class, bestie."

Ace in all my classes.

Ace involving Finn's brothers in pranks before they've had a single grade submitted.

Ace with a turkey baster in his backpack.

It's literally the first day of class, and Ace is already turning Dickson University upside down.

God help me. God help us all.

25

My Great Big Plan to win Julia's love is still in motion and still going great. My only complaint is that I really thought it'd go quicker.

Living across the hall and having access to her in all her classes has proven unbelievably useful in lessening her time with Drewbacca and increasing her time with me, and after a week and a half of working my ass off to prove I'll be more than dead weight to drag around on her schedule, Julia has warmed up to studying together too.

Things are moving along—but my heart is not what you'd call *patient*. I want the endgame now. I want forehead kisses and real fucking kisses and cutesy fucking nicknames and hand-holding and eating spaghetti noodles like we're Lady and the Tramp and being the person she thinks about when she sees a cute baby.

So… I've hatched a new idea. A genius-level acceleration tactic that came to me, oh, *twenty-seven minutes ago.*

See, being across the hall is fine, but being across the pillow? That's where the real progress happens. And in order to *stay* in her apartment, something has to go *horribly* wrong with mine.

Cut to: fire. Real fire. In a real trash can. Currently real-burning in my real apartment.

Fire licks in the trash can, burning the papers I torched just moments ago, and black smoke starts to billow from it and fill my living room. *Shit.* Fire is, like, intense. I mean, I've been around fire before since Gunnar is my brother, but I've never been the one in charge of the actual fire and this thing is feeling very… impulsive.

When the flames start to threaten to move their way out of the trash can and toward the carpet, I bolt across the hall to Julia's door, knocking frantically. She moves around inside, but every second feels like a lifetime as the fire I set in my apartment burns unattended.

I run back to my door and peek inside, but it's still contained for now, sizzling in the can.

Knocking again, I add a yell. "Julia! Come quick!"

I hear a groan and a grumble, followed by quick footsteps and paw steps as both she and Yoko jog toward the door. When she pulls it open, there's a wax strip on her leg and a tongue depressor in her hand and Yoko is bouncing around excitedly on all four legs.

"What? What is it that's so urgent?" she questions. "As you can see, I'm in the middle of something."

"I need your fire extinguisher," I say quickly, gently moving her out of the way and running for the cabinet under the kitchen sink. Yoko takes my hurried movements as excitement, following along with me and nipping at my ankles because I'm giving off playtime vibes. But all I can do is shoo him away as the expediency of the whole fire issue in my apartment is getting realer now.

You know, the real fucking fire that I set and that I'm now thinking might not have been the best idea.

"What? Where's yours?" she asks, running after me now, Yoko bouncing between the two of us as I head back across the hall, apparatus in hand. "What's on fire?"

"I checked that you had yours but didn't check that I had mine!" I explain quickly, knocking my pulled door open with a knee and running inside. My eyes bulge when I catch sight of the flames, and Julia outright screams her head off.

"Holy shit, Ace! There's a fire!"

Oh, trust me. I fucking know.

The fire has spread out of the trash can now and burns unchecked on both my rug and my curtains, climbing the wall toward the ceiling. If I don't get this thing out quick, it's going to be a hell of a lot more than a prank to move in with Lia—it's going to be a prison sentence for arson.

"Grab Yoko!" I instruct as I pull the pin on the extinguisher and spray wildly.

"The curtains!" Julia shouts the fire's progress from behind me, cuddling a now-barking Yoko to her chest. "Oh no! The rug now! Back on the curtains! Oh my God, your poster of Chris Evans!"

I foam and foam, coating the shit out of my entire living room until all that's left is the sound of sizzling, extinguished heat and sloughing fire retardant.

My heart races and sweat falls off every inch of my face as I drop to my knees and take in the damage. The entire back half of my living room is cooked.

Julia, still holding Yoko with one arm, wraps her other arm around my shoulders and squeezes, trying to reassure me. "It's okay. It's okay, Ace. You got it out." A startled laugh bubbles up, but she cuts it off before it can even finish rolling out. "I'm… sorry. I'll never doubt your urgency again."

"I…" I take a breath. I mean, the plan to have a reason for moving in with Julia is going strong. The damage, though? A touch more extensive. "Fuck, this isn't good."

"How in the hell did this happen?" she asks, her eyes still wide as she scans the charred living room.

It happened because I'm so in love with you that it's turned me into a moron, Julia.

"I think it's safe to say I spent too much on fire safety in your apartment and kind of forgot to do the same in mine," I mutter by way of an excuse. "Julia?"

"Yeah?"

"Can I…stay with you for a bit? I'm pretty sure they're going to need to do some repairs."

"Of course," she agrees easily. "Of course." Her voice drops to a whisper. "But what are you gonna say to your dad?"

A good question I didn't consider, and a reason nineteen-year-olds shouldn't be allowed to fall in love.

———

"Fire?" my dad barks out in question, his dark eyebrows melding with his hairline in a comedy sketch of expression via Zoom. Julia's out getting dinner takeout, and I'm mentally recovering by calling my dad from her bed. I guess I should just be thankful my mom is out to dinner with the girls, or I'd be getting the fat end of the stick from both of them at the same time. "You set an actual fire?"

"Yeah!" I snap, horrified and unentertained by this whole trip down memory lane.

"Did the fire department come?"

"Who the hell else puts out fires?" I ask with a groan. "Of course they came. I did have it out with a fire extinguisher, but it reignited, and I didn't have a choice."

"Oh, oh Jesus," Thatcher chokes out, his whole body rolling into a laugh that sends him careening off the couch and onto the rug. "Fire! You set fire to the fucking place!" his voice taunts from the floor, his entire being out of camera shot.

"It's not that funny," I complain on a grumble. "It's embarrassing, and it's whatever. We can move on now. Well, after you read me the riot act and decide what my punishment will be, I guess."

"Well, sure, we can move on, but that poor rug will never move on! It's dead. Burned. Will never live to see another day!" He's still on the floor, just straight up cackling through his words.

"You're not that funny, you know," I mutter. "You're not

doing stand-up on a fifty-city tour. You can tone it down a little bit and just be supportive."

"Oh, son, this is support. Support and laughter go hand in hand," he says and eventually finds his way back to his spot on the couch and in front of the camera. "You don't think I've been laughed at? That the things I did while I was trying to land your mother aren't worthy of their own set list? They are, buddy. Every motherfucker I know who's married has one too. Because we men are idiots when we fall hard. Can't seem to see straight, but I can't blame us. It's awful hard to have perfect sight when your head is that far up your own ass."

I sigh. "I just…normally have more game than this. I don't know what my deal is."

"That there is a true sign that you are, indeed, in love."

"Some good it's doing me. I'm not getting anywhere, and you're starting world wars with her father."

"Relax. Kline and I will be fine. You think we haven't had some spats over the years? We've been friends for a long time, and we're gonna continue to be friends until we're dead. The bastard might still be annoyed with me, but the lines of communication are there. We're texting. Phone chatting. You know, the normal shit but with him saying *shut up* and *fuck you* most of the time. You just keep up your end of the work with Julia. Though, I suggest you stop starting fires."

"I wanted to have to stay at her place." I admit the true intent behind the fire. "So… I thought a fire would help bring that desire to fruition."

"Ha!" he barks. "A classic move. But next time, son, may I suggest a pest control issue? Or landlord-ordered maintenance. A fake gas leak. There's a lot to work with here that doesn't require the same level of theatrics."

I let out a deep exhale. "Yeah, I guess—" The sound of the door opening cuts me off in mid-sentence. "She's back. I gotta go,"

I whisper. He gives the thumbs-up, but I end the call, way better for the wear than intended.

I thought he'd fucking kill me. And really, he should have. But love is Thatcher Kelly's weakness. He can't fight it. Can't deny it. Can't belittle it.

If I'd set fire to my apartment for any other reason, he'd have me by the throat. But love? It's the ultimate excuser of all behaviors in his eyes.

I sure hope when Julia finds out, she'll feel the same.

Julia

> **Drew: I need to see you again. Maybe we can make a date happen soon?**

"Julia! You have to see this! Come here!" Ace calls from the bedroom of my apartment, having officially moved in with me for the time being while the fire cleanup in his place is underway. I still can't believe he almost torched his entire place—this entire building—trying to get rid of a bug.

"One second!" I yell back, fingers poised on my phone to type a text back to Drew. I haven't exactly detailed the fact that Ace is staying with me to him, and I'm not quite sure I'm going to. There's not really a good way to explain to a guy you like that another guy is sleeping in your bed every night, even if he is your best friend with whom you've done it hundreds of times. Especially, given the history of how Drew feels about Ace's intentions. Ever since Ace joined all my classes, an extra layer of tension has spread between the three of us.

I also haven't had as much time to hang out with classes taking up my time too, and I know Drew's starting to wonder if I'm even interested anymore.

> **I don't know if tonight will work…or the next couple days… but maybe next week?**

I wince, deleting the text entirely. That sounds rude and like

I'm trying to brush him off in the worst way, and I'm not. I'm enjoying the time I've been spending with Drew a lot. I just…think the bed might be a little tight with three of us.

Not that I'm even close to sleeping with Drew. I'm not. We've barely even kissed for real, and physically, I just don't know if I'm completely ready to go all the way with someone. I know I'm technically an adult at eighteen—almost nineteen—but sometimes I still feel so young.

I blow out a breath and refocus, trying to think of a better message.

> **Me: I know. I miss seeing you too! It's just been so busy getting back into the swing of classes. Maybe next weekend?**

"Julia!" Ace yells again, and under the gun, I push send without overthinking it this time. I toss my phone to the surface of my kitchen island and power walk toward my bedroom, a tiny bit of apprehension about him accidentally setting my place on fire too making me move faster.

The door is pulled but not shut, so I shove through it and toward the bathroom and my walk-in closet, where the light shines out across my perfect comforter Ace made sure I got.

"Where are you?" I ask, choosing between the door to the bathroom and the closet with both interest and hesitancy when his voice calls out from the bathroom.

"In here!"

"You'd better not be pooping," I mutter under my breath as I push the door open and step inside. Thankfully, he's not by the toilet at all, but he is a familiar shade of greenish-brown, all the way down to the hair of his eyebrows, a low-slung pair of basketball shorts tucked into his underwear at the tops of his thighs.

I gasp, and he smiles even bigger.

"Oh my God, Ace. What are you doing?"

"I found your self-tanner!" he exclaims proudly, spinning around so I can get all the angles. "And I know using it without asking was a boundary crossed, but I've already found it online and ordered you two more bottles even though I didn't even use half of this one."

"Why is it in your eyebrows?"

Said eyebrows pull together. "Do you not do that?"

"I don't even put it on my face!" I shriek with a laugh. "How long have you had it on?"

"I don't know," he mutters. "Thirty minutes?"

"Oh my God! That's express tan!" I yell. "The max is an hour. We have to get it off your face now!"

My Apple Watch pings with a notification of a text message from Drew, but I clear it without reading it and lunge for the shower to get the water running. I grab a washcloth from under my sink and my face exfoliator, and I put them on the counter while Ace spins in a circle, clueless over what to do.

"In the shower, you're going to rinse off all the tanner thoroughly. Then, I want you to use this on your face and scrub it. Just trust me, you're going to wish it were Halloween if you don't."

"What if I need help?" he asks, waggling his brows at me, and I shake my head.

"No. You've got to strip down, and I'm drawing a line. Now get in there and hose down, quick."

"Yes, ma'am," he agrees, hooking his fingers into the sides of his shorts and starting to shove them down.

"And, Ace," I call from the door, pausing his motion just before I see all his goods.

"Yes?"

"You'd better scrub my shower to within an inch of your life when you're done with your body, do you hear me? If I come in here and find self-tanner staining even a speck of tile, I'm putting you out on the street."

He shoots a freaking finger gun at me. "I got you, girl."

I head out of the bathroom, through the bedroom and back toward the kitchen to grab my phone, but before I'm even through the living room, Ace is calling my name again. I sigh, turn around, and head back to help him through the door. My best friend is doing what my best friend does—adding the spice to life with self-tanner.

He's so unpredictable it makes me smile.

Drew's message can wait a little while longer.

———

"I'm sorry," Ace apologizes again from his side of the pillow wall I put between us before we tucked in to go to sleep tonight. The bedroom's been quiet for thirty minutes, and I thought he'd fallen asleep, but I guess I'm wide awake too, so I can't throw stones.

"For what?" I ask.

"For the tanner. And the kitchen towel I stained. And…for the best-friend kiss at the lake. I assume that's why you have the pillow fort between us tonight."

I sigh. "It's fine, Ace. All of it is fine. And the pillow fort is just because… Well, because I know we've done it before, but don't you think it's a little weird of us to sleep and cuddle? We're not dating, we're friends."

He rolls over to face me, smashing down the pillow between us to get a better view of me, so I roll over too. His eyes shine with innocence in the moonlight. "I don't think anything we do is weird, Lia. I just think it's us. Is Drew giving you crap about it?"

I shake my head. "He…doesn't know you're staying here."

"He doesn't? Why not?"

"I don't know. Because we're not officially a couple, so I don't really owe it to him to tell him, and I don't know… He's jealous. Thinks you like me, like me."

"And so what if I do?"

"Ace," I whisper.

"No," he says, grabbing the pillow and tossing it on the floor behind himself to clear the space between us. "I mean it. What's he care if I like you or not? Shouldn't he just be focused on his own shit? Treating you right, showing up when you need him, making himself memorable. He doesn't need to be worrying about me if he's not worrying about himself, right?"

"Oh, come on," I reason. "You can't tell me if all your little girlfriends knew we were in bed together right now, they wouldn't be jealous."

"I don't have any little girlfriends."

I roll my eyes. "You know what I mean. Your fan club."

He shrugs. "Conveniently for me, I don't give a fuck what anyone thinks."

"Yeah," I agree with a laugh. "You usually don't."

"What's that mean?"

"I just mean…you're not serious about dating and relationships like I am. And that's okay, it's you. But it means you're not going to understand where I'm coming from."

"I can be serious, Julia."

I shake my head, the overwhelming urge to tell him to prove it to me clamming me up tighter than a vise. "Let's just drop it, okay? I'm tired."

I roll over and face the window again, tucking my hands under my cheek and willing myself to be realistic. This is Ace. My best friend. My best bud. My comfort.

Five long seconds pass in silence before he wraps an arm around me from behind and pulls me tight into his front, and I let out a million pounds of air I didn't even know I was holding in.

It's peace. It's familiarity and friendship and, maybe, I don't know, a little more than that. I relax.

Within a minute, I'm asleep, Drew, once again, forgotten.

27

The quiet of my newly cleaned and restored apartment is depressing in the worst way as I open the refrigerator door for the tenth time, looking for food to fill my stomach with something other than feelings.

I miss Julia. I miss the strides I was making. I miss bedtime cuddles, and it hasn't even been two hours since I was still staying with her.

With questionable judgment, I pick up my phone off the counter and walk over to the couch, dialing my mom on FaceTime. Going to her for help is susceptible to all kinds of results, based on her mood and time of the month and how much my dad has been in her business that day, but I'm just desperate enough.

After making so much freaking progress with Julia in the last three days, I feel like it's worth the risk.

It rings three times before my mom picks up, and when she does, my dad's face is there too, his chin resting on her shoulder. It's a jump scare if I've ever seen one.

"Jesus. So I guess you guys are together."

My mom laughs. "It's Sunday. I can't keep him off me. But don't worry, he goes back to the office to be the provider I expect him to be tomorrow. Do you want to call back then?"

My dad frowns, offended, of course.

"No, that's okay. We can talk now. It's not like both of you don't know the Julia situation anyway."

"You're in loveeee, son," my dad corrects. "Don't be afraid to say it. Fear is the biggest cockblock I've ever met."

I sigh. "Fine. I'm in love. I'm not afraid to say it." I shrug and laugh a little. "Maybe to her, but not to the two of you."

"Well, that's step one, son. And if you inherited even half my ball size, you'll take it all the way soon."

"Wow, Mom, so glad I called you," I remark sarcastically, which makes my dad roll his eyes and pretend to zip his lips.

My mom laughs uproariously and shoots him the finger before focusing on me. "So, what do you need from me, Acer? Some fake STD results for the Chad kid? A couple hundred grand? What is it?"

"Jeez, Mom, no. This isn't the Brazilian black market or some shit. I just need advice. I really feel like I was getting somewhere with her while I was staying there. I was getting the one-on-one time, the connection. It was boxing out whatshisface almost completely all on its own."

"And you don't want the advice to be to just tell her that you're in love with her?"

"No." I groan. "Pretty sure I've established that Julia isn't ready for that kind of knowledge yet."

"Well then, it sounds to me like you need to move back in. I can cut off your money if you want. Make a big scene about evicting you?"

"She'll never buy that," I argue. On a whim, I navigate off the FaceTime screen and onto my texts, and shoot one to Julia quick, asking her to come over when she gets a chance. If I'm not off the phone, I'm sure my parents will come up with something to throw out on the fly.

"All right. I can get you robbed pretty quickly," she offers. "I know a couple F-list actors I had during a photo shoot last week who are absolutely desperate for work. Wouldn't even cost us very much money."

Good grief, this advice is getting darker by the second. And I'm not convinced it wouldn't land me in jail.

"Never mind. Forget I called." There's a knock on the door and Julia's voice on the other side, so I try to beg off. "I gotta go. That's her at the door."

"No!" my dad protests. He even pretends to unzip his mouth and then zip it closed again for dramatic effect, opening it once more to add, "I have an idea."

"Fine," I grumble, taking them with me as I jump up and run to the door. As I pull it open, I steel my nerves, willing my ever-present gift for bullshit to rise to the surface like cream on coffee.

"Hey," I say as casually as I can manage, holding the phone out to the side so Julia can see the screen when my parents start screaming their hellos.

"*Juliaaaa!*"

"*Hi, hi, hi!*"

"Hi, Mr. and Mrs. Kelly," she greets with a wave before bugging her eyes out at me and whispering. "You said to come over when I could. What's up?"

I open my mouth to answer, but my dad gets there first, yelling out, "Bugs, Julia! He's got bugs!"

"Bugs?" she asks, and immediately, her eyes go wide as she scans my living room, her body tight with fear that said bugs are going to start crawling up her legs.

"Uh, yeah," I ad-lib. "Remember the bug I was trying to kill with the fire? Well, turns out he's not alone. There's a whole family of bugs."

"A whole family of bugs?" Julia screeches and jumps back two steps before immediately reversing the action to get as close to me as humanly possible as her gaze darts around my apartment.

Okay, so maybe this bug plan isn't such a bad plan…

"Yep. Practically seventeen generations worth of bugs," I answer, really laying the fake bug thing on thick now. Hell, maybe she'll jump into my arms next. "They found them in the freaking walls, Julia, while they were doing cleanup from the fire. Now I need to have the place fumigated. Which is no bueno for the lungs, so they say I need to stay somewhere else again."

"You're kidding!" she exclaims, but she's still huddled close to me. "How long?"

"Three days," I lie, going with the first number I can think of on the fly.

"Jeez, Ace."

"I know, I know. I just moved out. You just got your space back. I understand completely if you'd rather me go to a hotel or try to stay with Finn and Scottie or something. I can be a lot."

"No, no. I mean, of course you should stay with me. You know I love being around you. You're my best friend." She shakes her head as if trying to clear it, and selfishly, I'm really hoping she's shaking whatshisface all the way out. "And how about we go ahead and head on over to my apartment, like, now?" A shiver rolls up her spine. "I'd prefer not to come face-to-face with the bugs."

"Yeah," my dad chimes in. "I wouldn't hang around in there too long. The exterminator said these bugs like to cling to shit and go from apartment to apartment."

"Oh my God." Julia cringes and grabs a hold of my shirt with a tight grasp. "Let's go, Ace. Let's freaking go."

"I'll talk to you guys later," I say, glancing down at the screen of my phone where both my mom and dad are flashing me secret smiles.

"Bye, Julia!" my dad yells, my mom adding, "We love youuu!"

"Love you guys too!" she says as she practically drags me out of my apartment and into hers.

Three more days, and the next level of the plan officially unlocked.

Maybe, just maybe, I'll manage to convince her to be with me before we're actually twenty-five.

ce digs through the cooler in the kitchen of the Tau Kappa Epsilon house, which is an absolute freaking mess, despite the new brothers having only moved in at the start of school. This is something like their eighth party in just under three weeks, and evidently, they don't have the number for a cleaning crew on speed dial.

I wait patiently until Ace hands me a sealed bottle of Mike's Hard Lemonade, twisting off the cap before he does. I smile gratefully and turn it up to my lips, excited by the tolerable taste. I know some people are seasoned drinkers by the time they're my age, but I'm still getting my boozy legs under me.

Ace takes a bottle of beer for himself and nods to Finn, nudging me forward to follow his roommate from last year as he exits the kitchen.

I weave through the crowd of rowdy partygoers, reaching up to hold my ear as we pass one of the giant speakers they have set up in the back sun-room area of the dining room and looking back over my shoulder to make sure Ace is with me. He puts his hand to my back in reassurance, and I smile as I force my way through the last little clump of people to get to Lexi, Scottie, and Finn.

Today was Lexi's official graduation from grad school. She's now the proud owner of two PhDs and will most likely be winning Nobel Prizes, curing cancer, and creating the world's most valuable AI technology in the next year or two.

There's smart, and then there's Lexi smart. Trust me, they're different.

I've known Lexi Winslow my whole life, and right now, she looks a little like a fish out of water. That shouldn't be a surprise, given Ace practically forced her here on the excuse that this will be the last college party she'll ever attend, but for as rowdy as these Tau guys get and as dirty as this place is, she's hanging in pretty well.

"Holy shit!" Ace exclaims from behind me, barreling forward to wrap an enthusiastic arm around Finn's shoulders and rock him back and forth. "Is Finnley Hayes enjoying an alcoholic beverage tonight?" Finn is holding a red Solo cup, which is out of character for him, given his family's abusive history with alcohol. I'd never judge him for drinking or choosing not to—and Ace wouldn't either. He just sometimes forgets his damn manners.

Finn rolls his eyes. "It's Mountain Dew."

"Fuck me." Ace groans. "And I thought you weren't going to be lame for once."

"Stop being a dick, Acer," I chastise, shoving Ace in the chest. He's extra hyper tonight, and while I know good and well he's not an asshole, he has a tendency to get overly excited and sound like one. "You're like one of those bullies on an after-school special, trying to get everyone to drink his parents' booze."

Ace cracks up. "Damn, Jules. Don't hold back."

I smile, saccharine and sugar all at once, and he moves to me, wrapping me under his arm tightly and tucking me into his armpit. I roll my eyes but melt into him, looking up at the jubilation shining from his handsome brown eyes.

He only moved out of my apartment yesterday afternoon after the extermination fogging took two days longer than expected, and as much as it pains me to admit, I miss having him in my space and bed all the time. He looks down at me like he might feel the same, and an unexpected flock of butterflies skims the inside of my stomach with frantic wings. Kayla sidles up to the group and says her hellos, and Ace seizes my teasing as an opportunity to take a trip down memory lane.

"Remember when we got drunk on your dad's scotch our sophomore year of high school?"

I laugh. "Remember? I still hear about it to this day! We filled his Oban single malt with water, for Pete's sake. We didn't even put food coloring or anything. A couple of idiots. He found it, like, the next night and reamed us into next week."

"Is your dad scary?" Kayla asks, and I shake my head.

"No. My dad is like the nicest guy on the planet. But we both felt bad about making him feel bad, and ultimately Ace's dad ended up punishing us for making his best friend weepy."

"Weepy?" Kayla cracks up.

"Yeah, that's all my dad," Ace interjects. "Leave it to him to call a man like Kline Brooks weepy. He wasn't, by the way. He was the scariest I'd ever seen him when he talked about me needing to do a better job of protecting Julia and that I should have taken the fall completely. He's a real man of respect, you know? Car doors, sidewalks, trouble—he thinks the guy should always take the fall. And truthfully, I agree with him. I can't believe I didn't then, but I was a dumbass high schooler. It was a good, very important lesson to learn."

"What, now you'd take the fall for me any day?" I ask, my voice undeniably cocky.

"In a fucking heartbeat," Ace responds without hesitation. "Yes, Officer, I am the murderer, and yes, I do wear red lipstick."

I laugh, smiling up at him, and take my purse off my shoulder to slide it on his. "Cute purse, sir."

He poses boisterously. "Thanks. I have impeccable style."

Finn rolls his eyes when Scottie looks up at him to smile, but when I glance over at Lexi to make sure she's doing okay, I find her staring across the room, her expression mildly horrified.

I follow her line of sight and find Blake dancing with some

sorority girl, and just behind him, a group of frat brothers pull their pants down to do questionable things in the open bowl of punch.

I don't know which one is scaring her, but both choices are valid, given the secrets Ace and I know.

I elbow him in the stomach, jerking my chin at Blake and the girl on the other side of the room, and he frowns before glancing back at Lexi. I know Blake's been an absolute wreck for a couple of weeks now, and judging by the depressing nature of their avoidance, I have to assume it's because something happened between them. Like a breakup of their secret relationship or something.

I don't like seeing either of them this upset, and in some ways, it's a cautionary tale against getting close with someone who's already a huge part of your life. Seeing the person who got away on repeat for the next one million years sounds like the worst kind of torture.

"Hey, Ace, I'm gonna go," Lexi cuts in suddenly, giving a half-hearted wave to the rest of the group. She shares a look with him I don't understand, and he nods as though there's an actual answer to their silent communication.

I don't understand it.

"What's that about?" I ask, turning under his arm and lowering my voice enough to keep the conversation between the two of us.

He leans down, speaking directly against the shell of my ear. "I'm guessing she's upset seeing Boden exercising his popularity with the ladies."

"No, I know that. I meant the look between the two of you."

His eyes glaze for a brief second, and then he smiles, kissing the side of my head. "It's nothing."

I don't feel like he's telling me the whole story, but I have no option other than to accept it. Though, it's probably just the loud, party environment.

He'll tell me when he can. I'm sure of it.

Because Ace has never kept anything from me before, and he knows it's important enough to me that he never will.

29

"**L**adies and gentlemen, please stand up from your seats!" the announcer exclaims, the energy in the stadium building into a roar. "And get ready to welcome this year's Dickson Dragons to the field!"

We all stomp and scream and hold up the middle finger when Georgia's fans start booing, and I wrap an arm around Julia to shake her from side to side. She laughs and smiles, though the sound is muted in the noise of the crowd as people start to chant, "*BBE! BBE!*"

It's the best of wordplay on BDE—*Big Dick Energy*—and halfway through last year, I masterminded reworking the phrase to include Blake Boden's initials.

One by one, the Dickson Dragons players make their way out of the tunnel, escorted by cheerleaders like they're doing a fucking wedding march. It's tradition for the first game of the year, and for as amazing as the high of today is, it's also fucking bittersweet. Scottie sits in a wheelchair spot at the end of the row next to Finn, thankfully watching with a giant smile on her face.

She's so strong—stronger than the rest of us, that's for damn sure. I'm really proud to call her a friend and impressed beyond belief that my buddy Finn was smart enough to turn his life upside down for her last year.

If life weren't so cruel, she'd be down there with Kayla and the rest of the cheerleaders.

I grab the fabric of my navy-and-gold T-shirt and billow it in and out to get some air moving around me. I'm hot and sweaty, and with everyone standing, waiting for the captain of the Dickson cheerleaders, McKenzie, and the quarterback of the Dragons, my good buddy Blake Boden, to finish the line of players and take the field together, the air feels stagnant.

I need game action. I need movement. I need something.

It's been a little more than a full week since Lexi sent me a cryptic message about her retirement from all things Dickson and the need to fill a *very important role* with someone capable of handling the pressure. I agreed to the terms of complete secrecy—I can't know the details of literally anything and am in no way allowed to ask questions or tell anyone else Lexi even exists, let alone is texting me cryptic messages—and so far, I have been doing nothing but waiting with a metaphorical sock in my mouth.

Between that and my never-ending quest for Julia's love, it seems like everything in my life is hovering above me in midair.

Julia reaches over and pats me on the stomach before turning back to the crowd, and instantly, I don't feel so claustrophobic anymore. With Drew nowhere in sight and my girl smiling beside me, maybe my secret plan to make her love me, as unorganized as it's been, is finally pulling into its destination—success.

Julia stops by my apartment every chance she gets, and when I return the favor, I'm always greeted by a smile. We spend our evenings together and our mornings together, and two times, I've caught her staring at my lips.

If we hadn't been interrupted by our furbaby son Yoko, I would have taken the opportunity to kiss her both times. As it is, I'm dangerously considering taking the opportunity right now…

Focusing on her mouth, I turn my body gently toward her in the raging crowd, positioning my back hand at her hip and pulling her just a little closer.

Fuck, she's so beautiful and her mouth is so perfect.

She glances from the crowd to me and falters, but before

locking her gaze with mine, she jerks her head back to the field on an abrupt swing. "Wait!" she yells. "Is that…is that Lexi? In a cheerleader uniform?"

It takes me a minute to shake off my Julia-focused stupor, but Scottie's laugh, point, and nod is the final shove I need to turn back to the field.

"Holy shit!" I exclaim, taking in Lexi's signature blond hair, blue eyes, and the very out of place blue-and-gold cheerleading uniform. She and Boden move toward the center of the field, his clearly shell-shocked gaze locked on Lexi as he walks sideways.

I cup my hands around my mouth and howl, and Julia puts her fingers to her lips to whistle beside me.

Even Finn is vocal, screaming obscenities at the top of his lungs, his obsession over his twin brothers Jack and Travis exercising their right to mingle with the entire female population of our fine university fifteen rows down temporarily waning. I laugh and pull Julia in for a tight hug. The joy of watching this unfold spreads among the whole crowd, their understanding limited until we start explaining it to them.

"That's fucking Lexi Winslow, dude!"

"Boden and Lexi Winslow!"

It gets louder and louder until it's a roar, and Scottie starts a telephone chain of information that makes it to me via Julia.

"Scottie says, Lexi bought off McKenzie with a promised invite to Double C to make this happen. Lexi knew she needed to make a huge display to win Blake back."

A small dagger tightens my chest at the mention of Double C, but I smooth my face to cover it quickly. I want to tell Julia what's going on—that Lexi approached me about taking over as the president and chair this year—but there's a strict policy of secrecy I've been sworn to.

Still, normally, there are no secrets between us. Normally, I'd tell her anyway.

I don't know if it's the sense of propriety stopping me this time or what, but…I have to believe she'll understand when I can finally explain it all to her.

"Everyone, please rise and remove your hats to honor America with the playing of our national anthem."

We're all already on our feet, but the roar trickles to a hum of mumble as an auburn-haired girl steps up to the microphone in the center of the field and starts to sing.

Blake and Lexi face each other now, seemingly whispering to each other. I'd pay good money to have some spy equipment right now, but without it, I have to settle for making up their conversation in my head.

I whisper it aloud, just enough that Julia can hear.

"Oh Blake, my darling football star. I do love you so."

"You, uh, do? Really? Me?"

"Of course. You are the computer to my keyboard and shit."

Julia elbows me in the chest, but not before smiling and laughing. "I'm so happy for them."

Lexi grabs both of Blake's hands in hers, and Julia gasps, getting up on her toes and digging her fingernails into my arm. "Oh my God. I think they're gonna kiss!"

The crowd starts to clap as the national anthem comes to a close, and just on cue, Boden pulls Lexi into his arms, lifts her off the ground, and plants a kiss right on her for all of us to see.

"Hell yes!" I cheer, and Julia jumps up and down beside me, slapping high fives with Finn and Scottie before turning back around to hang off me like a spider monkey, slapping me wildly to look up to the jumbotron. There they are, front and center—our girl Lexi and our boy Boden getting their happily ever after.

I'm happier than I've ever been.

And so fucking jealous I can't see straight at the same time.

I'm happy for Blake, but I want that for me.

The girl. The moment. The dream.

I look over at Julia, take in her smiling face and every facet of her beauty. Her eyes, her hair, her mouth, her entire being.

I love this girl. So fucking much.

And I want to be with her more than I want to be able to breathe.

It's motherfluffing time to make it happen.

No more fires or bugs or dramatic situations. I'm going to tell Julia how I feel.

I'm going to find the perfect moment to lay it all on the line.

I mean, I have to, before the line strangles me to death.

30

"Yoko, buddy, don't jump," I say, my voice gentle and my hands too full to correct him physically. "Mommy will be home soon, and we need to get this dinner done before she is so it's a surprise."

He barks a growing-puppy bark, sounding more and more like a teenager every day, and I move my spaghetti sauce to the back burner and turn the temperature down to low. It's got ground chicken in it because Julia prefers that over red meat most of the time when she's not on her period, and I did my best to cook it until it seemed done.

I've never browned ground chicken before—truth be told, I've never really cooked much that couldn't just go in the oven before—so I was working strictly off YouTube and hope.

Dropping the noodles in the pot of boiling water on the other side, I slide the tray of garlic bread into the oven and set the bowl of bagged salad on the kitchen island along with the candlesticks I had delivered via Instacart earlier.

Yoko barks again, this time at the sound of the key in the door, and I hold my breath, the nerves over how Julia will react to the whole thing hitting me like a dart between the eyes.

It's not that we haven't attempted to cook for each other before—mostly her for me—but the candles and stuff kind of scream romance.

As the door opens, I wipe my hands down the front of her

pink apron and head toward her, a glass of iced tea in one hand and a bottle of white wine in the other.

She bends down to give Yoko a scratch, but her eyes are undeniably wide as she takes in the scene. "Ace, what are you doing here? What's going on?"

I smile. "Sorry for breaking and entering, but I wanted to cook you dinner, and as it turns out, I don't have all the necessary cookware at my place. Slight oversight, I suppose. Is this okay?"

She glances at the food on the stove behind me and then back to me, her face surprised but warm. "Yeah. It's…really nice, actually."

"Good," I say, relieved. "I think everything should be done in about ten minutes if you want to go change into something comfortable while I'm finishing up. You can pick between wine and tea." I set the choices on the island with the salad bowl.

"Wow," she remarks with a laugh. "Change into something more comfortable? Is this dinner or the start of a porno?"

I smirk. "Your choice."

She scoffs, sputtering. "Oh my God, Ace, stop. I'll be back out in a minute."

I wish us filming a porno together didn't sound quite so much like a joke to her, but I'll take it. It is a little outlandish, even if she finds my body sexy in all the ways that count.

The plotlines are always so outdated.

Kidding. I don't watch porn. I'm clearly far too fucking busy trying to make Julia fall in love with me to fit in that kind of screen time.

I swirl the noodles in the water as they start to stick together and peek in the oven at my bread. I can't tell if it's really toasty or not, but the butter is melting, so I think that's a good sign. I decide to leave it until the noodles are done, just for good measure.

The sauce in the back bubbles and splatters, so I turn it off and hope for the best. Julia returns from the bedroom in a pair of sweatpants and a tank top as I'm draining the pasta, and I have to do a double take when I realize she's taken off her bra. I can literally see the outline of her perfect nipples underneath her top.

Fuck me.

"Better?" I ask, swallowing hard against the many, many raging thoughts diverting my blood from my chest to head to a location farther south.

"Yes," she says through a relieved exhale that makes her breasts move deliciously under her tank top. "I felt like I was being strangled by the top for some reason."

"Uh…that's good. That's great." I honestly don't even know what I'm saying right now and force myself to avert my eyes from her body. "Well, grab your drink and make yourself comfortable at the table. Dinner's just about ready."

"You know, Ace, I'm really impressed. You've been working so hard in all our classes, and now this meal… It's almost like you're growing up."

I smile toward the stove, mixing the noodles and the sauce and putting servings on two plates. Garlic bread out of the oven and served up too, I grab Julia's plate and carry it to the table along with the salad bowl before going back for my own and joining her.

I sit down at the table with her and hold up my own glass of iced tea for cheers. She matches my energy with a tap of our glasses. "To us. To a lifelong, unmatchable friendship and years and years of more," I say just vaguely enough to carry the tone while I work up the nerve to really let it all out there.

Because that's what tonight is about, I've decided—telling her I love her. But not yet, not right out of the gate. I want to spend time first, taking interest in her, asking questions, diving into the woman she keeps tenderly locked away.

I know her better than anyone, and yet, I long to know her more.

I want the key to the secret garden. The access no one else is allowed to have.

She takes a bite, chewing completely before swallowing it down and meeting my eyes with a smile. "Wow, Ace. It tastes really good."

"Really?" I ask.

"Yes!"

She scarfs down several more bites, and then some of the salad, before taking a big swig of tea. And we just kind of eat in a companionable silence before I start asking her questions.

"So, Jules. After we're done with college, any idea where you see life taking you? Do you want to stay in New York or go somewhere else?"

Her eyebrows draw together. "I don't know." She swallows hard, her eyes glassing slightly before coming back into focus. "I don't know that I've thought about it that much yet. Why? What do you want to do?"

I chuckle. "That's why I'm asking you, silly. So I can decide by copying you."

She startles on a giggle. "Yeah, I guess that is becoming a pattern."

"That's because you're good at making the right choices," I compliment. "I trust you. You're—"

A burp suddenly bubbles up from her mouth, and she startles, putting her fingers in front of it and her hand to her stomach.

"Are you okay?" I ask, but before I can even finish the question, she jumps up and takes off at a run. "Jules?"

Yoko follows her first, barking from the bathroom, and I get up on shaky feet to follow her. My stomach suddenly feels a little queasy too, and then, in an instant, it lurches entirely.

Oh no.

Running and untying Julia's apron from my body at the same time, I bolt across the hall, through my apartment and into the bathroom, where I slam down to my knees in front of the toilet and violently throw up the last several bites of food I've just swallowed.

My stomach pitches and then falls, and I vomit again as realization sets in.

Oh hell.

Instead of declaring my love, I declared war…on our intestines.

What the hell did I do wrong?

31

Julia

I groan and roll over in my bed, reaching weakly toward the bottle of water Ace left for me on my nightstand in the middle of the night last night. He's been in several times to check on me, often with a puke bowl below his own mouth as he dry heaves.

After much frantic discussion between vom sessions about what he could have done to our dinner that made us this violently sick this quickly, we made a four a.m. discovery that he used the one brand of spaghetti sauce that sneaks in peppers—something we're both allergic to. Our shared food-sensitivity was uncovered at a family barbecue when we were in kindergarten. My mom had made stuffed peppers, and both Ace and I ended up in the ER together with full-body hives.

Truth be told, hives would've been a better outcome in our current situation, and out of pure survival, I declared that I'd be the only one cooking our meals from here on out.

He agreed, as best as he could through a groan, and we've both been fighting for our lives ever since.

I crawl across my comforter to get the bottle since it's not magically coming to me, sipping lightly from the rounded top. My mouth feels both brittle and sore, and I find myself wishing I had some ibuprofen to go with the liquid.

The door to my bedroom bangs open, revealing Ace shirtless and wrapped in a throw blanket and walking like a zombie. He stretches one hand out in front of him. "Here. Take these."

By the red color of the three little pills, I know it's ibuprofen. And I think in my mind about telling him how I was wishing for this exact thing, but nothing audible comes out. I'm too weak and dehydrated.

"What about kids?" he asks through a raspy, fatigued voice. "Do you want to have kids?"

"What?" I question, the ends of the word wrapped up in a re-markable moan.

"I was just…wondering…"

"Well, wonder some other time," I cry.

"I'm sorry I poisoned us, Lia. Really. I'm so, so sorry. I thought if anything would get us, it would be the chicken. I never thought it'd be the sauce—"

"I know you are, Ace. Just…shut up." I groan and shut my eyes. "Please. My ears hurt."

"Here," Ace whispers, his voice noticeably softening. "Take these."

I finally take the pills from his hand and shove them one by one into my mouth. And he helps tip my bottle of water up to my lips to take a drink and swallow them down. He brushes my hair out of my face with a gentle thumb and then jumps to standing. "Be right back," he yells, running, once again, for his own bathroom.

"Ughhh," I grumble.

My cheek vibrates, and I move my head slightly to see that I'm lying directly on my phone. I pull it out from under my face and hold it up, willing my eyes to focus on the screen.

Drew: Everything okay? Just got out of Calc and was surprised you weren't there.

I can barely type the words, but somehow, I manage.

Me: Sorry yeah. Got food poisoning and trying to survive

It's not entirely accurate, but it is the simplest explanation. I drop my head back down to the comforter, relishing in the coolness of the fabric.

Drew: I can come by if you want. Bring some soup or something to help you hydrate?

Ace's loud groan from across the hall, weirdly, makes me smile. Not only does bringing a third person into this unnecessarily seem like cruel and unusual punishment, but for some reason, it also feels…wrong.

There's something so special about Ace and me together, even in this state, that I can't put my finger on.

He feels different lately.

He's matured. He's still so fun, but he's also serious.

I don't know. Maybe…maybe the two of us could…

I shake my head and close my eyes.

Shh, Julia, that's just the hallucination of the sickness talking.

Or is it?

The uncertainty is enough to give my fingers the energy to type out one last message to Drew. He's sweet. He's considerate.

But right now, he's not needed.

Me: Thanks, but we're good. I'll see you tomorrow.

And just like that, I fall back to sleep. To dreams of Ace and me. To dreams of what could be.

32

At Lexi's prompting, I arrive at the back door of the Nash Mathematics Center on Dickson's campus at five o'clock on the dot, nothing but the clothes on my back, a condom in my pocket, and my phone back in my apartment.

The condom wasn't a requirement per se, but my dad raised me on the phrase *Don't be silly, protect your willy!*, and while I'm not at all planning to have sex with someone else because I'm in love with Julia, I also have no way of knowing what's about to happen to me tonight. What if part of the initiation ritual for Double C's head of operations is to dip your genitals in a bucket of wax and the past leaders weren't STI negative?

Anyway, it's better safe than sorry, and if they run me through a metal detector or pat me down, a lone condom isn't liable to bat any eyelashes.

I survey the door and test the knob, but it's locked, and the sun, still on its way down on the western horizon, pierces me directly in the eye. I cup my palm and hold it up in front of me to block it out, but just as I manage, a dark sack comes over my head and does the job for me.

I let out a muffled scream—instinct makes it hard not to—but catch myself quickly as I'm ushered off the curb, into a waiting car, and sped off quickly.

Holy hell, it's really happening…

When Lexi's text finally came in an hour ago, ending my

two-week dance in the dark void of curiosity and scrambling any other attention to a normal Friday night entirely, a part of me wondered if this would still be a precursor or a test of my willingness to wait.

But kidnappings don't speak to more stalling; kidnappings scream action.

And since I can feel the leather seats under my hands and smell the freshness of a well-maintained space, any fear that I'm being kidnapped for something other than Double C vaporizes entirely.

The moment has arrived. And I have a really good feeling that by the end of the night, I'll be more than halfway to realizing all my goals.

King of Double C? Check.

Recipient of Julia's love? Almost.

"Well, this is interesting," I remark, which earns me an unidentified chuckle from someone in the car. There are hushed whispers that follow, and then, silence.

I hum a song to myself as we drive and drive, and then we eventually pull to a stop on hard brakes somewhere else. The door beside me opens, and I'm lifted out and walked forward into the shade and air of a building. I march on sure feet, someone's hand at my elbow to steady me, and sigh when I'm shoved down into a chair somewhere within what feels like the recesses of a maze of hallways.

"Stay here until someone comes for you," a deep but sort of familiar voice says. "Do not take off the bag."

I nod. "You got it."

I can't quite pinpoint how I know the voice, but my mind strives to figure it out while I sit in complete darkness.

And I sit and I sit—and I sit some more.

I don't know what time it is, and I don't know how long I've been here, but eventually, I try to keep myself occupied by rolling through a few renditions of "Bad Romance" by Lady Gaga. It's Julia's ringtone, and I know the song like the back of my fucking hand.

I'm halfway through the chorus when I'm yanked from the

chair and instructed to stand. It's the same voice. The same distant familiarity that my brain still can't piece together.

As the bag is removed, the entire room goes dark, and a slim blindfold slides over my eyes instead.

My elbow is grabbed, and I'm instructed to walk again.

On slightly shaking legs, the muscles cold with disuse for God knows how long, I do as I'm told and walk.

The whole way, my stomach dances with excitement, and I rub my hands together as someone shoves me forward, leading me back through what feels like another maze of hallways.

As we walk, my smile grows.

This is so fucking cool.

I'm shoved down into another chair, this one soft and velvety from the feel of it under my hands, and a hush falls over the room, the sound of my breathing all I recognize.

"Ace Tobias Kelly, I'd like to welcome you here tonight," someone announces, the sound of their voice circling me. "This is going to be one of the most important nights of your life. Are you ready to take on the challenge?"

"I'm ready," I say confidently. "I'm so ready."

Someone steps toward me, and I hold my chin high as their hands work to undo my blindfold. As it leaves, I blink against the darkness of the candlelit room, trying to find my focus as quickly as possible.

The first thing I notice is that the chair I'm sitting on is more throne than dining room spindle chair, and two people in long robes are in front of me, their official nature unquestionable.

That's not that big of a surprise, but what is a surprise is the identity of the person on the left.

And not a little one. It's the biggest fucking surprise that's ever been sprung on me in all my nineteen years.

"Mom?"

"Hi, Acer," she says, a smile in her voice and a *fuck yeah* grin on her lips. She's just pulled the biggest fucking coup in Kelly history.

"What are you doing here?" I ask, looking around the room for Lexi and trying to make sense of it all. I don't find the brainiac former president, but my mom finds her voice with ease.

"Surprise, motherfucker," she says without hesitation. "Your clearly very cool mom is one of the secret chairs of Double C."

My eyes feel like they might pop out of their sockets if I don't shove them back in.

The man, whom I don't recognize at all, standing next to her in a robe of his own, turns and nods to the two cloaked figures in the corner, and they step forward, pulling off their hoods.

It's Lexi and Connor. Instantly, I put the pieces of the familiar but mysterious voice together and know that it was Connor back there. He's been friends with Lexi Winslow since they were thirteen. At one point, back in the day, he was her boyfriend. Basically, he's been around my family and parents' friends for years.

Not to mention, he was Lexi's right-hand man for Double C all last year.

But now, the two of them are no longer Dickson students and are passing the torch…to someone who appears to be a devilishly handsome guy whom a lot of people know to be Ace Kelly.

Holy fucking shit!

I discreetly inhale a calming breath and force myself to keep my cool. No need to blow my load of excitement before they even get this cloak-and-dagger secret ceremony show on the road.

"Tonight, we are gathered here for the ceremony of your initiation," Lexi announces, a cheeky smile the only indication that she knew about my mom—and how fucking surprised I would be— from the beginning.

"Tonight, you will be initiated as the current sitting president of Computare Caterva," Connor instructs. "Are you ready to take the oath, Ace Tobias Kelly?"

Am I motherfucking ready? I was born ready.

I glance from Lexi to my mom, and another rush of excitement floods my veins. Fuck yes, this is going to be incredible. I'm genetically destined for this. "I'm ready."

My mom moves toward me, leaning down to whisper briefly into my ear. "Julia won't be mad?"

Her question catches me off guard. I mean, it's not like I hadn't considered how Julia would feel that I've kept this secret from her, but I guess I didn't consider that my mom would be thinking of it either. I hate that I haven't been able to tell her—that I won't until it's all said and done and the first event takes place—but I've been putting in the work to show her how much I love her until now.

Surely it'll be fine.

Once I explain, she'll understand. She always does.

I shake my head. "She will," I whisper back. "But that's why we have the fifteen-minute rule. It's saved my ass more than once, and it'll save it again. I'm ready."

"If you're sure," my mom says softly. For a split second, the hesitation in her voice makes my heart falter. But then she steps back and says, "Then, we'll begin." Her tone has returned to normal, and I let it go—trusting that the universe will work everything out between Julia and me. It has to. We're meant to be.

"Ace Tobias Kelly, you hereby pledge your secrecy and devotion to the Computare Caterva at Dickson University from now until your successor takes their position. You will harbor, protect, and defend this organization against those who seek to destroy it. You will uphold our honor, and you will continue to create the magic this organization brings to this prestigious university," the mystery man who's still cloaked and standing next to my mom says.

Lexi walks toward me with a lit candle, and my mom hands me one of my own that, as of now, is flameless. Lexi comes to a stop in front of me, her long cloak trailing behind her.

"Ace, do you accept this pledge and the undeniable responsibility of the title of President of Computare Caterva?"

"I do."

"Do you swear your life to the secrecy required of you for both your position as president and the organization in its entirety, from this eve forward, until your death releases you?"

"Intense," I mumble teasingly. "But yes, I do."

"Then I hereby pass the torch. You, Ace Tobias Kelly, are officially the acting president of Computare Caterva at Dickson University. Wear your new role well."

Hell yeah, baby. Here comes the new president…motherfucking me.

Looks like it's time to celebrate.

"You know I will," I agree. "Come on, Lex. You and I are going for a drink."

It's nearly two in the morning, and I haven't heard from Ace since our last class at three yesterday afternoon.

No texts or calls *from* him and no responses to any of my texts or calls *to* him. And no sound from across the hall.

I even reached out to Finn and Scottie and Blake, but no one had heard from him. It's been radio silence and the worst-case scenarios building one by one in my head for the last few hours.

Drew texted me earlier to see if I wanted to go to a party on Frat Row, but I declined because I wanted to make sure Ace was okay. And I don't know, I guess I felt more excited about doing something with Ace on Friday night than meeting up with Drew.

But what if Ace is lying in a gutter somewhere after being violently mugged? Or he's been kidnapped by some kind of drug cartel gang and held for ransom?

My heart lurches. I'm so close to calling the cops and reporting him missing, it's not even funny. I even grab my phone and text him exactly that.

But when no response comes back, no Read notification underneath my words, I start to really consider contacting the authorities. Though, I guess I should call his parents first. Maybe my parents too.

I'm mere seconds away from calling Cassie when Yoko barks at a sound in the hall. I jump up from my spot on the couch and run toward the door. Unbolting the lock and undoing the chain,

I pull it open just in time to see Ace turn his key in his lock and twist the knob.

"Hey," I call, my heart in my throat as I work to calm down the racing feeling of it. He's obviously physically okay, which is what I've been the most worried about, but I'm still wondering where he's been—almost to the point of desperation.

He turns around slowly, loosely, almost like he can't really keep his feet beneath him, and his eyes are big and bloodshot. It hits me then that he's drunk—very much so—and if possible, my stomach plummets even more than before.

"Heys, Lia," he greets affectionately, his whole body swaying toward me as Yoko and I step out into the hall.

"Where were you?" I ask, cutting to the chase for the sake of my tired, stressed-out mind. "I've been worried. I…I tried to call you, but you didn't answer. And when I texted Finn and Scottie, they didn't know where you were either. I didn't want to text Blake because I know he has the big game against Pennington later to-day, but I've basically been waiting around here all night, worried about you."

He frowns. "Sorries, babe. Forgots my phone here. You were callin' my apartment, I'm afraid, not me."

He forgot his phone? What the hell? Ace Kelly never forgets his phone. Hell, what human being on Planet Earth forgets their phone nowadays?

I rub at my arms until Yoko jumps on my leg, and then I lean down to pick him up in my arms. He's getting heavy, but somehow, holding his flaily body feels less awkward than standing here, vul-nerable, without him.

"Where were you, though?" I press.

He smiles, looking up at the ceiling and touching a finger to his lips. "Out."

"Out? Out where, Ace?"

He chuckles then, shaking his head and letting out a long,

theatrical sigh before snapping his fingers. "With Lex-a-nator. Yeah, Lexi freaking Winslows."

I frown. "You were out…until two in the morning…drinking…with Lexi Winslow?"

"I knows, babe!" He cracks up. "Crazies, isn't it?"

"Yeah," I say quietly. It's too crazy to be believable, and *why does my heart feel like it's breaking into a million tiny pieces?*

I help him open the door when he fumbles and walk him inside, watching as he stumbles to take off his shoes. His shirt is sloppy and untucked, and a condom flies out of his pocket onto the floor.

Instantly, I feel like crying. I don't know why, but I do, and I have to shut my eyes for a brief moment to keep the tears at bay.

He's bumbling around in his living room, and wordlessly, I pull myself together and help walk him into his bedroom while Yoko bounces around us the whole time.

"Ah, yes," Ace cheers. "My bed. I love my bed so much." He awkwardly climbs under the covers, his stupid shoes still on, and I find myself removing them so he's more comfortable.

Ace never lies to me, but tonight, I'm certain he did. I don't like to make assumptions about anyone or anything without knowing all the facts, but my mind is telling me he was MIA tonight because he was out with another girl…or *girls*. And all of those things combined hurt like a bitch.

I look into his eyes and find myself longing for the future I was quietly starting to dream about for us. For me to think he was past that phase of his life was a foolishness I'll be feeling for weeks.

Still, he's Ace. He's my best friend. So, I tuck him in tightly and brush the hair out of his face as he closes his eyes.

"Mm," he hums. "I love you, Julia."

"Yeah, I know," I say. "I love you too." And right now, in this very instant, with my drunk, deceitful best friend half passed out in his bed, I'm starting to wonder if I've loved Ace more than it's probably ever been good or healthy for me.

Sure, we made all sorts of decrees and promises when we were a couple of hopeful kids, but we're not little kids anymore. We're adults. And it doesn't make any sense for me to be planning my future around something we promised each other when I was seven freaking years old.

I mean, that would be the epitome of naïve. Ever since we hit puberty, Ace has been very much into girls. Flirting with girls. Kissing girls. Dating girls. Hooking up with girls.

All girls who are not me, in fact.

His breathing evens as he falls asleep, and Yoko and I climb in beside him. I snuggle close and breathe him in, burrowing my nose into the skin of his arm and wrapping my leg with his.

He doesn't smell like himself at all, and my back breaks with the weight of the realization, turning his fancy $10,000 mattress into a bed of nails.

I force myself to move away from him, pushing up to sitting and crawling to the edge of the bed.

With one last kiss to his cheek, I climb out of the bed and retreat across the hall to my apartment, shutting and locking both his door and mine behind me.

Unfortunately, the quiet independence I once longed for feels a hell of a lot lonelier tonight.

34

My head pounds, my tongue feels like it's made of denim, and when I roll over on my bed, my face sticks to the pillow in a way that screams tequila regret. It takes me a full thirty seconds to piece together why I feel like I got run over by a frat bus.

Becoming Double C president is easily the greatest thing that's happened to me since birth. And last night, I celebrated accordingly—by getting drunk enough to forget half of it. There was liquor. There was beer. There was a lot of shouting. And Lexi, Connor, my mom, and my dad were all in attendance.

I was shocked to my fucking core that Lexi Winslow wanted to go out to a bar near campus to celebrate my new role as president of Double C—the details of my asking her aren't important here—and who was I to tell Ms. Smarty Pants no?

She kicked things off with a toast, but she kept it classy and exited early to go snuggle with her boyfriend Blake—yeah, that's officially a thing now.

My mom, on the other hand, was shoving shots into my hand, and my dad showed up halfway through the night purely because his FOMO is stronger than his sense of moderation.

I vaguely remember people shouting my name in the bar or stumbling into my building after my also-drunk parents had Nathan drop me off. I'm pretty sure Julia was there and that she was in my apartment at one point, but honestly, it's all mostly a blur.

When I finally manage to peel my face off the pillow and reach for my phone, I'm hit with a tidal wave of guilt. Twelve missed calls. Nine texts. All from Julia.

Shit.

I scan her texts quickly, and each one gets more panicked and worried as the night goes on.

> *Julia: Hey, hey, what are our big Friday night plans tonight?*

> *Julia: Acer…hello? Where in the hell are you? It's nearly six. You're not going to leave your bestie hanging, are you?*

> *Julia: Okay, I'm starting to get a little worried here. It's nearly 10 and I haven't heard from you. You're not in your apartment. Are you okay????*

The last and final text came in at nearly two in the morning, and she was so panicked that she was threatening to call the cops to report me missing.

Fuck.

She has no idea what I was doing last night. She has no idea that I was getting initiated as Double C's newest president or that I went out after to have drinks with Lexi and Connor and my mom. Now it looks like I ghosted her on a Friday night for no good reason. And to make matters worse, I'm still not supposed to say anything, thanks to my vow of eternal fucking secrecy until I die or whatever.

Double fuck.

I hop out of bed, pull on a hoodie, toss some more ibuprofen into my mouth, and head across the hall on quick but slightly unsteady feet. God, I hope she's not too mad to let me explain.

I knock on Julia's door like a guy facing a firing squad, holding my phone in one hand and a knot of regret in the other.

When it opens, she looks like she's ready to go somewhere. She's wearing her go-to athleisure, her favorite white Nikes are on her feet, and Yoko's leash is looped around her wrist.

Her beautiful face is poised in an unreadable expression. It's calm, collected, but it's not exactly warm.

Yoko barks once, then runs straight for my feet, demanding pets to his head. I oblige, but I never take my eyes away from Julia's face.

"Hey, Lia," I say, voice soft. "Can we talk for a sec?"

"I'm actually about to take him for a walk."

"Yeah, I figured," I mutter, then hold up my phone. "I just saw all your messages from last night."

"Okay…"

"Julia…you were really freaked out."

"Yeah. I was." She looks away and fixates her gaze on Yoko, who is now lying between us. "I was really worried, Ace. I hadn't heard from you since class, and you weren't responding to any of my texts or calls."

"I know. I know. And I'm sorry." I step a little closer. "I left my phone here, and I didn't mean to disappear like that."

"It's fine," she says flatly.

"No, it's not fine," I refute. "It was a really dick move to make you worry like that. I'm so sorry."

She shrugs. "It's over and done with now."

Oh boy. She's definitely pissed at me.

"Did you…uh…help me get inside last night?" I ask, desperate to piece last night's drunken puzzle together so I can find the right words to explain to her what happened.

She finally meets my gaze. "Yeah."

Fuck. "Again, I'm so sorry." I grimace. "How bad was I?"

"Not the worst I've seen," she says with another shrug, then adds, "but you weren't exactly holding a press conference either."

I wince. "Thanks for helping me."

"Of course," she says, too quickly. "That's what friends do, right?"

Right. Friends. My favorite prison.

"I wanted to tell you where I was last night. I really did. It's kind of complicated. I—"

"You don't have to tell me anything," she cuts me off as she leans down to clip Yoko's leash. She's avoiding my eyes completely now.

"Is that all you wanted to chat about?" she asks quickly. "Because I really should get him outside. Pretty sure he has to pee."

"No, actually, it's not…" I pause, trying to find the right words. Trying to figure out how to explain it all. Trying to figure out if I can let the whole pact-of-secrecy thing go and tell Julia everything.

I mean, I want to tell her I got inducted as the new president of Double C. I want to tell her that Lexi passed me a cursed phone full of ridiculous last-minute event notes and that my mom made me do tequila shots while my dad challenged a bartender to a push-up contest. I want her to know I wasn't out with someone else.

Yoko whines before I can even open my mouth again, and that urges Julia to step into the hall with him and shut her door. "I'd better get a move on it," she says, stepping around me with Yoko's leash wrapped around her wrist. He's bouncing around now, whining and trying to tug her toward the elevators. "Do you want to come?"

It's a lifeline, but it's a fucking lifeline I can't take because of all the shit I have to make sure gets confirmed before tonight's event. There are no fucking baby steps with taking over as Double C's newest president. Lexi has quite literally tossed me into the deep end of the shark-infested pool.

Last night, she handed me the President Phone—yes, that's a real thing—and said, "*Good Luck, Mr. President.*"

Inside that phone, there's a long, bullet-pointed and color-coded fucking list of all the crap I need to do and become familiar with. Calls and texts I need to make for tonight. Names and phone numbers of Dickson University campus security officers I need to reach out to and pay off to let us in places we most certainly shouldn't be.

It's a lot of fucking to-dos. All of which I'm completely responsible for now, and I have exactly eight hours to make sure a secret society event, complete with a custom scavenger hunt, goes off without a hitch.

No pressure.

"Or I guess you don't have to come…" Julia adds, her voice

quiet in a way that makes my chest ache. "You probably have more important stuff to do."

I want to tell her that there's nothing more important than her.

I want to tell her the truth. I want to tell her everything.

But she doesn't even give me the chance.

"Julia, I—"

"Ace, can we catch up later?" she cuts me off. "Yoko is getting antsy."

"Uh…yeah, but—"

"I'll see you later, okay?"

She doesn't wait for an answer. She turns and heads down the hall with Yoko all but tugging her toward the elevator.

I watch them go until she disappears around the stairwell, my hand still resting against the doorframe like a guy stuck between two realities—one where I tell her everything, and one where I don't.

Because this secret is only temporary.

But Julia? She's always my endgame.

35

Ace

I look fucking good.

Like, walk-into-a-room-and-start-a-slow-clap good. The shirt's black, the collar's sharp, and the diamond cuff links I stole from my dad are glinting just enough to say *my bloodline pays taxes in commas.*

I adjust the collar again, turn slightly, and admire my studly reflection one more time. It's giving presidential. It's giving dangerous. It's giving "this man controls the playlist *and* the legacy."

It's only a little after five p.m., and I'm certain I've never been ready for a Saturday night this early, but tonight is *the* night. There's a new Double C sheriff in town, and his name is Ace motherfucking Kelly.

As I run a comb through my hair with the goal of giving laid-back GQ model, I snort a little when I think about the fact that my fucking mom of all people ended up being a chair of the campus's biggest secret society. What are the fucking odds, man? I mean, seriously, if there was a spread in Vegas, the payout would have to be exponential.

I glance at my phone, fully expecting Blake and Finn to have finally texted back their Double C attendance confirmation or to have a status update from Julia who's been MIA all day since leaving with Yoko this morning, but the screen shows nada.

I frown briefly. I know Julia was upset this morning and not reaching out to go to the football game with her this afternoon probably made matters worse, but she'll cool down and we'll move on. She always does. We just need our fifteen minutes, even if this time, it's running a little closer to eight hours.

I sigh and click into to my message with Finn and Blake again.

Those fuckers need to be there tonight so I can get a load of their faces when they grasp the awesome reality we're heading toward this year. I can already picture myself standing at the helm—the handsome center of attention—and the crowd going batshit crazy when I tell them that I'm their new leader. But I need my best guys right there in the front when I make the official announcement that I'm the new prez.

I mean, no offense to Lexi Winslow—she was one hell of a Double C president—but this is me we're talking about here. If anyone can bring Double C to a level where it's world-renowned, it's this guy right here. The future event ideas I already have rolling around inside my head are equal parts this-might-be-illegal and oh-fuck-yeah.

I spritz on a little cologne, willing a new message to pop up in the thread from Finn or Blake, but aside from smelling fucking delightful, nothing has changed.

Unacceptable.

My debut as president of Double C is in six hours. I need my guys in position. Fully hyped. Properly dressed. Emotionally ready.

I grab my phone off the counter and start firing off texts.

> **Me: Reminder… if either of you bail tonight you're dead to me**
>
> **Me: And I'll fucking haunt your apartments. Knock shit off shelves and shit**
>
> **Me: Finn I saw the three dots. Don't play with me.**

Bubble. Bubble. Ding.

Finn: It's 5 p.m., bro. Relax. We've got hours until we're supposed to be there. In fact, I don't think we've ever even gotten a text this early before.

Relax? Does he think Lincoln was chill before the Gettysburg Address? This is my fucking Sistine Chapel!

And a critique on the text timing at this delicate moment? Fucking hell, it sure is good Finn is handsome because he's pissing me off. It doesn't matter that he doesn't know I'm the sender; we should be synced up like a couple of roommates approaching menstruation!

Me: All I'm asking is for a little confirmation of your attendance tonight Finnley. God forbid I'm trying to make sure our sophomore year is a good fucking time.

Boden: Not gonna lie, I'd rather stay home with Lexi. Today's game against Pennington kicked my ass.

What the fucking fuck?

Me: Boden I'm disappointed.

Me: The Campus Golden Boy should be high off his win today and ready to fucking celebrate. Not whining about wanting to stay home like a little bitch baby. What the hell bro? These are the best years of our lives. Now is the time to live it up.

Finn: You do realize Boden wants to stay home because Lexi is home, right?

Boden: Bingo bongo, buddy. And the same could be said for you.

Finn: Ha. I won't deny that.

Me: You two can makeout with your girlfriends any night of the week. Come out, you fuckers.

Finn: Again, I'd like to reiterate that it's 5 p.m.

Boden: Yeah, Acer. We've got time, man.

Fuck me. Not being able to tell these bastards that I'm Double C's new prez is proving to be a real pain in my ass.

Me: Fine, but I'm taking this as your official confirmation that you will be in attendance at Double C tonight. If you're not there, I will personally hire Gunnar to come find you.

Boden: You're really scary, you know that? But not in the way you think.

Me: I'm fully aware of all the ways I'm scary and I don't care. I'll see you tonight. PS: You've got six hours to emotionally prepare. I expect vibes. Excitement. Big ass fucking smiles. We're not dragging our way into sophomore year like a bunch of losers

Boden: HA. Big ass fucking smiles? I don't think Finn's face is capable of that.

That actually makes me laugh, despite the otherwise raw nature of my mood.

Me: That's where Scottie comes in. Finn can't not smile when she's around and I've also texted her to assure her attendance

Finn: My girl definitely makes me smile, but the idea of you texting her behind my back does NOT.

Me: Finn please. Behind your back? Be realistic and let's move on to more important things…Do either of you need help in your attire selection tonight?

Finn: You're a fucking clown.

Boden: I second this.

I head into my bedroom, but as I toss my phone onto the bed, it pings again. I half expect it to be Blake sending me a photo of him in socks and fucking sandals to screw with me, but I shouldn't be surprised when I see who it is.

After all, she's one of three people I can think of off the top of my head that are nuttier than I am.

Mama Cass: If you mess this up, I'm changing my emergency contact to Gunnar. And I think we both know I might as well make myself a DNR.

Me: Pretty sure Dad should be your emergency contact...

Mama Cass: Excuse me? Do you even hear yourself right now?

Me: Valid point.

Mama Cass: You're my favorite kid today. I love you. Have the best fucking time. PS: Don't ruin our legacy, or I'll kill you.

Me: Love you too.

I set the phone down, still grinning, and grab the mini speaker from my desk to blast my "Hype and Dangerous" playlist on Spotify. But I only get half a song deep before I hear a faint knock at the door.

"It's open!"

A moment later, Julia walks into my bedroom.

She's standing in the doorway in that off-the-shoulder gray sweatshirt she always wears when she's not trying, which makes it even more unfair that she still looks gorgeous. She blinks at me. Her eyes drop to my outfit. My shoes. My perfectly done hair.

"You're already dressed?" she asks, surprised, and I feel like an asshole that I've been too busy making phone calls and running over to campus to pay off two campus security guards to try more seriously to check in with her. I texted a couple times, but I should have hunted her down in person. I know we weren't in a fight per se, but she was—probably still is—upset with me. And our fifteen-minute rule should've been of the utmost priority.

"Oh…uh, yeah." I clear my throat. "Just, you know, heading somewhere before the Double C thing tonight."

Her brows lift. "Where?"

"Just a thing." I wave a hand. "For…uh…my parents," I lie, and I hate that I'm lying. "No big deal."

"Okay…so… When should I be ready to go tonight?"

"Is it…uh…cool if I meet you there?" I ask, trying to sound casual as I flip the speaker volume of my music down a notch.

Her expression shifts, and she tilts her head. "You want me to meet you there because of something for your parents?"

"Yeah. I know we always go to Double C stuff together, but this is one of those rare exceptions. I'm sorry about last night, and this morning, but we can—"

"I'll see you tonight, Ace," she cuts me off before I can finish.

Fuck, I can't keep doing this. This is dumb. I need to tell her the truth. So what if I'm supposedly sworn to secrecy? This is *Julia.* My best friend. "Hey…wait…" I move closer, trying to read her. "Jules, I—"

"See you tonight," she says and walks out of my bedroom, and I hear the front door to my apartment click shut a few seconds later.

I stand there dumbly for another ten, my heart sinking into my fucking shoes, before I jog out of my bedroom and out my apartment door.

"Hey! Jules!" I knock on her door several times, but there's no answer. I don't even hear Yoko barking in response.

Immediately, I grab my phone and shoot her a text.

Me: Hey where'd you go? I wanted to tell you something real quick before I head out

Julia: Taking Yoko to my parents' apartment.

I guess that makes sense. It's better Yoko is at the Brookses' rather than being locked up in Julia's bathroom while we're at Double C tonight, but my God, she moves fast.

I almost text her and tell her I got initiated as Double C's newest president last night—that I wasn't out with some random girl or some other unredeemable sin. I want to tell her a million things, but instead, I text, **Okay see you tonight.**

I took a vow of secrecy less than twenty-four hours ago. The least I can do is forgo the urge to break it via text.

I'll tell her in person. Soon. We'll make up, and this whole stupid misunderstanding will be tucked away in the past.

She doesn't message me back, but I tell myself it's because she's got Yoko on the subway and he's a fucking maniac. I tell myself she isn't really upset with me, and she'll understand the reason I had to lie to her.

I tell myself this is Julia—the most understanding, perfect human being I know.

She'll understand after tonight. I'm certain of it.

I mean, I'm only utilizing a measly few hours' extension on our fifteen-minute rule, and then we'll be back to normal.

Right?

Julia

The basement of the psych building smells like old textbooks and mystery mold, but apparently that's what qualifies as high society when it comes to Double C. The first official event of the year is in full swing, and our little group is gathered right in the center of it all.

Scottie smiles from her chair between Finn and me, Blake's across from us talking about today's big game, and Ace is right next to me—loud, laughing, completely in his element.

Everything is normal—except me.

I'm trying to play my part, and I think I'm succeeding as far as the friend group is concerned, but internally, it's a struggle.

Shit has been weird between me and Ace since yesterday and, quite frankly, hasn't even hinted at getting better.

From not hearing from him all night to putting him to bed drunk after seeing *the condom* fall out of his pants to his avoidant explanation this morning to skipping the football game we would normally go to together to stopping by to find him already dressed and ready for tonight to coming here *separately*, it's been one fucked-up moment after another.

And yet…

He's *glowing*. His aura is brighter than I've ever seen it, and we haven't had even a second of private conversation. He hasn't asked if the time is up on our fifteen minutes.

He hasn't asked *me* anything at all.

Since my arrival ten minutes ago, he's been working the room like a politician, high-fiving half the people who walk by and making everyone feel like they're part of something big. He's the life of the party as usual, but for the first time ever, it feels like I wasn't invited.

He's talking with Blake and Finn about the playlist that's blasting from the speakers by the stage and joking about "revolutionizing secret society party vibes now that we're sophomores," and everyone is eating it up.

Everyone but me, that is.

My brain keeps trying to play it cool, but deep down, the green-eyed monster whispers that he's lying to me about something. Maybe even more than one something. Maybe some new girl he's started dating. Maybe two new girls.

I don't know. I do know I shouldn't care if he's dating someone. I shouldn't. But I *do*.

I care more than I've cared in a very, very long time.

I clear my throat and force myself to focus on anything but the way my best friend's brown eyes look like melted chocolate underneath the fluorescent lights of this dingy basement and the corresponding sweetness some skanky girl may have spent Friday night swimming in.

"I wonder what tonight's big event is going to be," I say, trying to sound normal and participate in the conversation, like maybe it'll keep me from spiraling.

Before anyone answers, Ace turns to me with a grin and bumps my shoulder. "Be right back, okay?"

"Okay, weirdo," I say, playing my part even though my heart feels so heavy it's sinking out of my chest. I don't know why I don't bring it up—it's not like me to withhold my feelings from Ace. But this whole set of circumstances feels different.

Everything we've done for the last few weeks, everything that's happened…I thought… I don't know. It felt like we'd turned a corner.

And now we're speeding blindly in reverse.

He peels away from the group, I assume to schmooze some

people on the edge of the crowd. *Or maybe he's going to meet his new girlfriend at the door.*

But then he heads to the stage in front. And grabs the microphone.

What is he doing?

Finn squints. "What the fuck?"

Ace's voice cuts through the noise. "I'd like to welcome everyone here tonight. This is our first official Double C event of the year, and while I think we can all agree that our previous leader Lexi's shoes are big ones to fill, I am fortunate enough to wear a size fourteen. Tighten your seat belts and check your zippers, motherfuckers. It's going to be one hell of a wild year."

And just like that, the world tilts a little sideways. Ace is the new Lexi. Ace—*my Ace*—is in charge of Double C. It's arguably the most the dramatic realization of his very wettest dream to run our college's secret society—to be the most recognizable, noteworthy student on campus.

And he didn't bother to tell me.

There are cheers and whistles and some guy yells "President Acer!" like that's a thing now, and all I can do is stand there and try not to let my face give me away.

I'm hurt. Not a scratch on the surface that heals quickly—a deep, throbbing wound.

He lied to me. Last night, today, and moments ago.

He lied.

Our lives—our friendship—are what they are because of a level of trust most people can't comprehend. Because of truth-telling and bared exposure of all parts, weak, strong, wicked or otherwise.

As the world turns around us, we are the true north, we are the reset, we are the soul.

At least, I thought we were.

But by lying to me about last night, by hiding this—whether he was sworn to some secret code of something or not—he's irrevocably changed the way we operate.

Everyone else is smiling. Everyone else is thrilled. And I'm standing here like an idiot trying to figure out why this hurts so much. I swallow hard, eyes fixed on the stage. An uninvited moisture blurs Ace's image.

"You good, Jules?" Blake asks, his voice kind.

I turn to him and force a smile so hard it cramps my jaw. "Of course. Just surprised, you know?"

"You didn't know about this?"

"Nope." I shake my head, blinking fast. "Just found out right now…with everyone else."

Scottie, thank God, chooses that moment to turn to me and ask if I want to go to the bathroom. I don't hesitate. I grab the handles of her wheelchair like my life depends on it and steer us away from the noise.

We push through the crowd, past the halfhearted dance circle and the groups clumped together whispering about President Ace and finally make it to the hall near the bathrooms.

The second we're alone, I let out ten pounds of air in one forced blow.

Scottie twists to look up at me. "You okay?"

"Yeah," I say too quickly. "I needed a second. It's loud in there."

She nods, not pressing, and I'm grateful. We both go into the bathroom—her into the accessible stall, me into the one next to it—and I sit on the closed toilet lid and stare at the tile.

I'm mad. Not just at Ace but at myself too. Maybe even a little bit at the world.

I shouldn't care this much. I shouldn't be this *bothered*. But the truth is, deep down, I've been waiting on Ace Kelly for most of my life. I'm always the girl on his sidelines, forever waiting for him to notice me enough to put me first.

I'm tired of being the girl waiting around to be his *only* girl.

Point-blank, I'm tired of waiting.

I dig in my purse to find my phone, the ache of my bruised ego pulsing with unintentional reprisal. I scroll to Drew's name, eager to make myself feel better any way I can, but before I can even start to type, a new message buzzes inside the thread.

> *Drew: Julia, I miss seeing you and doing things with you. I just miss you. I feel like you're done with me, but I'm hoping that maybe you've just been so busy with school and shit… Tell me the truth, babe, have you moved on? Or do I still stand a chance?*

Normally, Drew attends Double C events, but I guess he's missing it tonight. A few weeks ago, I probably would've known why, but I've slowly distanced myself from him. *Because of Ace.*

Maybe this message coming right now is a sign. Maybe it's a chance to rework my choices and start fresh.

Drew has been trying. Really freaking trying. And I've left him hanging out in the wind. *All because you've spent too much time focused on Ace and what Ace wants and needs. All because you've been secretly hoping that Ace wants to be more than friends with you.*

I stare at the message, thumb hovering, heart and mind racing. But eventually, I make a decision.

> *Me: I miss you too. And I'm sorry if it's felt like that, Drew. I'm so sorry. Things have been crazy lately, but it's all starting to wind down.*

> *Drew: So…does this mean you're open to going on a date with me soon?*

> *Me: Yes. Let's do it.*

It's high time for me to stop waiting around.

37

If campus handed out crowns, mine would be gold, glowing, and studded with fucking diamonds.

Only a week has passed since I officially became Double C's newest prez, but it's safe to say, after tonight's event, I'm fucking crushing it.

Surely that's not a shock to anyone. I mean, this is me we're talking about. Ace motherfucking Kelly. My legacy speaks for itself.

The fountain water is still drying off my shoes after the big "death scene," and I've already been pulled into seven group photos, handed three beers, and been told I'm the best Double C president since the underground poker scandal of 2016. Which, honestly, I've heard rumors about that Double C era, and whoever was running shit back then had some serious range.

Prodigy or not, though, 2016's motherfucker is no match for me.

Tonight's Double C event was flawless. Our "Dead Man Walking" event turned into full-campus chaos in the best way. It was a murder mystery that spanned three buildings, two frat houses, and a suspiciously well-dressed janitor. And the ending? *Bro.* If Epic and Dramatic and Mind-Blowing had a polyamorous relationship that ended in a baby boy named Awesome who grows a goatee and muscles by their first birthday, that still wouldn't equate to what I pulled off tonight.

While everyone was scouring campus trying to figure out who

was the killer on the loose and who was the target, I got fake-stabbed on the quad lawn. My death was sudden but dramatic, fake blood spurting everywhere, and I fell into the fountain like a champ.

Honestly, if a Hollywood director would've seen that performance, I'd already have a free, first-class flight to LA.

Needless to say, shit popped off. And because I refuse to leave any party-stone unturned, now we're balls deep in the first official Double C after party.

Which is new. No other Double C president thought to cap an event with an actual after party.

But this, this is where the magic happens.

The lights are low, the basement is packed, music's good, and everyone's feeling high off the rush of the night.

You're a fucking god among men. I mentally pat myself on the back when I see how many Double C members are enjoying themselves. I've been plotting and scheming all week for this shit. It's not easy planning a secret society event without letting any secrets out of the bag or making university staff suspicious.

Hosting an after party inside the basement of the math building without any professors finding out? It's fucking diabolical. But thankfully, all my borderline-illegal hard work has paid off, and no one with the power to expel me from Dickson for good is any the wiser.

I may have had to skip several classes and slack on some of my coursework, but obviously, it's all been worth it. Plus, I'm sure beautiful tutor Julia will be kind enough to help me catch up. One week of slacking isn't going to erase all the hard work I did the first month of school.

Speaking of my favorite girl, now that the event is over and the after party is in full, successful swing, it's time to get shit back on track. My big plan to find the perfect moment—sans accidental poisoning this time—to tell Julia I'm in love with her had to be put on the back burner temporarily so I could get my presidential feet under me, but after tonight's success, I think it's safe to say I can realign my focus. And frankly, I'm such a natural talent at this shit, she's probably spent the week being impressed anyway.

I haven't seen her much since we've been like two ships passing in the night—me with wrangling volunteers in secret locations and figuring out how to stage death scenes and her with study groups, lunch with Scottie or Kayla, and some TA thing she's helping Scottie with that's focused on students with disabilities on campus. I'm pretty sure at one point, she even had to run home to Jersey to do a family dinner or something.

It's been *busy*. But I'm so fucking ready to see her I can hardly stand myself.

I move through the party, eyes focused on finding Julia within the crowd. A few girls try to chat me up, one chick in a pink dress that shows a lot of leg even wraps her arm around my shoulders, but I politely disengage and stay on task.

Sure, Ace Kelly is a lover of beautiful women. But Ace Kelly only wants to love *one* woman, so if your name isn't Julia Brooks, you might as well be as dead to me as I was in the fountain a couple hours ago.

I spot her eventually, near a kegerator, her pretty face scrunched up in hilarity as she laughs about something in that adorable way of hers. By default, I look for Scottie or Finn or Blake or Kayla, expecting them to be the reason for her joy, but instead, I find that douche Drewbacca standing close and moving some errant hair out of her eyes.

You've gotta be fucking kidding me.

I thought she was done with this guy. I mean, it's been weeks since she's mentioned him at all, and suddenly they're all cozy at my fucking party? Pfft.

Whatever. I've had to deal with his lame ass before, and whatshisface is boring anyway. He's predictable. He's clearly not the kind of man Julia Brooks falls in love with.

They're talking and laughing, and even though I want to barge in between and shove the bastard out of here and onto the third rail of the closest subway stop, I decide to be a gentleman and pause my steps. I don't need to interrupt. He'll time himself out soon.

And then, I'll step in and find a way to get my girl alone, away from the crowd and the noise.

I tuck behind a corner of the wall, leaning into the plaster and checking my fingernails for dried fake blood. I scrubbed hard, but that shit is invasive.

Peering around the corner, I look back to Julia and Boring Bozo, expecting them to be wrapping shit up any minute, but if anything, they seem to be standing even closer than before.

Her smile is still firmly in place, and his grubby fingers are dancing all over her hip now. I frown and shove away from the wall.

Drew finally pulls back a little, but instead of stepping away, he turns toward the crowd around them, his voice loud enough to cut through the music.

"Julia," he says, and he has this stupid half grin on his face. "I wasn't planning to do this in front of, like, half the university, but here we are."

They have the attention of more than me now, and the chill that runs down my spine is more reminiscent of December than September.

"What are you doing?" she asks. Her voice is much softer, and I don't miss the way her teeth dig into her bottom lip because she's feeling awkward, but she's still smiling—which isn't a surprise since she's too nice to be anything but a good sport.

I'm about two seconds away from stepping in and saving her when Doucheburger picks back up on his spiel.

"Julia Brooks, we've been out four times this week." Drew holds up his fingers as he counts. "Tuesday, dinner. Wednesday, trivia. Thursday, that family party at your parents' house. And tonight. That's four dates. And I think if we combine those four really fantastic dates with all the fun and amazing times we had together this summer, it feels like it's time for us to call this what it is, you know?"

They've been on four fucking dates this week? And he went to the Brookses' house? When did this fucking happen?

"Drew?" Julia's smile is timid but unmistakably charmed. I know because it's normally the one she points at me. "I don't know what you're asking me."

Drew takes her hand. "Julia Brooks, will you be my girlfriend?"

I'm sorry…what?

The air shifts, but I force myself to wait. Obviously, she's going to say no, right? I mean, why the fuck would she want to be that schmuck's girlfriend?

Julia hesitates for a second. But then, she nods. It's soft, it's small, but it's there. And when she says, "Yes," I have to look down at my chest to make sure someone didn't fucking stab me.

The small crowd around them erupts in cheers and awws and claps and whistles, and Drew's smile looks like a winning fucking lottery ticket. Overjoyed, he wraps his arm around my girl like it's the most natural thing in the world and kisses her right there for everyone to see.

My girl? Pretty sure she's Drew's girl now.

Suddenly, the party's too loud, too bright, too hot.

Fuck me. I want to rip Drew's arm right off his fucking shoulder. I want to step in between them. I want to flip tables and cause a fucking scene. I want to do a lot of things, but not a single one of them feels sane or safe.

I see Finn and Scottie and Blake on the other side of the room, taking notice of the group that's around Julia and her new fucking stupid dickhead asswipe boyfriend.

Before they can see me, I duck back through the crowd. I keep my eyes to the floor and try to avoid talking to anyone. Someone tries to high-five me, and I miss their hand completely. I hear a girl call my name, but I don't turn around.

Right before I make it outside, someone claps me on the shoulder and says, "Legendary night, Prez."

I smile without conviction.

When the still-warm night air smacks me in the face, I suck in a breath that doesn't help at all.

Tonight, I was supposed to tell Julia I'm in love with her. I was supposed to find the perfect moment to finally put my heart on the line and tell her how I feel.

I planned to die in the quad and get resurrected, but I didn't expect to be murdered at the after party.

Julia and Drew are official, leaving me with nothing but false hope and my dick in my hands.

So much for the plan. I was wrong.

Apparently, one week was absolutely enough to wreck it all.

Ace

I don't remember leaving the after party.

One second, I was inside, living it up and soaking in praise like it meant something. And the next, I was walking home, every footstep echoing louder than the last while my mind raced with the reality that Julia said yes to Drew's stupid fucking question.

"Will you be my girlfriend, Julia?" What a douche. What an idiot.

But she said yes…

She said yes. She wants to be Drew's girl.

Which is a total fucking mindfuck because she's my girl, right?

Wrong, buddy. Clearly, she's not your girl.

It wasn't supposed to go like this. I was supposed to find the perfect moment tonight to tell her that I'm in love with her. Instead, I stood in the middle of my own after party while someone else made Julia his girlfriend.

I didn't even get to say hi to her tonight.

I close my apartment door behind me and immediately regret how loud it slams.

But the silence after is worse.

I walk to the kitchen and open the fridge. Close it two seconds later without grabbing anything. I turn on a lamp and turn it back off. Fold the blanket on my couch and then scramble it like I'm Gordon fucking Ramsay.

None of it leads anywhere, and more than that, none of it helps.

I start fucking pacing. Back and forth across the same stretch of hardwood floor, like if I walk it enough times, it'll turn into a path that leads to a version of tonight where none of this happened.

I should let it go. I should sleep it off.

But instead, I stop by the front door and listen.

It's stupid. I know it's stupid. But her apartment's right across the hall, and some part of me—the part that hasn't caught up to what just happened—wants to know if she's home. If she's alone.

If she noticed I left the party and came to find me.

I wait and I wait and I wait. Before I know it, I've managed to shower, change my clothes, and pace my hardwood floor another fifty times while listening for any signs of Julia coming home.

But then, I hear it. The sounds of footsteps and keys and a soft laugh that I know better than my fucking own.

Stomach churning, I push my ear to the door, trying to listen harder.

Julia's voice is low and easy and so fucking sharp inside me I can feel the score. "Thanks for walking me back."

Drew's voice is a lot of shit, but mostly, it's closer than I want it to be. "Of course. Tonight was…yeah. It was perfect."

A beat of silence.

Then Julia says, "Good night."

I look through the peephole before I can talk myself out of it. Julia is standing there, and so is that asshat Drew. They're facing each other, smiling, eyes locked. And then, he leans forward and kisses her.

It's soft and quick, but adjectives don't matter when it's a fucking kiss that shouldn't be happening at all.

He says something I can't hear and walks off down the hallway, and Julia watches him go like she used to watch me.

I try to get a read on her face, try to figure out if she's happy. But this fucking peephole is so goddamn small it makes it hard to make out much of anything, and when she turns and walks inside her apartment, I can't make out anything at all.

Not her face. Not my feelings. Not any sense of this giant fucking mess.

Before I know it, I'm opening my door and walking across the hall.

I knock twice and wait with raging energy while she comes to the door.

As she opens it, surprise is written all over her face. "Ace?"

For as determined as I was to come over here, my words fail to do the same. I don't answer. I can't. My heart pounds so loudly I can hear it in my ears.

Effectively mute, all I can do is step inside.

Julia blinks. "Um…hi?"

I shut the door behind me.

She's changed out of her miniskirt and tank top combo that she had on at the party and is now wearing a faded Dickson sweatshirt that used to be mine instead. The one she claimed last year and refused to give back. Her hair's loose and her feet bare, and her perfect legs are covered by her favorite pair of sleep shorts that have girlie fucking pink bows on them.

She looks like home and heartbreak and everything I'm trying not to feel, and my limbs are suddenly fifteen-thousand pounds. I get it, Eminem. My arms are also so, so heavy.

Fuck.

"You have a new boyfriend." My words come back with rage.

Her head jerks back in surprise. "Excuse me?"

"Drew." My jaw ticks. "He's your boyfriend now."

"Yeah, he is." Her voice is soft but weighty, measured—filled with more than excitement and wonder, as I would expect. It's almost…*vengeful.* It challenges me in a way I don't understand and makes me angry at the same time.

I stalk toward her.

"What are you—"

And then—

I kiss her. I kiss her because I don't want anyone else kissing her.

I kiss her because I want to erase the fucking kiss I saw that douchebag give her from her mouth and memory.

I kiss her because I'm angry and jealous and so far deep in fucking love with her that I can't *not* kiss her right now.

My hands are on her waist and her breath catches, but then, she's kissing me right back.

Our lips and tongues dance against each other in ways I've only been able to feel in my dreams before this, and it's as if everything I've been holding in—every look, every almost, every second of waiting—ignites all at once.

The kiss is not careful. And it's not tentative. It's a *crash*. A detonation. I swear, sparks and stars and gravity and the whole fucking earth shift under my feet.

A little moan escapes her lips and her fingers curl into my T-shirt and my heart slams against my ribs.

I don't even know if I'm breathing. But I know she's kissing me back.

And I know I'm not letting go.

39

Julia

I hardly remember opening the door. I barely remember confirming my newly coupled status.

But I know with my entire being that Ace Kelly is *kissing* me.

And I'm kissing him back.

It's not gentle. It's not sweet. It feels like years of tension exploding all at once. It feels like we've both been holding our breath and this is the moment we finally let go.

His hands are on my waist, then in my hair, then sliding across my back like he can't decide where to touch me first, only that he *has to* touch me. And I can't stop touching him either—his shoulders, his jaw, the collar of his T-shirt that still smells like laundry detergent and some scent that's just Ace.

I feel like I'm on fire—like if I stop kissing him, I'll never breathe right again.

His hands are on my hips, and before I know it, my legs are wrapped around his waist and his big hands are cupping my ass and my back is pressed against the wall of my living room. And we keep kissing, our tongues dancing and our mouths crashing together like magnets.

A throb starts between my thighs, and I press myself tighter against him as soft moans escape my lungs. Ace is big and hard beneath his sweatpants. I can *feel* it. I can feel his arousal pressing directly against my core. My eyes roll back a little as he continues to kiss me, and his lips paint a trail across my jaw and down my throat.

I whimper, and when I press myself tighter against him, he squeezes my ass with his big hands and lets out a throaty groan. *"Fuck, Julia."*

I feel half dazed, half drugged, half in fucking fantasyland when he finally breaks the kiss enough to rest his forehead against mine. We're both breathing heavily, and his warm breath fans across my face.

"I'm in love with you," he whispers. "I'm so in love with you, Julia, that for the past few months I've been doing insane shit. I started a fire in my apartment so I could move in with you. I enrolled myself in all your classes. I broke your AC unit. I—"

"What?"

"I said, I love you, Julia. I'm *in love* with you," he says, but his voice is a little louder this time. "Break up with Drew," he adds. "Break up with him and be with me. I love you."

My entire body goes still, overloaded with too much to process at once.

"You...*did what?*" My voice comes out raw and confused, and my lips, as if taunting, still tingle. "You *started* the fire on purpose? You *broke* my AC?"

"Yes. And it's all because I love you, Lia," he says, eyes burning into mine. "I'm in love with you, and I want to be with you. I don't want you to be with anyone else."

My mind swims with the reality that Ace Kelly is saying words I've secretly always wanted him to say, at the least convenient time for him to say them. He waited. He taunted. He pushed me away.

But now...now that I'm taken, he suddenly has to have me?

I'm with Drew now. He makes me smile and laugh, and I never feel like I'm waiting on the sidelines for him. If anything, all summer long, Drew was waiting on the sidelines for me. Sure, we're new in our relationship, but we're still in a relationship. Tonight, I agreed to be his girlfriend. I agreed to be together. And what I just did— kissing Ace—is wrong on so many levels.

My chest tightens. Ace's lips on mine. The confession. The

secrets he's kept from me. The insane things he evidently did to insert himself into my life without my knowing. The *timing*.

The euphoria of our kiss is gone, and in its wake? Dystopia.

"Ace, this is bad," I mutter and step back, putting some space between us. "I have a *boyfriend*. Why are you doing this? Why *now*? Why have you been lying to me and doing all this crazy shit? If you started fucking fires, what else have you done? What else have you lied to me about?" I question, and Yoko bounds out of my bedroom, sleepy eyes and his hair all messed up. He walks straight over to my feet and lies down, reading my inability to give pets right now with a keenness Ace is lacking. "Do not tell me your lies also played a part in finding Yoko at Central Park," I say through gritted teeth. "Do not even tell me I've been sitting here thinking it was fate that he ran over to me, but it wasn't fate at all…"

He grimaces. "Julia, everything I did was because I love you."

"God, Ace! I feel so…manipulated. I feel so…violated. I feel so—"

"Violated? Manipulated?" His brows pull together. "Julia, come on. This is *me* we're talking about. All I want to do is protect you, respect you, love you."

"All these years, I've sat back," I say, heat building in my throat. "I've watched you date a million fucking girls. And now that I'm with someone—now that I'm *happy* with someone—you suddenly decide you want to be with me? You suddenly decide to take over my freaking life by straight up lying to me because you don't want me to be with anyone else? I can't believe it, and yet, I can. You *never* liked letting anyone else play with your toys."

"It's not like that. I love you, Jules. I fucking love you." He shakes his head and pushes toward me, but I hold him back with a straight arm.

"Are you seriously mad right now? That I love *you*?"

"Of course I'm mad at you!" I exclaim. "Not only have you lied to me and done some seriously insane things, but you also just kissed me, knowing full well I'm with Drew!"

"But you kissed me back."

"I know, Ace! Trust me, I know!" I shout. "Because, apparently, when it comes to you, I'm a little too desperate for your scraps."

"My scraps? What the fuck is that supposed to mean?" he questions and his jaw clenches. "Are you fucking kidding me, Julia? You're my best friend. You're my world. Everything in my life revolves around you."

"Are you sure about that?" I toss back. "I mean, come on, Ace. Really think about it. Really think about all the moments when I've been the girl on the side when it comes to you. Do you even realize how many moments that is? Do you even realize that for years I've barely dated anyone, while you've dated pretty much anything with tits and legs?" My hands flop out in front of me as the truth unfurls. "Because that's my reality, Ace. So, I'm sorry, but you don't get to do crazy shit to manipulate me into being closer to you because you saw me dating some other guy and *decide* now's the moment for you to *really* see me."

"Julia." He takes a step toward me. "I *do* see you. I've always seen you."

"No, Ace. You don't. You haven't." My voice breaks, and I hate it. "When I finally let it go—finally let go of the insane idea that you'd ever want me to be more than your best friend—*now* you want me?"

"Julia, I don't just want you. I fucking love you," he says, voice steady in a way that makes my chest ache. "I'm in love with you."

My heart splinters, but I know, I have to take the hammer to it once and for all.

"Are you, though?" I whisper. "Are you really in love with *me*… or are you in love with the idea of always having me on the side, waiting around for you?"

40

"You think I'm…" I have to pause and swallow hard against the bile because that question hits harder than anything anyone's ever said to me. "You think I'm just keeping you around for backup?"

Worse than getting dumped. Worse than losing a game. Worse than watching her kiss Drew.

Julia's question burns and consumes like lava because it's *her* saying it *to me*. It's her erasing my picture of reality for the last two decades and replacing it with doubt, hurt, and misunderstanding. It's her shattering the foundation of who I thought I was and replacing it with the worst version I can imagine.

I stare at her, stunned, grasping for the version of her that doesn't think I'm full of shit.

But she doesn't take it back. Instead, she crosses her arms over her chest like she's holding herself together. "You have a pattern, Ace."

"A pattern?"

She lifts her chin. "You date. You flirt. You play. You keep girls at arm's length and me in your back pocket. That's always been your thing."

"That's not fair," I refute. "You're my best friend, Julia. You've been my best friend my whole life. I wasn't keeping you in my pocket. I wasn't doing anything but wanting to be around you. And for the longest time, I thought it was because of our friendship, but I know it's because of more than that. It's because I have feelings for you. Deep, all-consuming fucking feelings." I take a step toward her. "You act like I've never cared about you. Like you weren't the one person who—"

"But you didn't care like *this*, Ace. Not until someone else did."

"This has nothing to do with that guy, Julia." I run a frustrated hand through my hair. My heart is pounding so hard I can feel the buzz in my ears. "I didn't plan this. I didn't wake up and decide to blow up your life."

"Then why are you doing it?"

"Because I'm in *love* with you."

She laughs—one bitter, breathless sound that hits harder than any slap. "You say that like it fixes everything."

"It's not supposed to fix anything," I shoot back. "It's just the truth."

Her arms tighten across her chest as she scoffs. "You know what's really messed up? You think this is some big, romantic gesture. You barging in here. Kissing me. Telling me you love me like it's a movie climax. You think it's *good*."

I blink. "It's not a movie."

"No," she says coldly. "It's real life. And in real life, you don't wait until I finally feel like I'm *enough* for someone else to decide I'm enough for you too."

I was wrong. That's the one. *That's* the line that will forever haunt me as the worst there's ever been. I have to take one step back to get a grip on my equilibrium.

And once I'm in motion, my heart stumbling to find the kinetic energy to keep pumping, I don't stop until my back bumps into the door.

She doesn't move to make me stop either. Hell, even Yoko doesn't get up from his perch by her feet.

"I don't even know what to say," I whisper, holding her sad eyes as intently as she'll allow. "I don't know how this got so fucking twisted. I don't understand how you can't see that what I feel for you is real, Julia. Sure, it might've taken me a while to realize that, but what I'm telling you isn't bullshit. It's fact."

"Remember the homecoming dance our freshman year?" she tosses out. "Remember how you were dating Tiffany, and I ended up going with Braden? I didn't really like Braden, but he was your friend and you were my best friend, and even though you were taking Tiffany, I decided I'd rather be with you not without you that night."

I start to open my mouth, but she cuts me off.

"What about prom our junior year?" she asks. "You were dating Kya Parker, and I ended up going to the dance with your buddy Sam Houston. I didn't really like Sam. I mean, he was nice, but I wasn't into him. I decided that I wanted to make sure I was able to hang out with you that night, so yeah. I went with Sam. Oh, and let's not forget senior homecoming and prom. You were on and off with Lydia Bukowski. Both dances, we were supposed to go together, but then you and Lydia got back together, and you took her. And who the fuck cares about who I went with, because *you know* we don't talk about him or what a shitshow that was that it probably only happened because I was so heartbroken over you and Lydia." She laughs, but it's not out of humor, and I'm also not finding any of it funny either. There's nothing humorous about her losing her virginity to some loser or the fact that she thinks my actions played a part in that decision.

"The whole point is that I've been your backup plan, Ace. Whether you want to face that reality or not. And now that I'm dating someone—*actually* dating someone—you, all of a sudden, decide that you want to be with me? That you're in love with me? And I'm supposed to just believe it? I'm supposed to tell Drew to fuck off and be with you? Is that what you expected?"

"I didn't expect anything, Julia." I shake my head and stare at the floor for a long moment before I lift my gaze to hers again, the deep pain of being the root of her life's evil shaking me exponentially. "I didn't expect anything, and I guess that's good because you've clearly decided you're better off without me."

She doesn't say anything.

On the inside, a battle is raging in my body. My heart is telling me to fight for her. To do everything I can to make her realize that we belong together. To get on my fucking hands and knees and beg her to open her eyes to see how perfect we are for each other. But there's another part of me, the one that's not used to being rejected—the one that's scared I've had this coming for a really long time—that thinks I should go.

"Good night, Julia," I say quietly, and this time, I mean it.

I don't slam the door when I leave. I don't throw anything. I don't scream.

I just go.

Back in my apartment, I sit on the edge of the couch, elbows on my knees, heart still racing a hundred miles a minute.

Fifteen minutes. That's our rule. Fifteen minutes to be mad, and then we fix it.

I check the time.

2:00 a.m.

I stare at the door.

2:10 a.m.

2:15 a.m.

I don't move. I can't move.

2:16 a.m.

2:17 a.m.

2:20 a.m.

2:32 a.m.

And for the first time in our entire lives, fifteen minutes come and go, and there's no happy makeup. No apology. No...anything.

Tonight, both of us know fifteen minutes won't make it better.

41

Sunday, September 14th

Julia

Seventeen hours and forty-two minutes.

That's how much time has passed since Ace left my apartment after kissing me and confessing to a laundry list of manipulative moves over the last few months, and I feel an emptiness in the space right beside my heart where I usually keep our friendship like you wouldn't believe.

I'm cold to my bones and shriveled where I used to bloom. Betrayal lingers at the edge of all our sweet memories, and a new fear, rooted in how cavalierly he lied to me, sinks claws into my innocence.

Ace has always been a pillar of trust for me, and with all his omissions and illusions, that strong foundation crumbled into a pile of rubble.

And now, it's been seventeen hours and forty-three minutes since he walked out my apartment door, and I'm fighting every naïve part of myself to keep my backbone from bending.

I love him. But I don't deserve to be anything but first in line.

I woke up this morning to several soft knocks on my door and Yoko barking because of them. Drew, smiling and holding up coffees and a bag of muffins, was on the other side.

I told myself not to be disappointed.

I'm still working on following the order.

I sit on the couch in my apartment and try to swallow a bite of blueberry muffin while Drew tells me a story about his childhood dog Betsy. His expression is soft. His hand is warm on my knee. He's everything I should want, and my mind knows it.

My heart is just a little bit behind.

But I nod at the right places. I even smile when I'm supposed to. I am fake-it-till-you-make-it live and in color. Yoko, the adorable traitor, decided it was too early to be up and went back to my bed to sleep it off, so it's just the two of us, and the newness of our relationship is helping me pull it off.

Seventeen hours and forty-six minutes now. And yet, there's no knock on my door. There's no text. No paper airplane through the window with *"I miss you"* written in Ace's scratchy handwriting.

Fifteen minutes. That's our rule. We fight. We stew. We cool off. But fifteen minutes later, we're back. One of us shows up. We say we're sorry. We fix it.

I glance at my phone again, not because I expect anything—but because I can't help it. I am programmed to beg for Ace's leftovers.

Drew notices. "Everything okay?"

"Yeah." I force a smile and pointedly set my phone down. "Just a group chat blowing up."

He leans in and presses a kiss to my cheek. "You're quiet this morning, babe. Maybe I should've let you sleep in."

"It's no big deal. I was basically tossing and turning all night anyway. Pretty sure getting up and getting moving was a good thing." Which is true. I slept like garbage. I dreamed of nothing, and I woke up feeling heavy, like I was drowning with my shoes on.

Drew gets up and brings me one of the coffees he picked up at Brower on his way here this morning and sets it in front of me. "Hazelnut, right?"

"Yeah." I nod. "Thanks."

He's good. Thoughtful. The kind of guy who remembers what you order and pulls out your chair and probably sends flowers on random Tuesdays.

And still, my chest aches.

Because Ace looked at me like I'd broken something he didn't know how to fix last night, and I fear his look is right. You can't lie to someone over and over and not expect consequences. And I can't disrespect myself so much I lie down and take it.

Last night, I lay in bed for hours replaying everything, hoping to find a sliver of regret. Something I could be the one to apologize for—something to build a ladder out of this hole.

But I don't have regrets; I spoke my truth. I've been waiting on Ace's sidelines for years. And even though I've always told myself we were just best friends, there's always been a part of me that's wanted more.

Looking back on it, I barely dated anyone in high school because of that. But Ace? He dated *everyone*. And I had to sit back and watch the cycle play out.

I guess it could be said that I helped create this situation by keeping my feelings to myself, but I didn't want to push him away. Selfishly, I wanted his attention however I could get it. I know that wasn't fair of me, but I can't go back and change the past. I can only move forward. And no matter how badly my heart aches over the idea of Ace not being around, I simply can't bring myself to implode my life all because Ace Kelly has decided for the moment that he wants to be with me.

His attention span is short when it comes to girls. He's a love-'em-and-leave-'em type. And what kind of emotional state would I be in if I let myself experience being in his rotation? One month of happy bliss for years and years of heartache?

I guess either way we'll never be the same. Not after this.

I swallow hard against a throat clogged with emotion and force myself to focus on Drew. I'm still warring with myself over telling him that I kissed Ace last night because I know it's the moral high road, but I know beyond a shadow of a doubt I'm too emotionally inebriated to drive it right now.

Maybe in a few days or weeks, it'll feel easier to navigate.

And I know that's wrong, but I've spent a lot of years putting myself last, and today, I can't do it.

"Did you have any pets before Yoko?" Drew asks, and I make a concerted effort to be present in the conversation.

"I did," I say with a little smile as I recall childhood memories of our Great Dane Stan and our cat Walter. "It's actually a funny story."

"I'm all ears."

"When my mom started dating my dad, he had a cat named Walter," I tell him. "And Walter pretty much hated my dad, but he loved my mom. And after they got married, while they were on their honeymoon, their best friends Thatch and Cassie were in charge of watching Walter."

"Wait…Thatch and Cassie…that's Ace's parents, right?"

Goodness. All of my roads really do lead back to Ace.

"Mm-hmm," I mutter and clear my throat.

"And what happened?"

"Well, Walter escaped their apartment—it's still unknown whose fault it was, but he ended up lost in the city, and ultimately, animal control got ahold of him and brought him to a local shelter," I explain. "Walter, being the grumpy cat that he is, gave the staff a hell of a time. But eventually, he set his sights on this Great Dane puppy that was in a kennel there. The rest is pretty much history. Walter and Stan fell in love, and when my parents got back from their honeymoon and went to pick up Walter, they ended up coming home with a new puppy named Stan."

Drew grins. "That story is so wild it almost sounds made-up."

"Yeah, well, Ace's parents were involved," I explain and hate that my chest spasms at the mere mention of his name. "Both Stan and Walter were around for most of my early childhood. And man, Stan was protective of both me and my sister Evie. And since Walter only cared about whatever Stan cared about, he was protective of us too."

Memories of Stan and Walter play behind my eyes like a movie, and I don't miss the fact that nearly every damn memory I have of them includes Ace.

"What do you want to do today?" Drew asks and I shrug.

I want to curl up in the fetal position in my bed and try to wake up again in a universe where Ace and I are still on speaking terms, but I don't think that's on the menu.

"You want to take these coffees to go?" he asks. "Take a little walk around campus and see if we can get into anything?"

"Sure," I say and rise to my feet. "Let me brush my hair real quick."

I head into my bathroom, but before I pick up my brush, my phone buzzes on the countertop. Of course, I grab it fast, heart already racing before I read the screen.

Instagram: Ace Kelly posted for the first time in a while.

I tap it without thinking, which takes me directly to his latest post.

It's a photo of the campus fountain—the same one he "died" in for the Double C event last night. It's blurry, taken at night, the water catching light in this weird, moody way. The caption is short: "Reincarnation is a myth."

That's it. That's all he wrote. But it feels like a scream from the universe that life, post-Ace-and-Julia-blowup, is really moving on.

My throat tightens, and I set the phone facedown, pressing my hands to my eyes.

Last night, I had a best friend named Ace. But today, he might as well be a stranger.

42

At the start of this semester, I looked forward to Mondays. The start of a new week where I was putting my big "make Julia fall in love with me" plan into action.

I rearranged *everything* at the beginning of this year to be as close to her as I could get.

And it was worth it back then. You know, when Julia smiled when she sat next to me and wore my hoodie to class like it was no big deal. When she shared her notes with me and studied with me because I am in no way smart enough to be in any of these fucking classes.

But that was back then—when Julia felt like she was mine.

Mondays now feel like sentencing day for a cruel and unusual punishment—class, with her not speaking to me, all day, every day, all week long. If there were a judge to beg, I'd be asking for a stint in maximum security instead.

I head toward my third class of the day, my feet dragging as I pass people I know. They wave and smile and try to stop me to chat, but I do my best to keep moving because it was hard enough to get myself out of bed today. Small talk and shit isn't something I can sit through.

I've already skipped my first two classes, was tempted to skip all my fucking classes, but Double C already has me behind on so much coursework, I forced myself to get it together today.

I walk into the lecture hall for English 111—an advanced

literary study course that, judging by my use of grammar on a daily basis, I should be banned from ever taking. Of course, I spot Julia instantly. She's sitting in the front row, and right beside her is her stupid fucking boyfriend, Drew. Normally, I'd be the one in the seat beside hers but not today. *Not anymore.* Now she's chummy with Drewchebag, smiling at something he's saying, and sitting there like this is any other day.

It's not. At least, not for me. It's been over twenty-four hours since I told Julia I'm in love with her and she all but stomped on my fucking heart.

It's as if the last few months never even happened.

It's as if all the time and effort I put into my big plan to make her fall in love with me vanished into her boyfriend's fucking bushy eyebrows.

Does he know we kissed the other night?

Does he know I told her I'm in love with her?

Does he know he doesn't fucking deserve her?

Does Yoko think he's his new dad because he's been at Julia's apartment and not me?

Fuck me.

So many questions that I don't have the answers to. But it's hard to get answers when the one person who can give them to you isn't talking to you. Though, I guess I'm not talking to her either.

I'm too busy living an emotional loop of her calling me manipulative and violating. I'm too busy coming out of my fucking skin.

I take the farthest seat in the room, behind some guy with a neck tattoo and a laptop covered in band stickers. Though, I don't bother pulling mine out. I don't think I could focus enough to type my own name, let alone take notes.

I almost forget that this is the one and only class I have with Scottie and Finn until they slide into the lecture hall a few minutes later, mid-conversation, and half-eaten bagels from the dining hall poised in Scottie's lap. Finn pushes Scottie's wheelchair to the row

I'm in and sits beside me, totally oblivious to the fact that I'm currently trying not to drown in my own chest.

"Did you read the article he assigned?" Scottie whispers around a mouthful of bagel and cream cheese.

"Hell no," Finn says and Scottie laughs.

"Finn!" she whisper-yells and slaps him on the shoulder. "What are you going to do?"

"Well, babe, I guess I'm going to wing the whole discussion with confidence and a smile."

Scottie rolls her eyes and looks over at me. "What about you, Ace?"

I blink. "What?"

"Did you read it?"

I stare down at my empty desk. "No. I didn't."

Finn narrows his eyes, studying me for a second too long. "You good, man?"

"Yeah," I lie. "Just didn't sleep much."

That part's true. I spent most of the night staring at the ceiling, checking my phone every ten minutes like maybe Julia would cave. Like maybe the fifteen-minute rule wasn't completely dead.

Spoiler: It is. *Over twenty-four hours have passed.*

Professor Dudley walks into class, drops his briefcase down onto his desk, and immediately starts talking about narrative dissonance and voice tension—ironically appropriate, considering how tense my chest feels.

I try to focus. I try to care. But every time Julia shifts in her seat or pushes her hair behind her ear or Drew smiles in her direction, it's like a knife under my skin.

Scottie and Finn crack quiet jokes throughout the whole damn lecture. And normally, I'd be all into that game, but I hardly even hear what they're saying.

After class, I pack up slowly. Julia and Drew are standing up near their seats, and he's talking with his hands and leaning in like he's performing, and she's smiling up at him like she wants to hear it.

Then he does it. He reaches out and brushes a piece of hair behind her ear. The move. The soft one. The kind of thing I've done a thousand times without even thinking.

Something in my chest fractures.

I walk toward the door without saying a word.

Scottie and Finn catch up to me as we head out of the building.

"Wanna grab lunch with us, Ace?" Scottie asks. "Taco bar at Brower. Finn's convinced they secretly use expired meat, and I want to test that theory with my life. Trav and Jack and Reece are supposed to meet us there too."

"I can't," I mutter. "I gotta go meet with my counselor."

"What? Why?" Scottie frowns.

Finn looks at me in the way he does. The one where he's trying to see inside my fucking skull because he knows something's up.

"It's no big deal." I shake my head and start walking faster. "Just thinking about changing some classes. Don't worry about it."

Neither of them says anything, but I can feel Finn watching me like he already knows more than he should. I'm not surprised. It's fucking hard hiding the fact that someone's ripped open my chest and is currently feasting on the carnage.

Especially since this is the first time in my life I've ever felt this way. Before now, no matter what else was happening, I had Julia.

Now. I have nothing at all.

Wednesday, September 17th
Julia

Ace walks into Calc 2 two minutes late, but basically right on time because Professor Emmsy is conveniently MIA. Of course, I see Ace the second he steps through the door—even though I'm pretending to listen to Drew tell me about the big tailgate plans for the Dickson game this weekend—because despite my best intentions, I'm not even close to over the nuclear fallout with my lifelong best friend.

My stomach flips and my pulse jumps, and I force myself to look away when Ace doesn't glance in my direction before he slumps into a seat in the back row like it physically hurts him to be upright.

Drew managed to get the girl who was sitting to the right of me to switch with him yesterday morning by bribing her with donut holes, but the seat to the left of mine is technically Ace's via Professor Emmsy's beginning of the semester assignments and, thus, remains poignantly empty.

It feels like a boulder is stuck inside my throat, and I swallow hard against it. The urge to cry is so strong that I have to shut my eyes briefly to keep the tears at bay. I do not want to be emotional right now. Actually, I refuse to be emotional right now. I'm in the middle of class, for goodness' sake. Now isn't the time to start sobbing in front of everyone, most of all Drew, who's been nothing but kind and understanding as I work through the turmoil of having an ex-best friend.

I still haven't gone into the details with him about what

happened with Ace, and even if it's selfish, I don't know that I ever will.

The wound full of questions I can't answer is too deep.

Is it really done? Our friendship? Our bond? Are we really no longer Ace and Julia but strangers who used to be best friends?

Instead, I made up a dumb lie about us being in a fight over something Ace's dad did to my dad.

Drew says something about the guest speaker our professor invited to class next week, and I nod like I'm listening even though I'm not. My brain never stops racing, no matter how tired I get, prepped, I imagine, by a lifetime of exposure to Ace's charisma.

Discreetly, I glance over my shoulder to check…something.

Ace is staring at the floor like it has personally wronged him. His shoulders are tense, his jaw tight, and his desk is completely clear of a notebook or pen or laptop.

He used to draw stupid stick figure comics in the margins of his notes and then pass them to me with captions like *"this is you falling asleep in class, but sexy."*

Now, he won't even pass me a glance.

I shift in my seat, and Drew's knee touches mine. I don't pull away, but I don't lean into it either.

Instantly, I wonder if Ace notices. *God, I hope he doesn't. But also, I hope he does.*

Hell, I don't know what I want. I only know this hurts.

I click my pen just to do something, but when that's not enough of a distraction, I check my phone. I hate that there's a huge part of me that hopes to find something from Ace, but there isn't anything. No texts or calls or emails. *Nothing.*

I look back again, and Ace is rubbing the space between his eyes like he's trying to press out a headache that won't go away.

He looks…wrong. Off. Like he's in the room but not *in* the room.

You did that, Julia.

Guilt and anger and sadness and heartache wiggle inside my

chest. I don't know what to think or feel or do or say. I don't know how to fix it. I don't even know if I want to fix it.

Ace might've told me he was in love with me, but he also told me things that showed me he'd been mind-blowingly deceitful.

The professor enters the room, tosses his briefcase down on his desk and starts discussing radial and interval convergences without preempt or greeting. I swallow hard and face forward again. I try to listen. Try to care. Try to pretend I'm not burning from the inside out.

After class, Drew asks if I want to grab coffee between my classes.

I make up an excuse that I have to meet with my adviser. I don't know why I do it, but I do. And while Drew is packing up his laptop, I look over my shoulder again—right in time to see Ace walk out the side door without looking back.

I've lost so much, and the bitter pill of it all is that there are some parts I don't know if I truly ever had.

44

It's Thursday morning and my ass should be in class, but instead, I'm storming down the hallway of the advising building, gripping the strap of my backpack like I'm about to use it as a weapon.

I only got through one of my classes before I couldn't do it anymore. I simply couldn't walk into another lecture hall, sit behind Julia and Drew, and pretend I don't see the way he touches her arm when he makes a joke. Every fucking time she laughs over something he says—which is probably fucking stupid—my mind reminds me that that laugh used to be mine.

I used to be the guy who made Julia laugh.

I used to be the guy who walked her to class and sat beside her in each one.

But I'm not that guy anymore.

So, like a fucking coward, I bailed on my second class of the day, and now I'm standing in front of Cynthia Patreetus's door, knocking once before pushing it open. I tried to come here Monday, but her secretary said she was out of the office until today.

She looks up from her computer, a little startled at first, but when she sees me, she immediately rolls her eyes and lets out a soft laugh. "Ace Kelly," she greets. "No appointment, no warning, and not even a coffee bribe this time? To what do I owe this mildly chaotic interruption?"

I drop into the chair across from her with a sigh. "I need to change my schedule."

She gives me a look that is equal parts amused and exhausted. "Nice to see you too."

"I'm serious," I say. "I want to go back to my original class plan."

She freezes, and her fingers hover over the keyboard of her computer. "You mean, the schedule you abandoned because, I quote, *'this version is more aligned with what I need to have a challenging, optimized, experience-driven academic structure'*?"

"Yeah. That one."

Cynthia leans back in her chair and crosses her arms over her chest. "Why the sudden shift?"

I stare at the corner of her desk and shrug. "I just think that was the better schedule for me."

She gives me a look that says she's not buying it.

"Personal reasons," I add quickly. "It's just not working out."

Cynthia squints at her screen and starts clicking. "You're six weeks in, Ace. Add/drop's been closed. You know that."

"I figured you might make an exception."

She raises an eyebrow. "On what grounds?"

I hesitate, then repeat, "I just think that was the better schedule for me."

"The better schedule for *you*," she repeats slowly, as if she's waiting for me to crack.

I don't.

She sighs. "You're lucky I like you, Kelly."

"I know." I smile, and hope starts to inflate my chest like a balloon.

That is, until her words pop that fucker like a pin. "But this isn't happening. You're locked in unless you've got a documented emergency. Death in the family. Medical. Academic probation. Time travel. Take your pick."

I lean forward and hold my hands together like I'm praying. "Come on, Cynthia. There's gotta be something."

"Ace, you're not failing anything. According to the portal, you're thriving. You're not being bullied. No one's reported emotional distress. So unless a doctor, therapist, or alien abduction expert signs off, I can't override university policy."

I let my head fall back against the chair. "So, I'm stuck."

"Afraid so." When I look up again, I realize her eyes are on me in a way that showcases her skepticism. She knows something is up. "Are you okay?"

"Yeah," I lie. The truth is, I'd rather crawl out of my own skin than sit through another fifty-minute lecture with Julia pretending I never kissed her and told her I'm in love with her. But looks like I'm going to have to find a way to suffer through it. Also, I'm probably going to have to get brainiac Lexi to help me study and shit because Julia was always my go-to tutor.

Basically, everything is fucked.

"Thanks anyway, Cynthia," I say and rise to my feet.

"Of course. Let me know if you invent time travel. Then I'd be happy to help you."

I'm already halfway out the door when I mutter to myself, "Yeah, funny thing, if I could time travel, I wouldn't need a new schedule. I'd rewind a couple months. To before I screwed everything up."

Zip's Diner smells like grease and burnt toast, which should feel comforting, but right now it makes me queasy.

Finn never texts first. Hell, Finn barely texts at all, but this morning after I left Cynthia's office, I got a text from him that said, **Lunch. Today. Zip's. Don't bail.**

So, even though I really wanted to bail, I didn't. Finn can be fucking scary when he wants to.

He and Blake are already in a booth when I walk in. Finn is drinking black coffee because he's a fucking masochist, and Blake is halfway through a plate full of eggs and bacon. I won't be surprised if that's only his appetizer. That bastard can eat a truck when he's in season.

"Hey," I say, sliding in across from them.

Blake looks up, but immediately, his smile drops to a frown. "Dude. What the hell is going on with you? You look like you've been sleeping in the back seat of your own grief."

"I'm fine," I mutter.

Finn gives me a long look. "Fine? Get real, Ace. You haven't been around all week. No texts. No party-pushing. No annoying late-night house calls where you try to convince Scottie and me to hide in the bushes in Central Park with you. Hell, you even skipped class this morning."

"How do you know I skipped class this morning?" I narrow my eyes. "You got surveillance on me or something?"

Finn taps the side of his mug. "Scottie ran into Julia outside Nash. Said you weren't in Calc."

In the span of ten seconds, I go through what feels like every emotion possible. *Julia mentioned I wasn't in class? So, she was thinking about me? Is she thinking about me?*

"Did she…uh…say anything about me?" I ask and immediately want to grab the words from the air and shove them back down my throat.

Don't be suspicious. Don't be suspicious. That stupid fucking TikTok sound blares in my head, and I do my best to pretend to look at the menu even though I know it by heart. Hell, a few months ago, Zip even named a burger after me.

Finn and Blake don't miss a fucking beat, though. Blake raises an eyebrow, and Finn is looking at me so closely I swear he might be able to bore actual holes into my skull.

"What's going on, man?" Blake asks.

"What do you mean?" I retort, choosing the defensive route. "Nothing's going on."

"Oh, something's going on, bro," Finn challenges. "So, you might as well tell us why you look like a kicked puppy in a hoodie."

Blake leans in slightly. "Did something happen with Julia?"

I stare down at my hands. I could lie. I could make it smaller than it is, but the words slip out, quiet and sharp, before I can stop them. "I kissed her."

The silence is immediate. Heavy.

"When?" Blake asks, like I just confessed to murder.

"Saturday night. After the Double C event."

Finn straightens. "And?"

"And I told her I'm in love with her."

"Holy shit." Blake chokes on his drink. "But that's good, right? I mean, you finally told her how you really feel."

Finn is still staring at me. Not judging. Just *watching*. "You finally did the thing. You finally told Julia Brooks you're in love with her."

"She didn't take it well," I say, voice dry. "Basically, the whole thing blew up in my fucking face."

"What?" Blake questions, shock highlighting every line of his features. "What do you mean, it blew up your face?"

I push at a napkin on the table. "She said…she's been waiting around for me. That all these years, I never saw her the way she saw me. And now that she's with Drew, she thinks I *suddenly* want her. Like some fucking puppy who's jealous someone else has his toy."

Finn whistles low. "Ouch."

"She's never been on the sidelines, not to me. She's always been *it*. The girl. My girl. I—" I stop, exhaling hard. "Deep down, I thought she knew. Deep down, I thought Julia understood that no one else compares to her."

Neither of them says anything for a second.

Then Finn says, "Did you tell her that?"

"I don't know." I shrug. "Everything got pretty fucked up after I told her I was in love with her and mentioned some of the shit I've done to be closer to her. She wasn't happy about any of it. She said she felt manipulated. Felt like I violated her."

"Oh shit. That's no bueno," Blake mutters.

"I know. And it's the furthest thing from the truth. I mean, I wasn't trying to manipulate her. I only wanted to be close to her. I just wanted to be with her."

Finn looks at me like he doesn't exactly agree with me, but Blake clears his throat and asks, "So…let me get this straight. You kissed her, told her you loved her, told her the wild shit you've been doing since you realized you're in love with her, and then she walked?"

"Not exactly," I answer. "I saw her agree to be Drew's girlfriend at the Double C after party, and that really fucked with my head."

"Scottie and I saw," Finn murmurs. "I was hoping you missed it."

"Oh, I fucking saw it. So much so that I left early and waited like a stalker by my front door for signs of her to come home. I had to watch Drew fucking kiss her, and the instant that asshole was gone, I walked straight over to her apartment and…kissed her. She kissed me back, and I told her I was in love with her and mentioned the fire I started in my apartment so I could move in to her apartment and how I broke her AC unit and—"

"You started a fucking fire in your apartment?" Blake booms. "What the fuck? How didn't I know this?"

"Probably because you were so far up Lexi's ass you didn't have time to do anything else."

He shrugs and nods. "That's valid." But then he smiles like a man in love because the woman he loves conveniently loves him back. Hell, they've officially moved in together and shit.

"Okay, so what happened after you told her all the shit?" Finn asks.

"I left."

"You left?" Blake questions. "What do you mean, you left?"

I shrug. "I left because it hurt too fucking much to hear her say the shit she was saying. I mean, she thinks I only want her as my backup plan. Like, what the fuck? You don't start a fucking fire for a woman if you want her as a backup plan."

Blake runs a hand through his hair. "Still can't believe you set your apartment on fire, man."

Finn leans back slowly, the realization sinking in. "So…you guys haven't talked since Saturday?"

"Nope."

"So, what, you're just not friends anymore?" Blake asks, his lips turning down at the corners.

I stare at the table. "I guess not."

That word—*friends*—feels too small for what we were. But it's the only word that mattered.

And now, it's gone.

Blake lets out a breath. "You and Julia not being friends is like… gravity not working. It doesn't compute."

"Fuck, Ace." Finn nods. "You've been locked in since birth. Matching costumes. Shared birthday parties. You and Julia not being friends doesn't make any fucking sense."

I try to smile. I can't.

"She was everything," I say. "And now I don't even know what we are."

Blake sighs and leans back against the booth. "Clearly, this is fixable," he says, and I shake my head.

"I wish I could tell you it is, but I don't think so." The moment we broke our fifteen-minute rule, it felt like there was no going back from it. It felt…final. "Can we talk about something else?" I toss out and run a hand over my face. "Anything fucking else?"

There's a pause, then Finn asks, "So…uh… Double C this weekend, Mr. President? Surely you're planning something big…"

Fucking Double C. I love it, and I hate it at the same time. Frankly, it was when I got initiated as president that everything went to shit with Julia.

"You know it," I say, but the words don't sound excited and shit. They're monotone as fuck. They're just there.

Blake perks up. "You gonna tell us what it is?"

Technically, I shouldn't tell them jack shit about what it is.

But instead, I hear my tired and flat voice say, "It's called Midnight Market. Everyone gets fake currency and has to buy their way to clues. Campus-wide black-light scavenger hunt. Live snakes, probably. A goat. Oh, and Finn, I added all three of your brothers to the text invite list."

"Greaaaat." Finn's not thrilled, but neither am I. And when Ace Kelly suffers, everyone suffers.

"Dude, that sounds wild." Blake stares. "But I'm pretty sure you weren't supposed to tell us any of that shit…"

I shrug. "Probably not."

Finn pushes his plate toward me. "Eat. You sound like you're hallucinating."

I pick up a fry. Bite it. It tastes like nothing. I don't even bother dipping it in ketchup, but that's mostly because I feel like the fucking ketchup bottle is standing there judging me.

I know I should be hyped. Double C events are *my thing*. And I'm the fucking prez, for fuck's sake.

But right now, everything but Julia feels like white noise.

Saturday, September 20th
Ace

The goat got loose twice.

The snake handler showed up forty-five minutes late, demanded to be paid in cash, and only answered to *The Viper Whisperer.*

And the three rugby bastards who found their way into Double C during Lex's tenure as president tried to bribe their way to the final clue with actual money. It was a bold move, but it was clearly denied. They were also disqualified from the event. I swear, Dickson's rugby jocks are on another level.

Even while in a deep depression, I find a certain kind of high that comes with covertly running events that aren't university-approved. My mom told me I'm lucky that I'm ruling in the era after Lexi Winslow created an app that allows encrypted text messages to be sent out to all members, but I'm not entirely sure I wouldn't vibe with a little police chase these days.

I'm both melancholy and evil, and as it turns out, the combination is one of the universe's most dangerous.

Tonight's text was simple. **Midnight. Dickson Garage. Don't bring your goat.**

When Cassie Kelly—back then, she was Cassie Philips—was running Double C, it was basically the Stone Age. Hell, Nokia was the popular phone brand, and unlimited text messages weren't a thing. I don't know how the fuck she got the word out without leaving a paper trail, but knowing my mom, her crazy ass had to get real creative.

Tonight's Double C event, Midnight Market, consisted of the kind of challenge that will keep campus buzzing with rumors for weeks. The final clue glowed under black light and was hidden inside a vending machine with a rigged QR code. And that vending machine was located in the most obscure part of Beckley Theater.

I don't know how I pulled it off, but I did. Hell, there were even flickering lanterns on the practice soccer field beside Dickson Stadium and a trail of Hollywood-worthy market stalls made out of plywood.

It was chaotic. It was covert. It was fucking perfect.

I should be celebrating, patting myself on the motherfucking back for pulling off such a stunt. But right now? I'm not feeling it at all.

I'm currently standing in the basement of Pi Gamma's frat house at the *after-after-party*, where it's nothing but strobe lights, beer, and heat. The music's so loud it rattles your bones, and everything's glowing under black light—paint, teeth, shirts, secrets.

And people keep stopping me, clapping me on the back, tossing out fist bumps whenever I get in their vicinity.

"Kelly! That was unreal, man."

"I still don't know how you pulled that off."

"Was that snake even legal?"

All I can do is smile and nod. I try to let the praise soak in, try to savor a night like this, but it all bounces off me like I'm good-time repellent.

Across the room, I spot Blake, Finn, Travis, Jack, and Reece, all leaning against the wall near the pool table. Scottie's with them, glowing under the lights with a streak of pink paint on her jaw. Blake lifts his bottle of water like a toast, and Finn motions for me to come over while Jack and Trav shove each other playfully. Reece frowns before tripping Jack, and I shrivel at the mere thought of trying to match their energy.

I raise my empty cup in the air instead, letting them know I need a refill before flashing a grin over my shoulder that I don't feel at all.

I duck out of the room, slipping past a crowd of sweaty juniors dancing to a remix that would make my dad's favorite movie, *Dirty Dancing*, look like an Amish after-school special.

Down the back hallway, I walk until I reach the keg room. Technically, it's a converted laundry space with three tapped barrels, a fridge, and a fluorescent Pi Gamma sign.

I push the door open, and I'm relieved to find that it's empty. *Thank fuck.*

For the first time all night, I exhale.

It's quiet in here. Just the soft thump of bass through the walls and the buzz of a broken ceiling light. The black-light paint on the walls is splattered like crime scene art—handprints, words, shapes, a glowing dick or two. But no one else is here. No eyes. No pressure. No need for me to pretend I'm happy and shit.

I lean back against the counter and let my head fall against the cabinets. My fingers tap the side of the empty cup.

I should feel good. I should feel *electric.*

But instead, all I can think about is Julia.

She was at Double C tonight with her meathead boyfriend. And I did everything in my power to keep my fucking distance. Though, it wasn't easy because Julia is friends with everyone I'm friends with. The complications our rift has created feel endless.

I don't know how long I stand in here by myself, but I don't move from my perch until the door creaks open. I turn my head, expecting someone looking for beer, maybe one of the rugby guys yelling for a funnel, but instead, I'm face-to-face with Julia.

The second I see her, something sharp and breath-stealing catches in my chest.

Fuck, why does she have to be so beautiful?

Her blond hair is bright under the black light, and I know by the soft waves that hang down her shoulders she spent at least forty minutes curling it. Her blue eyes shimmer like fucking diamonds, and she has green and pink neon paint across her collarbone and down one arm.

She's dressed in her favorite pair of Converse sneakers and an all-white dress, remnants of her tan from all the days we spent at the pool this summer still visible.

It's as if the universe has taken up its own personal interest in my misery and is making damn sure Julia looks like a fucking angel.

The door has a mind of its own and slams shut behind her. She jumps a little, and it takes her a good twenty seconds to even realize I'm in the room.

Though, when we make eye contact, she stops.

We stare. Neither of us moves. Neither one of us says anything.

Fuck, Julia. What is happening to us? my mind screams. *What does everything feel so fucking fucked?*

I almost ask her just that, but two frat guys barge in behind her, yelling about someone named Crackers and a broken toilet seat. One of the idiots accidentally bumps into her shoulder, and she stumbles.

I'm on her in half a second, my arm around her waist and my hand on her elbow as I catch her before she falls.

She gasps, and her hands find my chest.

We don't move. We don't breathe. The fear of getting sucked back into the bleakness of our friendship's black hole is too strong.

Her big blue eyes stare up at me. I brush the strand of hair from her cheek, and it's as if I've touched a live wire. She doesn't flinch or pull away, and my mind races with a million and one thoughts—sadness, relief, love, anger, want, desire, need. Everything I've been trying to bury all week.

Her lips are barely parted, and I've never been this close to her and wanted something more than I do right now.

I tilt my head a little, and my hand slides behind her neck. My thumb grazes her jaw, and she doesn't pull away. Ever so slightly, she leans in, just barely, just enough.

My mouth is inches from hers. I could kiss her.

I *should* kiss her.

My heart punches at my ribs.

"Julia…" Her name cracks out of me, low and wrecked. It's the first word I've spoken to her since I walked out of her apartment a week ago—the first word either one of us has spoken to each other in seven days.

I naïvely hope it conveys much more than its length. A paragraph, a page, a chapter—something, anything from my novel of bottomless grief.

I know it's only a name.

But it's *her* name. And I miss her more than life itself.

Julia

ce's eyes are wild and gentle and begging, and my heart's pounding so loud I'm scared he can hear it.

I don't move. I can't move.

His gaze searches mine, silently asking me if he can kiss me again.

Can I? Should I? his eyes plead.

I hate myself for wanting him to so much, but *God, I want it so badly it hurts.*

I am desperate for our healing—raw for his hugs. I miss who we were. Miss my life before he left it. But I also want to scream. *Because how dare he. How dare he do this now. How dare he try to do this again.*

His lips part like he's about to say something else. My name again, maybe. Or maybe he's going to kiss me again. Maybe he's going to press his lips to mine.

I should pull away. I should put distance between us, but all I find myself doing is leaning in closer and savoring the way it feels to have his hand on the back of my neck.

I swear, for ten full heartbeats, he's all I can feel. He's solid and warm, and he feels like home in this black-lit cave of fluorescent handprints and pounding bass.

My palms flatten against his chest, and his heart is hammering beneath my fingers. Or maybe it's mine, rattling through both of us? I don't know.

He reaches up again—careful, almost reverent—and tucks a

strand of hair behind my ear. His fingers graze my cheek, and everything in me goes hot and electric. I can't breathe. I can't even remember why we haven't been on speaking terms for the past week.

Say something, Julia.

I swallow.

And then, the door slams open.

Suddenly, the room is filled with more frat guys shouting and laughing. Their voices echo off the cement walls of the small room as they barge inside. Someone bumps into Ace, jostling him, and then there's space between us.

I step back, gulping air that'll pull me back to rationality. It tastes like stale hops and regret.

My skin aches from the loss of contact, but I revel in it, willing it to make me stronger.

And then I feel Drew's arm slide around my waist. "There you are, babe. I've been looking everywhere for you." He looks down at me and then over at Ace. "Hey, man," he greets, half smiling, clueless and oblivious to the wreckage in front of him. "Unbelievable event tonight, by the way. You're a fucking evil genius."

"Thanks." Ace's eyes never leave mine, too bright in the black light, like bottled storm clouds. I want to reach across the two feet between us and drag him back, but my feet stay planted, cemented by guilt and fear and all the words I said that night in my apartment when he kissed me and told me he was in love with me. Words I meant for better or for worse.

Drew's saying something about the snake—*Was it real? Did anyone freak out?*—but all I can hear is my pulse in my ears and the silent thunder of things Ace isn't saying.

His gaze flicks to the hand at my waist, and something cracks across his face. Without a word, he steps sideways through the doorway, and he's gone.

My breath whooshes out like someone punched me.

I stare at the empty space where Ace was, neon paint still

glowing on the wall behind him, and the room is suddenly too loud, too hot, too *everything*.

"Jules?" Drew squeezes my hip. "Everything good between you and Ace now?" he asks, his eyes searching mine curiously.

"I don't know." I shrug it off like it's no big deal. Like the dismal state of our friendship isn't slowly eating me alive. "But I'm sure we'll figure it out eventually."

I'll never be whole again if we don't.

47

Ace

My phone buzzes in my pocket as I'm walking through my door. My heart hitches in speed as I fumble to see the notification on the screen. But it's not who I was hoping to hear from, and the corresponding disappointment is my own damn fault. Frankly, I'm an idiot for thinking she'd reach out to me at this point.

Boden: Dude. Where are you?

After I left my pathetic heart beating on the floor in the keg room beside Julia's feet, a bleeding third wheel to her and Drew, I headed to the room in the Pi Gamma house that holds all the liquor. I took four shots of tequila and forced myself to mingle at the party.

The booze might've given me a buzz, but it didn't quell the racing thoughts inside my damn head. All I could think about was Julia. Julia with Drew. Julia kissing Drew. Drew with his stupid arm around her waist, grinning down at her like she belongs to him and his eyebrows.

I have to squint to focus on the fucking screen, and my fingers stumble a little as I type out a text.

Me: Left earlys. At my plaz..

Before I know it, Finn is chiming into our group chat.

Finn: Fuck, Ace. You okay?

Am I okay? The question makes me burst into laughter.

Me: I ams fabulus.

So fucking fabulous that I've found myself leaving another party early. Another party I fucking planned, mind you.

Things are going really fucking well!

My phone buzzes again, but I ignore it and snag my headphones off my bed, sliding them over my ears. I tap on a random Spotify playlist, hit play, and crank the volume up as high as I can tolerate.

Frankly, I'm not in the mood for music, but I really don't want to hear anything right now. Not Julia's door opening or her voice in the hallway or the sound of her coming home from the party… with Eyebrows.

But when the silence around me still feels like too much, I turn up the volume a little more while an aggressive beat blares in my ears.

I can't handle silence right now.

The silence lets me think. And all I can think about is how her big blue eyes looked when she stared up at me. How good she felt in my arms. How badly I wanted to kiss her and how close I was to kissing her.

How I told her I was in love with her a week ago and she looked at me like I set fire to everything we ever were.

Like I set fire to everything? Hahahaha. I mean, I did light my apartment on fire for her.

Julia's rejection feels like more than a fucking rejection—she erased us.

I plop down on my sofa, close my eyes, and lean my head against the back of the couch. The music's pounding so hard in my ears a headache threatens at my temples, but it doesn't touch the hollow in my chest.

God, I miss her.

I miss her so much.

But the more my mind races, the more thoughts I have about

Julia and us and everything that's happened, the more I start to feel really fucking angry.

My chest grows tight, and each breath I release feels more and more restricted. I told Julia I love her, and she basically told me she didn't believe me. She told me that the only reason I was saying that was because she was with Drew.

And that is so fucking far from the truth, it's not even funny.

I pull my phone out of my pocket, and my thumbs fly across the screen.

Such such bullshit Lias. The whole fuckin thing is shits. We best friends for our whole lives…! I told you I love you and now you wants me gone. You wants me to poofs be a ghost.? Fuck, Julia Julia Julia. This is so fucked

I stare at it.

Then I delete the whole damn thing.

Give it another try, man. You can do it. You're Acer.

i wants to hold you and hugs you and kiss you all the times. I miss you. I miss us.

Okay, you're maybe too drunk for this…

Delete.

I drop my phone on the couch beside me and let my head fall back again.

Everything is so fucked, and I might be a little boozed right now, but even my inebriated brain is convinced I can't change any of it.

I can't fix it because Julia doesn't want me. Not even as her best friend.

Julia

Drew's hand is warm in mine as we walk down the hall, the leftover glow of the black-light paint still clinging faintly to our clothes and skin. My stomach is tangled in knots, but it's not from the beer I drank or the noise of the party. It's from what almost happened in the keg room.

From *Ace*.

My mind won't stop replaying that moment in my head. Won't stop thinking about how close I was to kissing him…again. Won't stop reminding me that I have a boyfriend and that I'm a slimeball for even considering doing something like that.

I've never thought of myself as a cheater. I've always thought I was a loyal kind of girl. But evidently, I do stupid things when it comes to Ace Kelly.

"You okay?" Drew asks as we step off the elevator and onto my floor. I know I've barely said anything since we left the party.

"Yeah." I nod too quickly. "Just tired."

He watches me for a beat but then eventually gives a small smile. "Tonight was fun. Though, I feel like I didn't see you much."

"It was chaotic." I force a smile. "I mean, that goat ate my fake money and then decided that I was enemy number one and proceeded to chase me halfway across campus."

Truthfully, I wasn't even planning on going to the Double C event tonight, but between Scottie telling me I needed to be there and Drew wanting to be there, I couldn't say no.

"The goat ate your money?" Drew asks, an amused chuckle leaving his throat.

"He was a pushy little bastard."

"Damn, Julia. You should've texted me. I would've come and saved you." Drew chuckles again and pulls me into a hug when we stop in front of my door. "So, I was thinking," he says, and his arms are still wrapped around my waist as he looks down at me. "I could come in for a bit? Just hang. Nothing major."

I hate that my eyes flick to the apartment door over his shoulder. I don't even mean to look, but I do. And instantly, guilt flashes through me like a spark to dry grass.

It feels a lot like Ace almost kissed me again tonight, and there wasn't a single part of me that was trying to stop him.

Wow, Julia. You're kind of a bitch.

I can't even find a reason not to agree with that thought. I mean, I am being a bitch to Drew. I've agreed to be his girlfriend, but it's like I'm not all the way into being his girlfriend. Which feels insanely cruel.

Crueler than I ever thought I was capable of.

Goodness, I need to get it together. I need to figure my shit out. I need to reflect on all the things rolling through my mind. I can't agree to be someone's girlfriend and then spend most of my time lying to them.

You shouldn't be someone's girlfriend when you're in lo—

I cut off my rogue thoughts and discreetly move a breath of oxygen in and out of my lungs, forcing myself to focus on Drew.

I meet his eyes again. "Can I take a rain check again? My head is kind of pounding, and I have to get up really early tomorrow to have breakfast with my mom and grandma."

Thankfully, none of those things are lies.

"Oh. Yeah, of course." Drew's smile falters a little, but it's still there.

"Maybe we can grab dinner tomorrow night?" I offer immediately when more guilt starts to creep in.

"That sounds like a plan." He presses a gentle kiss to my forehead. "Call me tomorrow?"

I nod.

He leans down and presses a soft kiss to my lips, and I hate the part of myself that doesn't let the kiss linger into anything more.

Drew smiles at me one last time before heading to the elevator, and I give a little wave as he steps onto the cart and the doors close.

For too long, I stand there in front of my apartment door, staring across the hallway at Ace's door.

I'm still pissed at him for turning our entire friendship on its head a week ago—so angry, I think I'd be a degree hotter if I checked my temperature—and yet…

Thoughts of him consume my every waking moment.

God.

Tears threaten at the corners of my eyes and my spine tingles with the fight to keep them at bay.

Will it ever end?

It's all such a mess, and the thing that's the most messed up out of everything is I really miss my best friend.

Eventually, I make myself go inside and lock the door. I kick off my shoes, head into my bedroom, and plop down onto my bed. My phone feels like it weighs fifty pounds in my hand as I stare down at it.

Next thing I know, I'm pulling up our thread. There are years and years' worth of text messages inside this thing. A snapshot into our best friendship that started the instant our parents agreed to let us get cell phones. And it's still pinned at the top of my text inbox. I haven't been able to unpin it.

Do you want to talk?

I stare at the words I just typed, wondering if the pain of the rift is worth the pride of finding my backbone.

But before I hit send, a banner flashes across the top of my screen.

Ace Kelly posted on Instagram.

My heart stutters.

Immediately, I swipe away from the message draft and pull up his profile. The new post is vague, cryptic, and a carousel of moody images. One is of a goat with glowing paint streaked on its back. Another of fog curling around the base of a bonfire. Another of hands—his hands—lighting a candle behind a black curtain.

Double C.

It's a nod to what happened tonight without ever saying it.

Before I know it, I'm snooping around his profile, through all his previous posts—a lot of them have photos of us in them—and then, to all the photos he's been tagged in by other people.

He's already tagged in a bunch of photos from the party tonight. One of them is him with a pretty brunette I recognize from a sorority—his arm slung casually around her shoulders. Another of him laughing with two girls who are a year older than us and who I know are members of Double C.

He looks happy in the photos, like the Ace I know so very well. The Ace who's the center of the party. The Ace who I loved with my whole being all while he never stopped to realize that his best friend felt like she was always on his sidelines.

I go back to the message I typed and delete every word.

For tonight, my pride wins.

Sunday brunch at the Plaza Hotel is supposed to be a decadent, indulgent experience. Think French jazz in the background, champagne flowing by eleven, little silver butter dishes that shine like they've never seen a fingerprint in their lives.

But when you're brunching with your mother, your smartass little sister, and your sex therapist grandmother who has written four best-selling books on sexual liberation and once said the phrase "clitoral blooming" in a TED Talk—it's less Audrey Hepburn fantasy and more HBO dramedy with a side of eggs Benedict.

My grandma leans forward, her silk scarf billowing like a cape in the air conditioning, and points her mimosa flute at me. "So, Julia. Are you still experiencing regular orgasms?"

I choke on my orange juice, and my mom is quick to chime in.

"Mom!" she hisses, appalled by my grandmother's question. Which is wild, honestly, that she can still get that worked up over her sex therapist mother's random sexual health questions. I'd think she'd be used to it by now. Expected it, even. "Can we please not with the climax talk? This place has white tablecloths."

"Relax, Georgia." My grandma rolls her eyes. "It's the Plaza. Not the Vatican."

My sister slouches dramatically in her velvet chair, stabbing her fruit salad with a fork. She doesn't look up, but she does join in the conversation. "Honestly, I was wondering the same thing."

"Evie!" my mom shrieks.

Grandma just smiles. "See, Georgia? Even Evie is concerned about Julia's sexual health."

"Why do I come to these things?" I mutter, half laughing, half dying inside.

Grandma takes a quick drink of her mimosa but doesn't hesitate to answer my rhetorical question. "Because you know we love you, and brunch without me shocking your mother is just overpriced toast."

By the time our food arrives—smoked salmon this, truffle aioli that—the chaos has mellowed into something warm and fizzy like the champagne. We're laughing about how Evie managed to get Big Boobs McGee Heather to take down the website that scandalized our father by contacting one of our parents' best friends Caplin Hawkins, a very successful lawyer, and serving her lawsuit papers while she was in the middle of class.

Technically, Thatch is the one who served the papers, and that honestly makes it ten times funnier, even though the mere thought of anyone related to Ace sets my chest ablaze.

But then Savannah turns her full therapist gaze on me again. "So. Are you seeing anyone, Julia?"

"Uh…yeah," I answer around a bite full of eggs. "I am. And you met him, Grandma."

She stares at me, confused. "Met who?"

"Drew," I say. "I brought him to brunch at Mom and Dad's."

"You brought a boy to brunch? Why don't I remember this?"

"Probably because Julia's boyfriend isn't very memorable," Evie mutters, and I roll my eyes.

"Drew is really nice," I say. "He goes to Dickson."

"Is it serious with this…?" My grandma pauses, already forgetting Drew's freaking name.

"I've known *Drew* since freshman year, but we just started dating this summer so it's still pretty new," I add.

"Cassie met him at a party Gunnar threw at their house," my

mom chimes in. "She thought he was very charming and had clean fingernails."

Damn, the night of Gunnar's wild party feels like ages ago.

That's probably because it was before everything with you and Ace went to shit.

"Clean fingernails?" Evie repeats with a furrowed brow. "I call bullshit. There's no way in hell Aunt Cassie said he has clean fingernails."

"*Evie,*" my mom chastises. "How about we keep the language PG? We're at the Plaza, for goodness' sake."

Evie shrugs, but she doesn't let up. "What did Aunt Cass really say about Julia's new dude?"

Our mom sighs. "Does it matter?"

Evie grins and points a finger in Mom's direction. "I knew she didn't say clean fingernails!"

"Are you monogamous with Drew, hun?" Grandma asks. "Or are you giving yourself room for sexual exploration?"

"Really, Mom?" Mom sighs audibly.

"What? It's a fair question," Grandma says, munching on a croissant. "Julia isn't exactly glowing with postcoital energy."

I sigh. "How about we play a little game of let's be silent while I eat my eggs in peace?"

Savannah narrows her eyes like I'm a patient in denial. "Julia, my sweetheart. Women always get a specific look when they're in love and being sexually satisfied. Like their whole aura is humming. But right now, I'm sorry to say, you look more like dial-up internet than high-speed Wi-Fi."

"I'm happy," I say, but I can't deny it feels like a lie coming off my tongue. "Drew is great. Clean fingernails. Amazing sexual prowess. Fully satisfied and happy, that's me." The last part is most definitely a lie. Drew and I haven't done much besides make out, hug, and hold hands. Our relationship has maintained an incredibly PG status, and I'm not sure if that's a good thing or a bad thing.

Girl, it's a bad thing.

I refuse to entertain the thought and distract myself with a drink of orange juice.

"Mm-hmm," Savannah comments, but her scrutinizing eyes say she's unconvinced. "And what about my favorite college stud, Ace? Is he dating anyone? What does he think of your new boyfriend, Drew?"

Her question lands like a fork dropped on a glass plate.

I blink and swallow hard against the irrational emotion that migrates into my throat. "I...I don't know. I don't really know what Ace is up to these days."

Even my own voice sounds wrong. Too light. Too practiced.

"What?" my mom questions, her eyes very much fixated on me now. "What do you mean, you don't know what he's up to? It's Ace, Julia. The two of you have been inseparable since you could walk. He lives across the hall from you."

When I look across the table, I see that Evie's eyes are on me now too. *Goodness, is it hot in here?* You'd think the Plaza would keep their shit comfortable, not sweltering. "Isn't Ace with Dad today?" she questions and Mom nods.

"Yeah. He's playing golf with Kline and Thatch and Wes."

"Well, if they're golfing together, it's safe to say that big fight between Kline and Thatch has officially come to an end," my grandma chimes in. "Glad to hear that's resolved. I know Thatcher is an emotional kind of guy. Always wearing his heart on his sleeve."

"Yeah, he is, but he's also a troublemaker," my mom adds in defense of my dad. "It's not every day someone tries to give you a crocodile."

"Did that idiot Gunnar go golfing?" Evie asks, rolling her eyes. Evie and Ace's little brother Gunnar have a bit of a love-hate relationship.

"I'm not sure," Mom responds, and Evie refocuses back on me.

"Are you and Ace in a fight or something, Julia?"

"No… I mean…" I pause and look down at my plate as if it holds answers. "He's got a new thing…a club of sorts that he's running." I skirt over the Double C truth I'm not supposed to talk about. But I also skirt over the harsh reality of the state of our friendship. "We're both just really busy these days."

Evie's eyes are judging me from across the table, but eventually, she picks up her phone and goes back to ignoring all of us.

But while Mom and Grandma start chatting about a DIY disaster in their trailer that involves our grandfather Dick and a sex swing, my phone buzzes on top of the table.

> **Evie: You're lying about something. I can tell.**

I roll my eyes.

> **Me: What are you talking about? Don't tell me you're drunk off those two mimosas I saw you chug behind Mom's back…**

Evie flips me the middle finger, and I go back to pretending that everything's fine.

And I do a pretty good job of it until my phone buzzes again with a new text message.

> **Aunt Cass: I need my weekly Ace update, Jules. Don't hold anything back. Give me all the details, even the horrible ones where I realize my son is an idiot like his father. Oh, and I know you're currently at brunch with Georgia and Savannah. I'll buy you a new Chanel if you ask your grandmother about the hump pillow your mom had when she was a teenage girl. I'll only accept video evidence of the conversation as proof.**

I love Chanel as much as the next girl, but knowing Cassie, that conversation would lead to more trauma than it's worth, and I've got my fill of emotional cutting these days. Even this message from Ace's mom—a regular weekly occurrence for years now—makes my stomach dive to my feet.

Our parents, our siblings, our families aren't aware of the current state of our friendship—our nonexistent friendship, that is—and somehow that hurts as much as the fight itself.

Our lives are so intertwined…what else will we lose if we can't find a way to fix this?

50

It's a warm, overcast Sunday morning at Winged Meadow, the kind of private NYC-exclusive golf course where memberships cost more than most people's cars and the grass looks like it gets Botox.

My dad invited everyone out for a casual round. Though, Gunnar already bailed, and only Kline and Wes showed up to suffer through the experience that is golfing with Thatcher Kelly.

Not to mention, nothing is casual when it comes to him.

He's wearing limited-edition Jordans on the green, teeing off like he's trying to launch satellites, and putting with his driver "for efficiency." He slices every third ball into oblivion but insists he's having "an off day."

Wes is trying to pretend it's not getting to him, but I see the muscle twitch in his jaw every time Thatch skips a wedge and takes a full swing out of a bunker.

Which leads me to believe this round of golf might have nothing to do with bonding and everything to do with my dad finding an opportunity to prank my uncle Wes.

And clearly, it's working.

My own golf game? Utter trash today.

We're currently at hole five, and I step up to tee off. I take a swing, and the ball slices hard left and disappears into the trees.

Thatch whistles. "You trying to tee off or snipe a bird out of a tree?"

"Like you should talk," Wes chimes in. "I feel like I'm out with the Temu version of Tiger Woods today with your incompetent ass."

"You talking about my game, Wesley?" my dad counters, and Wes nods.

"Yeah, Thatch. I am. It's shit."

"I'm warming up," Dad retorts. "Just wait until we hit the back nine. That's always where I catch my fluffing stride."

"That's if you have any balls left to tee off with," Kline interjects.

It's pretty clear that my dad and Kline are back to being friends, though one might complain the timing is complete shit now. I mean, it would've been nice if the bastards could've sorted their crap out when I still had a shot at making Julia fall in love with me.

Now, I'm out of her life, and our stupid fathers are the only ones with a fucking friendship.

I tune out the Three Stooges, reset my stance, and try again. This time, the ball soars straight down the fairway, landing clean.

"There he is!" Thatch cheers. "Only took some warm-up swings and a minor emotional crisis, but we're back, baby!"

I don't bother to respond. My head's not in it—not with Kline casually mentioning back at the first hole that Julia was having brunch with her mom, grandma, and sister at the Plaza. Said it like it was no big deal.

Which, it shouldn't be a big deal. But it is. I used to be part of those brunch recaps. Used to know what she ordered, how annoyed Evie was through the whole damn thing, and how Savannah kept trying to sex-therapist Julia's mom.

Hell, there've been plenty of times that I've tagged along. Today, I probably would've. Golfing with my crazy fucking dad is always a last-option kind of gig.

But now, I'm finding out about the brunch through her dad, and I'm not a part of it all.

I'm not part of anything when it comes to Julia.

My dad and Wes and Kline walk ahead, arguing about whose

turn it is to pick up lunch at the clubhouse. And I hang back and pull out my phone.

Julia's name is still pinned at the top of my messages.

Still no new texts from her.

Before I know it, I'm typing.

How's brunch?

I pause and backspace each letter away.

What the fuck is going on with us, Julia? Everything feels wrong

Delete.

I miss you so much it hurts

Delete.

I stare at the blinking cursor until it disappears, and then I lock the phone and shove it in my pocket.

"Acer!" Thatch is waving me forward. "You good?" he calls out.

"Yeah," I say and start to jog to catch up with them. "All good."

But it's a lie. I'm not good.

I'm not good at fucking all.

51

Two weeks.

That's how long it's been since I was face-to-face with Julia and said her name and almost kissed her at the Double C black-light after party.

Fourteen days of radio silence between the two of us. I guess she and Drew are still going strong, though I'm doing my best to avoid them entirely. It's too fucking painful at this point.

It's already October, and the weather is turning crisp with fall. The air outside is colder, but inside this lecture hall for English feels like a padded cell. I'm seated two rows behind Julia—close enough to count the strands of hair she pulls into a high ponytail, but far enough that I can pretend I'm not memorizing the delicate length of her neck like a madman.

For once, though, the seat next to her is empty.

Maybe she and Drew aren't still going strong?

Hope blooms in my chest, and for one reckless second, I consider walking up and sitting beside her. I don't even know what I'd say. But maybe I wouldn't have to say anything. Maybe she'd look at me like she used to. Maybe she'd smile.

But all my hope pops like a fucking pus-filled pimple when Drew walks into the lecture hall. His eyebrows are bushier than his fucking hair, and he even slaps me on the fucking back like we're buddies and offers a "Yo, Ace" as he passes by my seat.

Of course, he slides into the empty seat next to Julia like he's right where he belongs and says something low in her ear that makes her lips twitch into a smile. But it's not the smile I know. The one I've seen a million times. It's polite. It's…nice. I feel like I'm watching a scene from a rom-com no one asked for.

Though, I'm not the love interest. I'm the fucking punch line.

My phone buzzes, and I glance to check the screen.

> **Gunnar: Can you drive a city bus?**

There is only one appropriate response to this text message.

> **Me: Absolutely not. Whatever this is I'm out.**

> **Gunnar: Wow. No vision. Sad.**

I pocket my phone and lean back in my chair because it's the only thing keeping me from falling apart and try to think about anything but the girl sitting two rows in front of me.

I've got plenty of shit to think about when it comes to Double C. I'm currently balls deep in planning two events—one for this weekend that's still unnamed and disorganized and the big one for Halloween night—and if I have any hope of passing these classes without Julia, I should probably think about some fucking academic shit too.

I groan and allow my mind to wander back to the big Halloween event for Double C.

That one, I've actually got plans for. I'm talking masks, code names, no phones, cloaks. It has all the elements to be the best Double C event I've planned thus far, which is saying a fucking lot because every event has brought its A game.

I should be fucking pumped, but I'm a shell of chaos. I have too many tabs open in my brain, and keeping them organized is harder than ringleading a Barnum and Bailey circus.

Because nothing is the same without Julia Brooks by my side.

Class starts, and I don't hear a single word of it despite knowing how badly I need to.

Halfway through the lecture, I glance up to find Scottie watching from across the room. She doesn't smile. Only tilts her head like she's trying to solve a puzzle. Sadly, the puzzle she's trying to solve is probably somewhere in the NYC dump by now, being piled on by other fucking trash.

But because Finn is conjoined with his girl at the dick, I already know I'm going to get texts from him about her theories.

And sure enough, when class ends, my phone vibrates in a fury.

Finn: I think Ace needs an intervention.

Boden: Oh shit. He's spiraling?

Finn: He's close. Two feet on the ledge, man.

They keep going, but I ignore whatever they're saying and shove my phone into my pocket, purposefully heading out the side exit of the building.

I skip my next class and head back to my apartment, halfheartedly going over logistics for Double C's Halloween event. And since the university can't know it exists, planning it feels like coordinating a heist but with glitter and fog machines.

Honestly, this is the only thing keeping me going right now. I might not be enjoying it per se, but it's at least given me a purpose while everything else in my life feels like a bag of sweaty ballsacks.

My fingers move through spreadsheets and equipment lists, but my mind's on the pretty voice that used to narrate my life in dumb impressions and whispered jokes. That used to say things like "You're such an idiot" but in a way that always felt like it meant "I love you anyway."

Before I know it, I'm pulling out my phone and scrolling past the new text notifications from Finn and Blake, ignoring them completely. I open my voice memo app instead, my mind wanting to take a walk down memory lane when everything felt happy.

And there it is. **Untitled** and dated **March 6 at 11:24 p.m.**

I barely remember recording it. I'm pretty sure it happened

during one of our late-night walks home from a party. One click to the screen and Julia's laugh fills the quiet. It's not her sweet, giggle laugh but the kind of laugh she only does when she thinks something is insanely hilarious. Tears and snorts are always involved.

I close my eyes and let it sink in.

And being the masochist that I am, I let myself pretend that everything is okay. That Julia's still my best friend. And that I didn't ruin the only thing in life that ever felt like it was worth being serious over.

Sunday, October 12th

Julia

Zip's Diner is packed and buzzing with lazy Sunday energy. The scents of butter and maple syrup cling to the air, mixing with the occasional clatter of silverware and laughter from the corner booths.

Scottie dunks a forkful of hash browns in hot sauce. "We should've known once Ace Kelly became the prez…things would go off the rails."

Kayla grins. "Right? Last night was insane. How many ferrets were there? Ten? And what was with the dude in the gorilla costume on the skateboard?"

Scottie laughs. "I saw that guy crash and burn so many times."

I laugh because I'm supposed to. But my smile is brittle, and my coffee's long gone cold.

Ace was barely visible last night. Just flashes. A glimpse of his profile across the room. A low laugh from somewhere down the hall of the chemistry basement. And always with someone beside him. Usually a girl, and never but never me. He didn't come over to try to make up or explain again, he didn't pull me aside and apologize for keeping something from me for the first time ever and for fucking everything up with his timing, and he didn't let me have my fifteen minutes to be upset and then check on me to call it to an end. I know he was never good at telling time, but three weeks ought to be long enough to tell the difference.

The worst part? I noticed.

I noticed *all* of it.

I stir my coffee for too long. The spoon clinks the sides of the mug in a repetitive rhythm I don't even notice until Scottie shoots me a look.

"You okay?"

"Me?" I blink, and when I realize her eyes are on me, I quickly nod. "Oh yeah. I'm good."

"You sure?"

"Mm-hmm."

Kayla's too busy face-diving into her pancakes to notice, but Scottie doesn't look away. She lowers her voice. "So…how are things with Drew?"

I bite the inside of my cheek as I realize that I haven't thought of Drew once since we sat down. And the worst part is, I have to force myself to scroll through my brain to find the file labeled *boyfriend.*

"They're…fine."

Scottie raises her eyebrows.

"They're good," I add and force a smile to my lips. "Great. Things are great."

Scottie gives me a look but lets it go.

I pick at the corner of my napkin and try not to think about how I haven't heard Ace's voice in three weeks. Or how it feels like the loudest silence of my entire life.

Kayla's phone buzzes, and she groans. "Ugh, study group. I gotta go."

She hugs Scottie goodbye and waves at me. "Text me later!"

Scottie and I are left in a quiet lull. She takes a long sip from her coffee, eyes never leaving mine, and I just sit there, wishing I could be more conversational. Wishing I could be more present and not lost in my own freaking head.

"Girl, I know you're not okay," she says softly.

I stiffen. "I'm fine."

"You know you don't have to lie to me, right?"

I shake my head. "I'm not lying."

"Julia, from the moment I met you last year, you and Ace were a package deal. And now, all of a sudden, you don't sit by each other in class. You don't go to parties together. You're strangers."

I open my mouth to deflect again, but something in me cracks. And instead, I whisper, "We're not okay."

"Damn." Her mouth turns down at the corners, but her eyes are unsurprised. "I figured. And also…Finn might have told me some things."

I swallow against the lump rising in my throat.

Scottie doesn't push. She sits there with me in the silence, letting it stretch out between us.

"I don't know what to say," I finally admit. "I don't even know what happened."

Scottie frowns, and I redirect my lie toward the path labeled reality.

"Okay, that's not true. I do know what happened, but I don't know *how* to deal with it. The fight between us…it's a long time coming and brutal in the most unshakable form. I want to forgive and forget. My body *longs* for it. But I know I shouldn't." I shake my head. Without context, I must sound baffling. "Anyway, I know that's vague, but I don't think I can talk about it right now. Not without losing it."

"Just know…" Scottie reaches across the table and squeezes my hand. "When you're ready to hash out the details, I'm here."

"Thanks, Scottie." I try to lift my lips into a smile but fail miserably. "It might not seem like I appreciate that, but I do."

"Oh, what?" she teases. "You think your current state of resting bitch face isn't showcasing your true emotions?"

A small laugh bubbles up from my lungs. "I don't know why my face does that. It's either giving friendly or I-might-want-to-kill-you."

Scottie grins. "Don't worry, I know and love the true woman behind the RBF. She's one of the sweetest, kindest, supportive, most loyal friends there is."

Her words are meant as a compliment, as reassurance, but they might as well be sharpened nails that slice my chest right open. I don't feel like I'm any of those things right now. Not to Drew. *Not to Ace.*

My mind races over the current facts of my situation. And it feels pretty dang dismal when I start stacking everything up. Drew is my boyfriend, but I'm not exactly all in to the relationship. We've kissed, but that's about it. And that's really freaking weird because we're not in middle school. We're in college. We're in college, and I'm basically abstinent…from my boyfriend. And not loyal at all because even though Ace initiated the kiss in my apartment, I very much kissed him back.

Ace told me he was in love with me. And I can imagine from his POV, he feels like I rejected him. Which doesn't feel like anything remotely sweet or kind or supportive.

What if I was too hard on him?

"Hey, so," Scottie says, dragging me out of my own head. "I have some news."

I clear my throat and sit up straighter. "Yeah?"

"It's about my surgery," she updates. "After all the testing, Dr. Raines thinks I'm a great candidate, and I've decided I'm going to do it. In November. It's scheduled for the Monday before Thanksgiving."

"Oh my God, Scottie." There's shit in my life that very much feels like a dumpster fire, but nothing, and I mean nothing, can compare to what my girl Scottie has been through. Right now, her stuff is way more important than my stuff. "That's incredible. And a really big deal. Huge, *huge* deal. Are you…excited? Nervous? I can't even imagine the emotions you have to be going through."

"I'm terrified, but…excited. I'm ready, you know?" she says, and her mouth twitches up like she might be afraid to fully smile. "I'm ready to do the damn thing."

"You're brave," I say and mean it. I reach out and squeeze her hand. "So fucking brave."

She squeezes back. "Thanks."

We talk a little more about her surgery, but eventually, she needs to go to do something with Finn and his brother Reece. So, we pay the check and head out of Zip's.

The air is cool and crisp on my face as we move down the sidewalk. It's that in-between stretch where fall hasn't committed yet but summer's starting to let go.

"You good?" Scottie asks before she heads in the other direction to Finn's and her apartment.

"Yeah," I lie again. "I'll see you later."

I finish the three-block walk to my apartment, but once I'm up the elevator and on my floor, instead of going into my apartment, I stop outside *his* door.

The paint is still chipped on the bottom corner from where Yoko got a little too excited. There's a faint scratch across the doorframe I remember from when his dad helped him move a couch inside. And somehow, the silence on the other side of the door is louder than noise.

I don't knock. I *can't* knock. I…stand there.

Eventually, I turn and go into my apartment.

Yoko greets me like the wild man that he is, and once I give him some treats and pets, I cuddle with him on the couch. The TV is on, but my mind is still in the hallway, standing outside Ace's door. My phone is in my hand before I even realize it, and I'm typing up a message inside the eerily silent chat with Ace.

I hate this.

Delete.

Are we ever going to talk?

Delete.

I miss you. I hate that we're not okay. I don't want it to be like this, Ace. I really don't. Can we…talk?

Before I hit send, I open Instagram. Sadly, it's the only place I still see him. And yes, I'm aware this is very stalker-esque behavior.

There's a new photo that he's tagged in. A blurry, too-dark party pic. Ace is in the center, mid-laugh, and a girl with glitter under her eyes is kissing his cheek. Her hand is wrapped possessively around the back of his neck.

He looks happy. Too happy.

I use two fingers to zoom in like a fool. Like it matters. Like if I look hard enough, I'll find some sign he's not as okay as he looks in the photo.

But all I see is a girl kissing Ace's cheek and him smiling into the camera like he's enjoying it.

And I go back to my text thread with Ace and delete the last unsent message I wrote.

Even if you were too hard on him, looks like it might be too late to take it back now…

53

It's 1:12 a.m., and I should be asleep because I have an eight a.m. class, but I'm staring at the ceiling like it's got something to say and might suddenly form into words and explain why everything feels like it's slipping through my fingers.

My phone is on my chest, screen still lit from the Instagram post I shouldn't have opened again, but I did. Third time tonight. Fifth, if I'm honest. I'm not even sure what I'm hoping to find. It's not like the photo's changed.

I look fine in it. Better than fine, even. That same easy grin I've had since high school, arm slung around a girl I barely remember. She was laughing and kissing my cheek at the same time. Truthfully, I don't even know the girl. Don't even know her name. She just wanted to take a picture with me.

But it's all a fucking lie.

Because I am *not* fine.

And I shouldn't feel guilty about that photo, right? I shouldn't care. Julia's the one who walked away. She chose someone else.

Except…I *do* care. And I do feel guilty. Because if Julia saw it, then maybe she'd think I've moved on. Maybe she'd think that I'm perfectly happy and fine and not at all slowly dying in my misery.

Clearly, I'm not fine.

I haven't been since the night I kissed her. Since the night I told her I was in love with her. Since she looked me in the eye and basically told me that she's always been the girl on the sidelines in our story. That I didn't really see her. That I never have. She told me she didn't believe me that I'm in love with her.

God, I don't know how to explain it. I didn't even realize what I was feeling until a few months ago. And once I knew…once I *knew* I was in love with her, it felt like it had always been that way. Like I'd been blind and suddenly I could see and everything made sense.

But now, I'm the ghost of a guy who thought he had a shot. I see her across rooms, in hallways, sitting in class—right fucking there—and it's as if my body doesn't know what to do with itself. As if some part of me still thinks I get to walk over and make her laugh.

And then I remember I don't.

I unlock my phone and open a new note. My fingers hesitate over the keyboard, like they know I'm about to say shit I'll never have the balls to send.

But I start typing anyway.

I know this is dumb and you probably don't give a shit, but I was tagged in a picture on IG last night that doesn't sit right with me. If you saw that picture, it'd make you think I'm doing okay. Which is a fucking lie.

I don't even know the girl's name. She asked for a photo and I said yes because it was easier than saying no. She kissed my cheek right as the flash went off. I don't know if you saw it, but I feel fucking guilty that it even happened.

I feel like I cheated on you or some shit which is fucking stupid, I know, because you probably don't care and you've moved on with Drewbacca. But I can't change the fact that even though you don't want to be mine, I still feel like I'm yours.

Fuck, I hate that I look okay in that stupid fucking picture.

I'm not okay, Julia. I'm fucking miserable without you.

I meant what I said, Julia. I meant all of it.

I AM IN LOVE WITH YOU.

I know I should stop thinking about you.

I know I should stop hoping.

But if you knocked on my door right now? I wouldn't ask a single question.

I'd let you in. And I'd pull you into my arms.

God, I miss us.

I miss you.

But again, you probably don't care about any of this shit and that's probably why I shouldn't bother sending it to you.

I stare at it for way too long. The screen dims, and I tap it back on. I even copy and paste the fucker into my text chat with Julia. My thumb hovers over the send button like I'm going to push it.

But I don't.

Instead, I select all and hit delete.

And *poof.* The words are gone.

I flip my phone over, screen down, and press the heels of my hands into my eyes.

I miss her so fucking much, it's physically painful.

But I guess that's the price of loving someone who doesn't love you back.

To: julia.brooks@dickson.edu

Subject: SOS

One month and four days, Jules.

That's how long it's been since I told you I'm in love with you. Since we kissed. Since you chose someone else over me.

I still sit behind you in class. I still know the way you tuck your hair behind your ear when you're thinking really hard about something. I still catch myself waiting for you to turn around and smile at me like none of this ever happened.

But you don't. You never do.

It all feels like a really horrible fucking nightmare that I can't wake up from.

Every fucking day, I want to call you, text you, talk to you, share something stupid about my day with you. I can't tell you how many times I've even reached for my phone before I remember this shitty reality where we're not talking at all.

Hell, I talk to your mom more than you. I still get her nearly daily check-in text messages. And now I have to respond with some vague shit because I don't know what you've told your mom and we're basically strangers, even though our families have been best friends for our entire fucking lives. I've even talked to Evie more than I've talked to you. Yes, fucking Evie texts me more than you. I helped her arrange some lawsuit over Kline's dick pics. My dad and your dad are friends again. The Crocky rift has been officially laid to rest, you know, just in time for our friendship to fucking implode into smithereens.

But you laugh with Drew now. You kiss him goodbye in front of our building like I'm not standing twenty feet away pretending to talk to Blake or Finn on the phone so I don't have to look like a complete idiot.

And maybe I am an idiot.

Because despite all of it, I still check my phone like you might text. Like maybe you'll remember how we used to talk about anything and everything and spend hours doing absolutely nothing together and still call it the best part of our day.

We were best fucking friends, Lia.

BEST FUCKING FRIENDS. OUR WHOLE LIVES.

Fuck, the silence is so loud.

And I guess I get it. I mean, I crossed a line, right? I broke the rules.

I fell in love with you.

I just wish I knew if there was ever a second, just one fucking second, when you felt the same way.

This is the tenth email I've written you this week. I've yet to send one of these fuckers to you and I probably won't send this one either.

-Ace

Unsent. Saved to drafts.

Friday, October 25th
Julia

"Y ou want anything?" Drew asks, stretching as he stands and nodding toward the vending machines. "They've got those weird sour gummy worms you like."

"Uh…" I pause, my distracted mind needing a minute to catch up with his words. "Only if they're neon," I murmur, still staring at my laptop screen.

"A woman of taste." There's a smile in his voice, but I don't look up to see it. "Be right back."

For the past hour, we've been camped out in one of the quieter corners of McKinley Library—laptops open and notebooks scattered between us. Drew's been helping me study for our upcoming calc exam, and I've been pretending I'm not distracted. That my thoughts haven't been drifting. That I haven't checked Ace's Instagram three times today.

It's not who I am, and it's embarrassing. Calculus is something that comes easy to me. All last year, in Calc 1, I didn't have to study for a single exam. But this year, I don't know, my focus is that of a squirrel trying to fight its way out of a tube sock.

But once Drew is gone, I glance up from my laptop and move my eyes toward the large window by our table that looks out over the quad. And out of all the people I spot moving across the sidewalk, I don't expect to see Ace. It's like the universe is playing tricks on me.

He's walking fast across campus in his favorite black hoodie with his headphones on.

He's heading somewhere.

Or maybe he's heading to someone?

The thought slips in before I can stop it. *Is it going to be a meet-up with her? The glitter girl from the Instagram photo?*

My stomach twists, and before I even realize what I'm doing, my eyes are back on my laptop screen and my fingers are on the keyboard.

I open my school email inbox.

I click the button to start a new message.

To: ace.kelly@dickson.edu

Subject: Just So You Know

I almost texted you last night.

Actually, that's a lie. I **did** text you. I typed out the whole thing. Twice. But I deleted it. Twice.

And sadly, that's not the first time I've done that. I do it a lot.

I don't know what we are anymore. Strangers? Enemies? A thing we can't talk about?

Everyone keeps asking if we're okay. Scottie asked. Kayla asked. My mom asked. Even Drew asked me last week if I still talk to you. I said no. And then I couldn't breathe for an hour after.

You're everywhere. You're in my classes. You're in the way your mom still texts me every day, trying to make sure that you're not, like, in jail or on drugs, and I have to give some half-assed response back because I have no idea if you've told her what's happened between us. You're in the way my coffee order gets made because you used to pick it up for me without asking. You're in the background of every laugh that doesn't quite reach my chest anymore.

And maybe you don't care. Maybe you're out there living your best President-of-Double-C life and you have a new random girl who loves, I don't know, stupid glitter eye shadow, and maybe you don't miss me at all.

But just so you know…I miss you, and there's a part of me—one that gets bigger every day—that wonders if I was too harsh on you when you told me you're in love with me.

But it was all such a shock, Ace. You had been lying to me, keeping stuff from me, and then, you told me a bunch of insane things that you'd done. And for years, I guess, I was secretly waiting for you to come to that realization and want to be more than friends with me, but you didn't come to that realization until I'd finally let myself lean into the idea of not always being the girl who is silently waiting around for you to want more.

But it's all probably too late, huh? I'm with Drew. You're with glitter girl. And our friendship doesn't feel like a friendship at all. It feels like…nothing. Which is the most painful thing of all.

-Julia

Unsent. Saved to drafts.

I *should've stayed in bed.*

It's what I keep thinking as I take a seat two rows behind Julia. It's not like I haven't spent the past month watching the back of her head and wondering what the hell she's thinking—but today already feels worse. There's something in the air. The professor is too chipper for a fucking English lesson. And I swear to God, Drewchebag is humming. Fucking *humming*.

I really hate that guy.

"Okay, everyone!" Professor Dudley claps his hands like we're in kindergarten. "We're doing something fun today!"

I brace for it. I swear, every time a teacher says *fun*, it ends up being some social torture experiment in disguise.

"We're starting a multiweek group project," Dudley announces. "And I've already preassigned the groups."

The entire room groans, but Finn's sigh can be heard above it all.

I can't deny I can relate to the sentiment. The last thing I want to do is fucking group project. I honestly thought this shit was done once I graduated high school.

Dudley starts listing off the assigned groups, and I zone out until I hear, "Group 3: Finn Hayes, Scottie Bordeaux, Julia Brooks, Drew Bettencourt, and Ace Kelly."

"Oh fuck," Finn mutters.

Yeah, my thoughts exactly, bro.

My eyes go to Julia, but she's not looking at me. She stares straight ahead like she didn't hear it.

Drew, on the other hand, glances over his shoulder in our direction—Finn's, Scottie's, and mine—and grins at us like he won a fucking cruise as he wraps his arm around Julia's shoulders.

Scottie leans over to Finn, whispering something that I don't bother trying to overhear. Surely she's wondering if this is going to be a problem.

Which, it already is. *Trust me, it's a huge fucking problem.*

"Professor," I say, raising my hand. "I've always been a bit of a lone wolf, so I'm sure you can understand why I'm going to go ahead and do this group project solo."

"Ace Kelly? A lone wolf?" Professor Dudley laughs. "Very funny. Before you even arrived in my class this semester, other professors referred to you as the mayor of Dickson U. Most would say group projects are where you thrive."

"I'm trying something new," I retort. "It's always good to switch it up, you know?"

"It's a group project, Ace. End of discussion." His smile is smug. "And this is important. It's my job to prepare you for the real world, where you'll have to collaborate with other people."

Tell that to my fucking blood pressure. With the way my heart is pounding so goddamn hard beneath my ribs, I might end up being the only healthy nineteen-year-old who keels over from a heart attack.

Dudley hands out the assignment sheet and gives us time to group up and discuss scheduling. I drag my chair over, reluctantly, while Drew's arm snakes around Julia's shoulder again like he has a fucking claim on her. At this point, I feel like this fucker is doing it on purpose.

But I force myself to focus on neutral ground, safe territory like Finn and Scottie. But with the way Finn is eyeing me with concern, I eventually have to avert my eyes from him and fixate on a random crack in one of the ceiling tiles.

"So…you guys want to meet at our place?" Scottie jumps in first. "We've got the space."

"Our place? Really, Scottie?" Finn groans, but Scottie playfully slaps him on the shoulder.

"Yes, Finn. Our place. And don't be so grumpy about it."

He smiles at her like a man in fucking love, because he is. Though, he's a man in love who gets to be with the woman he loves, so I guess that makes it pretty goddamn easy to be happy all the fucking time.

"Appreciate the hospitality, Finn," Drew says. "Though, maybe next year, Julia and I will be able to offer our apartment up for group projects and let you guys off the hook."

I'm sorry, *what?* Did that motherfucker just say *their* apartment?

"*Your* apartment?" Scottie chokes. "You guys are going to live together?"

"No, no, no," Julia blurts out with a fast tongue. "We're not living together."

"I was just messing, babe." Drew laughs like it's a joke. "I guess it was a little wishful thinking on my part. At least, for now."

For now, he says.

For now?!

I feel my pulse in my teeth.

Julia is staring at the table now. She's avoiding everyone's eyes, especially mine. And every cell in my body wants to throw a chair through a window.

Finn elbows me, but it's subtle. I think it's supposed to mean *chill*, but it confirms that he can see me unraveling.

Julia still won't look at me.

The rest of the group chat is a blur. I say nothing. Just nod at the time we agree on to meet at Finn and Scottie's place late next week.

And I bolt out of the lecture hall the second Dudley dismisses us.

In the hallway, I have to pause for a brief moment to suck in

air like it might help. *Julia and Drew...moving in together? It's ei-*
ther the biggest joke of the century or the universe has started to
plan my funeral.

It's not like she's had serious boyfriends before. Not really. Not
like this. And she's planning a future with this guy? The one who
wears loafers to fucking parties and says *epic* unironically?

My phone buzzes with a few texts from Double C members who are helping me work on setup for tomorrow night's big
Halloween event. But I temporarily ignore them and focus on speed
walking back to my apartment so I can be alone with my rage.

*Julia and that fucking asswipe have been together for like a month,
and he's already saying shit about moving in together next year?*

What the actual fuck?

I do my best to ignore shouts from across campus, trying to
get my attention. Eyes on the cement, I walk. Hell, maybe I'm running. I don't know.

Truth be told, I have no idea what the hell I'm doing anymore.

57

Finding one hundred cloaks in New York City without raising red flags has turned out to be harder than smuggling a goat through Grand Central Terminal.

Which, for the record, I've also done. And that was easier.

It's one thing to say "Halloween party" when you're buying a couple cloaks. People usually nod and smile. But it's a whole other thing when you're hunting for cloaks in bulk, preferably hooded, all black, and preferably *not* with red satin lining or embroidered pentagrams. The more I ask around, the more I get side-eyes like I'm the leader of a local death cult.

I've already gotten flagged by at least one Etsy seller who messaged me: ***"Hi, just checking… You're not trying to perform a ritual, right?"***

No, bro. I'm just trying to host the most epic, secretly sanctioned university Halloween bash in Double C history. One where no one can know it's me behind it—except everyone kind of does.

My arms are full—two more delivered boxes of party supplies balanced badly on my hip—and I'm half thinking about how I still need to bribe someone at the farmers market in Chelsea for hay bales when I hear a loud crash from across the hall.

It's sharp and sudden, sounds like glass on tile, and it's loud enough to echo off the walls of our quiet hallway.

I freeze, and my eyes dart straight to Julia's door.

And within a second or two, I hear an *"Oh shit"* muttered from the other side of her door.

A few seconds after that, I hear a thud.

My chest tightens as the boxes in my hands hit the floor.

"Julia?" I call, already crossing the hallway, everything else but the building panic in my gut disappearing.

No answer.

"Jules, open the door." I knock several times, my fist pounding against the wood of her door harder each time. I jiggle the locked knob. "Julia, open the door!"

Still nothing.

Something's wrong.

Immediately, I rush into my apartment, kicking the boxes on the floor in the door as I go, and snag the spare key I still have to Julia's place and sprint back over to unlock the door.

The living room is dim, soft light glowing from the kitchen, and I spot Julia instantly. She's in the kitchen, on the floor, and slumped against a cabinet. Blood is dripping from her palm, and broken glass is everywhere.

"Jesus, Julia." I'm already moving toward her, my heart in my throat. "What the hell?"

Her eyes are wide and dazed as they flick up to mine. "I dropped it. A glass. I just wanted water, and it slipped and…and…"

She sees her own hand. The blood. And she starts to sway.

"Hey. No. No, no, no." I crouch beside her, voice steady even though my insides are unraveling. "Look at me, Lia. Not your hand. Me."

"I think I'm gonna—"

She doesn't finish. Her eyes fall closed and she slumps forward, and I catch her before her head can hit the floor.

Shit. She passed out.

I ease her down gently, careful not to jar her hand, and grab the dish towel I know she keeps in the top drawer by the sink. I press it to the cut and keep talking to her in a calm voice, trying to make her come to again without putting her in a full-blown panic. "Hey, Jules. It's okay. I got you, all right? I'm here." And the entire time, I keep monitoring her hand. It's still bleeding, even with the pressure I'm putting on it. So much so that I have to switch towels.

"Ace?" She stirs a few moments later. Her lashes flutter as her eyes meet mine. "Did I pass out?"

"Yep, babe. You did. Full drama-queen blackout," I say softly, giving her a crooked smile. "Don't worry. You still looked hot doing it."

Her lips twitch like she wants to laugh but isn't sure she can.

"I forgot..." she breathes. "I hate blood."

"I know. It's okay." To me, none of this is a shock. I've seen Julia pass out several times over the years. One time, when we decided to try a blood oath when we were, like, six. One time when Barry Donahue skinned his knee so bad that blood was dripping into his gym shoe. And one time when her late dog Stan got a stick stuck in his paw.

I inspect her hand again, and I'm not liking what I'm seeing at all. I didn't get a great look at it, but I know the cut is pretty deep and the bleeding doesn't appear to want to stop anytime soon.

Her head rests against the cabinet behind her. Her color is still all wrong.

"Julia, where's Yoko?" I ask when I realize I haven't seen or heard him the entire time I've been in here.

"He took a little road trip with my grandma and grandpa in the trailer."

"Okay, here's the plan." I tighten the towel with careful pressure. "I'm going to pick you up."

"No," she mutters. "Just the couch. I can—"

"You could." I nod. "But I got a new couch over at my place. It's practically ergonomic. NASA technology. Reclines. Heated. Sings lullabies."

She blinks up at me, unconvinced.

But I ease one arm behind her back, the other under her knees, and lift her gently into my arms.

She doesn't resist. She just rests her head on my shoulder like it's instinct.

I grab her phone and purse from the counter, and I hook it over my shoulder like it's mine and carry her to the door.

She starts to stir again as I press the elevator button.

Her brow furrows. "Where are we going?"

I don't answer right away.

I glance down. Blood's already soaking through the towel again. Not pouring, but enough.

She follows my gaze. Sees the red.

Her breath catches. "Oh God—"

And then she's out cold again.

Shit.

———

St. Luke's Hospital ER wasn't busy, and they got Julia back and into a room in no time at all.

Now, she has six stitches in her hand, and I'm pretty sure I have permanent nerve damage in mine from how hard she gripped it during the procedure.

She passed out twice—once in the elevator and again when the nurse unwrapped her hand. Then she damn near bit a chunk out of my arm when they numbed the area. Not on purpose, of course. Julia's never been great with blood. Even worse with her own.

Thankfully, before the doctor started stitching, they gave her something to calm her nerves—something mild, but it hit her *hard.*

Now she's curled up on the tiny ER hospital bed, high as a kite and still cute as hell. Her hair's a mess, her eyes are heavy lidded, but she's smiling at me like none of this ever happened. Like we haven't been strangers for nearly two months.

"You're really nice," she says, slurring slightly. "You're always so nice to me. Even when I'm...you know. A blood fountain."

My throat tightens.

"You've always been a drama queen," I say quietly, brushing a piece of hair away from her face.

"You love it."

I love you.

She shifts a little, squinting at me like I'm hard to place. "You smell good. Like, unfairly good. What is that?"

"Uh…soap? I don't know. You asked me that once in high school too." I laugh. It's forced and my chest aches, because even though she's talking to me in the way Julia always used to talk to me, she's high. She's numbed. She's not fully aware.

She giggles. "Did I?"

I nod. "Right before prom. You told me I smelled like confidence and bad decisions." *Simpler times. You know, when you were still my girl.*

She lets out a sleepy laugh and reaches out like she's going to grab my hand but ends up swiping at the air. "I like that. I like you. You're warm. Stay here."

Fuck. I wish I could. I wish I could stay here forever if it meant getting her back. The real her. The version that used to crawl into my bed when she had nightmares and fall asleep with her mouth open and her foot shoved under my thigh.

I sit beside the bed and take her hand carefully—her unstitched one—and she immediately curls her fingers around mine. Like muscle memory.

"I miss you," I whisper.

She doesn't answer. She's staring at the ceiling, smiling lazily. "Can I have my phone?"

I hesitate for a second but pass it to her from where I set it down in the little bin by the bed. "I already texted your mom. She's on her way."

"Thanks," she says, unlocking the screen and scrolling. I see her typing something but don't think much of it. Probably her sister or something. Maybe she's ordering pizza. Honestly, it wouldn't surprise me.

She sets the phone down and leans her head toward me again. "Hey. Can you kiss my forehead? Just once?"

God. She's going to ruin me.

But I can't deny her request. I want to do it as much as she wants me to do it or more. I lean down and press my mouth to her skin, and I let my lips linger for no less than ten seconds.

She sighs like that's all she needed in the world. "Perfect," she says.

"Yeah," I say hoarsely. "Perfect."

The curtain rustles, and Julia's mom bursts into the room. Georgia's voice is half panicked and half relieved as she moves toward where Julia is lying in the bed. "Julia, oh my God. Are you okay?"

"I'm a hemorrhage," Julia announces proudly. "But Ace fixed it."

Georgia steps in, taking Julia's face in her hands, checking her like a worried mom would. And then, my mom walks in right behind her, all energy and zero subtlety.

"What the hell happened?" my mom asks, already making a beeline for the bed. But once she gets an eye on Julia's face and sees the dopey, adorable smile, she laughs. "Oh honey, they gave you the good shit, huh?"

"Yep." Julia giggles. "The nurse got me high with drugs. I'm going to try to take some home. I feel gooooooood."

My mom snorts and runs her hand over the top of Julia's hair. "Maybe the doctor will give us a twofer and I can take some home too."

Georgia groans. "Seriously, Cass?"

"What?" my mom questions, but Georgia rolls her eyes.

They're talking over each other now, bustling around her bed, and Julia's loving the attention, grinning at them like everything is right in the world. And then she's grinning at me. Her smile so damn adorable I feel my chest tighten from it.

It's been forever since she's smiled at me like that.

"Ace is the best," Julia says, and both of our moms look at me. "He's also really handsome, you know? Like, it's almost not fair."

My mom smiles at me like she's in on a secret, and I do my best to ignore her. I haven't told her or my dad shit about what's gone down between Julia and me, but Cassie Kelly is sage. She doesn't miss a fucking beat…over anything. I know that she knows something is up. Hell, my dad even knows something's up, but I refuse to have that conversation right now.

"Cass, you and Thatch have hot genes," Julia rambles.

Georgia snorts.

My mom is still smiling.

"Every girl on campus wants to date Ace Kelly." Julia huffs out breath. "It's annoying."

"You know, Julia, I think Ace Kelly only wants to date one girl," my mom says, and she's running her hand over Julia's head.

"Who?" Julia asks, looking between my mom and me.

"Don't even think about it, Cassie," I warn, and my mom shrugs at me and looks back at Julia.

"Maybe you should ask him," she tells Julia. "But, like, maybe do it when you're not so high, okay?"

"Okay!" Julia yells toward her phone that's now sitting by her hip. "Siri! Remind me to ask Ace who he wants to date!"

"I'm sorry, but I didn't understand that," Siri responds, Julia's phone lighting up.

"I said, remind me to ask Ace who he wants to date!" Julia shouts.

"Searching for pizza-date ideas," Siri responds.

"Oh my God!" Julia groans and drops her head back against her pillows.

For a moment, it feels like everything is perfect in the world. Like maybe nothing's broken. Like maybe Jules and I will find a way back to each other. Like maybe she loves me back.

But then, the curtain rustles again, and the last fucking person on the planet I want to see right now steps into the room.

"Julia?" Drew's voice is all concern and breathlessness as he appears, eyes wide.

Instantly, my little bliss bubble is popped, and I'm catapulted back down to fucking reality. You know, the one where she's dating this bag of tools and we're not friends.

"Drew?" Julia looks at him, her expression a little more guarded. "What are you doing here?"

He's at her side in a flash. "I came as soon as I saw your text back. Are you okay? What happened?"

"It's no big deal," Julia says and adjusts her now-bandaged hand in her lap. "Only a little cut."

"A little cut?" Drew responds with wide eyes. "You got stitches."

And I stand there, watching him run his hand over the top of her head and looking down at her in a way only a boyfriend does with his girlfriend. Because, yeah, Julia *is* his girlfriend.

I feel it all like a punch to the gut.

And I… I can't be here.

Not with him. Not with her pretending like everything's fine. Not with the taste of her skin still fresh on my lips and the ache of everything we've lost weighing me down.

While my mom and Georgia and Drew hover around Julia's bed, I back away slowly. I make an excuse of going to grab a coffee that no one really hears.

And then I leave the hospital and head back to my apartment. Alone.

The smell of maple syrup and bacon grease and cinnamon hits me first. For a second, I think I might still be dreaming. My head's foggy, my body feels like a wet paper towel, and there's a dull, throbbing ache in my left hand.

And when I open my eyes, I spot the bandage around my palm. Oh. *Right.*

Last night. The glass. The blood. *Ace.*

I push myself up slowly, my brain swimming from whatever they gave me at the ER. I can hear my mom humming from the kitchen of my apartment, and sure enough, when I shuffle out, she's standing at the stove like she's hosting a brunch for twenty instead of only one daughter recovering from blood-loss-induced fainting spells.

She turns the second she hears me. "You're up!"

"Barely," I croak.

My mom walks over and kisses my forehead like I'm six years old again, brushes my hair back, and inspects me like she's searching for leftover trauma.

"You scared the hell out of me," she says. "But Ace kept it together like a champ."

My heart lurches at the sound of his name.

"He told you what happened?"

Her eyes soften. "He texted me on the way to the ER and kept me updated the entire time until I could get there."

I search my brain for memories, but the whole night is a fog. "I don't even remember you being in the ER."

"Pretty sure that was the drugs they gave you so they could get your hand stitched back together." She grins at me over her shoulder as she flips bacon on my stove. "You were pretty loopy, girlfriend, when Cassie and I showed up."

"Oh God." I drop my face into my good hand. "Please tell me I didn't say anything awful."

"Oh, you did," she says cheerfully, returning to her army of pans. "But it was adorable. Also slightly alarming. You told the nurse she looked like Harry Styles's sister and then cried when she wouldn't sing 'Watermelon Sugar' for you."

"That's embarrassing," I say through a groan. "Have you been here all night?"

"Yep." My mom nods. "Cassie helped me get you home. I slept on the couch."

My mind silently wonders where Ace fits into that story, but the sound of my front door opening stops me from asking.

"Morning, ladies." My dad's voice floats through the apartment. "I hear someone decided to become a human blood fountain last night and figured I'd pop in this morning to check out the aftermath myself before heading into work."

"Hi, Dad." I can't not smile as he crosses the room and wraps me in a gentle hug, kissing the top of my head.

"How are you feeling, sweetheart?"

"I'm good."

"Well, I'm glad you're okay." He leans back, looking me over. "Leave it to my daughter to faint at the sight of blood."

My mom snorts. "She gets that from your side."

My dad laughs. "Oh, Georgia. Shall I remind you of the night of our first date? Benadryl ring any bells?"

"Kline," my mom chastises, but she also giggles. "Pretty sure Evie has interrogated us enough about how we got together. Let's move on from it."

He walks over and wraps his arms around my mom, pressing a kiss to her temple, and she giggles again like they're newlyweds.

I slam my head into an imaginary wall.

They've always been like this. Loud and in love and embarrassingly affectionate. I used to roll my eyes at it as a teenager, but now, I understand their brand of happiness is the goal we're all shooting for one day.

It's normally romantic, but with the state of my life right now, it makes me seethe with jealousy. I want it for myself, and unfortunately, I want it with the one boy it feels like I can't have.

God, last night. My memories are foggy, but I do remember Ace picking me up off the floor and distracting me with terrible lies about new couches. He carried me like I weighed nothing and held my hand while they stitched me back together.

And then he was gone. I don't know when he left, but at some point after the chaos and the laughter and the pain meds, he apparently slipped out of the ER. No goodbye. No message.

I check my phone instinctively.

One unread text.

> **Drew: How are you feeling this morning, babe? Think you're going to make it to class?**

My heart sinks.

No texts from Ace. No calls. No nothing.

I stare at my phone for a long minute, debating if I should walk across the hall and knock on his door and ask him why he left. But mostly, I want to thank him for being there for me last night.

Ace has always been there for you.

My phone vibrates in my hand as another text comes in.

> **Scottie: I know you weren't planning on going tonight, but pleaseeee come. What time should we meet up with you for Double C?**

The big, not-confirmed-but-we-all-know-it's-happening Double C event for Halloween.

No one knows the time or place yet—it's always kept secret until the last minute—but the Halloween party is going down. People are already buzzing about it. Another event. Another night Ace will be the center of the universe.

Another night you'll have to force yourself to stay focused on your boyfriend and not mentally keep tabs on Ace.

I stare at Scottie's text. The other day, I told her I wasn't planning on going to it, and even though I didn't want to be honest with myself on why I didn't want to go, the Instagram picture of Ace with Glitter Girl was front and center in my mind.

I could still say no, but I don't.

> **Me: Okay. Yeah. I'll go. I'm eating breakfast with my parents, but I'll text you later.**

My mind isn't thinking about Drew or texting Drew when I respond to her.

It's thinking about Ace.

It's tempting fate. It's playing with fire.

But I'm already the walking wounded, right? *What's a little burn?*

59

If someone had told me at the beginning of the semester that I'd be hosting an underground, costume-mandatory Halloween party in a historic campus theater, I'd have laughed and then immediately started figuring out how to make it happen. Because yeah, that sounds exactly like me.

Still, as I slip past a pair of fire performers doing synchronized tosses in front of the Beckley Theater, even I have to admit, *I've outdone myself tonight.*

Beckley is old and creaky and technically off-limits after ten p.m., but a few greased palms and one carefully worded anonymous email about "emergency art student access" and voilà—Double C's Halloween bash is live. Music echoes from the theater's old stage, lights are pulsing, and black-robed bartenders are passing out color-coded drinks from cauldrons. The whole place is a chaotic fever dream of cloaks, corsets, smoke machines, and strobe lights.

And I'm wearing the most ridiculous thing I could find. A velvet pirate coat, boots, a silk shirt unbuttoned far too low, and a fake sword that I've already whacked into three people. It's not subtle, but then again, neither am I.

"You look like a bad porno version of Johnny Depp!" Blake shouts over the music, his tone both horrified and impressed.

"Get real. Even Johnny Depp himself would be proud of the Captain Jack Sparrow I've managed to pull off." I smirk, tugging at the collar of my coat. "Plus, jealousy's a bad look on you, Weiner Man."

Blake looks down at his half-assed "Hot Dog Vendor" costume—literally a striped apron and a cardboard sign that reads HOT DOGS 4 SALE. "I didn't know we were going full Broadway production, man."

Before I can reply, I feel a hand on my arm.

I turn to look and spot Scarlett standing there. She's in a crimson devil costume with glitter horns and a neckline that defies the laws of gravity. She twirls a fake pitchfork in her hand and leans in close, her voice purring in my ear. "Well hello, Captain Kelly. I almost didn't recognize you."

Blake snorts and backs away like he wants zero part of this.

I give Scarlett a polite smile. She's always been confident and a little dangerous in that way that makes most guys lose their minds. Last year, before everything with Scottie went down, I probably would've tried to see where things went with her. She flirted, I flirted back, but then everything happened.

And now, I see her and feel…nothing.

Well, not nothing.

I feel *Julia*.

Even when she's not here.

Scarlett steps closer. "You look good," she says, eyeing me like I'm on the menu. "Really good. You have plans after this?"

Before I can formulate a smooth let-down, the crowd at the front doors stirs. There's a flutter, a hush that spreads like a wave. I don't even know how I know it's her, but I do.

I turn.

And there she is.

Julia Brooks.

She walks into the theater like a goddamn vision, dressed in a black lace mask and a costume that hugs her like she was born for it.

She's flanked by Scottie, who's in an angel getup with gold wings, Finn in a skeleton suit and LED glasses, and whatshisface dressed like he thinks he's charming in a tuxedo shirt and vampire cape.

He puts his hand on Julia's back, steering her toward the bar.

I swear I see her stiffen, only slightly, but fuck, I could be imagining it.

Scarlett says something beside me, but I don't hear it.

All I can think about is last night and how I got to be the guy by her side, taking care of her. I held her in my arms. I calmed her down and distracted her with dumb jokes while the ER staff worked on her hand. And I watched her look up at me with those sleepy, loopy eyes and smile like none of the last two months happened. Like she didn't reject me when I told her that I'm in love with her. Like I haven't nearly gone crazy trying not to text her, call her, knock on her apartment door every single goddamn day.

And now, here she is. Looking like every dream I've ever had of her and none of them at the same time. But of course, she's standing beside someone else.

I should look away. I should go back to my dumb pirate act and the overzealous girl practically drooling beside me.

But I can't.

Because no matter how many cloaks I order or parties I throw or girls like Scarlett who try to get close—there's only ever been one person who always has my full attention, even if she doesn't want it.

Julia

The Beckley Theater doesn't even look like Beckley Theater anymore. It's unrecognizable in the most ridiculous, over-the-top, badass way. The velvet curtains glow under strobe lights. Jack-o'-lanterns line the aisles. There's a DJ in the orchestra pit and actual fire dancers twirling onstage like we're in some underground club in Europe instead of a campus theater.

Seeing all of this makes a surge of pride fill my chest. Ace has taken on the responsibility of Double C, and he's doing it in a way that only he can do. Lexi was a fantastic president, but Ace, well, he's taken Double C to another level.

He's made it his own. And I'm really proud of him for that.

"Holy hell, this is unbelievable, but I guess it shouldn't be a surprise," Scottie says next to me, eyes wide. "Once Ace Kelly became the president, shit was gonna get wild."

I don't answer her. I'm too busy searching the room.

And then I find him.

He's standing near the stage, wearing a pirate costume—if pirates wore sexy velvet coats and partially unbuttoned shirts that showed off stupidly perfect collarbones. He's chaos and confidence wrapped into one hot package.

And he's not alone.

Scarlett is standing beside him.

My stomach twists at the sight of her. She's in a devil costume, all legs and boobs and red lips and high heels. She's draped over him, laughing like he's the funniest person she's ever met, touching his arm like she belongs there.

My hand aches. I flex my fingers against the bandage, the gauze still wrapped around my palm. The throb is dull but insistent, and not because of the stitches.

It's because of him. Because of last night.

Because Ace took care of me without question, like he's done so many times before.

And I didn't feel scared last night. Because Ace was there.

I force myself to look away. My eyes land on the bar, where Drew is ordering drinks. The female bartender is smiling at him, laughing, and leaning a little too close. She flicks her hair over her shoulder, and it's a very flirtatious move.

I know that move. Every girl knows that move.

And yet, I feel…nothing. Not even a flicker of emotion.

Which is somehow so much worse than jealousy.

Because if I cared—if I still really cared—I'd be mad. I'd feel something. Instead, I feel like I've been holding my breath for weeks, pretending this thing with Drew still has life in it.

I glance at Scottie, my voice barely above a whisper, but the words fly out of my mouth unchecked. "I think I need to break up with him."

Scottie jerks her head toward me. "Wait. What?"

I keep staring at the bar. "I can't do it anymore. It feels cruel."

Scottie doesn't say anything. She threads her arm through mine and gives it a quiet squeeze.

Before I can say anything else, Drew is already walking back over with two plastic cups of beer.

He hands me one, and I down half of it in one go. It's not even good beer, but I don't care. I need something in my hands.

"Thirsty?" he asks with a laugh.

Scottie's watching us with wide eyes, like she's witnessing something she's not supposed to be seeing. She sips her drink and avoids eye contact like it's her job.

And I stare down into my cup like the answers might be floating in the foam.

What the hell am I doing?

Sure, Drew is good guy. A nice guy. He likes me, and he wants to be with me. But I don't feel it. Not the way I'm supposed to. Not the way I feel when Ace looks at me like he's gravity and I'm free-falling straight toward him.

I glance across the room again—back at Ace.

He's still talking to Scarlett.

He's out of reach. Maybe moving on.

Except, last night, he wasn't. Last night, he was right there. He was with me.

I turn back toward the stage, letting the music pulse through me like it can drown out everything I don't want to feel. The bass. The lights. The bodies packed around me.

My heart pounds in time with the beat.

I've made a mess. A complete mess. And it's all because I've spent years pretending I haven't been in love with Ace Kelly my entire damn life.

And now, it's like I don't know how to stop.

"I think I need another drink," I announce to Drew and Scottie, but my feet are already heading toward the bar.

Getting drunk isn't the best idea I've ever had, but it sure seems like the easiest option.

The party is still pulsing all around me—lights flickering, bodies moving, music so loud it vibrates in my ribs—but I feel like I'm stuck behind glass. Like I'm watching it all happen from somewhere else entirely.

Drew leans in close, shouting to be heard over the noise. "You wanna dance?"

I blink at him, my cup long since empty. I've chugged three shitty beers in the last thirty minutes, and while I'm definitely buzzing, it's not the kind of drunk that makes anything feel easier. Just fuzzier. Louder. More complicated.

I look past Drew, my eyes drawn to wherever Ace is.

He's on the dance floor. There's a circle of girls around him. Sorority girls. Double C girls. I don't even know. They're all dressed in some version of sexy and supernatural. A vampire. A witch. A fairy. Scarlett's back too—looking like she was poured into her devil costume and like she knows exactly what to do with it.

Ace isn't dancing with any of them, not really. He's just there. Laughing. Smirking. Moving in rhythm while they orbit him like he's the fucking sun.

My stomach clenches. My chest aches. My fingers curl into fists at my sides.

Drew's voice cuts through the fog again. "Wanna dance?"

And it's all too much. The reality is too glaring. "I can't do this anymore, Drew."

He frowns. "What?"

"This. Us." I confess the truth, and his brow furrows in confusion.

"What are you talking about?"

"I can't be with you anymore."

"Julia?" He takes a step back. "Are you drunk?"

"Yes," I admit without hesitation. "But I'm also right."

The music is pounding, and there are people everywhere—laughing, shouting, dancing—and suddenly, I can't breathe.

I grab Drew's hand and tug him with me, weaving through the crowd until we find a quiet alcove off to the side. It's dark and half hidden behind one of the giant velvet curtains.

"I'm sorry, Drew. I know this feels like it's coming out of left field, but I can't be with you anymore. It's not fair to you," I say, and tears well in my eyes when I realize how badly I've strung him along. It doesn't matter if Ace is moving on; the fact remains that I'm in love with him. I have been in love with him since before I even knew what love was. And I can't, in good conscience, be in a relationship with someone when my heart wants someone else.

"What do you mean, it's not fair to me?" He tugs his hand away. "I don't understand."

"You were right," I say. "You were right about Ace having feelings for me. But you weren't aware that I have feelings for Ace too. The night you asked me to be your girlfriend, he came over to my apartment and told me he was in love with me. He kissed me and I kissed him back, and I'm so sorry I did that. I know it was wrong, and I should've been honest with you, but that's what happened."

"You fucking kissed him? While we were together?"

"I'm sorry, Drew. I'm so, so sorry."

"And you decided now, in the middle of a fucking party, is the right time to tell me all of this? The right time to break up with me?"

"I'm so, so sorry," I say again, my voice barely audible. "I didn't plan this. I didn't want it to go like this with us, but I feel like I'm lying to myself. And I'm lying to you. And I don't want to keep doing that."

"So, this is it?" His face hardens. "You're literally breaking up with me?"

My eyes sting. "You're great, Drew. You're kind. You've been patient with me, and I've been trying so hard to be the girl who deserves that. Be the girl who you deserve. But I'm not that girl for you."

I look down at my bandaged hand, the reminder of everything that's happened in the past twenty-four hours pressing down like a weight on my chest. "I don't want to hurt you," I say. "But I think staying with you would hurt you more."

He stares at me like he's trying to find the version of me he thought he knew somewhere inside this mess.

And then he simply…shakes his head. He doesn't say anything else. Doesn't yell. Doesn't argue. Doesn't call me a bitch for kissing another guy while we were together.

He just walks away.

And leaves me standing there alone.

Tears slip from my eyes almost immediately. I blink them back, trying not to let them fall, but it's impossible. Everything feels like a disaster. A slow-motion, heart-wrecking disaster of my own making, and I am definitely the bitch for breaking the heart of an actual good guy.

I step out of the alcove and glance toward the dance floor again.

Ace.

He's still surrounded by other girls. Scarlett's with him again, all long legs and fake horns and devilish confidence. She leans in close, wraps an arm around his shoulders, and whispers something in his ear.

And then he looks up. Right at me.

Our eyes lock—for just a second.

But it's enough to make my chest cave in on itself.

I look away first, and I don't wait around. Don't stop to explain or fix anything.

I hightail it to the nearest exit and leave.

61

My head's still pounding, and I swear there's glitter in my *ear canal.*

I've showered twice, but somehow, I still feel like I smell like fog machine and stale beer.

And now, instead of sleeping in or eating my weight in hash browns at Zip's Diner, I'm walking into my parents' penthouse because my mom texted me no fewer than fifty times this morning to get here. She said it was a 9-1-1 emergency.

The elevator dings, and I step out to my mom standing in the foyer like she's been waiting for me.

"Finally," she says, stepping aside and waving me farther into the penthouse like I'm late for a court-ordered appearance. "Come collect your crap."

"Wow, Mom. Good morning to you too."

She huffs out a breath and leads me to the kitchen, where a box is sitting on the island. It's busted open and overflowing with ancient Ace artifacts like old charging cords, faded notebooks, and a paint-stained hoodie from high school.

"I figured since you're such a grown man now," she says, dramatically flipping her hair over her shoulder, "you can finally take responsibility for the museum exhibit you left in your closet."

"I don't even remember owning half of this stuff."

"That tracks."

"And why in the hell is it so important that I come get this box *today?"* I question. "I mean, from what I can see, it seems like you can throw it all away."

"Acer, don't fucking sass me," she snaps. "Go through your shit."

Good grief. What's crawled up her ass? I don't dare ask the question and start halfheartedly digging through the box. My brain's still fried from last night. I don't even know what time I got home. I only remember seeing Julia across the room. Seeing her *with him.* And feeling like I couldn't breathe.

"I found this too. Seems important." Mom slides a folded piece of paper across the counter toward me. It's wrinkled and soft from time, and I recognize the handwriting before I even touch it.

Pink marker. Loopy letters. Hearts dotting every i.

I don't have to unfold it to know what it is.

She says nothing. Just sips her coffee and watches me read it.

Ace and Julia get married at 25 years old. No matter what.
J U L I A
A C E

My throat feels tight.

I refold it slowly. Carefully. Like it's fragile in more ways than one.

My mom doesn't say a word. She simply turns to the fridge like she didn't drop a memory bomb on my morning.

And my dad strolls into the kitchen, shirtless, whistling, and his favorite mug is in hand that reads **I LOVE CASSIE'S TITS** in big block letters. "Morning, Acer," he says, clapping me on the back so hard I stumble a step. "How ya doing, buddy?"

"Fine," I mutter, my skin still stinging from his big fucking meaty hand.

Dad refills his coffee mug, leans against the counter, and says, "Saw Kline yesterday. He said Jules and that guy Chad are getting pretty close. Real fluffing cozy. Know anything about that?"

My stomach twists, but I keep my face flat, and my silence only spurs him on further.

"Apparently, Julia brought him to brunch and shit several weeks ago. I guess if they're doing meet-the-parents shit, they must be getting close." Dad takes a sip. "He also mentioned something about next year. Julia maybe moving in with the guy…"

I freeze. The paper's still folded in my hand. My name written in pink. Hearts over the i's.

"Really?" I ask, and it's the first word I've said since he started fucking gabbing.

"Who knows." He shrugs. "Might just be Kline being paranoid. Or maybe it's happening. Either way, it's feeling a lot like you're letting the love of your life slip through your fingers. But what do I know, huh?"

"You know what? You can go through the rest of that later," my mom says as she slides the rest of the box full of junk she demanded for me to come over here and look at down the hall behind her and away from me.

To my surprise, they don't say anything else. At least not to me. To each other, they talk about Thanksgiving plans and bicker about who left the fancy olive oil uncapped. There are boob squeezes and nipple pinches and my dad talking about how olive oil makes his balls smooth.

But it's nothing more than chaotic background noise as I stare down at the paper in my hands and think about the love of my life.

This may just be paper—our silly marriage decree—but what it stands for is so much more.

Even when Julia Brooks isn't mine…it still feels like I'm hers.

62

Julia

I'm wearing an old hoodie and socks that definitely have a hole in the toe.

My hair is…questionable. My eyes are puffy. And I've been standing in front of my mirror for a full five minutes now, pretending I'm brave.

Not *brave* brave. Not save-a-kid-from-a-burning-building brave. But like…walk-across-the-hall-and-talk-to-the-guy-who-used-to-be-your-best-friend-and-you're-in-love-with-him brave.

Which feels harder, honestly. I clear my throat and try again, staring at my own reflection.

"*What is your fucking problem, Ace?*"

I wince. "Okay. Nope. Aggressive. Very aggressive."

Deep breath. New attempt.

"*Why did you do all that crazy shit? Set your apartment on fire? Put yourself in all my classes? Why didn't you tell me you were in love with me, you moron?*"

I blink. "Oh my God."

I wave that one away so hard it's like I'm trying to bat it out of the air.

I try again.

"*I miss you.*"

"*Kiss me, you idiot.*"

I groan and slap my own forehead. "Jesus, Julia. You sound like Rory Gilmore."

I take a deep breath and give it one more shot.

"Tell me that you're really in love with me and not that I'm just a girl you want to keep as a backup. Tell me that you feel for me the way I feel for you. Tell me that we can fix this. Tell me that we can fix us. Tell me that I'm not too late and you haven't moved on."

It's so honest, so painfully honest, that I feel like I could throw up. Which means it's perfect.

But I choose to pace my apartment instead. Last night at the party was the most emotionally violent moment of my entire adult life. I had to see Ace with girls hanging all over him, and it hurt so damn much I could hardly breathe. I broke up with Drew, which was definitely needed, but not easy telling someone how shitty of a human being you've been toward them and that you're in love with another guy.

I slept like shit. And now, I'm a disaster in a hoodie, talking to herself in the mirror.

Screw it.

I grab my phone off the counter and march across the hall before I can psych myself out again. I knock once. Twice. And then step back, heart practically in my throat.

No answer.

I wait thirty more seconds. Press my ear to the door like a total weirdo.

Still nothing.

Of course, my brain takes the open invitation to spiral.

Maybe he's at Scarlett's apartment.

Maybe she's in *his.*

Maybe I waited too long. Dated Drew too long. Said all the wrong things, held everything back for way too many years when I should've let it out. Maybe I was too harsh on him when he told me he was in love with me.

Maybe *I'm* the problem. Maybe I ruined this. Us—if there even is an "us" anymore.

I exhale shakily, step away from his door, and pull out my phone again.

I send a text to the people who might be able to distract me from this identity-level tailspin.

> *Me: You guys around? I need greasy food and friends who won't let me cry into mozzarella sticks.*

Three dots pop up immediately.

> *Scottie: I'm in.*

> *Kayla: Say less. Zip's in 20?*

> *Me: See you there.*

I look back at Ace's door one more time before heading back to my apartment and throwing on some clothes for lunch.

I'm wishing I had a plan. I'm wishing I knew what to do. But mostly, I'm wishing and hoping and praying that whatever's broken between us can be fixed.

Julia

The coffee at Zip's tastes like it was brewed in a 1970s radiator, and I love it for that. The booths are cracked vinyl, the syrup is exceedingly sticky, and the burgers are basically perfect.

But none of it is helping with the pit in my stomach.

Scottie wheels up to the table, and Kayla slides into a chair across from me. Both of them look suspiciously cute for people who supposedly woke up hungover.

"Okay, before you even try to pretend this is a normal lunch," Kayla says, tossing her purse down, "your text sounded like a cry for help."

"It wasn't a cry for help," I lie. "I just wanted to see you guys."

Scottie lifts a brow. "C'mon, Jules."

"Okay, fine." I laugh, but it's a weak one. "Maybe it was a little cry for help." I wrap my hands around the mug in front of me like it might anchor me to the earth. "Not sure if you noticed…but Ace and I aren't exactly on speaking terms."

Both of them blink at me.

Then they laugh. *Hard.*

Scottie points a fry at me. "Girl, we *noticed.*"

"The tension between the two of you for the past month and a half could power the entire New York electrical grid." Kayla's shaking her head. "So…what happened between you guys?"

My cheeks burn, but I find the courage to lay it all out there. Some of this, I'm sure Scottie already knows because of Finn, but

Kayla is most certainly in the dark. "Right after he became Double C prez and I agreed to be Drew's girlfriend, Ace kissed me and told me he loved me. He also told me all this crazy shit he'd been doing to be closer to me. Really insane kind of stuff."

"Whaaaaa?" Kayla chimes in with wide eyes. "And what did you say to him?"

"I basically told him it was too late."

"Oh shit," Scottie mutters.

"I know." I sigh. "But in my defense, I feel like I've been waiting my whole life for Ace."

"Wait…you've been secretly pining for him all this time?"

I sigh again. "Cat's outta the bag."

They both go quiet.

"Everything just got so…complicated. And now I think I messed everything up."

"Does Drew know you have feelings for Ace?"

"I don't think that matters because I broke up with him last night."

Kayla lets out a low whistle. "Damn, girl. No wonder you texted us."

"Do you want to be with Ace?" Scottie asks.

"Yes. But mostly, I want my best friend back."

"You do know that Ace isn't dating anyone, right?" Scottie adds.

I blink. "Oh, come on. I *saw* him with Scarlett last night."

Scottie *snorts.* "Last night? Seriously? The only person Ace went home with last night was himself. I was there. Hell, I haven't seen Ace with anyone since, like, early June, Jules. And I'm pretty sure Scarlett went home with Seth Maddox."

Kayla groans. "Who is, like, stupid hot but also a total sleaze. So I guess they're kind of perfect together."

I stare at them.

I mean…*really* stare.

Because somehow, I'd convinced myself that Ace left the party and went straight to bed with Scarlett. I *saw* them together, so it must've meant something. But now I'm realizing that might've been…fear. Insecurity. Projection.

"Oh my God," I whisper, voice catching in my throat. "I know Ace didn't handle shit well, but I think I've been a bit of an asshole."

"No," Kayla says immediately, reaching for my hand. "You've been confused. And scared. And trying to protect yourself. That doesn't make you an asshole. I mean, we've all seen the ladies' man that Ace Kelly has been since he set foot on campus freshman year."

"Yeah," I say quietly. "But I still hurt him. And I didn't mean to."

Scottie nudges a plate of fries toward me. "Eat something before we get deep into this emotional spiral. You're going to need the carbs."

I smile faintly and take one, but the moment's already slipping. My thoughts are spiraling fast.

I'm back in that hospital room. Ace kissing my forehead and carrying me in his arms.

I'm back at the Beckley Theater, watching him laugh with someone else while I fall apart inside.

"I don't know if I can fix it," I murmur.

Kayla squeezes my hand. "You can."

"Trust me, Julia, you can," Scottie says. "Ace loves you. To the point of madness. You just need to tell him how you feel."

"Oh! You should do it tonight! At the Gamma Pi Halloween party they moved because they were fucking scared everyone was going to the Double C thing last night!" Kayla exclaims, and they launch into a conversation about the party—apparently someone's older cousin is DJing and there's a rumored confetti cannon—but I barely hear them.

Because I'm stuck on one and only one thing—how can I get my best friend back?

We split the check and say our goodbyes outside Zip's, but I linger for a second on the sidewalk after Scottie and Kayla disappear around the corner, both already talking about outfits for the party tonight.

I should go home. Do laundry. Wallow.

Instead, I pull out my phone and text the one and only person I want to talk to right now.

> *Me: Are you busy?*

Her reply comes two seconds later.

> *Mom: Currently in the city. Crashing one of Cassie's photo shoots in Central Park. She's taking photos of Theo Damon.*

> *Mom: Wait. Is something wrong?*

> *Me: No, but I think I'll swing by to see you. Is that okay?*

> *Mom: Julia, sweetheart, of course that's okay. We're at the Mall. It's shut down for the shoot.*

I shove my phone in my purse and head to the nearest subway stop. And I have to ride the train for six stops before I reach Central Park. By the time I'm back on the sidewalk and in the rush of people, it only takes me another ten minutes or so to reach the park's famous entrance.

It's surreal walking through the closed-off stretch of Central Park. The Mall looks like a movie set, all curated lighting and fashion chaos. There's a makeup tent. Stylists with clipboards. Cameras on dollies. Security.

And there, right in the middle of it all, is my mom holding a cup of coffee and chatting animatedly with someone holding a reflector.

When she spots me, her brows furrow, and she waves me over immediately.

"Julia? What's going on?"

"Nothing," I say when I reach her, and she sets the coffee down on the bench.

"Honey. I wasn't born yesterday. I can tell something's wrong."

"Am I that obvious?"

"Well, my very independent college girl who sometimes forgets to call and text me back tracked me down in the middle of Central Park…" She eyes me knowingly. "I think it's safe to say something's going on."

I let out a deep exhale. "Mom, I think I messed everything up."

Her face softens. "Messed what up?"

"I broke up with Drew."

"Drew?" She blinks. "Who's Drew?"

I laugh weakly. "The guy I was dating."

"Ohh. The one from the hospital? Right, right. I don't know why I thought his name was Chad. Cassie is always calling him that."

I half laugh, half sigh, but before I can say anything else, a familiar voice cuts through the chaos.

"You broke up with Chad?"

Cassie Kelly has her camera slung around her neck and is walking over, hair up in a messy bun, oversized sunglasses perched on her head like a crown. Behind her, the celebrity being photographed is literally *waiting*. But Cassie's focused entirely on me.

"Drew," I correct on a sigh. "His name was Drew."

Cassie waves a hand. "Whatever. It's about fucking time."

My mom's eyes go wide. "Cassie!"

"Don't act surprised. That boy had placeholder energy." Cassie shrugs. "Tell me I'm wrong." Then she looks at me. "And tell me you broke up with Chad because you realized your heart wants someone else…"

"I'm in love with Ace." I blurt it out, and Cassie whoops in excitement.

"Well, it's about time you realized," my mom says like she's known all along. Which, apparently, is the story of my life when it comes to Ace. While she's smiling sweetly, she also mutters, "Poor Kline."

"I just…don't know what to do now. I feel like my life is a

clusterfuck," I say, voice smaller than I mean it to be. "Ace and I aren't talking. And I don't know how to fix it."

Cassie tilts her head, assessing me the way she probably does her photography subjects. "There's a Gamma Pi party tonight, right?"

My eyebrows shoot up. "How do you know about that?"

"Because I'm Cassie motherfucking Kelly," she says, smiling. "I know everything."

"I don't even know if Ace is going to be there," I tell her the same thing I told Kayla and Scottie when they told me it would be the perfect place to talk to Ace.

Cassie smirks. "He'll be there."

"How do you know?"

She pulls off her sunglasses and points them at me like a mic drop. "Again, because I'm *Cassie motherfucking Kelly*, that's why."

My mom groans but also laughs. "Remember that Halloween where you and Ace dressed up like Sandy and Danny from *Grease*?"

I nod, my chest squeezing. "Of course I do. It's Ace's favorite movie."

"You looked amazing," my mom says.

"You *did*," Cassie agrees, eyes twinkling. "And if you're serious about wanting to fix things with my son…" She leans in. "I've got a pair of fantastic leather hot pants at home you could borrow. Just saying."

Before I can answer, a deep voice from the direction of the camera setup calls out, slightly bewildered. "Uh…Cassie? Are we still doing this? Or…?"

We all turn.

Theo Damon. As in, *the* Theo Damon. Star of *Criminal Bloom*, *The Stolen Coastline*, and that one rom-com everyone was obsessed with last year.

He's standing in front of the lighting set in a perfectly tailored navy coat, wind machine going, brows furrowed in mild confusion. He's movie-star handsome with the kind of jawline that could slice a watermelon.

Cassie waves at him like he's a mildly annoying extra. "Just stand there and look pretty!"

He blinks. "Okay…cool."

Then she turns right back to me and my mom as if nothing happened.

I glance between her and Theo freaking Damon, stunned. "Did you just…"

Cassie shrugs, nonchalantly adjusting her camera strap. "You know, Jules," she says casually, "those leather hot pants I mentioned really deserve an encore."

I can't decide if this is the best or worst idea I've ever had, but I decide I need to do it. I need to show Ace that not only am I sorry for how everything has gone down, but that I'm all in when it comes to him.

By the time I'm back at my apartment building—after a quick pit stop at the Kellys' penthouse to get Cassie's leather hot pants— my entire body is vibrating with nervous energy.

But when I unlock my door and step inside, my feet kick something on the floor.

It's a white envelope, and my name is written on the top of it in handwriting I've known for what feels like my whole life. Handwriting I've seen change over the years from messy and unreadable to scribbly and sharp.

My hands shake as I open it.

Julia,

There are so many things I want to say to you. So many things I need to say to you. Honestly, I've tried. I've written so many unsent texts and emails to you, it's not even funny.

I'm sorry for how I handled shit. I'm sorry for all the wild situations I put you in because I didn't have the balls to tell you that I'm in love with you.

I'm sorry for that night I came home drunk and didn't

tell you about Double C and made you think I was out with some random girl. I wasn't, by the way. Frankly, Julia, I can't fathom the thought of being with another girl who isn't you.

I'm so fucking sorry I made you feel manipulated and violated. God, the mere thought of that makes me want to vomit. That's the last thing I want you to feel.

And I'm sorry if I made you feel like I took you for granted throughout our friendship. If I made you feel like you were the girl on my sidelines. If you felt like you were some kind of backup plan.

I can be fucking self-involved and self-absorbed and selfish, and I can see how those piss-poor qualities could make you feel all the things you did. I took for granted that you were always there. Not because I didn't care, but you were a given for me. You were always it, Julia.

You're still it for me. You're still the love of my life, even if it's not reciprocated on your end.

In my mind, no one compares to you. No one is more important than you.

I know you're with Drew now. I know you're in a relationship that's possibly getting serious, and I'm not trying to ruin something if it's making you happy. Because Julia, I really, truly want you to be happy. I wish more than anything I could be the guy who makes you happy, but I'll gladly take you being happy with someone else if it means you're safe and protected and content.

I miss you. I miss us.

I miss my best friend. And I hope one day she'll be able to forgive me.

I hope one day that she'll want to be my best friend again.

I know it's not much, but I've been working really hard

to learn where to put commas and asking myself the hard questions the old me would never ask.

The one question that comes up every day is simple: "Do you love her, Ace?"

And the answer is always the same.

"More than myself. More than existence. More than the stars."

I hope one day, when you ask yourself the hard questions, your answer says you love me too.

Love, Ace

Tears fill my eyes and hope blooms in my chest.
Maybe we're fixable after all.

64

Ace

I'm not proud of how I've been living.

There's a half-eaten takeout sandwich on my coffee table that's probably growing a new strain of penicillin. My couch has swallowed me whole, and my TV has been playing a loop of old basketball highlights for…a while. It's dark. Maybe on purpose. And I might smell curdled milk on the shirt I haven't washed in I don't know how long.

I've only left my apartment once today to grab some food. But the entire time, I couldn't get the vision of Julia and Drew—or the fact that they're supposedly moving in together—out of my fucking head.

When the door buzzes, I ignore it.

When it buzzes again, I groan and shout toward no one, "I'm not dead, but I'm working on it!"

It buzzes forty times in a row, so finally giving in, I shuffle over and crack open the door, only to be met by the smug, judgmental smirk of my father.

"Well, shit," Thatch says, stepping inside uninvited. "You look like warm sushi in a dog's asshole."

I try to shove the door closed as I reply, "Come back later. After someone in the building calls about a smell coming from my apartment that's my rotting corpse."

He stops the door with his big clown foot and shoves his way inside, and I wrap the blanket I'm wearing as a cloak around myself tighter.

"Holy fuck, Acer." He sniffs the air and instantly recoils. "What actually died in here?"

"My will to live?"

Thatch kicks aside a pile of laundry with his boot. "Christ. You're sulking."

"I'm not sulking."

He raises a brow. "You're sulking *with texture*. C'mon, get dressed."

"What?"

"We're going out. I made a dinner reservation."

I look down at myself. "You think I'm in any condition to be seen in public?"

"You're almost twenty years old. Being disgusting is literally your whole personality," he says. "And here—wear this." He throws something at me. I catch it. It's a cardigan. Like…a varsity-style letterman sweater.

"Are you serious?"

"It's vintage," he shrugs. "Your mom bought it. Said it would make your shoulders look broad. Get your ass dressed."

I don't know why I listen to him. But twenty minutes later, we're in his Range Rover, pulling up in front of—

"…Gamma Pi?" I blink. "You said dinner."

"This *is* dinner."

"This is a fucking frat house."

"Don't be such a prude."

"You brought me to a frat Halloween party?"

He throws the car in park and unbuckles. "You need to get out of your own head. Drink something that isn't carbonated depression. Maybe touch a boob. Whatever kids do these days."

"I'm not going to a frat party with you."

"No, you're not." He grins. "You're going by yourself."

He walks around the back of the SUV, opens the trunk, and pulls out a full gorilla suit.

I stare. "What the fuck?"

He starts putting it on.

"*What the fuck*, Dad?"

"You don't go in—" he shrugs as he zips up the suit "—I go in."

I groan and drag my hands down my face. "Good grief. Chill, old man. I'm going."

"Have fun, Acer!" he calls as I storm off toward the door. "I'll be in the bushes! I see you leave early, I'm climbing in that window!"

My feet drag through the mud of my messy feelings, but the threat of my dad's attendance keeps me moving until I'm fully ensconced in the foyer.

Inside, it's chaos.

There are strobe lights and laser lights, and people are packed wall-to-wall. There's a foam graveyard in the corner, and a guy in a werewolf costume is doing body shots off a nurse. Someone else is crowd-surfing in a full inflatable T. Rex suit.

The vibes are all fucking wrong for my piss-poor mood, but the mess of the place serves as decent camouflage at least.

I spot Blake and Finn near the bar while I'm searching for a hiding spot, and for some reason, my dumbass feet take me their way.

Blake lifts his bottle of water, smiling at me. "Nice letterman sweater."

"Thanks. My dad dressed me."

"No shit?"

I shrug. "Long story."

Scottie and Kayla wave at me from across the room, both dressed as witches—though Kayla's witch hat has tiny beer cans dangling from the brim.

My eyes scan the crowd, but the one person I want to see isn't here at all. But maybe that's a good thing. I smell a little like cottage cheese, and surely that fuckwad would be following her around like a puppy.

The music shifts to a song I know like the back of my fucking hand. It's the song from *Grease* that I've made Julia duet with me at more karaoke bars than I can count, and I instantly have visions of driving a car off a fucking cliff.

I'm here, alone, in a letterman sweater, and the universe thinks it's a good time to play one of my fucking wet-dream songs?

Fuck off, fate, you bastard.

Determined to face whatever consequences Gorilla Bush Thatch doles out, I head for the door on quick feet with nothing more than a muttered expletive over my shoulder.

I'm surprised when Blake jumps in front of me and blocks me—surprised and fucking pissed.

"Get out of my way, superstar. I'm not staying."

He shakes his head. "Sorry, dude. No can do. Turn around."

When I don't comply, he puts his hands on me and makes me, and a rage boils so quickly I'm practically a scientific marvel.

And then Julia appears from the crowd. But she looks like a fucking fever dream. Tight leather pants. Black heels. Curled hair. Red lips. Smoky eye.

I blink. My brain malfunctions. "Julia?"

Blake or some other bastard pats my shoulder from behind, and I gulp and gawk at the sight of my best friend—the love of my life—embodying a *Grease*-inspired Sandy in front of me.

She smirks and pretends to take a long drag off a fake cigarette, then flicks it to the floor and stomps it out with the toe of her shoe. "Tell me about it, stud."

My heart relocates to my throat and my excitement to my balls as Julia steps right up to me smelling like strawberry lip gloss and every single good memory I've ever had. She is heaven and home all wrapped up into one gorgeous package.

And then—without warning—she kisses me.

Hands in my hair, lips on mine, completely, absolutely, *Julia* kisses me.

I don't think. I don't even know if I'm breathing, but I do know I'm kissing her back. I grab her waist and pull her closer. The crowd around us might as well not exist. All I can focus on is the taste of her mouth and the thundering of my pulse and the voice in my head screaming finally, finally, *finally*.

And when we part, her eyes flick up to mine like I'm the answer she's been searching for.

"Can I tell you a secret that I don't want to be a secret anymore?"

I stare at her. My voice cracks when I finally speak. "Anything."

"You smell horrible for the first time ever."

Julia

"But bad smell and all, I'm in love with you, Ace."

Ace blinks at me. Rapidly and repeatedly, like he's trying to reboot.

The flickering orange lights from the jack-o'-lantern string above us catch the gold flecks in his eyes, and I swear to God, my heart is going to punch a hole through my chest.

For half a second, I panic, and my skin heats like I've been dropped under a spotlight. The silence is scary.

But then, he steps forward. His movements are slow and deliberate, like the rest of the party has gone quiet—even though it hasn't. It's still loud and wild, and someone's screaming along to a Pitbull remix in the corner. There are body shots happening on the kitchen counter.

But Ace is only looking at me, and all my doubt flies through the window like a guy dressed as Zorro did an hour ago.

He brings his hands up, framing my face, thumbs brushing my cheeks. His eyes scan over me—Sandy wig, red lips, tight black outfit that suddenly feels like it might combust under the heat of his stare.

"I guess the letterman sweater makes sense now," he murmurs.

I huff a nervous laugh. "Yeah."

"I'm sorry for all the bullshit I've tossed your way." He lowers his voice, steady and serious.

"I know you are," I whisper. "And I'm sorry too. I didn't handle things right either. I should've never dated Drew when, deep down, I knew I had feelings for you."

"You're not with Drew anymore?"

I shake my head. "I'm sorry, Ace. For everything."

"Lia, I've been in love with you my whole life," he says. "I didn't know it, not really. Not when we were kids and you cried when Petey Dillon took the last chocolate milk at lunch and I got detention for kicking him in the dick. Not when we were twelve and you punched a boy in the throat for calling me a loser. Not even when we were sixteen and you danced with me at prom in that sparkly pink dress that made you look like a fucking angel."

His smile is small. Reverent.

"But now, I see it. All of it. Every moment—every stupid, beautiful, ridiculous moment—I've ever loved you."

Tears well up in my eyes.

"I love you," he says again.

"I love you too."

He leans in and kisses me.

It's soft at first. Sure. Steady. But the second I melt into it, Ace deepens the kiss like he's making up for every second he waited too long. I fist my hands in his sweater, he wraps his arms around my waist, and we…fall.

We fall all the way in. To each other. To our hearts. To the love we've *always* had for each other.

Behind us, someone lets out a whoop.

"Finally!" Blake shouts.

Finn claps. Scottie cheers. "Get it, Sandy!"

Kayla starts chanting something that might be our names mashed together, and Finn yells something that might be "You've gotta be fucking kidding me, Trav! Right now?" but I don't hear any of it enough to pass a test.

For me, it's just Ace and this kiss. When Ace finally pulls back and rests his forehead on mine, I'm breathless.

"So…can we get the fuck out of here now?" he whispers, "I want to kiss you in more places than your mouth."

My brain short-circuits. "Oh boy."

He smirks. "That a yes?"

"Obviously."

We're already walking out before the word fully leaves my mouth. His dad, dressed like a gorilla, is pulling off the mask to wipe tears of joy from his eyes and waves from his spot in the bushes as we go.

It's no Cinderella story, but it's ours—and I wouldn't change a single thing.

Ace

I don't remember much after she said it. Not the music. Not the crowd. Not the ridiculous frat-party chaos happening around us. All I remember is Julia Brooks, in a blond Sandy wig and skintight black pants, looking me in the eyes and saying, *"I love you."*

Everything tilted. My heart, my head, the fucking axis of Earth.

She loves me.

She. Loves. Me.

Thank fucking everything.

Still in our stupid costumes, still drunk on the high of that moment, and riding the elevator up to my apartment like we're trying not to combust before we make it to the finish line.

She's standing close, her Sandy curls brushing my shoulder, red lipstick a little smudged from where I kissed her senseless in front of all our friends.

And I can't stop looking at her.

God, she's beautiful. Beautiful in that devastating, once-in-a-lifetime kind of way that makes your chest ache and your future reorient.

When the elevator dings, I don't wait. I scoop her into my arms like some love-sick Danny Zuko on steroids.

"Ace!" she shrieks, arms flailing before they wrap around my neck.

I grin down at her. "This is me carrying you over the threshold."

"We're not married," she says, laughing.

"Well, duh," I say. "We're not twenty-five yet."

She goes quiet for half a second—just long enough for our eyes to meet—and then she shakes her head, cheeks flushed, smile wide. "I can't believe you remember that."

"I remember everything when it comes to you."

I stop outside my door and shift her slightly in my arms. She tightens her legs around my waist, threading her fingers through the hair at the back of my neck.

"You sure about this?" I ask, quieter now. "Because once I step through this door, I'm not letting you go."

She doesn't hesitate. "Don't ever let me go."

Fuck me sideways.

I push the door open with my back, step inside, and kick it shut behind us.

Then I kiss her. And it's mayhem.

Months of wanting. Years of not knowing. A lifetime of feeling something I couldn't name—all of it crashes into me at once.

I kiss her like she's air and I haven't been breathing right for years.

She clings to me like she feels the same. Her lips chase mine. Her hands are everywhere—my neck, my jaw, the buttons of my letterman sweater. I don't even care when she pops one off and it bounces somewhere under the couch. She could set this whole place on fire, and I'd say thank you.

We stumble into the living room, never breaking contact, and I drop to the couch with her in my lap, legs tangled, hands greedy, lips desperate.

"Fuck, Julia," I curse softly against her neck, and she giggles.

"What?"

"You're in my arms," I whisper, kissing her collarbone. "After all this time, you're actually here."

"I know." She lets out a soft, breathless laugh that's equal parts joy and disbelief. "It almost doesn't feel real."

"It doesn't," I agree, brushing my nose against her cheek. "But then you touch me, and…yeah. It's real. It's so fucking real."

"You know, I used to secretly imagine this." Her fingers find the back of my neck, tugging me closer. "You and me together."

"You did?"

She nods and glides her lips against mine. "I did."

"I've imagined this too," I tell her. "A thousand times. A hundred different ways."

She leans her forehead against mine. "We're really doing this, huh?"

"Fuck yes, we are," I murmur and kiss her again—deeper this time and slower.

Her hips shift against me, and a soft moan escapes her lips.

Fuck.

She's kissed me before, but not like this.

Not like someone who loves me back.

Not like someone who's *mine.*

I lean into her, mouth at her ear. "Tell me again."

She pulls back enough to meet my eyes.

"I love you, Ace."

I'm gone.

Totally and completely.

And fuck, I want it to be more than this. More than frantic touches on my couch. I want to remember everything. I want to feel everything. I want to fucking worship her.

I stand, lifting her with me, and she wraps her legs around my waist like it's second nature. I carry her down the hall to my room. I kick the door shut with my foot, and she's already pulling at my shirt and letterman, fumbling with the hems, laughing when they gets stuck over my head.

Once both are gone, I guide her to the bed, laying her down gently. I remove her wig and her heels, kissing her feet as I do. Her shirt and bra are next, and her pants and lacy underwear come off shortly after that.

I have to pause to catch my breath. Naked Julia is inconceivable. Undeniable. *Fucking perfect.*

My heart pounds so hard inside my chest it might as well be a playlist—the soundtrack of our love.

Julia is beautiful in the way that you feel to your damn bones. She's beautiful in the way that makes me wonder if I'm going to die of a heart attack before I reach twenty fucking years old. She's beautiful in the way that I know with absolute certainty, years and years later, the vision of her like this will be so ingrained in my fucking brain it'll probably have to form a new goddamn lobe to remember any other shit.

"I love you," I tell her. "I love you more than I've ever loved anyone or anything."

"I love you too," she says and moves to kneel on the bed before me. With quick hands, she removes the rest of my clothes until I'm completely naked. My cock juts out like it's willing to disconnect itself from my fucking body to be closer to her.

I crawl onto the bed, urging her to lie back again, and start kissing every inch of her. Her feet, her legs, her upper thighs, her belly, her breasts, her arms—my lips and tongue and mouth touch every part of her skin.

My kisses are greedy and desperate, but they're reverent too.

I memorize her body, her panting breaths, and her little moans and sighs.

"*Ace.*" She reaches out to pull me toward her until my body hovers over hers. Until my chest brushes against her breasts and the tip of my hard cock can feel how wet she is between her thighs.

"I need you." She looks up at me, her hand on my jaw, eyes so full of emotion it nearly levels me.

"I've always fucking needed you, Julia," I tell her, my voice a little hoarse. "You should've been my first."

Her eyes soften. "You should've been my first, too."

"You should've been my first everything." I brush my lips against hers. "But now, you're something better."

She searches my eyes.

"You're my last," I say quietly, stroking my thumb across her cheek, "You're my always. You're my forever."

"You're mine too." Her eyes glisten. "Let me feel you," she whispers. "All of you. Inside me."

Every piece of us, together. Every piece of us forever.

67

Friday, November 7th
Julia

It's been almost a week since I told Ace I loved him and we went from being best-friends-who-weren't-on-speaking-terms to together. As in, *together* together.

Six days of waking up tangled in his sheets or him tangled in mine. Of toothbrush-sharing and takeout dinners and watching half a movie before one of us can't take the tension anymore and climbs on top of the other. Six days of sneaking kisses between classes, falling asleep with my head on his chest, and wondering how the hell I survived college life before this.

Tonight, we're headed to his parents' penthouse for dinner because Cassie Kelly insisted. And when Cassie Kelly insists, you go.

It's barely a fifteen-minute walk from our apartments, but Ace insisted we take the subway instead of walking. Something about "adding spice to our foreplay." He's been holding my hand the entire time, his thumb grazing my knuckles while his other hand rests lightly on my thigh. His eyes keep drifting to my mouth.

"You know," he leans over and whispers, lips brushing the shell of my ear, "if I weren't such a gentleman, I'd already have you pressed up against that pole."

"Ace," I hiss, scandalized but smiling.

"You're right," he says solemnly. "Too many witnesses. But just know, I've been mentally undressing you this entire ride."

"Only mentally? That's disappointing."

He grins like I told him it's his birthday. "Lia. You can't say sexy shit like that in public."

"You started it."

"True. But I'm finishing it," he says as the train slows at our stop. "Hop on."

"Hop on what?"

He turns, crouching slightly. "My back. Obviously."

"You are not giving me a piggyback ride through Manhattan."

"I absolutely am. Come on, it's a tradition now."

I laugh but oblige, wrapping my arms around his neck and letting him lift me off the floor like it's nothing. "We've been dating for one week."

"One week, and, like, almost two decades in the making. That's tradition-worthy, baby."

We draw a few stares as he jogs up the steps of the subway station with me on his back, dodging tourists and shouting about how I owe him a back massage after this. When we finally reach the elevator in his parents' building, both of us are breathless from laughter, and Ace is still grinning like he won the lottery.

Which, according to him, he did. "Finally," he mutters, pressing a kiss to my wrist. "You're mine."

The elevator doors slide open, and we step directly into the penthouse.

And that's when it happens.

"*Surprise!*"

I jolt, nearly falling off Ace's back as a wave of sound and confetti hits us like a brick wall.

Everyone—and I mean everyone—we know is standing in the Kellys' massive living room.

And a giant balloon banner stretches across the room in bold letters: **FINALLY!**

Lexi and Blake are here, and so are Finn and Scottie, and all of Finn's siblings. My sister Evie and Ace's brother Gunnar. The Winslows are here. Ace's parents are here, looking more excited and happier than I've ever seen them. And my mom is smiling, though my dad kind of looks like someone just told him Ace knocked me up.

Ace lets me slide off his back gently, one arm still wrapped around my waist. "Is it just me, or does this feel like overkill?" he whispers toward me, but his dad hears him.

"Overkill? Acer, I've been waiting years for this. Literal years," Thatch says, refilling champagne flutes in a tuxedo T-shirt.

My dad glares at him like he wants to file a noise complaint with his soul.

Thatch wraps an arm around my dad's very tense shoulders. "Don't stress, K. Think of this as the start of something beautiful. Us? One big, *official* family someday soon."

"Oh God," Ace mutters into my ear. "Should we remind them about the crocodile incident before things escalate?"

"Don't you dare," I whisper back.

Everyone starts coming forward to hug us, pat Ace on the back, or whisper "about damn time" in our ears. The party kicks off around us with music, drinks, and so many appetizers that I briefly consider a second piggyback ride to the dessert table.

But then Ace turns to my father. "Hey, Mr. Brooks."

My dad arches a brow. "Ace."

"I just wanted to say…" Ace pauses, scratching the back of his neck in mock nervousness. "I'd like to formally ask for your daughter's hand in marriage."

Kline nearly drops his champagne flute. "Excuse me?"

My mouth falls open. "Ace!"

Thatch whoops from across the room, now wearing a cone-shaped party hat and blowing a noisemaker like it's New Year's Eve. "This is the happiest day of my motherfluffing life!"

Ace holds up both hands. "Kidding. I'm kidding. For now." He winks. "But I'll be back in five or six years."

Kline Brooks does not look comforted. If anything, he looks eerily close to a cardiac event or a stroke or, I don't know, seeing red and killing Ace with his bare hands. "Remember that time you asked me about a shotgun, Ace?" my dad tosses out before my mom grabs his wrist to purposefully tug him to the other side of the apartment. "Keep that in mind!" my dad still calls over his shoulder.

Oh jeez.

As the party buzzes around us, Ace leans in and kisses me softly with a brush of his lips before he whispers, "Love you, Lia."

"Love you too."

"And just so you know…" He reaches into his pocket and pulls out a folded piece of worn notebook paper. "I still have the marriage contract you signed when we were kids."

My eyes widen. "You do not."

"Oh, I do. A contract that binds Julia Brooks to me in marriage when I turn twenty-five? Like I'd ever lose that. Hell fucking no."

He tucks it back into his pocket like a treasure map.

And I laugh.

Because somehow, in a room full of boisterous people who love us…being with Ace feels like the calmest, happiest place I've ever been.

Saturday, November 8th
Ace

The Double C after party is still raging when I duck out the side door of Perkins—otherwise known as the history building—and head to the nearest subway stop.

I don't even pretend to be sorry that the prez of Double C is leaving his own after party.

But that's because my girl is at home with a migraine, and ever since she said she felt too sick to go to the Double C event tonight, I've been busy checking in on her every hour on the hour. Sometimes every half hour, to be honest.

Julia's been sick maybe four times in the entire time I've known her, and even then, she refused to miss school. So, yeah, I'm concerned. Hell, she practically had to shove me out of her apartment to make me come to Double C tonight, reminding me that I'm the one in charge and I have to be there.

But I stayed as long as I needed to stay, and I'm currently in the elevator, headed up to our floor, texting as I lean against the mirrored wall.

Me: You up?

It only takes a second before her response pings.

Julia: Yes. Come to your apartment.

She's in my apartment?

My brows pinch as I shove my phone into my pocket and walk the short stretch down the hall.

And the second I unlock the door and step inside, I know something's up. The lights are dim, the room smells faintly like vanilla, and right there, perched in the center of my leather couch like a perfectly wrapped gift, is Julia.

Wearing nothing but *my* black Hermès tie.

It's tied loosely around her neck, barely brushing the tops of her thighs, and her legs are open. Her hair's a sexy mess of wild curls, and she's smiling at me like she already knows she's going to wreck me tonight.

Oh fuck me, I love this woman.

She leans back on her elbows, lifts her chin, and with a perfectly smug little smirk, says, "How was your day, dear?"

My jaw drops. Not because I don't get it, but because I do—*instantly.*

I bark out a laugh. "Nice tie."

She grins. "Thanks. I got it for you."

"Yeah?"

She nods and giggles. "Straight from your closet."

God, I'm obsessed with this girl. Fully, completely, can't-see-straight obsessed.

"You're quoting *Pretty Woman.*" I start walking toward her slowly, like she's something sacred and I'm not sure I'm worthy.

She shrugs one bare shoulder. "It's your favorite."

"It's one of my favorites," I correct, pausing right in front of her. "Not *the* favorite."

"You've made me watch it five hundred times."

"And you've argued with me five hundred times that it's not a rom-com."

"Because it's not, Ace."

"It literally is."

She purses her lips. "There's prostitution and trauma."

"There are also shopping montages and a happy ending. Classic rom-com formula, Lia."

She rolls her eyes, but her smile says she loves this. Loves me. God, I'm a lucky bastard.

"Also…" She pauses, and her voice drops to this sexy, seductive tone. "I have a confession to make."

"Yeah?" I sink to my knees between her thighs, breath catching as I finally let myself touch her—only her knees at first, brushing slow circles over her skin with my thumbs.

"I didn't have a migraine."

My eyebrows rise. "No?"

She shakes her head, and the tie shifts slightly, barely grazing the perfect pink of each of her nipples. "I had plans."

I grin. "To do another reenactment of one of my favorite rom-coms?"

"Something like that," she says, wicked glint in her eye. "I mean, the lead actress is named Julia."

I laugh, but it's a strained kind of sound because I'm not just worked up. I'm reverent. I'm fucking floored. I'm so goddamn grateful that she's mine.

And when I lower my mouth to her, tasting her, devouring her, worshiping her, I do it like a man who's been starving for years and finally gets to eat.

She moans. Her head falls back. Her thighs tighten around my shoulders.

And me? I think *this* is what heaven tastes like.

McKinley Library is nearly silent, except for the low hum of the ceiling lights and the occasional squeak of someone's sneaker on the tile floor. Ace is slouched in the chair across from me at one of the back study tables, a pencil stuck behind his ear, one hand tangled in his hair, and absolutely no clue what I'm talking about.

"For the third time," I say, tapping my pen on his notebook, "if you increase the angle of the incline, the parallel component of gravitational force increases too."

Ace stares at me blankly.

I sigh. "That means it'll slide faster."

"Ohh," he says, grinning. "You mean like how I slid right into your DMs freshman year?"

I throw my head back and groan. "You never slid into my DMs."

"Because I was already in your life since we were kids," he says, leaning forward on his elbows and lowering his voice. "Living right in your heart and you didn't even know it."

I stare at him.

He grins wider. "You know, it was all part of my plan…getting into all your classes. Moving across the hall from you. Studying with you. I was playing the long game of trying to make you fall in love with me. If that doesn't prove that what I feel for you is true, all-consuming love, I don't know what does."

"Or it proves you're insane," I reply.

He shrugs. "Insane for you, baby."

I try not to laugh. "Ace. Focus. You have to pass this exam, or you'll blow your GPA. And a shitty GPA could quite literally fuck your title as president of Double C."

He sighs dramatically and drops his forehead onto the open physics textbook. "Then teach me the sexy way."

I raise a brow. "The what?"

He looks up at me, eyes mischievous. "I'm just saying… I'd retain a lot more if you were, I don't know, maybe whispering formulas in my ear while you undressed me."

"Oh my God."

"I'm serious. You have a gift, Julia. Use it."

I roll my eyes, trying not to smile. "You're impossible."

"And yet, here you are. In love with me."

"You're lucky I am," I mutter.

"I really, really am." His voice softens at that, and when I glance up, he's looking at me like I'm the only thing that's ever made sense in the whole universe.

Which is why I get a ridiculous, impulsive idea.

I glance around, confirming no one is close by, and stand up. "Come on."

Ace straightens. "Where are we going?"

"Just follow me."

I lead him down a quiet hallway near the staff offices and find the door I clocked earlier. The janitor's closet. Unlocked. I pull it open and motion him in.

He looks delighted. "Oh, hell yes."

Inside, it smells faintly of lemon cleaner and old books, and there's only enough space for two people to stand shoulder to chest. Which is exactly what we're doing.

I press him back against the wall and reach up to run my fingers through his hair. "Maybe I need to teach you using the laws of physics."

"Oh?"

I smile and slide my hands down his chest, fingers teasing the hem of his shirt. "Let's start with the law of universal gravitation."

Ace's breath catches. "Which is?"

"All objects attract each other with a force that is directly proportional to the product of their masses…" I lean in and press a kiss to his jaw, then lower "…and inversely proportional to the square distance between them."

"God, I love you."

I grin. "I know. I love you too."

I sink to my knees.

His breath stutters as I tug at the button of his jeans. "Are we still…studying?"

"Oh, we're studying," I murmur. "This is kinetic energy in motion."

"I think I love kinetic energy." He lets out a shaky laugh, but it turns into a groan as I pull him free and run my fingers along the length of him. He's already hard and swollen and begging for my lips. "Holy shit, Jules—"

"Shh." I look up at him. "We're in a library."

He gently cups the back of my head as I take him in my mouth.

He tastes sweet and salty and something distinctly Ace. *My favorite freaking flavor.* And he tightens his hands as I hollow my cheeks and move slowly and methodically, taking as much of him into my mouth as I can.

"Fuck." His head thumps gently against the wall. "Best. Study session. Ever."

70

It's the Monday before Thanksgiving, and I'm spending it in one of St. Luke's Hospital's waiting rooms because Scottie is having her surgery.

Dr. Raines, Lexi's brilliant dad, is the one doing it. I don't know much about what the surgery entails, nor could I even understand it if I tried, but I know it's an extremely cutting-edge procedure on Scottie's spine.

The whole goal? To make Scottie walk again.

The fluorescent lights in this waiting room are giving me a headache, but I don't say anything. Compared to what Finn's going through right now, I don't have a single right to complain.

It's been over eight hours since they wheeled Scottie into surgery.

Eight. Fucking. Hours. I'm not even sure I've sat still for this long in my entire life. I keep getting up, pacing, checking my phone, texting Julia even though she's sitting right beside me. Just…doing anything to distract myself.

Julia's flipping through some random celebrity gossip magazine, legs crossed, one foot bouncing, her free hand laced tightly in mine. I haven't let go of her since we got here this morning. Don't plan to either.

Finn's sitting across from us, and Jesus—he looks like he's holding on by a single frayed thread. His knee's been bouncing for the last two hours, and his eyes haven't left the double doors that lead to the OR.

I watch him for a second. Watch how pale he looks, how stiff. I don't think he's even blinked in the last minute. The love of his life is back there—under anesthesia, under a scalpel, under more risk than anyone should ever have to face. And he's just here. Waiting. Praying.

I glance over at Julia again. Her lashes flick as she turns a page, completely unaware that I'm watching her like she's my lifeline. Because she is.

God, I can't imagine being in Finn's shoes. Can't imagine Julia in that OR. Can't imagine the idea of anything happening to her, ever. She's my whole fucking world.

My throat gets tight with emotion, and I squeeze her hand harder.

She glances up, surprised. "You okay?"

"I'm always okay when I'm with you, Lia," I whisper.

Her lips twitch like she's trying to smile but doesn't quite make it. She leans her shoulder into mine and goes back to flipping the page.

The room is full of people. Everyone who loves Scottie. Everyone who loves Finn. And somehow, we all showed up in this one room, together.

Scottie's dad is sitting quietly in the corner, his hand resting on the backpack Scottie arrived with like it's some kind of emotional tether. Her sister's pacing, muttering something under her breath and occasionally peeking at the clock like it might give her answers.

Finn's entire family is here—his mom Helen, looking like she's aged ten years overnight. His sister Willow and his eldest brother Reece sit side by side, whispering to each other. His twin brothers, Jack and Travis, are off in the corner trying—and failing—not to look like they're about to fall apart. It's the most serious I've ever seen them.

The Winslow family is all here too. Wendy and Howard, every

one of their grown kids—Remy, Ty, Jude, Flynn—with their spouses and kids. The kids are currently in a full-scale battle with the vending machine.

Jude finally has to get up and shout, "Hawk, stop kicking it before you break your damn foot!"

"But it stole my money!"

"You're gonna steal my sanity," Jude grumbles as he digs out a five and feeds it into the slot.

Wes and Winnie are here. So are Lexi and her boyfriend Blake, who's currently rubbing her back in slow circles as she watches the door like the rest of us. It's weird seeing them together sometimes. They were like oil and water, and now they're solid and quietly in love.

Kayla scrolls her phone in the corner, but I know by how quiet she's been, she hasn't seen even one word on her screen.

My parents are here too, sitting across from Julia's. My mom has a crossword puzzle on her lap that she's not even pretending to finish. My dad is chewing gum like it owes him money. Georgia is whispering something to Kline that's making him frown. Probably about Gunnar—aka convincing Kline not to kill him for coming back from the bathroom earlier and pranking him by putting wet hands on his face while complaining about his lack of aim while peeing.

Speaking of.

"Has anyone seen Gunnar or Evie?" I ask out loud.

Julia doesn't even look up. "Last I heard, Gunnar was trying to convince a nurse to let him scrub in."

"Christ," I mutter. "If that idiot so much as picks up a scalpel—"

The double doors swing open, and everyone goes still.

Dr. Raines walks out, still in scrubs, mask pulled down around his neck. His expression is calm—almost too calm. But then he smiles.

"She's in recovery," he announces. "And the surgery was a success. It couldn't have gone better."

The room erupts.

Finn stands, frozen, like his brain hasn't caught up to his ears. Julia stands and throws her arms around him, and then I'm moving too. I wrap him up in a hug so tight I think we both stop breathing for a second.

Then Blake and Lexi and Kayla and all of Finn's siblings join in. One after another, we all pile into this messy, overwhelming group hug, all centered around the guy who's held it together for way too damn long.

"She did it," Julia whispers to him. "Scottie is okay."

Finn doesn't say anything, but I see the tears in his eyes, and I know what that means.

Relief. Gratitude. Love.

We all fall back into our seats, laughter echoing around the room, tears running down faces, smiles stretching wide.

Everything is okay.

Scottie is okay.

And that means everything is exactly the way it should be.

Thank fuck.

71

I'm lying on my bed surrounded by wrapping-paper carnage and half-eaten birthday waffles when my phone buzzes with a text from Scottie.

> *Scottie: HAPPY BIRTHDAY, JULIA!*

> *Scottie: And I have to know…what did Ace get you for your birthday???*

I snort and start typing.

> *Me: Girl, what didn't Ace get me. My morning started with, like, twenty-seven presents exploding out of my room the second I woke up.*

> *Me: Then breakfast in bed. Waffles. Heart-shaped. Fruit arranged into a smiley face.*

> *Me: And then. THEN. He opened the window to a live band.*

> *Scottie: A live band???*

> *Me: Yes. A live band. Outside my window on the freaking sidewalk performing an acoustic version of the entirety of Taylor Swift's Midnights album.*

> *Scottie: Holy shit.*

Me: I KNOW. My boyfriend is nuts in the best way. I'm supposed to go to dinner at my parents' tonight, but he left twenty minutes ago to "run an errand" and wouldn't say what the errand entails. I'm a little terrified I'm going to walk into my kitchen to a mariachi band or a freaking Broadway play.

Scottie: I wish I could say that wasn't possible, but this is Ace Kelly we're talking about.

Scottie: But also, I'd pay actual money to see a mariachi band in your kitchen.

I grin down at my phone, the warmth of it radiating through my whole body. I'm nineteen
today, and I feel spoiled in the best ways. Loved. Lucky. *So damn happy.*

Me: Okay, but for real, how are you doing today?

Scottie: Honestly? Pretty good. I had PT this morning, and my therapist said I'm healing ahead of schedule. I'm still sore and tired, but it's a good kind of sore. First time I've felt like myself since surgery. And I was even able to wiggle my toes this morning.

Me: Holy shit, Scottie! That's incredible. God, I'm so proud of you. You're a superhero, girl.

Scottie: Yeah. Yeah. All I need is a cape. LOL.

Me: Don't even tempt me. LOL.

I'm still smiling down at the screen when I hear the front door creak open.

"Evie?" I call out, assuming my little sister has arrived uninvited again to loot my closet or complain about Heather Donovan. No answer.

Then I feel arms around my waist.

"It's me, Lia," Ace whispers, his voice low and warm in my ear.

I suck in a breath. "You have *got* to stop sneaking in like that."

He presses a kiss to my cheek. "Don't scream. And don't fight me."

"What? Ace, what are you—"

He slides a blindfold over my eyes before I can finish.

I start to laugh, but my heart is racing. "Are you serious right now?"

"Dead serious."

"You're kidnapping me?"

"Technically," he murmurs, "yes."

"Because that's totally normal behavior on someone's birthday."

"Just trust me, Lia."

"Trust you to *kidnap* me?"

"Yeah. Actually."

I sigh like I'm annoyed, but I go willingly because it's Ace.

The car ride is short, but long enough for me to spiral.

"Where are we going?"

"Is there going to be a crowd?"

"Oh my God! I'm still in my pajamas, Ace! Do I look okay?"

Those are only a few of the random questions I practically screamed at Ace when my brain started to overthink the whole "just trust me to kidnap you" thing.

By the time we come to a stop, Ace helps me out of the car and guides me forward, one hand on the small of my back, the other laced through my fingers.

A door opens, and warm air brushes my skin. It smells like citrus and candles. Somewhere, soft music is playing.

Then, footsteps and whispers.

"Seriously," I whisper. "What is this?"

Ace doesn't answer. He pulls off the blindfold.

I blink. And then gasp.

We're standing in a cavernous room that is composed of tall stone walls, golden candlelight flickering everywhere, and in the center, draped in black velvet, is a Double C crest the size of a table.

And surrounding us are cloaked figures in a semicircle.

"Oh my God," I whisper. "Are you making me join a cult on my birthday?"

One of the cloaked figures pulls their hood back, and Cassie Kelly's face comes into view. "Not a cult, Julia," she says with a big grin on her face. "But a secret society." She winks and my jaw drops.

"Wait…you're a part of Double C?"

Cassie's smile grows. "You bet your cute ass, I am. And its technical name is Computare Caterva. Remember that, you're going to need to know it."

I look at Ace, and he simply grins down at me. "Julia Brooks, as the current sitting president of Computare Caterva, it is my honor to offer you an official initiation to be vice president."

"You're joking," I say with big, shocked eyes.

Ace shakes his head and leans down to press a kiss to my lips. "So…what do you say, VP? Want to run the world with me?"

I grab the center of his cloak and pull him back toward me to kiss him hard. "Hell yes, I do."

"Happy Birthday, Lia," he says, and I kiss him with the power of every kiss we've missed out on until now.

Man, Ace Kelly sure knows how to make all this girl's dreams come true.

72

There's something about the smell of a real Christmas tree that makes you feel like a kid again.

Pine and cinnamon. Wrapping paper and sugar cookies. Laughter and something soft playing on the speaker—probably Nat King Cole, because Wendy Winslow doesn't allow modern Christmas music under her roof.

The lake house is glowing and packed to the fucking brim. A fire crackles from under the mantel, and everyone is bunched into the living room with blankets and fuzzy socks and Christmas-themed pajamas.

All the Winslows. All the Hayeses. Blake and Lexi. Scottie and Finn. Lexi's parents and my parents and Julia's parents, and of course, Jules and me. I don't know how this lake house manages to fit all these fucking people, but it's like Mary Poppins's bag.

We're all passing out presents and drinking from mugs of hot chocolate and just enjoying the ambiance that is Christmas Eve.

Blake's wearing antlers, while Gunnar keeps trying to hang an ornament from one.

My mom is snapping photos like she's been hired by a magazine.

Julia's curled up near the tree, her legs tucked under her, our dog asleep across her feet.

And Scottie is in her wheelchair, grinning at something Finn whispered to her, cheeks flushed with that kind of fierce, quiet joy that makes you pause mid-sip of cocoa and remember life is big and beautiful and fragile.

I move toward Julia—let's be real, it's my favorite hobby—and settle in next to her and Yoko as Scottie wheels herself into the middle of the room and says, "Okay. I have one more present."

Everyone turns to look with astonishing quickness. She's been working so hard since her surgery with Dr. Nick, both physically and mentally, and all of us have enjoyed watching her like the gift it is.

I'm a mentally tough fucker, but Scottie outpaces me any day. She's as tough as they fucking come.

Finn rises like he's about to help her, but Scottie lifts a hand.

"No," she says. "Just…watch."

And then…

She stands.

Scottie fucking stands up!

With one hand braced on the armrest of her chair, she pushes herself upright until she's fully standing. Silence falls like snow across the room, shock and awe and outright surprise robbing the energy we'd otherwise use for noise.

I wait with bated breath, Julia's fingernails clawing my arm like talons, as Scottie takes two steps on slightly wobbly feet before she grabs Finn's outstretched arms for support.

Julia's eyes are wide and brimming with tears, and I feel a scream building in a very violently loud place in my throat. I hold it—but I know it's going to pop out soon.

Scottie smiles and giggles and says, "Merry Christmas, assholes."

The room erupts in laughter and cheers, and we all surge toward Scottie like it's old-school Black Friday at the local Circuit City.

Finn reaches her first, arms wrapping around her like he'll never let go again, and Julia and I pile on top of him.

My mom takes pictures rapid-fire, my dad is blubbering like an emotional fool, and everyone else spins in place, beside themselves with excitement.

Scottie can fucking walk.

"It's a motherfluffing Christmas miracle!" my dad sobs. "And I am all up in my motherfluffing feels! Hold me, Cassie!"

The whole thing feels like fucking magic. A fairy-tale Christmas if we've ever had one.

———

The house is still.

Everyone's asleep. After presents, Wendy insisted on more hot chocolate and sentimental Christmas movies, which means most of the group passed out halfway through *It's a Wonderful Life.*

But I'm wide awake.

I sneak up the creaky stairs as I've done a thousand times before, only this time, I'm not a dumb eleven-year-old on a dare.

I'm a man who needs to see the woman he loves more than anything.

The bedroom door to the girls' room is cracked, and I peek in to find Julia curled up on the bed on her side, and Yoko lifts his head from his spot curled up against Julia's back.

Julia is scrolling her phone in the dark, her face lit faintly blue.

Everyone else appears to be asleep.

"You're supposed to be asleep," I whisper toward her.

She jumps, and Yoko scurries away to take refuge at the foot of the bed. "Ace! Goodness! You scared me!"

I grin and close the door behind me. "That's no way to greet your future husband."

She sets her phone aside as I crawl into her bed, lifting the blanket and sliding in behind her like it's the most natural thing in the world. Probably because there is nothing more natural than Julia and me together.

"I missed you," I murmur against her neck.

"You just saw me," she whispers, smiling.

"I know. But that was like an hour ago. I missed you."

She turns in my arms, our noses brushing. Her fingers find the hem of my T-shirt and curl there.

We lie in silence for a beat, just breathing, just being.

And then she says, "Do you remember the year Santa Dick knocked over the tree?"

I laugh into her collarbone. "Yeah. Because Santa Dick's big sack was too big, and he kept swinging that fucker around. We're lucky he didn't take out a kid."

"Goodness, my grandfather is nuts."

"Let's not forget when we found him and Mrs. Santa Dick making out like teenagers," I say, and Julia snorts.

"Evie cried for like three hours straight over that," she says and then adds, "But Gunnar thought it was so cool that Santa Dick was such a ladies' man."

I grin and press my forehead to hers. "God, I love you."

She goes quiet.

And I use that moment to pull out a piece of crumpled paper from the pocket of my flannel pajama pants.

"Oh my God, Ace," Julia mutters in surprise when I unfold the paper to reveal the marriage contract we created when we were kids. "What, do you just carry that thing around with you now?"

"Pretty much." I smile and smooth it out between us. "I want to marry you now. Is that crazy?"

"Yes," she says softly. "But it's also sweet."

I touch the corner of her mouth. "Promise me forever, Lia."

She traces her pinkie across mine. "Promise."

It's no royal decree or fifteen-minute rule, but I'll be damned if it won't do.

Ace Kelly and Julia Brooks may grow and change and get old enough to need canes and dentures and menthol patches. But there's one thing we'll be for the rest of time, and that's together.

EPILOGUE

Thursday, July 2nd

Julia

It's ninety degrees in the middle of the city, and the only thing hotter than the air outside is the inside of Ace's and my new apartment. Filled to the brim with our parents, our furniture, and about fifty pictures of Ace and me being hung at various angles on the walls, there's barely enough space for a breath, let alone a breeze.

I'm relieved when I see my dad fiddle with the AC temperature, hopefully turning that baby down to a cool sixty degrees, but that relief is short-lived when I look around the room and see the current state of our move.

Boxes are everywhere, half opened, stacked like a game of Jenga, and threatening to fall over every time someone brushes past them. Cassie and my mom are fluttering around our new apartment like it's the set of an HGTV show, hanging framed photos of Ace and me with alarming enthusiasm.

I don't even know where they got all these pictures. Some of them look like they've been pulled from the depths of our childhoods, and others must've been ripped straight from our Instagram stories and printed off at CVS when we weren't paying attention.

"Oh my God, look at this one!" Georgia says, holding up a photo of Ace and me at the lake house last summer. I'm laughing with my mouth wide open, and Ace is dripping wet beside me, flipping off the camera.

Cassie grabs it like it's a family heirloom. "That's going over the toilet in the guest bathroom."

Our new place is only a block from Dickson's campus, in the

same building where we lived last year—but we've upgraded to a two-bedroom this time. Ace insisted we needed a "study room," though we both know, if I'm not careful, he'll turn into a snack closet and nap spot by midterms.

Still, we've got more space. A bigger kitchen. A real living room. And a little terrace that looks out over the street.

It's our first apartment together. And it's freaking perfect.

Meanwhile, my dad and Thatch are locked in what I can only assume is a testosterone-fueled competition over who can carry the most furniture without throwing out their backs. When Ace started to make it look too easy, they told him to fuck off and find something else to do.

"Tell me again how I ended up moving my *daughter* into an apartment with *your* son?" my dad mutters as he drops our coffee table onto the rug.

Thatch grins and claps him on the shoulder. "It's a beautiful thing, Kline. A Kelly and a Brooks under one roof. It's like fate and karma had a beautiful baby. We should get matching family shirts made. Ooh, or a crest."

My dad glares at him but says nothing.

But Thatch isn't done. "I mean, first college sweethearts… Next stop, wedding bells."

Ace's smile is soft and easy as he turns to my dad. "Mr. Brooks, should I get your approval now—or wait until we graduate?"

"Are you serious right now, son?" My dad blinks.

Ace keeps on smiling—so much so, he's even nodding now too.

"*Shotguns*," my dad says pointedly, even raising one eyebrow in Ace's direction. "I have two now."

Oh boy. Here we go.

"Dad, can we hold off on the threatening to murder my boyfriend talk until we finish moving?" I quickly question, hoping a little levity might defuse the tension.

"Yeah, Kline," Thatch adds, but he stops talking when his phone starts ringing loudly from his pocket. He pulls it out, glances at the screen, and groans.

"It's Gunnar," he mutters as he puts the phone to his ear. "If you're not on US soil, I'm going to call the US Embassy and tell them to keep your ass wherever you are."

There's a pause, and then his eyes widen. "What do you mean, you're at the Manhattan police station?"

Ace turns toward his dad, brows raised.

"I have a license, Dad!" I hear Gunnar's voice yell through the phone.

"You don't have a fucking *CDL* license, Gunnar!" Thatch yells back. "You can't fluffing drive a semitruck through Times Square!"

Cassie looks up from her decorative pillow arranging. "What happened now?"

Thatch slaps a hand over the speaker and mutters, "Our son's been brought in for driving a tractor trailer through the city. He says it was for his business."

"His business?" Cassie questions in confusion. "He doesn't have a fucking business."

My dad shakes his head, whistling sharply and counting his blessings all at once. "I guess I should just be thankful Julia's dating Ace and not Gunnar."

"Cass," Thatch says, pointing at her like he's delivering devastating news. "We have to go down to the Manhattan police station."

"*We?*" She snorts as she holds up another photo of Ace and me toward the wall. "You mean *you*."

"Yes, *we*." Thatch sighs. "He's your son, Cassie."

"Yeah, but Ace is my favorite son today."

"Shall I remind you that our son could be going to jail?"

"Thatch, you and I both know jail is the *last* place Gunnar should be. He'll learn too much. Make too many friends. I'll end up entertaining men with teardrop face tattoos named Snake and Meathead. I'm not cut out for that life. I don't even know how to make toilet wine."

"Is there a point to this?" Thatch questions, both hands on his hips now.

"Yeah," Cassie retorts. "The point is that *you* better get your big ass down there and fix it."

Thatch turns toward Kline with a hopeful look. "Kline? A little help?"

Kline sighs the loudest dad-sigh in history. "Let's go get your delinquent."

As they head for the door, I hear Thatch already calling his lawyer. "Caplin Hawkins, my guy. I've got another problem…"

I turn back to the chaos of the apartment, now quieter with half the parents gone. Cassie and my mom are still hanging framed memories like they're trying to turn our apartment into a museum of "The Love Story of Ace and Julia."

Ace sidles up beside me and grabs my hand, tugging me gently.

"Come here," he whispers before pulling me into our walk-in closet and pointedly shutting the door.

I giggle. "What are you doing?"

"Is it creeping you out a little bit how many framed pictures of us our moms are hanging?"

"Creeping me out?" I laugh. "It's like Chucky started a romance magazine. I already planned to take some down after they leave."

He grins and leans in to kiss me. "Hello, roomie."

"Hey, yourself," I say, smiling up at him. "You ready to live with me?"

He nods and rubs his nose against mine.

"You do realize that means you'll never be able to escape me, right?"

He nods again and presses a soft kiss to my lips.

"You're going to have to wake up to me every morning. And I'll be the last face you see every night. I'm going to be—"

"Jules, babe, you're making me hard," he interrupts, grinning like the menace he is. "So, if you don't mind, let's keep the dirty talk to a minimum until our mothers leave."

I burst out laughing, burying my face in his chest.

And Ace wraps his big, strong arms around me, pressing another kiss to the top of my head. "Love you, Lia."

I smile against his shirt. "Love you too, roomie."

Man, life sure is good. You know, besides Ace's brother possibly going to jail. Really, though, that's another sign that everything is right in the world.

Saturday, July 4ᵗʰ

Ace

Fourth of July at Aunt Paula and Uncle Brad's lake house is always a big deal.

And this year is no different.

The whole crew is here. My mom and dad and my brother Gunnar, who is miraculously *not* in jail. Julia's parents, Kline and Georgia, and her sister Evie. And Wes, Winnie, Lexi, and her little brother Wes Jr.

Lexi and Blake Boden are still together, stronger than ever. Blake will be joining the NFL draft this year, and all eyes are on Wes Lancaster and the New York Mavericks to see if they're going to draft him. Word on the street is that he's a first-round draft pick, but there's obviously no good in counting chickens before the eggs are hatched.

The entire Winslow clan is scattered across the lawn and deck—Wendy, Howard, Remy, Flynn, Ty, Jude, their wives, their kids. It's chaos, but it's our chaos. The Hayes family is here too. Finn, his mom, his brothers Reece, Jack, and Travis, and his sister Willow.

Basically, it's a full house in the best way, and it's exactly how Fourth of July should always be.

I'm standing on the deck, watching the lake shimmer under the July sun. It's hot as fuck outside, but I can't stop grinning.

Julia is out on the water, floating in an inner tube, her hair slicked back, sunglasses on, laughing at something Scottie just said from the tube beside her. Scottie's recovery has been nothing short of miraculous. She's walking again—slowly, with a cane—but she's walking. And every day, she gets stronger.

My mind flits back to last year, when I was standing right here, watching Julia the same way. I knew I loved her then. I just hadn't told her yet. Hell, I even kissed her that night and called it a best-friend kiss because I was too much of a fucking coward to tell her the truth.

But now, she's mine. And I get to kiss her every damn night. Every morning. Every chance I get.

Thank fuck.

Behind me, the deck creaks with new arrivals, and I pray to the fire marshall and whoever constructed it that it can handle the load. I glance back and see Gunnar strutting toward the drinks table like he owns the place. He grabs a glass of lemonade and hands it to Finn's sister Willow like it was his idea all along.

"Seriously?" Evie huffs from her spot in the shade. "What about me?"

"You have legs, don't you?" Gunnar shrugs, already walking away.

Evie flips him off.

Before she can rise out of her chair in dramatic teenage fury, Reece—Finn's eldest brother—slides a glass of lemonade in front of her like it's nothing.

"Thank you," she says sweetly, her voice gone soft as she stares up at him like he's the fucking sun and the moon and the stars. It's a teenage fantasy daydream happening right in front of my eyes, and I find myself blinking hard to make it go away.

Slow your roll, Evie. Reece is definitely too old for you.

I turn my attention back to the lake. Scottie and Finn are joined by Blake and Lexi, but there's no sign of my girl. I start scanning the waterline, frowning.

Where the hell did she go?

Arms wrap around my waist from behind, soaking the back of my shirt. "Hey, roomie," the voice of the girl of my dreams whispers against my spine.

I turn to find Julia grinning up at me, soaked and glowing.

"Hey, roomie," I say, brushing her wet hair off her face.

"Don't you want to come swim with me?"

"I was enjoying the show from here. Very *Baywatch*, Jules."

She laughs. "Were you watching me like a stalker again?"

"You know it, babe."

She plants a kiss on my chest. "Well, now that I'm up here, I think I'll make a sandwich."

"Nope." I scoop her into my arms. "You're gonna sit your cute little ass right here while I go make you one. The AC is cranked in there. You'll freeze your tits off."

She rolls her eyes but melts into the chair I lower her into.

But as I head toward the door, it swings open and out walk Jack and Travis Hayes. But they're not alone. There's a girl following behind them. A girl I've never seen before. She's petite, brown-eyed, and nervous as hell, glancing around like she's one deep breath away from bolting.

Jack and Travis are too busy arguing over God only knows what to introduce her, but Julia doesn't miss a beat.

My girl stands and smiles. "Hi, I'm Julia."

"Piper," the girl says, reaching out. "Hi."

"Oh shit," Jack mutters. "Everyone, this is Piper."

Piper smiles awkwardly but also elbows Jack in the stomach.

Jack chuckles and wraps his arm around Piper's shoulders. "Piper just transferred to Dickson, so Trav and I have taken her under our wing."

Piper smiles up at Jack like a girl who *really* likes Jack.

"I'm currently trying to talk Piper into being our roommate next year," Travis chimes in, and now Piper is smiling at Travis like a girl who *really* likes Travis. "We have the extra space in our apartment, and the dorms are all filled."

"You do not have the space," Piper says quietly. "One of you would be sleeping on the couch all year."

Travis shrugs and smiles. "I already told you, babe, I don't mind."

"I also don't mind," Jack adds.

I look toward Julia, my mind a little confused on what the arrangement is here and if we're about to be in the middle of a Why Choose-style romance, but when Julia discreetly widens her eyes at me, I know I'm not the only one.

Eventually, Jack and Travis lead Piper down to the lake, where everyone else is located, and Julia moves as close to me as she possibly can, whispering, "What the hell was that?"

"No idea, Jules." I shake my head and run a hand through my hair as I watch the trio head for the lake. "But it seems like Dickson is going to be interesting this year."

She snorts. "Let's hope those boys don't take a page from your book and start fires in their apartment."

I laugh. "Jules, honey, it feels like they're already playing with fire as we speak."

She rolls her eyes and stands up on her tippy-toes to kiss my lips. "So…about that sandwich?"

I kiss her again. "I'm on it."

"I sure do love a man who knows his place in the kitchen," she teases, giving me a light smack on the ass before sitting back down.

But I can't let her have the last word.

I stride back over, lift her into my arms, and kiss her hard. "Oh, Jules," I murmur against her lips. "You're gonna pay for that later."

"A girl can hope," she says, and I kiss her again.

Is it just me, or am I the luckiest son of a bitch in the entire damn world?

Yeah, I thought so too.

This isn't the end of Dickson University...

The next book in the highly addictive Dickson
University Series is coming soon!
Subscribe to our newsletter to not miss when the next
book is announced!
www.authormaxmonroe.com/newsletter

Haven't read the other two books in the series yet?

Start reading *Learning Curve*—aka Finn and
Scottie's book—today!

Start reading *Playing Games*—aka Blake and Lexi's book—today!

Sign up for our newsletter, and we'll keep you up-to-date on any
Dickson University Series news, AND a lot of times, we share
fun teasers and excerpts!

www.authormaxmonroe.com/newsletter

Plus, our newsletter is hilarious! Character conversations about
royal babies, parenting woes, embarrassing moments, and shitty
horoscopes are just the beginning! If you're already signed up,
consider sending us a message to tell us how much you love us.
We really like that. ;)

Need EVEN MORE Max Monroe before our next release?

Never fear, we have a list of nearly FIFTY other titles to keep you
busy for as long as your little reading heart desires!

Check out our Suggested Reading Order on our website!

www.authormaxmonroe.com/max-monroe-suggested-
reading-order

Follow us online here:

Facebook: www.facebook.com/authormaxmonroe

Reader Group: www.facebook.com/groups/1561640154166388

Twitter: www.twitter.com/authormaxmonroe

Instagram: www.instagram.com/authormaxmonroe

TikTok: m.tiktok.com/ZMe1jv5kQ

Goodreads: goo.gl/8VUIz2

ACKNOWLEDGMENTS

To all the most important people in our lives.

You know who you are.

We couldn't do this without you.

We love you.

To the first characters we ever wrote together. Our OG Billionaires. Our Kline. Our Thatcher. Our Wes. Our Georgia. Our Cassie. Our Winnie. We love you assholes so much.

To all our reader friends, THANK YOU FOR READING. You're the best.

And last, but certainly not least, to our dream team. The people who surround us and help us turn our words into books. The people who help us reach our readers. The people who support us every step of the way in this industry. Mark Gottlieb, Lisa Hollett, Stacey Blake, Kim Greene, Rick Hambright, Peter Alderweireld, Joanne Cote-Felaccio, Kristina Hassaker, and so many more amazing people, we are forever grateful for you.

XOXO,
Max & Monroe

* 9 7 9 8 9 9 1 8 4 3 5 9 1 *